Prai

"Abundant details
series launch into a

on
Where Secrets Sleep (starred review)

"Crisp writing and distinctive characters make up Perry's latest novel. *Where Secrets Sleep* is a truly entertaining read."

—*RT Book Reviews*

"Perry's story hooks you immediately. Her uncanny ability to seamlessly blend the mystery element with contemporary themes makes this one intriguing read."

—*RT Book Reviews* on *Home by Dark*

"Perry skillfully continues her chilling, deceptively charming romantic suspense series with a dark, puzzling mystery that features a sweet romance and a nice sprinkling of Amish culture."

—*Library Journal* on *Vanish in Plain Sight*

"*Leah's Choice*, by Marta Perry, is a knowing and careful look into Amish culture and faith. A truly enjoyable reading experience."

—Angela Hunt, *New York Times* bestselling author of *Let Darkness Come*

"*Leah's Choice* is a story of grace and servitude as well as a story of difficult choices and heartbreaking realities. It touched my heart. I think the world of Amish fiction has found a new champion."

—Lenora Worth, *New York Times* bestselling author of *Code of Honor*

Also available from Marta Perry and HQN Books

Sound of Fear

Echo of Danger

How Secrets Die

When Secrets Strike

Where Secrets Sleep

Abandon the Dark

Search the Dark

Home by Dark

Danger in Plain Sight

Vanish in Plain Sight

Murder in Plain Sight

MARTA PERRY

SHATTERED SILENCE

Recycling programs for this product may not exist in your area.

ISBN-13: 978-1-335-00700-1

Shattered Silence

This edition published by arrangement with Harlequin Books S.A.

For questions and comments about the quality of this book, please contact us at CustomerService@Harlequin.com.

www.HQNBooks.com

Printed in U.S.A.

CONTENTS

Dear Reader,

I hope you've been enjoying my Echo Falls books as much as I've enjoyed writing them. It's always a little sorrowful when I come to the end of a series, but soon I'm looking forward to the next project.

This story came out of a conversation I had with another writer a few years ago, when we discussed the difficulty of someone actually pretending to be Amish. While it's fascinating to think of a hero or heroine hiding from danger in an Amish home, it would be very hard to pull off in reality because of the language. The Amish speak Pennsylvania Dutch to each other, and young children don't usually learn much English until they start school. So the average person would be totally lost in an Amish home, since very few people outside the Amish community know Pennsylvania Dutch.

But my heroine, Rachel, is different. The child of a runaway Amish mother and an English father, Rachel grew up spending her summers with her mother's Amish family on the family farm. So when danger thrusts its way into her ordinary life and she needs a place to hide, she can sink back into the world she loved as a child. Her time spent on the farm allowed me to contrast Rachel's fear and anxiety with the calm, peaceful life at the farm, and I found it fascinating to write about the differences.

I hope you'll let me know how you like my book.
You can find me online at www.martaperry.com and at www.Facebook.com/martaperrybooks. If you'd like to receive a signed bookmark and my Pennsylvania Dutch recipe brochure or sign up for my newsletter, just let me know at either place.

Best,

Marta Perry

SHATTERED SILENCE

This story is dedicated, as always,
to my loving husband.

You appreciate the light much more
when you have come through the darkness.
—Amish proverb

CHAPTER ONE

THE CHANCES OF catching her ex-husband at work were slipping away as Rachel Hartline sat in rush hour Philadelphia traffic. She gripped the steering wheel, frowning against the October sun dazzling her windshield, willing the cars to move. Only one last thing remained to be done between her and her ex—for Paul to sign the agreement to put their house on the market. That would end the connection between them.

Would that end the grief and the pain of failure that had dogged her since the divorce? Somehow she doubted it. It would take more than selling the house they'd bought together to do that.

Rachel couldn't help wincing at the thought of strangers walking through the home where she and Paul had started their lives together, commenting about her decorating and her taste. The Craftsman bungalow in West Chester had been the only real home she'd ever known, the only place that had been truly hers. The prospect of losing it was a stone in her heart. Still, she had no choice. She couldn't afford the payments on a teacher's salary.

Paul had, after much delaying, agreed to meet her after work at his office in Attwood Industrial Designs. But the renovated warehouse that housed the small company was in another of Philadelphia's suburbs, miles from the charter school where she was the kindergarten teacher, and traffic on the Blue Route was going from bad to worse.

She couldn't have gotten away any sooner, not with one of her kindergartners standing there in tears because her mother hadn't come to pick her up. Alissa was already shy and withdrawn, struggling to adjust to a new home and a new school. Rachel couldn't find it in her heart to leave her, even with Lyn Baker, the head teacher and her closest friend, staying, as well.

Traffic finally started moving again, and Rachel fought to control her impatience. She'd tried to call Paul from the school to let him know she was running late, but as usual he hadn't answered, so she'd left a message. She wouldn't call from the car. People did, of course, but she would never take the risk of one of her students seeing her doing something dangerous. A teacher had the responsibility to do the right thing.

And if she didn't settle this today...well, she'd just have to hope Paul had waited.

When she pulled into the nearly deserted parking lot, she glanced at her watch. Half an hour late. Well, she'd waited longer than that for Paul before. Rachel slid out and hurried to the door, but a yank told her it was locked.

Suppressing the urge to pound, she pulled out her cell and keyed in a quick text. Paul might still be in the building. She waited, seconds ticking away, for a response that didn't come. Of course not. Paul was a master at avoiding unpleasantness. If something threatened to be uncomfortable, he'd slide out of it with that charm that had captivated her the first time she met him. But charm, she'd discovered, did not mean a man was marriage material.

Glaring at the glass panel in the door, she started to turn away when she caught a glimpse of movement inside. Charlie Booth, the elderly security guard, was coming slowly around the corner from the workrooms. She pounded on the door and waved frantically.

Charlie looked her way, did a double take and then hurried to the door. In a moment it swung open, and he stepped back in invitation.

"Ms. Hartline. Haven't seen you in an age." His broad smile slipped, as he obviously remembered why he hadn't seen her. "I mean…"

"I know. It's all right."

She was touched by his concern. Charlie was probably not the most effective security guard in the world, with his failing vision and his tendency to fall asleep on the job. But he'd been with James Attwood from the beginning, and Attwood showed an unexpected loyalty to the old man.

"I was supposed to meet Paul here after work, but I'm late. Do you know if he's still in?"

She nodded upward, toward the offices on the second floor. The rest of the sprawling cement block building was taken up by the workshops, where Attwood's designs were implemented and tested.

"Haven't seen him leave," Charlie said, and then turned toward the desk as the phone began to ring. "If you can wait until I get that…"

"No need to trouble yourself." Rachel hurried toward the metal stairs that were probably left over from warehouse days. She was eager to get this over with. "If he's not there, I'll be right back down."

For a moment Charlie looked as if he'd object, but then he nodded, grabbing the phone.

Rachel rushed through the glass door that led to the executive assistant's domain.

No one was there, and that in itself was a relief. Claire Gibson—an elegant, polished redhead—always made Rachel feel like a grubby teenager. Not, she had to admit, that she looked all that great in her school garb of khaki pants and a cotton sweater, her long hair in a braid, but a kindergarten teacher had to dress for practicality and for small, sometimes dirty, hands tugging at her.

No lights were on, but enough illumination came from the high windows to see that the complex of offices had a deserted look. Rachel let out a long breath. It was quiet, almost too quiet for comfort. She'd been here only during the workday, when all the doors were open and the clatter of metal could be heard from the workrooms. The stillness seemed wrong, like the school building when emptied of its cargo of lively young bodies and high voices.

Shaking off the thought, Rachel crossed to Paul's office and eased open the door, her rubber-soled shoes soundless on the carpet. No one was there. As marketing director, Paul often worked long hours, but apparently not today. He'd always said he had to adjust his schedule to the whims of Attwood, whom he described as an eccentric genius who was going to make them all rich.

If Attwood did, Paul would gamble his share away, just as he had already gambled away practically everything else they'd owned. It had taken too long for her to recognize it as the addiction it was, and longer still to understand that she couldn't help him. Despite her grief and pain, Paul was the only person who could change himself.

So far, it seemed his compulsive gambling hadn't affected his work. Maybe gambling was easier to hide than some other addictions.

She crossed to the desk, thinking of leaving a note. No, better not. A note would be too easily ignored. She'd send Paul a text and insist on a meeting tomorrow. If he didn't respond to the text, she'd keep calling him until he found it easier to deal with her than avoid her.

Funny that he was dragging his heels on this final step of severing what had been between them. They'd been apart for over a year. She'd actually expected him to be eager to get his hands on his share of the house's value. Maybe that was a sign that he felt more regret than he showed.

She closed the door behind her as she stepped back into the outer office, not giving in to the impulse to see if he'd replaced the photo of her on his desk with something else. It wasn't her concern, not anymore.

The smallest of sounds reached her—no more than a click, coming from Attwood's office. Chilled, she froze where she was. It might be foolish, but she'd always been awed and a bit intimidated by James Attwood. It wasn't the genius part that troubled her. The man had the coldest pair of eyes she'd ever seen, and he looked at other people as if they were a lower form of life. She was not eager to explain what she was doing here to him.

Rachel had made up her mind to retreat as quickly as possible when a muttered exclamation, in a voice she knew only too well, reached her. Paul. He was still here. But what was he doing in Attwood's darkened office?

She didn't care. He was here, and at least she'd be able to settle with him. Hand on her bag where the contract rested, she moved quickly toward the noise.

As she touched the knob, some instinct made her hesitate. What *was* Paul doing in Attwood's private room? Something he preferred to do without turning a light on, it seemed.

Rachel turned the knob gently and eased the door open a couple of inches. Paul stood at the massive mahogany desk, an oddly furtive look on his face. His fingers were on a flash drive inserted in Attwood's computer.

"Paul! What are you doing?"

He jerked compulsively at the sound of her voice. Rachel pushed the door the rest of the way open, staring at him.

The hastily arranged smile he gave her was a dead giveaway. She'd seen that same smile too often before, such as when she'd caught him taking the only piece of valuable jewelry she owned, a diamond bracelet he'd given her, from her jewelry box.

"Rachel. I'd about given up on you. I thought you were eager to get my signature."

"Never mind about me. Why are you copying something from Attwood's computer?"

"This?" He pulled out the flash drive and slid it into his pocket. "Nothing, nothing. James asked me to look over some thoughts he had on a new project."

He turned away for a moment to exit the computer file, but Rachel had seen enough. Paul had lied to her so often that she couldn't fail to recognize the symptoms, and her stomach churned. How had she ever been so naïve as to believe him at all? For a woman who claimed she valued honesty above every other trait, she'd been remarkably stupid about Paul.

And beneath her anger, she knew she still longed to believe in the man he'd once been.

He came toward her. "Did you bring the papers?"

It wasn't her business, not any longer. She should just get his signature and walk away. But somehow, she couldn't.

"I don't believe you. Honestly, Paul, of all the foolish tricks—I thought this company was everything you'd always wanted. If Attwood finds out you've been in his files…"

Paul opened his mouth, probably to deny it, but no words came. Rachel heard the sound at the same time he did. Footsteps, moving slowly up the metal stairs. Charlie was coming to see what was taking her so long.

Before she realized what he was up to, Paul had shoved her out into the reception area and was hurrying toward the door that led to the cavernous work area.

"Don't say anything," he whispered. "Please, Rachel. I'll call you and explain. Just don't give me away."

He flashed her a pleading smile and was gone before she could refuse to tell any lies for him. Not that he'd have believed her, anyway. That sweetly boyish smile of his had been getting him out of trouble all his life. Even now, he wouldn't believe she was immune.

Anger swamped the remnants of pity she felt for him. Fighting the urge to throw something, Rachel reached the outer door before Charlie could. He stopped partway up, looking at her with a question in his face.

"I'm so sorry." She hurried down to him. "I didn't mean to make you walk clear up here."

"No problem." He let her precede him down the flight. "Paul gone already?"

She nodded. That, at least, had the virtue of being true. He was gone by now.

"I'll have to call him later." He had a lot of explaining to do. "So how's your grandson? This is his senior year of high school, isn't it?"

A glance over her shoulder told her that Charlie's lined face was wreathed in smiles. "That's right. Out for track, he is, and with a good chance for a scholarship, the coach says."

Rachel responded appropriately, and the talk of his grandson's prowess on the track and in the classroom lasted until Charlie had locked the outer door behind her. Only then could she let the smile slide from her face.

Paul was in trouble. She had no doubt about that, because she'd seen it too often in the five years they'd been married. He was in trouble, and thanks to her deplorable sense of timing, she'd landed herself right in the middle of it.

CLINT MORDAN WALKED toward the century-old brick building that housed the Fairfield School. Clever placement. He knew from his background research that the charter school had existed for less than five years, but the gracious old building suggested stability and tradition.

Rachel Hartline had been one of the original teachers at the school, so he had to assume that she was dedicated to the motto of cooperation and growth that adorned the arch over the front gate.

Would that cooperation extend to assisting Clint in his investigation into her ex-husband's activities? Hard to say. In his experience, ex-wives could be vindictive or they could have remnants of faithfulness. Either way, they weren't usually neutral judges of their exes.

Logan Angelo, his partner, had done a very preliminary rundown on Paul Hartline this morning when he'd turned up missing at the same time that certain very sensitive files from Attwood Industrial showed signs of tampering. Attwood, who'd been remarkable only for his insistence on doing everything his own way since he'd hired Angelo and Mordan a few weeks earlier to advise him on security, had been predictably furious and inclined to blame them.

Fortunately Logan was in charge of dealing with irate clients, not he. He didn't have the necessary tact, as Logan frequently reminded him. Clint was more comfortable driving straight over any obstacles between him and the facts.

Clint pressed the buzzer at the front door of the school. Logan had also wanted him to wait until the end of the school day to approach the Hartline woman, but that wasn't Clint's style. His years as a cop had taught him to move in fast and take control of the situation. And that included getting to the ex-wife before she had time to hear about this from other sources and prepare a story.

The presentation of his credentials was sufficient to move him quickly past the school secretary and into the presence of the head teacher, but there things stalled.

Lyn Baker regarded him skeptically from behind the

barricade of her desk, handing his credentials back to him with a dismissive air. Calm, cool and collected, she looked as if she'd be equally at home dealing with irate parents and difficult kids. To a woman like that, a private security agent presented no particular challenge.

"Ms. Hartline is in the middle of the afternoon kindergarten session. Why can't your business with her, whatever it is, wait until dismissal time?"

He'd been deliberately vague about why he needed to see Ms. Hartline, but this woman wasn't one to be awed by a set of credentials. He could use a little of Logan's tact right now.

"I can't discuss the specifics with you because of client confidentiality. However, an important matter has come up regarding her husband, making it imperative that I speak with her at once."

"Ex-husband," she corrected. She studied him for a long moment…long enough to make him nervous. Just when he thought she was going to kick him out, she nodded. "Very well. If you'll come with me, I'll ask her if she's willing to talk with you. If so, I'll take over her class while you speak with her."

Since the woman didn't seem inclined to converse during the walk to the classroom, he had time to assess the school. Despite the venerable look of the exterior, the inside seemed to have been completely remodeled to make it efficient and attractive to children and, probably more important, their parents. Bright colors, cheerful murals and appealing furnishings created an up-to-date impression.

"This area is our primary section." Ms. Baker's gesture took in the wing of the building. "The kindergarten classroom is down here, across from the library. You can speak with Ms. Hartline there, if she agrees."

He nodded, feeling no response was welcome. One wall of the hallway leading to the kindergarten room was adorned with what were apparently self-portraits of the children—most grinning, some with gaps where baby teeth had been. Ms. Hartline's pupils? He supposed so.

They stopped outside a closed door that had been surrounded with colorful cutout balloons, each with a child's name printed on it.

"Wait here." The woman's tone left no room for doubt.

Clint waited. But he could see into the room through the glass panel, and what he saw intrigued him.

Rachel Hartline sat cross-legged on a rug, a cluster of children around her. Telling a story, he assumed, judging by her animated face and gestures. She was smiling, enjoying herself, and her audience leaned forward, intent on every word.

The head teacher's entrance had all the faces turning toward her. He watched for signs of apprehension on the Hartline woman's part, but saw nothing other than polite interest until Ms. Baker bent and murmured something. Then she gave a quick, startled glance at the door before turning back to the children with another smile and what was probably an explanation.

A moment later she rose gracefully and walked toward him. Apparently he was going to get his interview. Good. There was no way he could have pushed it if she'd refused.

He had just enough time for a quick assessment of the woman before she reached out to open the door.

Average height, slim and fit-looking in khakis and an aqua knit shirt. She wore no jewelry but for a pair of gold studs and a businesslike watch. Her thick blond hair was pulled into a single long braid that hung down her back to between her shoulder blades.

Then she'd reached him. She closed the door to the classroom behind her, looking faintly apprehensive. He concentrated on the words he'd speak. The first few words were important when it came to someone who might be an adversary or a source of information. After all, he didn't have the authority of a police badge now.

"Ms. Hartline, my name is Clint Mordan. I'm a partner in a security firm, and Attwood Industrial Designs is one of our clients. I'd like to talk with you about your husband."

"Ex-husband," she corrected, as the Baker woman had. She frowned at him, lips pressed together as if to prevent any question or comment. If there'd been a flicker of some emotion in her eyes, it was quickly gone. "Come over to the library. It should be empty at this hour."

The library, a few steps down the hall on the opposite side, was sunny and welcoming, with bright murals of children's book characters and child-size furniture. But his attention was on the woman beside him, rather than the surroundings. Did she know that her ex-husband was missing, or had he gotten in first with the news?

Before she could ask the question that obviously hovered on her lips, he fired his own query.

"Where is Paul Hartline?"

She stiffened, attempting a look of disinterest she couldn't quite master. "I have no idea. Paul and I are divorced."

He studied her face, considering before he spoke. Her face was strongly contoured, with deep green eyes under arched brows. She had a straight nose and full lips that were firm and level at the moment. All in all, she looked like someone who might appreciate plain speaking.

"You're fairly recently divorced, I understand. Since you still own property together, I assume you've kept some track of his whereabouts."

Her green eyes darkened, her frown deepening. "You seem remarkably well informed about my personal life, Mr. Mordan. What business is it of yours?"

So she was going to battle him every step of the way. He moved toward her, deliberately invading her personal space. "I told you. My security firm represents Attwood Industrial, so Attwood's employees are of vital interest to us. Especially when they turn up missing."

The warm peach of her skin faded, to be replaced by a pallor she couldn't possibly have faked. So she really hadn't known Hartline was gone.

"What do you mean, missing? I just… I heard from him yesterday. How can he be missing?"

He'd caught the hitch in her voice that told him that wasn't what she'd intended to say. What was she hiding?

"He didn't show up for an important meeting this morning. His office tried to reach him, but there was no answer on his landline or cell. Attwood sent someone over to his apartment to check. Hartline was gone." He pounded the facts like nails and then paused, letting them sink in. "It looked as if he'd left in a hurry."

She took a step back, fingers clenching into fists, obviously fighting for composure. "I had no idea. Some…

some emergency must have come up. Or I suppose he might have had an accident."

He was shaking his head already. "As far as we've been able to determine, he went back to his apartment at around eight last night, packed up a few things and left. What would make him do that?"

"How would I know what he was thinking?" She evaded his glance and answered a question with a question.

So she knew, or suspected, something. And she didn't want to talk. Guilt? Or an instinct to protect her ex-husband? He wouldn't have expected loyalty, given how recent their divorce was, but he knew nothing yet about the circumstances. Maybe theirs had been unique, leaving no harsh feelings on either side.

He tried again. "Come now, Ms. Hartline. You two live in the same area, own property together—you probably have the same group of friends. You must hear something about him at times. When was the last time you saw him?"

Clint knew instantly that this was the thing she didn't want to answer. For just an instant she looked...what? Lost? Bereft?

"Well?" He didn't want to give her time to think up a convenient lie. "When?"

She stiffened, her chin coming up, ready to go on the offensive. "I don't see any reason why I should answer your questions. Anyone can flash an identification card and claim to be official."

There was no arguing with that. "Fair enough. You can call Attwood's yourself and check on what I'm telling you."

"I'm in the middle of a school day, and it's time I got

back to my class. There's no way I can help you. My ex-husband may be away on perfectly legitimate business of his own."

"Taking with him a file of valuable information that belongs to Attwood Industrial?"

That staggered her, and he had to suppress a surge of sympathy before he could push her further.

"We're taking about theft, Ms. Hartline. If you hold back information, you're just as guilty as your ex-husband is. When did you last see him?"

Clint had expected fear for herself, but he didn't see it. Instead, the implied threat seemed to feed her resistance. Her chin firmed, and he realized how very stubborn it was.

"I don't know that anything you're telling me is true, and I'm too busy for this. You could be making this whole thing up." She swung away from him.

He caught her arm, got a flash of fury from those green eyes and released her. He lifted both hands in a gesture of surrender.

"Like I said, it's easy enough to prove." He pulled out his cell phone and held it out to her. "Call Attwood's. Talk to the head man himself. He'll confirm everything I've said."

The woman looked at the cell phone as if it were a snake. Then she glared at him. "I am going back to my class to complete the school day. When it's over, I'll call James Attwood on my own phone. I have nothing else to say to you."

He couldn't keep her here, not unless he wanted to end up in jail. He let her reach the door before he spoke.

"School ends at three fifteen, I understand. I'll be waiting to talk then." By then he'd have the results of further interviews with the staff at Attwood Industrial, along with the security camera footage that might have caught Paul Hartline in action. Too bad Attwood wouldn't allow the cameras in the offices, or Hartline's guilt might be established if they could see what he'd done there.

No answer. She went out the door and disappeared from view.

One point for Rachel Hartline. The head teacher would be here momentarily to escort him out, and he'd have to go.

This was one of those times when he had to remind himself that he wasn't a cop anymore. Cold swept over him like a wave, and he was back in uniform again, flat on his belly, gasping for air. The dirty alley, concrete hard on his cheek, the pain ravaging his body as he fought to hang on to consciousness. Tony…where… Then he saw him, just a glimpse as the darkness closed in, lying in a pool of blood, his body twisting…

Sweat broke out on Clint's forehead as he grabbed the closest table, leaning heavily on his hands as he fought the attack. He jammed the memory back into the recesses of his mind. Slammed the door on it.

Damn. He took a steadying breath. That had been a bad one. He'd thought he had those flashbacks under control. Looked like he was wrong.

At the sight of movement beyond the glass door, Clint sucked in another breath and strode out into the hall. Okay. Focus on the thought that Rachel Hartline was wrong, too. She hadn't gotten out of this situation, not yet. He pushed aside the appeal of that hint of vulnerability in those green eyes, the appeal inherent in the way that slender body had straightened to fight back.

When the kids poured out of school at the end of the day, he'd be waiting for her.

WHEN SHE'D WAVED goodbye to the last of her kindergartners, panic poured into Rachel's mind. While her students had been there she'd been able to compartmentalize, keeping memories of that strange confrontation with Clint Mordan at bay. But now the implications flooded in on her.

Her original instincts had been on target. Paul had been doing something wrong, and now it was catching up with him. She tried to think of an innocent reason why he'd have copied apparently important material that belonged to the company and came up against a blank wall of ignorance.

She'd known a little about Paul's job, of course, but when he talked, it was about the marketing he did, not about the devices that were created by the company. She knew they'd invented devices corporations needed and couldn't create in-house. But from what Paul had said, Attwood's biggest interest had been in working on original ideas and then finding a market for them. That was where Paul had come in, with his background in marketing.

Rachel rubbed her aching temples, pushing back the curling strands that had escaped from her braid. It shouldn't hurt and surprise her, but it did. The last time they'd talked, he'd said that he was trying hard to turn things around. She'd actually thought he meant it, because he had accepted that their marriage was over. He no longer had any need to lie to her about it. Now, to find out this…

She had to talk to Paul. She couldn't go stumbling

around in the dark. If he had stolen a file, he'd have to return it at once.

He'd know that would be her attitude. Maybe that was why he'd ignored her messages all day. Clenching her teeth, Rachel grabbed her cell phone, this time leaving a voicemail. "Call me. At once."

Glancing up at a sound, she saw Lyn hesitating at the door. "Do you want me to vanish while you make a call?"

"No, come in." She dropped the cell phone on her desk. "He won't call me back."

"Sorry." Lyn put a comforting arm around her in a quick hug. "I take it Paul's misdeeds have finally hit the fan."

No point in trying to keep anything from Lyn. She already knew everything there was to know about Paul and the divorce. Rachel leaned her hip against the desk.

"It looks like it. That man…Mordan…claims that Paul stole valuable information from his company and has vanished."

"Is it true?" Lyn was practical as ever.

"Maybe." She paused, rubbing her temples again. "I've got to talk to someone from Attwood's and find out what's going on there. And what authority this man has."

"In the meantime, you're going to be talking to Mordan again if you don't move quickly. That's what I came in to tell you. He's been parked on the street since he left here, and I spotted him coming toward the school."

Rachel snatched up her bag and phone. "I can't deal with him again right now. I've got to get out—"

"Not in your car," Lyn said. She held out a set of keys. "Mine is parked behind the school. We'll switch and change back later." She shoved Rachel toward the door. "Out the back, quickly. I told Maggie to delay him, but I don't know how long her ingenuity will hold out."

"You're a saint, Lyn." There was no time for the thanks she owed her friend. She tossed her car keys to Lyn. "I'll be in touch later."

Rachel hurried to the door, took a quick look down the hallway and then scurried toward the back of the building. At least this would give her breathing space. She had to talk to someone from Attwood Industrial, but she didn't want it to be the man himself.

Ian. Ian Robinson had been friends with Paul since college, and she and Paul had socialized with Ian and his wife before the split. Ian would tell her what was going on.

She slid into Lyn's compact car and pulled out into the alley. She'd have to go the long way around if she didn't want to run into Clint Mordan before she was ready to talk to him.

Rachel shivered a little at the thought. Hard-edged, tough, aggressive… Maybe those were necessary qualities for his job, but they certainly didn't leave any room for excuses. Or empathy. He was the kind of person who'd keep barreling straight toward what he wanted without even noticing what or who he went through.

It wasn't fair that Paul had entangled her in his situation, forced her to defend him to that man. Not fair, but very like Paul, unfortunately.

A few miles from the school she pulled over into a convenient mall parking lot. If she went straight home, she'd probably run right into Mordan, who'd undoubtedly go there when he realized he'd missed her at the school.

He wouldn't stay there long, would he? Surely he

had other avenues to explore—she wouldn't think he'd waste all his time on her. She quickly called Ian. Would he answer, or would he try to avoid her, too?

But Ian picked up promptly. "Where are you? Have you heard from Paul?" His voice sounded guarded.

"On my way home from school, and no, I've been trying to reach him. Ian, what's going on? I've had this man, Clint Mordan, dogging my steps all afternoon. Is he really who he claims?"

"Security firm. James called them in just a couple weeks ago."

"Because he suspected Paul of something then?" The thought leaped to her mind.

"I don't know." Before she could respond, he hurried on in little more than a whisper. "I can't talk here. I'll come by your house later, on my way home. We'll talk then." He ended the call on those words.

Rachel was left with a host of unanswered questions and a load of frustration. But at least Ian hadn't turned against her. He'd be honest with her. Once she knew exactly what the situation was, she'd know how much to reveal.

Her cell phone gave the ding that announced an incoming text, and Rachel nearly dropped it in her haste to unlock her phone. From Paul, at last.

It's not what you think. I just need time to decide what to do.

Call me. I'm being questioned about you. What is this?

She waited for more, but nothing appeared. Apparently Paul wasn't ready to be honest with her.

She frowned. Was she imagining it, or was there something a little panicky about Paul's words? She wasn't sure, and in the meantime she was left still confused and uncertain about what to tell that investigator.

Rachel started the car, glanced into the rearview mirror and got a jolt right to her heart. Clint Mordan was in the vehicle right behind hers. Clint Mordan. He seemed to catch her look in the mirror, since he nodded slightly.

A faint sense of admiration flickered. He'd found her remarkably fast, given how clever she thought they'd been. She'd underestimated him.

Well, he could follow her home if he wanted, but that was all he could do. If he tried to push his way into her house, she'd call the police, no matter what the consequences.

CHAPTER TWO

CLINT EYED THE woman in the car ahead of him. He'd seen the movement of her head when she spotted him in her rearview mirror. Was she going to confront him here and now?

No, apparently not. Rachel Hartline pulled out, signaling as if he were any other driver close behind her. If she was shaken that he was on her tail so quickly, she didn't show it. She might still try to lose him, but he was ready for that…even grimly amused at the thought.

But Rachel made no move to do any such thing, and after a couple of turns, it was clear she was headed home. Good. There were a few things they had to talk about.

He'd checked in with Logan to learn that according to the watchman, Rachel had visited the offices last night. The security camera had caught her arrival and departure. It hadn't shown anything of Paul Hartline, after he'd supposedly left for the day. If he'd been there, he must have left by an unmonitored hallway. And if Attwood had taken their advice, that wouldn't have happened.

When he'd heard about Rachel's visit, the flicker of sympathy Clint had felt earlier was extinguished. Obviously she knew something, even if she hadn't been involved. And he intended to know what that was.

Clint frowned. Logan had questioned the night watchman, who'd insisted she'd been in the offices alone only for a few minutes. He could have been covering up for his own laxity in letting her in, but the film bore out what he said. Even so, if she knew how to get into the files, it would take only that long to make a copy.

As for his insistence that she hadn't been carrying anything but her handbag when she left...a flash drive wouldn't take up much space at all. His jaw hardened. Yes, Rachel had a lot of explaining to do.

They reached the quiet suburban street she lived on, and Rachel pulled into the driveway leading to the garage. Leaving her car outside, she got out quickly. She headed for the front door, a set of keys in her hand, and she pointedly didn't glance his way.

Ignoring him wasn't going to help her now.

Clint parked at the curb and followed her up the walk while assessing the house she and her ex-husband owned. A small Craftsman-style bungalow, it was undoubtedly one of the older houses on the block, but it was also in immaculate condition—freshly painted, the planters overflowing with mums in bright oranges and yellows. Nice place, making him wonder how she could afford it on a teacher's salary. But maybe Hartline was still paying his share.

He overtook Rachel before she reached the door. "We haven't had our little talk yet," he reminded her.

She stiffened, then spun and flung an annoyed glance at him. "We can have as many little talks as you want, since you seem prepared to make a nuisance of yourself to get them. But I still can't tell you what I don't know."

The last sentence came out loudly, and he glanced toward the next-door neighbor, who'd stopped clipping his hedge to stare at them. Best not to give the man any excuse to interfere.

"Sorry," he said, not meaning it. "But the situation is too serious to wait."

Rachel met his gaze briefly and then looked away. He thought he read resignation in the movement. "I suppose you'd better come in."

Success, it seemed. She fumbled with the key as if her fingers were cold, and he moved closer to her, just in case she had any idea of bolting inside and slamming the door in his face.

She finally got the key to turn. "I didn't—"

The words cut off, and he followed her shocked stare toward the inside of the house. The door opened directly onto what had probably been a neat, pleasant room, judging by what he'd seen of the outside.

Not now. It had been tossed, and by someone who hadn't bothered trying to hide his actions.

"No." The anguish in the word was as acute as if she'd been attacked herself. She started in, but Clint grasped her arm.

"Wait. Someone might still be there. Call the police first." He suspected bringing the police in might not sit well with James Attwood, but Clint was still too much of a cop to do anything else.

Rachel shook his hand off, her green eyes stormy. "You—you probably did this yourself."

"I didn't." He hung on to whatever patience he possessed. "If I had, would I be telling you to call the police?"

The logic seemed to get through to her. A little of the anger left her face, leaving it strained. "No, I suppose not." She paused, and he could almost see her weighing the options. "I'd better see if anything is missing. There have been a couple of recent break-ins in the area."

She turned away from him, obviously intending to do this on her own.

"The police—" he began again, and he could almost hear his partner's voice in his mind. *People use our agency because they don't want to call in the police.*

"I said I want to see if anything's missing first. There's no point in filing a report until I know that."

"Not by yourself," he said, stepping past her into the living room. "It's not safe. And if this has anything to do with the current situation..."

He didn't believe in coincidences. But if the search of Rachel's house was connected with her husband's disappearance, he'd better proceed carefully. Attwood wouldn't be happy to have police in the middle of his problem, to say nothing of Clint's partner's reaction.

He moved carefully across the living room, assessing the scene automatically. Who had been here? Someone from Attwood Industrial, impatient already with the pace of their investigation? Or someone else, like maybe the person who'd bought Paul Hartline's loyalty?

That presented a fresh set of complications on its own. If true, that must mean that the information hadn't been turned over to the buyer yet. There may still be time to prevent that from happening, but only if he and Logan found the man first.

He'd have to talk it over with Logan, but he had to deal with this now. "Stay there, please. Let me make sure no one is in here before you come in."

She hesitated, obviously reluctant, and then nodded. "How many rooms?"

"Just the living room, kitchen, sunroom and the two bedrooms. No basement, and the attic is just an attic."

Nodding, he moved into the kitchen. Small, sunny, cheerful. An expression of Rachel's personality? Someone had obviously had a thorough look around. He opened the closet door carefully, to find only a broom, a mop and cleaning supplies.

Moving on, he went through each of the other rooms. The house was small and compact, and there weren't many places for an intruder to hide. He—whoever he was—had probably struck while Rachel was at school.

Returning to the living room, he nodded at her. "It's all clear. You can come in now." He studied her face as she did, watching for anything out of the ordinary. But all he saw was stunned bewilderment.

"The intruder jimmied the back door. Easy enough to do. Why don't you have dead bolts on these doors?" He felt a spurt of irritation. Why did people neglect the most elementary precautions? She was an attractive young woman living alone, and she seemed oblivious of the simplest safety precautions.

Rachel moved slowly to the middle of the room, lifting her hands in a helpless gesture and seeming to ignore his question. "Why would anyone do this? I can't imagine there's much here that would interest a thief."

Did she honestly not see the connection with her husband? Ex-husband, he corrected himself.

"An ordinary thief would go straight for the electronics," he pointed out. "They don't seem to have been touched."

She picked up a ripped needlepoint cushion and hugged it against her, staring at the drawers pulled out of a lamp table, their contents strewn on the floor. "You think someone was looking for something." She said it as a statement of fact, not an accusation.

He had the feeling this violation of her home had knocked the stuffing out of Rachel, as well as her cushions. "What else? Someone is searching for whatever it was your husband has. Or for what he knows, but I'm guessing a specific object, judging by the search. Something small."

"Why here?" It was almost a cry. "I'd expect them to search Paul's apartment. He hasn't lived here in over a year."

"They probably did that first." He made a mental note to check if Logan hadn't done it already. "They didn't find whatever it was, so they tried here. And you know what they're looking for, don't you?"

Rachel seemed to try, and then fail, to summon up some indignation. "You know I was at the office yesterday, don't you?"

"We learned from the night watchman. And the security cameras. You must have realized we would."

She nodded. "Charlie. I talked with him for a bit."

Her reaction brought him back to being perplexed by her, and he didn't like it. He wanted to put her in a simple category—innocent bystander or criminally involved, one or the other. But she didn't fit.

"Why didn't you tell me this afternoon? You must have known we'd find out. It makes you look guilty."

Now she was back to looking at him with dislike. "I wasn't too concerned with what impression I was making on you. I felt I should talk to someone from Attwood's first. And I still haven't had time to do that with you trailing me around."

"Sure you weren't waiting to hear what your husband wanted you to do?"

Her rounded jaw suddenly looked remarkably firm again. "Ex-husband. And if I wanted to talk to him, it was to find out what he knew about this."

"Didn't he tell you when you saw him at the offices yesterday?" That was a shot in the dark, but he suspected it was true. That would explain a lot.

"No." She pressed her lips together on the word.

At least she wasn't denying that she'd seen him. That was progress, he supposed, but not enough.

"Why were you there?" He shot the question, hoping to get an honest response, or at least some hint that she was lying.

But Rachel looked more confused than anything else. She shook her head as if trying to clear it, and the long braid swayed against her back. For an instant he imagined that blond hair loose and curling down her back instead of confined in a braid, inviting a touch.

He pulled his mind back to the business at hand. "Well?"

She rubbed her temples again. "I had a paper for Paul to sign—the agreement to put this house on the market. I couldn't move on it until he agreed, but… Anyway, I was supposed to be there earlier, but I was late in leaving the school, and the traffic was terrible."

He could believe that. Anyone who'd experienced Philadelphia traffic at rush hour would. "So what happened when you did get there?"

"Charlie—the night watchman—let me in. He knows me, of course. He said he hadn't seen Paul leave, so I wanted to see for myself."

She seemed to come to a halt, and he prompted her. "And what did you find?"

"He wasn't in his office," she answered readily enough, maybe hoping he'd go away if she did. "But..." Rachel seemed to hit a stumbling block.

"But what? Did you see him or not?"

Rachel pressed both palms against her eyes. Trying to block out what she'd seen? Or just create a diversion?

"Did you?" He took a step closer, trying to push her to answer.

But that was the wrong move. Once again her anger flared. "I can't do this. Not now. You'll have to wait."

"Not a chance. You..."

"Rachel? What's going on here?" The intrusion of another person had both of them swinging toward the door.

Ian Robinson. Clint had seen him last at Attwood Designs. Attwood's right-hand man, so he'd understood. Clint's eyes narrowed. What was he doing here?

Robinson recognized him, of course. He nodded, his eyes skittering away from Clint.

Rachel moved toward the other man. "Ian, I'm glad you're here. I've had a break-in." She gestured at the chaos.

"I see." Robinson gave him a speculative look, probably wondering if he'd been the breaker-in. Then he walked in and took Rachel's arm, aligning himself with her.

Clint didn't bother trying to explain. Obviously he wasn't going to get anywhere with the man here. He shoved down his irritation.

"Here's my card. Call me if you think of anything. Or if you hear from your ex-husband." He held out his business card, but she made no move to take it. Finally he dropped it on the lamp table. "I'll drop by in the morning, Ms. Hartline. We can finish our conversation then."

"I leave for school at seven thirty," Rachel said. "Later..."

He shook his head. "In the morning. I'll be here at seven. Don't stay here alone without taking some precautions. It's not safe, and anyone could walk in that back door."

She didn't respond. He wasn't even sure what he said had registered. He eyed Robinson. Whatever their relationship, he'd have to hope the man would urge her to protect herself. She was not going to pay heed to anything he said. And why was it bugging him so much, anyway? Rachel Hartline wasn't his responsibility. He walked out.

Robinson closed the door decisively behind him, and Clint stared back at it for a moment. He'd give a lot to know what they were saying. Was Robinson's interest in Rachel Hartline professional? Or personal?

He glanced at the houses on either side. He wanted to talk to the neighbors, see if anyone had noticed anything, but not while Rachel could see him doing it. He'd find out in the morning if she'd notified the police. He scoured his memory for any contact he might have with the local force. There'd be some way of finding out the police response.

He got in the car, turned the key and discovered a reluctance to leave. The truth was, he didn't think Rachel was safe, and telling himself she wasn't his responsibility didn't seem to be doing a thing to lift the sudden protectiveness he felt.

RACHEL SUCKED IN a deep breath once Mordan was gone, feeling as if she hadn't breathed the entire time he'd been there. "Thanks for..." Her voice wavered, and she stopped, clutching at her vanishing poise.

Ian put his arm around her shoulders in a reassuring hug. "You're upset. It's no wonder with everything that's going on. You should see people at the office. What was he saying to you?"

She shrugged, taking a step away. It was tempting to lean on Ian, but she had to be careful about confiding in anyone until she'd had an explanation from Paul. She kept telling herself she didn't owe him loyalty, but despite everything, somewhere in Paul was the man she'd fallen in love with.

Despite all his faults, he never wanted to hurt anyone. He just couldn't stop believing that luck was going to turn his way and make everything all right—like one of her kindergarten children wishing on a star.

"The same thing everyone is wondering about, I suppose. Where is Paul?"

"If you know..." Ian stopped, looking worried and maybe apprehensive. Afraid of being involved? Probably. He had a job to consider and a family to support, after all.

"I don't," she said firmly.

Ian ran a hand over his fair hair and massaged his neck. Memory flickered—Paul used to tease him about looking like a male model with his clean-cut features, blond hair and blue eyes. Ian was certainly good-looking, and he used to be the center of attention with women. But that had been before he was married, of course.

"You must have some idea what he's up to," he said at last. "You saw him last night, didn't you?"

"Just for a minute or two." She picked her way forward with caution, not sure if it was necessary to tell him yet about the flash drive and Attwood's computer.

If there was some way Paul could manage to undo what he'd done, she wanted to give him that chance, at least. "He was supposed to sign the papers allowing me to move ahead with the sale of the house."

She looked around, another hurdle looming. The house would have to be restored to pristine condition before it went on the market. But since she hadn't succeeded in getting Paul to sign on the dotted line, that didn't really matter.

"Will you really have to sell?" Ian's voice went deep with sympathy. "I know what this place means to you."

She swallowed a rush of emotion. "I can't afford it on my salary." She shouldn't have to say more. Ian was Paul's best friend. If anyone else knew about Paul's gambling problem, it was he.

"I'm sorry." He moved as if he'd put his arm around her again, but seemed to think the better of it. "If there's anything Julie and I can do, just name it."

In happier times, she and Paul had often gotten together with Ian and Julie, usually at their house, because Julie didn't like to leave their baby daughter with a sitter. She'd enjoyed those times of socializing as a couple, but she couldn't expect Ian and Julie to feel the same now. The break-up of a marriage changed a lot of things, forcing people to pick sides, and Ian had been Paul's friend first.

"It can't be helped. I just wish I knew what Paul is doing."

She smoothed the mutilated needlepoint cushion she'd made. It had taken her most of last winter to finish it. Needlepoint was one of the many things her mother hadn't had time to teach her. Any sewing she'd learned had come from her grossmammi. For an instant the image of that Amish farm where she'd spent her child-hood summers shimmered like a mirage of peace and security beyond the current chaos. It had been a haven during her hectic childhood, and like a child, she longed for it now.

"Haven't you heard from him at all?" Ian's voice chased the image away.

"Just a brief text, saying he could explain."

She closed her lips against the temptation to say what she'd thought about that response. It was what Paul had always said when the checking account was overdrawn, or the credit card was over its limit, or the diamond earrings he'd given her had inexplicably disappeared.

The explanations were rarely credible, but in the beginning, she'd persuaded herself to believe them. Eventually she'd learned better. They weren't explanations, they were lies.

"If he contacts you again, will you tell him to get in touch with me?" Ian's gaze held hers. "Please, Rachel. He's my friend, and I'll do anything I can for him."

"I know." It couldn't be easy to keep on being Paul's friend. Though not quite as bad as being his wife and watching him plunge into disaster and nearly drag her with him.

Ian shook his head. "If only I could talk to him, maybe I could make him see sense. He's got to come forward right away. That's the only way out of this fix. I can talk to James—I'm sure he wouldn't press charges if Paul came back."

"You've tried to call him?" Of course he would have. She was tempted to tell him about the flash drive, but something held her back.

"He doesn't answer. Or respond to my texts." Ian sounded as frustrated as she felt.

He bent to pick up a sheaf of paper from the floor, putting it neatly on the desk, and then looked around for the missing drawer. It lay several feet away, and he went to retrieve it.

"You don't need to bother with that," she protested. "I'll have to go through all of it to see if anything is missing, not that I think there will be. I imagine whoever did this wasn't interested in my bills or letters."

Ian shook his head, smiling a little. "You don't think I'm going to run out and leave you to deal with this mess, do you? I'll help you clean up."

"Julie will be expecting you." It was a halfhearted protest. She had no desire to face this alone.

"I called and told her I had a stop to make, so she won't be worried. I'm sure she'd come over, if you want..."

"No, no. She won't want to leave the baby, and it's not necessary." She tried to find a bright spot in the situation. "At least so far it doesn't look as if there's too much actual damage, but I haven't checked the rest of the house yet. That man...Mordan...looked around to be sure no one was here, that's all."

"You let him walk around by himself?"

"Well, yes. Why not?"

"Nothing, nothing. I suppose it's his job. But I'll take a quick look, just to see if there's anything I need to break gently to you."

She smiled, thankful for a light touch in this mess. "There have been several minor break-ins in the area, and I imagine I'm just the latest victim."

"What have the intruders been taking? Do you know? Cash? Electronics?"

"Just cash, apparently. I've heard they think it's probably kids." She swung around and hurried to the desk. "I keep cash in here..." She held up the bank envelope. Empty. "Well, I *did* keep cash in here. There probably wasn't more than fifty dollars."

"Well, that answers one question, anyway. I don't suppose they'll come back, but if you'd like to stay the night with us, we'd love to have you."

The offer warmed her. "That's good of you, but I'm not afraid to stay here. As you said, they won't come back." She firmly dismissed the idea that it had been anything other than a random break-in. Mordan was seeing shadows where none existed. This couldn't have anything to do with Paul.

"At least I can rig something on that back door so no one can walk in. And you probably should have some dead bolts installed." Ian headed for the kitchen. His hand on the door frame, he stopped and looked back at her. "Rachel, if you do hear anything from Paul, tell him to get in touch with me right away. There's not much time."

"Time?" She stared at him, puzzled. It didn't seem there was any way this situation could get worse.

"The security firm is bad enough, but if they don't get any results in a day or two..." Ian paused, his face grim. "I'm afraid Attwood will call in the police. Then it will be too late for Paul to make amends."

Too late. The words were still echoing in Rachel's mind after a sleepless night. If she'd hoped the wee hours would bring an answer, she'd been disappointed. The situation still looked as bad as it had before.

If Paul ended up in jail, or worse, if she was also

charged with aiding him… Rachel struggled to face the possible consequences. She'd have to resign from the school immediately, of course, and even that might not be enough to keep enrollment from suffering. Fairfield School had been the dream of her heart as well as Lyn's. If she were responsible for its failure, how could she live with that?

Trying to concentrate on what she was doing instead of on what might happen, she finished making coffee and got out two mugs. Although why she should offer any hospitality to Clint Mordan, she didn't know. Given how antagonistic he'd been, she might be better off greeting him with boiling oil.

But when she opened the door to him a few minutes later, he didn't look quite as grim as he had when he'd left the previous day. He held up a white paper bag as if it were a peace offering. "Bagels. I hoped you might have coffee."

She ought to be suspicious, but she was so relieved to see that forbidding face relaxed that she almost smiled in return. *Careful*, she warned herself. If Mordan wanted to start over with her, it could be only because he thought that would get him what he wanted.

"Come into the kitchen. I don't have a lot of time." Half an hour. A lot could happen in half an hour.

"Looks like you spent the night cleaning up in here." He glanced around the living room before moving into the small kitchen, where the morning sun slanted through the windows, brightening the colors of the scarlet mums she'd put in the window boxes.

"Ian stayed for a time and helped me. The other rooms didn't seem quite as bad as the living room."

She shrugged. "Or maybe when I reached them, I was getting over the shock."

"Any serious damage?" He stood next to the pine table, obviously waiting for her to take a seat.

She waved him to a chair as she poured the coffee into mugs. "Milk? Sugar?"

"Just black, please." He opened the bag. Without waiting for such a frivolous thing as a plate, he slid bagels, napkins and cream cheese containers out onto the table.

"No, nothing bad." But she still felt violated. "The cash I kept in the desk was missing. That's what happened in the other break-ins, so I'm sure it was the same kids."

She added a couple of small plates and knives to the mix and set coffee in front of him before taking a seat.

"I'm glad it wasn't worse." He seemed almost conciliatory. "People can cause a lot of problems if they're intent on vandalism." He sipped at his steaming coffee, giving her a moment to study him.

The previous day she hadn't had time to do anything but react. He'd come across as harsh, antagonistic, stiff, with a stoic face that seemed to be carved from granite.

Now, she tried to look without prejudging. Dark brown hair, thick and cut in an almost military style. His eyes were nearly as dark, but they had fine lines around them that told a story of tension, stress, possibly pain. The planes of his cheekbones and jaw contributed to the sense of someone stripped down for action. Formidable. That was the overall impression that emanated from him. Wonderful, if he happened to be on your side, but he wasn't on hers. It shook her, knowing that strength was aligned against her.

He set the mug on the table. “It’s still possible your visitor had an objective in mind other than theft or vandalism.”

She nodded. There was no point in denying the obvious. “It could be, I suppose, but that wouldn’t explain the missing money. And if you’re assuming Paul left something here, I can assure you, he took everything to his new apartment.”

“Did you change the locks after he moved out?”

“Of course I did.” She wasn’t dumb enough to leave Paul access to something he could convert to ready cash. “He couldn’t…” She stopped, suddenly realizing how he could have, if he’d thought of it.

“Missed something?” But Mordan sounded sympathetic, not sarcastic, so she didn’t flare up.

“I never thought of it, but Paul knew where I hid the key to the garage. I suppose he could get in the garage that way, and the extra house key is hanging in there.” Annoyed with herself that she’d had to admit it to him, she snapped, “But there’s no sign he did. The key is still there, and I’ve never noticed any signs that someone had been in the house.”

He studied her face for a moment, and she felt her cheeks warm under that intent gaze.

“Believe it or not, I’m not the enemy here. We’d like your cooperation. And telling me what we want to know is the best way of proving you’re innocent of theft.” His tone was uncompromising. He struck her as a man who wouldn’t tolerate any wavering from the truth.

And of course he was right. Rachel fell back on what was the last line of defense. “Since Paul was a partner in the business, he may have the right to access any material belonging to it.”

"Partner?" He snapped the word, his face tightening. "We haven't been told anything about a partnership."

Rachel took a gulp of the coffee and tried to think how to explain something she didn't fully understand herself.

"Maybe I shouldn't have said anything. I don't know how formal it was, but the four of them—Paul, Ian, James Attwood and Claire Gibson—had all been in college and grad school at the same time. Attwood had the idea for the business, but he needed help to get it off the ground, so the others agreed to work for a share of the profits until they got established. They apparently had some lean years before contracts started coming in." She shrugged. "At least, that's the way Paul told it."

Mordan's expression hadn't changed, and she had no idea whether he found that a good defense or not. He didn't give much away with that stoic expression. At least he was listening.

"I'll check on it. Now let's get to what happened when you went to the office to meet your ex-husband."

Her stomach turned over. It was one thing to decide she couldn't lie for Paul and another to be the one providing evidence against him.

Seeing her hesitation, Clint Mordan's eyes became a little less frosty. He reached across the table to touch her hand lightly. "Look, you must realize that Hartline is already in deep trouble. We know he was there, we know he accessed Attwood's personal computer. We know he's disappeared, and judging by the fact that someone was in your house, someone could know he took something away. What was it, a flash drive?"

Rachel let out the breath she'd been holding. "Yes." Her voice sounded weak, and she cleared her throat. "I found him in James Attwood's office. I heard him make a sound and went to look. He was just disconnecting a flash drive from the computer."

There. It was done. Whatever came of it, Paul would have to face the consequences of his action. But if she'd done the right thing, why did she feel so guilty?

"All right." Those steely eyes were still fixed on her face. "Did you question him? What did he say?"

Obviously he wasn't going to be content until he'd extracted every bit of the memory. She took a gulp of the hot coffee to ease her tight throat.

"I don't remember exactly. I think he tried to act as if it were nothing, but I knew he was lying. When I confronted him about it…" She shook her head. "That was when we heard Charlie coming up the steps. Paul ran out the back way, though the workrooms."

"Taking the flash drive with him."

She nodded.

"Did he say anything else before he went?"

Rachel sucked in a breath, her throat tight. "He asked me not to give him away." But she had. They both knew that now.

"He didn't explain?"

"No. There wasn't time." Didn't he understand how quickly it had happened? "It couldn't have been much more than a minute or two. Then he was gone, and I went out to the stairs before Charlie could come all the way up."

Mordan leaned back in his chair, still watching her. Whatever he saw seemed to satisfy him, because he nodded slightly.

"I'm sure you've tried since then to call him. That would be the natural thing to do."

She shot him a look of dislike. Just when she thought it was over, there was more.

"Yes, I tried. He's not answering."

"What about a text?" He wasn't leaving her any room for evasion now.

"I did get a short text. It basically said he could explain. That's all. Ian…" But she didn't want to involve Ian.

"What about him?"

She suspected he'd know if she tried to evade saying the words. "Ian mentioned that he'd also tried to call, but that Paul hadn't answered."

"No, I guess he wouldn't."

He seemed to be taking it for granted that Paul was guilty, and her temper flared.

"You don't know yet that he's guilty of anything."

His gaze was almost pitying. "Sorry. But it's our job to find out the truth of what happened. If your ex-husband took that copy for some legitimate reason, wouldn't he have come forward by now?"

"I suppose something might have happened to prevent him." But she didn't really believe it. There didn't seem to be anything else to say. She glanced at the clock. Time was up.

Mordan stood, indicating that the interrogation was over. "For your sake, I hope that's the case. I know this wasn't easy, but maybe we can stop bothering you now. Call me if anything comes up." He hesitated, looking down at her, and then reached out to put a hand on her shoulder.

She was startled at the comforting feel of that strong grip, and for a moment she was aware of him as a man, not just an antagonistic force. Their gazes met and clung, and he seemed as startled as she was. The warmth of his hand seemed to flow through her, reminding her of how long it had been since she'd had someone to rely on. If only…

Clint pulled his hand away as if he'd touched something hot, swung around, and walked off. After a moment she heard the front door open and close.

CHAPTER THREE

"SO I ENDED up telling him everything I know. I just wish I felt sure it was the right thing to do." Rachel had arrived at school in time to tell Lyn all that had happened.

Lyn had listened with gradually increasing concern. "I don't see what else you could do," she said, when Rachel had come to a reluctant halt. "Not even Paul could expect you to lie for him in a situation like this. Although nothing that man does would surprise me."

Rachel couldn't help but smile at her friend's partisanship. "You never did trust him, did you?"

"Nope. But nobody in love wants to hear warnings of doom and gloom. They only blame the messenger." She ran her hand through her short brown locks, tugging at them as if trying to force herself to think. She leaned against her crowded desk. "Wish I had some brilliant idea."

"Me, too. After all, you're the head teacher. You're supposed to be full of good advice." She smiled again, but the lighter moment passed quickly, leaving Rachel stuck in a morass of doubt.

"You've called the police about the break-in, haven't you?"

Rachel felt obscurely guilty. Naturally Lyn would call the police. But Lyn wasn't involved in her ex-husband's murky affairs. "No. And I know you think I should, but I hate to get them involved, especially if it's anything to do with Paul."

"You're still covering for him." Lyn's tone was accusing.

"Not exactly." The protest didn't sound convincing, even to her. "I know what you think of Paul, but he did have his good side. No one could be sweeter than he was, and he never wanted to hurt anyone. Unfortunately that usually meant he ended up lying about things."

Lyn didn't say anything. She just showed her disapproval.

Rachel hurried on with the story. "And wouldn't you know, no sooner had Clint Mordan left than I got a text from Paul."

"What did he say? Any explanation?"

She shook her head. "Too much to expect, I guess. The text just said I should pick up a disposable cell phone and text him from that."

"Did you do it?" Lyn's look of concern grew deeper.

"Not yet, but I suppose I'll stop after school and buy one, if it'll make him talk to me. But I don't know what he's worrying about. It's not as if anyone could get their hands on my phone."

"I suppose, but you hear about all kinds of ways of spying on people. For all I know, someone like your security agent has some means of listening in on your calls."

"He's not *my* security agent," Rachel pointed out. "If anything, he's James Attwood's."

"Yes, and you'd better remember that," Lyn warned. "From the way you talked about him, he must be an expert at getting people to trust him."

Lyn could read her pretty well. She supposed she had begun to feel as if she could…what? Confide in Clint? Those moments when he'd pressed her shoulder, seeming to reassure her… Was she reading too much into that?

"Don't look so grim," Lyn said, apparently doing it again. "I wasn't trying to scare you. But I wouldn't tell him anything you don't want Attwood to know. Mordan isn't bound by the same regulations as the police. And I still think you should go to the police. Or come and stay with me for a few days." She glanced at the clock and straightened. "And as for your position here, of course you can take as much time off as you need, but don't start thinking you're going to resign for the good of the school. We'll ride it out together."

Absurdly, Rachel felt her eyes fill with tears. She turned away quickly to hide her emotion. "Thanks, Lyn. We can talk about it later."

She wasn't going to be the iceberg that sank Fairfield School, not matter how loyal Lyn was. If she was in any legal jeopardy because of her involvement, the publicity could hurt the school. A private school like theirs could be successful only if its reputation was spotless. Parents had plenty of other choices. "I'd better get to my classroom before the kids drive the new aide under the nearest table."

Lyn grinned. "She's not that bad. Just new. Everyone was new once."

As she headed for her classroom, Rachel realized she was thinking of Lyn's words in a different context. She was certainly new to the situation in which she found herself, and there was no comfortable road map to help her through it. If she could trust anyone…but she couldn't, and she had to remember that.

Once Rachel became involved with the children, the familiar absorption took over. If she had to give this up… Pain cramped her heart for a moment. Lyn's brave assurances were what she'd expect from her friend, but the fact remained that she would resign before she'd bring any harm to the school. Maybe she was being oversensitive on the subject, but she'd never take chances like that.

The morning flew by, and when she opened the door to take her pupils to the lunchroom, the school secretary was waiting for her.

"A call for you. Lyn sent me to supervise lunch so you could take it. Okay?"

"Right, thanks, Maggie." She tried to give the grandmotherly secretary the impression that this was just routine, but she suspected every staff member knew something about her troubles by this time. The school was a very small community.

Lyn was waiting in her office. "Attwood's assistant called to say he'd like to see you as soon as possible. I just said I'd give you the message." She gave Rachel a worried smile. "In case you wanted to ignore it."

"Tempting," she admitted. "But I guess it was inevitable. I'll call her and set something up for after school."

Lyn shook her head. "If you're going to do it, you may as well get it over with. We'll cover your class for the afternoon."

Rachel didn't argue the point as she punched in the phone number. Lyn was right. She'd never be able to focus on her class with that interview looming over her.

It was the work of a moment to tell Claire Gibson she'd be there in an hour, and she clicked off.

Since she was out of school at an unusual hour, she decided to get the pay-as-you-go cell phone. She had to pass the mall anyway, and it wouldn't take long.

Of course there wasn't a nearby parking space, and even when she found the phones, the young salesman in the department seemed determined to tell her the advantages and disadvantages of each model, most of which she didn't understand.

Finally getting the phone paid for, Rachel stayed long enough to set it up. She sent the number to Paul, and then hurried to her car, afraid now of being late.

If Paul wanted to make peace with his erstwhile friends and colleagues, now was the time. If only he'd talk to her, she might be able to convince him. He was digging himself deeper in trouble the longer he delayed.

Fortunately she didn't hit much traffic the rest of the way to Attwood Industrial. She raced inside to find Claire Gibson standing at the top of the steps leading to the office area.

"James is waiting for you." She started to lead the way and then hesitated, giving Rachel a quick, side-long glance. "I'm sorry about all this. I don't suppose it's your fault."

"No. It's not." She got ahold of herself before she could say anything she might regret. "People seem to be forgetting that I'm not Paul's wife any longer. What he does isn't my business, and he doesn't tell me anything."

Claire eyed her for a moment and then nodded. "I guess you're right. If James comes on too strong..." She paused and then gave a rueful shrug. "I seem to spend most of my time preaching sensitivity to him. Without much success."

Rachel supposed that was an apology. Or maybe an explanation. Still, she could hardly expect a warm welcome here, and she'd never found Claire very congenial, anyway.

"I guess we shouldn't keep James waiting then, should we?" Rachel tried to stiffen her backbone. All she could tell them was the truth, and she knew little enough of that. If the reason behind what Paul had done was anywhere, it was here.

Without another word, Claire led the way to Attwood's office, tapped lightly and opened the door. "Rachel Hartline is here, James."

When Rachel stepped inside, the memory of the last time she'd been here flooded back. She had to force herself not to stare at the computer on Attwood's desk, but it seemed to lurk at the edge of her vision.

Attwood didn't bother standing, but then, he'd never been one for the normal politeness that eased social interactions. For that matter, she wasn't sure he understood the whole concept.

"Please, sit down, Rachel." Claire pulled forward a couple of chairs. When Rachel had taken one, Claire sat down next to her. Apparently she was going to be a part of this meeting.

At least Clint wasn't there. She'd more than half expected it, and it was a relief to think she wouldn't have his eyes on her throughout this ordeal.

"What is Paul up to?" Attwood snapped the question at her, not bothering to lead up to it.

"I don't know." She'd have to force herself to be as

blunt as he was. "As I was just reminding Claire, I'm not his wife any longer."

"You were here the night my computer was tampered with. You watched Paul copy my file."

Obviously Clint had told him everything she'd said. Well, what else could she expect? It was irrational to think he'd do otherwise when he was employed by Attwood.

"I came here to talk to Paul about the sale of our house. I just happened to see him with a flash drive. I had no way of knowing what it was."

Attwood surveyed her coldly. "You must have known he shouldn't copy something from my computer. Does he think he can get away with stealing from the company?"

"I haven't talked to him. Your investigator probably told you all that I know about it." Her mind scrambled through alternatives, trying to come up with the best approach. She couldn't let Attwood's manner make her defensive. "If he took something of value away with him—"

"Value?" Attwood interrupted her. "Did he tell you it was valuable?"

Rachel tried to hang on to her dwindling supply of patience. "He didn't tell me anything. But you'd hardly be so upset if it weren't."

"Any new advancement in our business is potentially valuable," Claire said, giving him a warning glance.

"Potentially," Attwood echoed, taking his cue from her. "*My* new technology," he said, stressing the possessive. "Our competitors would love to get their hands on it. If it pans out, of course."

"Naturally, we don't want to believe Paul has any

such intent of selling it," Claire said quickly. "We've been friends for so long."

"Yes, you have." That was what she didn't get. She'd have said Paul valued that relationship more than anything else in his life.

"That's what makes it so hard to understand. Why would he do such a thing?" Claire seemed genuinely disturbed.

Claire obviously thought she understood him, but Paul was an addict, and addicts lied. It was the first lesson any addict's friends and family had to learn. Once that was accepted, it made life a little easier. Not better, but at least one knew not to rely on the addict.

Rachel hesitated, thinking about the new cell phone lying in her handbag. Surely Paul wouldn't have told her to get it if he didn't intend to call her. She looked at Claire, finding that easier than confronting Attwood.

"If Paul does contact me, do you want me to tell him anything?"

"Tell him to come back. To explain." Claire spoke before James could, maybe afraid he'd make things worse. "We don't want to bring in the police. We can settle this among the four of us, like always."

"And if he doesn't come back?"

"We'll prosecute," Attwood snapped. "If you're involved, you're liable. So you'd better hope he does."

Rachel's stomach clenched in a spasm of fear. Attwood meant it. Somehow she had to convince Paul. But she had a growing sense that anything she could do would be too late.

WHEN CLINT REACHED his office late that afternoon, Logan was talking on the phone and studying something on his computer at the same time. He glanced up, ended his conversation and looked at Clint with raised eyebrows.

"You look like you need a drink."

"More like a decent meal. And maybe some sleep. What have you found out?"

Logan shoved his chair away from the desk, stretching and wincing a little. The muscles of his upper body flexed, mirroring the time he'd spent rebuilding them after a roadside bomb in Afghanistan came close to ending his life.

"Mostly I've learned how hard it is to get any substantial information from our client. You'd think we were spies, the way he guards every word."

Clint grunted, sinking into a chair. "He's worse in person. No feedback at all. Did he give you any better indication of who might be interested in acquiring whatever information Paul Hartline might have walked out with?"

"He won't name any names, but I gathered his new project might be of interest to either the government or any of several kinds of corporations. Something to do with the way wireless devices store power, and that's as specific as he'd be. Which tells us nothing that's of any help." Logan sounded as frustrated as he felt. "But he does seem confident that whatever it is, it hasn't been passed on yet."

"I wish he'd let us in on why he thinks that." He frowned, not sure why he felt so depressed about the whole investigation. "Any suggestion as to what it could be worth?"

Logan shrugged. "Not committing himself. But plenty, the way he acts." He reached out to click open a file on his computer. "I've been digging into the backgrounds of those four, since Attwood insists no one else knows anything about the project."

"Any red flags?" Clint straightened, interested.

"Nothing on Claire, the assistant or whatever she is. Always well dressed, a casual social life, but no close female friends that I can find. No social media presence at all, which suggests she likes her privacy. According to one of the neighbors, she often goes away on weekends, but the neighbor has no idea where."

"It's something to dig into, anyway. What about Ian Robinson? And Attwood himself? Any weaknesses that might have been exploited?"

"Attwood's not the type to show weaknesses. If he has any, they're well hidden," Logan said. "And even so, he's the biggest loser if Hartline passes the information on. I just don't see him being involved."

"Right. Still, if there was something in their past that would account for Hartline wanting to do in his friend, it might explain his motivation."

"That's what you're always telling me," Logan said. "Don't take anybody for granted. Okay, why would Attwood be involved in stealing his own project?"

"I don't know. But it wouldn't be the first time a client tried to manipulate us."

"If so, he won't succeed. Okay, we include him in our probing. What else?"

"Robinson," Clint reminded him. "What about him?"

"Robinson should be doing well, given his salary and a nice little nest egg from his parents, but there's nothing flashy about his lifestyle. Wife, baby girl, own their own home in a nice subdivision, but nothing conspicuous."

"Nothing turned up on anyone else employed there? Someone who might be a plant or might know more than anyone thinks?" Logan was the research point man. If he didn't know where to find something, he'd find someone who did.

"Not as far as I can tell. What about you? Anything turn up today?"

"Not much. His apartment was searched. But I'm guessing the searchers didn't find what they were looking for."

"What makes you think that? Whoever wants to buy the info on that flash drive might have decided Hartline was too greedy and decided to cut out the middleman after he'd picked up the information they wanted."

"Maybe, but it doesn't have that feel to me. If so, I'd expect Hartline to give up and clear out. Instead, he's apparently trying to get in touch with his ex-wife."

"How do you know?" That caught Logan's interest.

"Because Rachel Hartline made an unscheduled trip when she should have been at the school this afternoon." He didn't like the taste of the words. He'd actually begun to believe Rachel was the innocent she seemed to be. More, he'd begun to trust her, to want to protect her. But if she was lying to him, he'd come down hard. "She picked herself up a nice little burner phone. And if you can think of any reason for a respectable kindergarten teacher to be doing that other than to stay in touch with someone on the run, I'd like to hear it."

RACHEL'S REPEATED TEXTS on the new phone hadn't borne any fruit by the time Lyn called, insisting they go out for supper. It was easier to agree than to argue. Besides, she had no desire to sit at home alone waiting for a call that didn't come.

They met at a favorite Italian restaurant, where the candles cast a soft glow and the server recognized them. The murmur of voices formed a background to their talk, but no one sat close enough to overhear, so Rachel could unload.

To her surprise, once she'd shared her frustrations and uncertainties with Lyn, she actually relaxed. A plate of lobster ravioli accompanied by the wine Lyn insisted on ordering finished the process.

Seeming to know that what Rachel needed most was to forget for a time, Lyn steered the conversation to school matters—the tiresome parents, the challenge of teaching students used to instant gratification and the endless paperwork that ate up too much of a teacher's time.

She was laughing at Lyn's description of her recent interview with a prospective student and her parents, when she heard a cell phone tone. Not her usual phone—it was the new one, and an actual call rather than a text.

Rachel scrambled to her feet, yanking the phone out of her bag in a fever lest Paul should lose patience and hang up before she could respond. She managed to pick up while hurrying toward the restroom—the only place she might have the privacy this call demanded.

"Paul, is that you?" She kept her voice low as she threaded her way between tables and reached the relative sanctuary of the women's room. "Don't hang up. Okay, now I can talk. Where are you?"

"Never mind that. What did you say to Attwood?" Paul's words came out in a rushed whisper.

"What could I say? They already know you were there and that you copied something from his computer."

"Nothing more? Didn't they ask you?"

"They asked, but I didn't know anything else. All I could say was that you'd said you could explain."

She heard the sharp intake of his breath. "You told them I'd texted you."

Rachel closed her eyes briefly, trying to press down that vague sense of guilt. She had nothing to feel guilty about. "I won't lie for you, Paul. Don't ask it."

"No, no, of course not," he murmured hastily.

"Besides, they just want you to come back. Claire said…or implied, at least, that they wouldn't bring in the police if you did. And Ian said the same."

"I can't."

"Why not?" Exasperation mounted. How could he ignore the possible consequences?

"There's more to it than you think. Listen, I can't talk here. I'll stop by the house around nine. But not inside. Meet me out by the garage."

"Why outside? Don't tell me you think someone bugged the house—that's ridiculous." Really, this was starting to sound like a bad spy film.

"Just do it," he snapped, then began again in a different tone. "Don't let me down, Rachel. Please." He ended the call.

Rachel was tempted to call back, to demand answers, but that never worked with Paul. It would just put up all his defenses. It was only when he was assured that her feelings were positive that he'd been able to tell her the truth. What had happened to him as a child that had left him so desperate for approval? She'd never known.

And now she hadn't even had a chance to tell him

about the house being searched. A chilling thought struck her. She had ridiculed the idea that the house was bugged, but how would she know? The disorder could have covered up a more devious act.

When she returned to the table, she told Lyn what had happened, who didn't hesitate to share her opinion on men who tried to get their ex-wives to bail them out when they'd gotten themselves in trouble.

Everything Lyn said was only too true, but Rachel couldn't just walk away and do nothing. She deliberately didn't tell Lyn that she was going to meet Paul. If Lyn knew, she would insist on being there, and the last thing Rachel wanted was to pull Lyn further into Paul's misdeeds.

Nine o'clock found her turning into the driveway, her headlights revealing nothing out of the ordinary. Rachel pulled into the detached garage and came out, closing the door but not turning on the light that illuminated the walk to the front porch.

For a moment she lingered by the garage, listening for any sound. Then, realizing that her figure was silhouetted against the white garage door, she moved a few feet toward the house, preferring the shade of the rhododendron bush that was overgrowing its allotted space.

The neighborhood was quiet, almost too quiet. The house to her right was empty and dark, while on the other side a flickering light announced that the elderly couple who lived there, the Bartons, were watching television. A month ago they might have been sitting on their patio, but people didn't go outside in the evenings now that the weather was cooler.

Even as she thought it, their door opened, sending a rectangle of light onto the sidewalk. Mr. Barton, no doubt putting his cocker spaniel out. Buster never intruded into her lawn, thanks to the picket fence, but she knew he'd trot around restlessly for a time, probably thinking his humans were foolish to prefer the indoors on a night like this. He was a sweet animal, but she wished he weren't out just at this moment.

She pressed back into the bush, wondering if he'd set up a racket if he scented her. If so…well, she'd deal with that if it happened.

She strained her ears for any sound. The dark seemed to press in on her, and the neighborhood was quieter than she'd have thought possible. Every slight rustle of the shrubbery seemed to announce her presence.

Or someone else's. The discovery that someone had been in her house still lingered like a nightmare she couldn't quite wake up from.

She began to regret not turning the light on. Would Paul show up, or was this yet another time when he failed to deliver on his promises? The glow of the Bartons' porch light, coming from her left, lit up a section of her yard, and she turned away from the garage to scan it.

Something, maybe the scrape of a shoe on the pavement, alerted her. She started to turn toward the garage, a greeting forming on her lips, when there was a rush of movement. An arm encircled her, a hand clamped down hard on her mouth and she was pulled hard against a man's body.

For an instant shock paralyzed her. Paul—but it wasn't Paul. This was someone bigger, taller. She struggled to free her mouth enough to scream, trying to remember the elements of the self-defense class she'd once taken.

The arms dragged her backward, toward the darkness that ran along the side of the garage. *No!* She couldn't let that happen. *Kick, bite, scratch—do whatever you have to.* With a spurt of panic, Rachel fought back, struggling to get a hand free to claw at his face. But he held her too tightly. She couldn't get loose… Sagging down, she made herself a dead weight, hoping to distract him. If he thought she'd passed out, he might relax his grip for an instant.

But the deadly pressure of the hand blocking her mouth and nose was too strong, and the darkness began to swirl around her. Frantic, afraid she really would pass out, she kicked backward again, connecting with what felt like the hard bone of his shin. His hand slipped momentarily.

Momentarily, but it was enough. Rachel managed a choked scream before it was cut off, and a volley of barking burst out from the next yard. Loud, frantic—it sounded as if Buster was attacking the fence. The Bartons must hear, they'd come out—she fought with a fresh burst of energy.

The door opened in the next house, Buster's barking increased frantically, and she was thrown violently to the ground, the breath knocked out of her.

When she could breathe again, Buster, tail wagging furiously, was licking her face. She drew in another breath, pushing herself to her hands and knees.

"Ms. Hartline, are you all right? What happened?" Mr. Barton hurried toward her, panting at the exertion. "Are you hurt?"

She sat back on her heels, hugging the spaniel. "I'm okay. Thanks to Buster."

"I heard him and I just knew something was wrong." Mrs. Barton had joined them by then. Short, white-haired and rounded, she and her husband looked like a matched set. "Goodness, Blaine, don't just stand there, help her up."

"Yes, yes." Galvanized, he put his arms around her shoulders, puffing.

Afraid he'd strain himself into a heart attack, Rachel managed to get her feet under her and push herself up despite her shaking legs. Her breath still came in gasps, and her heart raced. "Thank you so much. Did...did you see what happened?"

"Not enough to recognize." Barton shook his head, absently patting her back. "Just a shadow. What was it, a burglar?"

"This neighborhood gets more dangerous every year," his wife declared. "Let's get you inside your house where we can find out if he hurt you. Then we can call the police."

Her first instinct was to say no, but that would make them suspicious of her. Besides, did she really want to refuse?

Then she thought of Paul and wavered. By the time they were in her house, she'd made up her mind.

"Looks like he didn't get inside, anyway. You must have scared him off before he could." Mr. Barton looked around, and she could only be thankful that he hadn't seen it after the previous search.

Rachel pushed back tumbled hair. Succumbing to Mrs. Barton's urging, she sank into the corner of the sofa and let the woman check her for injuries. Aside from a scratch on her face and what would probably turn into a couple of colorful bruises, she was all right. Just shaken. All the self-defense classes in the world couldn't prepare her for the real thing.

"I should have left the lights on. I went to dinner

with my friend, and I hadn't planned to be this late. I suppose he must have thought the house was empty."

That obviously didn't explain the fact that she'd just pulled into the driveway moments before. Any intruder would surely take alarm at that.

A chill went through her. This hadn't been a search, not this time. This time they'd gone after her directly. But who?

"I'll call the police." Mrs. Barton, taking charge, headed for the phone.

"No, wait." She thought furiously. It hadn't been Paul, so who had it been? And what had happened to Paul? "I'll do it, but I want to check first to see if anything is missing. If…if he…they never got into the house, I can wait until morning to report it."

Mrs. Barton exchanged glances with her husband. "Wouldn't it be better to do it now?"

"I'm just so shaken." She let her voice tremble, and it wasn't hard. "I don't want to get into a long ordeal of talking to the police at this hour. I'd rather deal with it when I've rested."

"But surely…" Mrs. Barton wasn't easily deterred.

"Now, Alice, if she wants to wait, that's her business." But she could sense Mr. Barton's doubt at her hesitation.

An unspoken understanding seemed to pass between the elderly pair. Then Mrs. Barton nodded.

"All right, dear. Just as you say." She patted Rachel's shoulder. "Do you want anything—a nice cup of tea, maybe?"

"Or a stiff drink," Mr. Barton added, blue eyes twinkling a little. His wife gave him a pretend slap.

"No, I'm fine. I just came from dinner. I want to curl up and relax."

"All right, but if you get nervous tonight, you just call and we'll come right over."

"I'll be fine." Rachel tried to infuse her voice with an assurance she didn't feel. "Thank you so much for coming to the rescue. And thank you, Buster." She bent to ruffle the spaniel's silky black ears. "You're a real hero."

"First time I've ever been proud of him for raising a racket," Mr. Barton said gruffly. "You take care now."

It took a few more assurances that she'd be fine, but her helpful neighbors finally left. Rachel closed the door, locked it and leaned against it, exhausted.

All she had were questions, no answers. The first one was obvious. What had happened to Paul? He could have come, she supposed, and been frightened off if he'd seen someone lurking outside. If so, he'd been more observant than she had.

Rachel fished out the cell phone and called his number. It went straight to voicemail. "What happened to you? Someone attacked me when I was waiting for you. Tell me what you're involved in." Afraid she was starting to sound panicky, she disconnected.

Panicky. That was a good description. Her home no longer felt like a haven. Her safe, normal world had turned upside down, and she'd begun to think there was no one she could trust who was capable of dealing with a situation like this.

Clint Mordan slipped into her thoughts, and she pushed the idea away with a shudder. He was capable, all right, but as Lyn had pointed out, he wasn't on her side. He might even have been the one who attacked her, hoping to frighten her into depending on him.

She rubbed her temples, collapsing limply into the nearest chair. She needed time—time for Paul to settle his affairs, time for Paul to clear her of any involvement. And she needed safety. Security.

There was only one place in her life that had ever offered her security. Few people knew of her connection to the quiet Amish farm a lifetime away from here. Paul knew, of course, but he never talked about it. He'd actually found it a little embarrassing that his wife's history was so unconventional. Besides, his interests had always been in the here and now or in the future pot of gold, not in her childhood summers.

The familiar picture formed in her mind—the serenity of the farm, fields golden now in the fall sunshine. The quiet, steady routine of Amish life, grounded in the habits of centuries. Her pounding heart slowed. The figures of grandparents, aunts, uncles, cousins, each one dear to her but anonymous to anyone else—dressed alike, looking alike to strangers.

She could hide there. The idea formed in her mind, growing stronger by the moment. What she needed was a place to be quiet, to regroup, to figure out how to cope with the mess Paul had involved her in. She shivered, thinking of Attwood's threat to prosecute her for complicity. She couldn't prove she hadn't been involved with Paul's actions. The very fact that she hadn't immediately reported him weighed against her.

She couldn't have done that, even in a moment of anger. How could she jump to turn in a man she'd once loved, a man she'd promised to honor and love for the rest of their lives? She couldn't just turn that off and forget it. Her grandparents had taught her well, and even if she hadn't listened to them, seeing the mess her mother had made of her life would have done it. She might never be able to live with Paul again, but she didn't have it in her to betray him without hearing his side of it, at least.

That was at the heart of her reluctance. Paul should have a chance to defend himself. Despite all the lies he'd told, she'd never been able to see him stealing from his closest friends. He'd have rationalized that the money in their joint account was his as much as hers, but he couldn't have thought that about the company.

Unless, of course, he really did hold an actual partnership in the company, but if that were true, then what he'd done couldn't be described as theft. *If* it were true.

Would it make sense to go to the police? But once she'd reported the assault, where would it end? The police would obviously want to know why she was a target, and that would lead inevitably to Attwood, to Paul's copying the file and to the fact that she'd known. She could end up charged with complicity, and even if it never went to trial, just the charge could be enough to ruin her future as a teacher here.

Rachel rubbed her forehead tiredly. She was starting to think in circles. *Get back to what your instincts tell you. Get to a safe place, contact Paul and find out what he was doing.* She was already so involved that she'd never be free of this until she knew.

She'd go to her grandparents' farm. That would give her a breathing spell, but she had to be careful. Clint had found her laughably soon after her last attempt at evasion. It would take some doing to get to Echo Falls without leaving a trail for him to follow.

But once she was there, she could sink, unnoticed, into the placid routine of Amish life. She could stay there, undetected, until she'd clarified things with Paul and decided what she could do to salvage her life.

Determination flowed in, strengthening her. No one would know where she was, *especially* Clint.

CHAPTER FOUR

BY SEVEN THE next morning Clint was pulling up at Rachel's house, intent on confronting her about the burner phone. He'd have been there the previous night if Logan hadn't advised caution, afraid she'd call the cops if they pushed her too hard. He'd had to agree, but still, it rankled, maybe all the more so because he'd begun to sympathize with her. He should know better than to fall for the wide-eyed innocent act.

After pulling into the driveway he headed for the front door, determined to get the truth out of her.

Leaning on the doorbell, he listened to it chime inside the house. No response. He knocked, taking a step sideways so that he could look through the living room window. Neat, orderly, with nothing to indicate that the house was occupied or that anything was wrong.

Clint gave it another try, knocking hard enough that the door shivered. Nothing. He eyed the lock. No dead bolt, just an ordinary lock in the knob, the easiest thing in the world to open.

Tempting, very tempting, but he wouldn't. Rachel might have left early for school this morning for all sorts of reasons. If so, he'd catch up with her there, preferably before class started, so he didn't have to have another encounter with the head teacher. The woman was entirely too reminiscent of his third-grade teacher back home—a woman with eyes in the back of her head and an uncanny ability to sniff out trouble before it started.

Texting Logan to let him know, Clint joined the work-bound flow of drivers attempting to get from one side of Philadelphia to the other. Later than he had hoped, he reached the school just ahead of a school bus.

He had to be buzzed in, of course, and by the time he reached the office, the secretary was obviously prepared for him. Unsmiling, she ushered him straight into the head teacher's office.

Lyn Baker's expression was not only unsmiling, it was openly antagonistic.

"This is a school, Mr. Mordan. We really can't have persons unrelated to school business haunting our building. You'll have to leave."

He tried to produce a disarming look, holding up his hands in surrender. "Believe me, I know, and I wouldn't have come if I'd had a choice. But Ms. Hartline had already left her house when I arrived this morning, and it's important that I speak to her."

"Important to you. Not, perhaps, to her." The icy tone gave no hint of thawing.

"It's in Ms. Hartline's best interests that she speak to me. The sooner we get this situation cleared up, the better for her."

The woman wasn't noticeably buying it. Instead, she stretched out a hand toward the phone, and he suspected it would give her great pleasure to call the police. "If she wanted to speak to you, I'm sure she'd be in touch."

"Suppose you ask her now if she'd give me a few minutes." All this stalling was beginning to make him more suspicious than he'd already been.

For a moment she hesitated. Her hand touched the phone. “That’s impossible.”

“Why?” He snapped the word, beginning to see the truth. “She’s not here, is she?”

“No, she’s not here. And it’s about time you weren’t here either, unless you’d prefer I call the police.”

He grabbed onto his rising temper. “Look, it’s obvious you’re her friend. If you know where she is…”

“I don’t. Ms. Hartline asked for a personal day. I granted it. That’s all.”

“You must have some idea…”

She lifted the receiver to her ear.

“All right, I’m leaving.” It was no part of his plan to end up under arrest. “But when you speak to her, tell her I’m looking for her.”

If that sounded threatening, at this point he didn’t much care.

Clint left the building fuming. He’d trusted her—that was what rankled most. He must be getting soft now that he was in the private security business. His cop’s instincts said she’d gone on the run…probably meeting her ex-husband even now. And where? He had no clue.

Mixed messages. Rachel was full of them. There’d been moments when he’d thought her honestly baffled by what was happening, making his protective instincts go into high gear—those green eyes troubled, her lips trembling a little as she tried to make sense of the situation. Had that all been an act?

After jumping in the car, he headed back to her house. On this visit, he wasn’t going to let any consideration keep him from checking inside.

Traffic had lessened by this time, and he made it back to the quiet neighborhood fairly quickly. Quiet was just what he needed. Most people were out at work at this hour, and there was no one left to see when he made a neat, quick entry.

Clint stepped inside, closed the door gently and stood motionless. If she'd been here all along, refusing to answer his knocks, she'd make a move when she heard the door open.

But the small house was still, the room frozen in a kind of unnatural order. No sign here that she'd left in a hurry, but that meant nothing. The disorder, if there was any, would be in the bedroom.

He moved through the house, observing but not touching. In the kitchen all was as it should be, and the dishwasher had a load of clean dishes waiting to be put away. No cup in the sink, and the coffee maker was cold, clean and dry. It looked as if whenever she'd gone, it hadn't been in a rush, which probably meant she'd been gone when he'd come by earlier.

His jaw tightening, he moved into the bedroom. He didn't know her well enough to know what clothes had disappeared, but there was a gap on the top shelf of the closet between a suitcase and a carry-on bag…just about big enough for a backpack or a duffel bag.

Rachel had fled. He had to face it. So much for the half-formed notion that she was an innocent pawn caught in the middle between her ex-husband and his angry employer. She'd been stringing them along until she could make arrangements with her ex to take off.

Did that mean the information had been passed on? Possibly. He hadn't heard from Attwood this morning. How much could they rely on his conviction that he'd hear something if his creation had surfaced?

Clint had no idea. The limited info they'd received

had been beyond his grasp, and his only concern was to retrieve the file and Paul Hartline, in that order of preference. If Attwood got his precious project back safely, he probably wouldn't bother chasing after Hartline.

There was nothing else for it but to trace Rachel Hartline and hope she led him to the prize. With that in mind, he began a methodical search for any clue as to when and where she'd gone.

At the end of an hour, he was no further along than he'd been when he walked in the door. All he had to show for an intensive search was Rachel's cell phone, hidden inside a boot in the closet. She must've been afraid he could trace her from it, so she'd just taken the burner phone.

He slid the cell phone in his jacket pocket and went out the front door, locking it behind him. He'd take a cursory look through the phone before passing it on to Logan to work his technological magic on it. If there was any hint or information there, Logan would find it.

Clint had barely started out the walk before a woman came rushing from the house next door, waving her hand to stop him. A small spaniel ran in circles around her, entranced by this new game.

"Goodness, I'm so glad you're here. We told Rachel she should call the police last night, but she insisted on waiting until this morning to notify you. I was afraid she wouldn't do it." With a sudden onset of caution, she eyed him. "You are the police, aren't you? I mean…"

"I'm an investigator," he said quickly. Obviously something had happened the previous night, something that had concerned Rachel's elderly neighbor enough to have her in a flutter. What? She thought he knew already, so he'd have to be careful.

"Have you seen Ms. Hartline this morning? I'm eager to get her firsthand account, you understand."

"Yes, of course." Her white curls bounced as she nodded vigorously. "Just like on television. The detectives always want to hear it all over again." She shook her head regretfully. "I looked out in particular this morning because I wanted to see how she was after her ordeal. But she must have left early for school. Or to stop at the police station, of course."

How early? It seemed clear the woman hadn't seen her at all this morning. But what ordeal? He had to get her to tell him without betraying his own ignorance.

"She was very upset by what happened, wasn't she?"

"Goodness, yes. I wanted to stay with her, but she wouldn't hear of it. Kept insisting she was all right, but she had to be shaken. I mean, anybody would be."

The woman was maddening. She was the type who'd talk all around a subject without ever getting to the meat. His nerves were stretched to the breaking point. So much for his conviction that Rachel was just a manipulator. All it took was a hint of danger to her, and he was right back to being protective.

"And my husband said it was so fortunate that we'd put the dog out just at that time. It was his barking that scared off the burglar, I'm sure of it." She patted the dog. "He's a good baby, isn't he?" she crooned.

"It's not quite clear from the report I saw whether the man actually got into the house or not," he said, trying to sound like someone who'd consulted a written report on the incident.

"No, no, my husband looked all around when we helped Rachel inside, and there was no sign. She said she must have arrived home just as he was trying to get in. He actually knocked her down trying to get away. It's amazing she wasn't hurt more than she was, but she *said* she was fine. Bumped and bruised and scratched, and it stands to reason she was shaken up." She made it clear that she'd have relished the chance to fuss over Rachel a bit more.

"Now, dear, if Rachel said she was all right, she should know." The man approaching them looked like a perfect fit for his wife, with the same round face and curly white hair. Some said long-marrieds grew to look alike, and these two were the perfect example.

"Mr.…Barton," he said after a quick look at the name on the mailbox. "I take it you folks came to the rescue last night."

"Mostly it was Buster," he said, bending in his turn to caress the spaniel that sat panting, one silky ear flopped up. "He raised such a fuss I knew something was wrong." He turned to his wife. "By the way, I noticed that soup you're cooking was boiling pretty hard."

The woman made a clucking sound. "And you didn't turn it down? If that isn't just like you." She hesitated, obviously torn.

"I'll tell the officer anything else he needs to know," he said, giving her a gentle push toward the house. "You go on."

When she'd gotten safely out of earshot, he turned back to Clint. "I didn't want my wife getting any more upset. She'll be nervous any time she's alone in the house, thinking someone's trying to break in."

"I can understand that, sir. Did either of you get a good look at the man?"

Barton shook his head, regretful. "Wish I had. If I'd thought to bring a flashlight out with me—but I didn't, and there's no use regretting it now. Rachel's all right. That's the important thing."

Clint studied the shrewd wrinkled face. "You saw a little more than your wife did, I take it."

"Nothing helpful, I'm afraid. But my wife jumped to the conclusion that Rachel had fallen when the man rushed past her trying to get away."

Clint stiffened. "It wasn't that way?"

"Well, the thing is, I couldn't see very well. And I don't want the wife getting all upset and thinking we're going to be murdered in our beds."

"I'm sure I won't need to bother her again." Clint answered the unspoken concern. "If you'll just give me your impressions."

"Judging by the time it took me to get out here—" Barton spoke carefully, as if concerned not to give any false impressions "—and taking the way the dog was carrying on, well, it seemed to me that Rachel was actually struggling with the man. It wasn't just a matter of him running off when she spotted him." He hesitated, and then gave Clint a questioning look. "Didn't she say anything more in her statement?"

"People are often inclined to minimize things like that after they're over," he said. "I suppose it's a way of rationalizing something that seems unthinkable."

That seemed to satisfy him, because he nodded. "Well, like I said, I wish I'd helped more, but it was dark, and I don't see all that well. The guy went running off the other way. I did notice I didn't hear a car start up, so if he drove here, he didn't park real close." He shook his head. "Rachel's a nice woman—not somebody bad things happen to, I'd have thought."

"Random crime can happen to anyone," he said

vaguely, holding out his hand. "Thanks for your help. I'll do my best to clear this up. You can count on it."

The man gave him a firm handshake, seeming satisfied. Clicking his fingers at the spaniel, he headed back toward his own house.

Clint strode to the car. Rachel was on the run; he was sure of that. But given what had apparently happened the previous night, it was no longer safe to assume that she'd just gone to meet her erring ex.

Who had reason to attack Rachel? Her ex-husband, for reasons he couldn't even guess? Nobody from Attwood Industrial, he felt sure. They wanted their property back, but reputable professionals didn't go around acting like hit men.

He was beginning to wonder if Hartline had double-crossed his prospective client. Or were they dealing with a middleman who specialized in industrial espionage and might not be above such tactics?

More was going on here than they'd yet discovered. He didn't know from whom or why, and he needed to find out. But one thing was clear—Rachel Hartline was in danger.

AFTER THE WAY Clint had found her so quickly when she and Lyn traded cars, Rachel knew she had to take every precaution she could. She might not be a match for a professional like Clint Mordan, but she wouldn't make it easy for him to follow her.

She'd called Lyn, explaining as little as possible and carefully not telling her where she was going. Lyn had caught on to all the things she didn't say.

She'd rather keep her friend out of it entirely, but

she couldn't risk having Lyn go to the police when she didn't turn up for school the next day.

So far so good. She settled into a bus seat, averting her face from the passenger across the aisle. The older woman looked the type to while away a tedious trip by endless conversation, so Rachel slid over to the window and stared fixedly out. She couldn't afford to do anything that might cause someone to remember her. The jeans and sweatshirt she wore were the sort of thing every other young person would have on, and she'd pulled the hood up over her hair.

She had driven her car to the Philadelphia airport before the sun was up, escaping most of the usual morning traffic on 95. Leaving the car in the long-term lot, she'd waited for a shuttle to take her to the train station, fearing a taxi might be too easily traced to her.

Surely Clint would first assume she'd taken a flight when he found her car at the airport. She didn't doubt he'd find it—that was probably child's play to a man like him. That's why she'd switched to a train to Harrisburg, and now she was on a bus to State College. The bus service was often crowded with students going back and forth to Penn State, and at the moment she welcomed the idea of losing herself in a group.

The bus filled up gradually, and she slid the new cell phone from her bag and checked it. But it remained stubbornly blank. No reply from Paul to her texts. Was he even receiving them? Not being able to contact him was a constant irritant, separate from all the other fears and frustrations she felt.

Exasperation had her biting her lip. What was Paul playing at? She'd texted him about the attack, told him she was leaving town until he straightened out this mess. It was hard to believe he wouldn't be alarmed that someone had come after her.

Paul might figure out where she'd gone. But he had visited the farm at Echo Falls only once, and the visit hadn't been a success. Not that her grandfather would say anything against him, but Grossdaadi's silence on the subject spoke volumes. Even Grossmammi's voice had sounded hollow when she'd wished them happiness.

If Rachel had taken their opinions more seriously, she might not be in this predicament today. It had been useless to expect good advice from her several-times-married mother, but despite their restricted lives in the quiet Amish countryside, her grandparents understood people. She could have trusted them.

It was far too late for regrets of that sort. All she could do now was focus on staying out of Paul's affairs as best she could.

The bus began to move, lumbering slowly through traffic. The large young man who'd taken the aisle seat next to her propped his knees against the seat in front of him and fell asleep. That left her plenty of privacy to focus on her own problems. Her mind returned, inexorably, to Clint Mordan. For a crazy moment or two after the attack, she'd almost called him.

That would have been a mistake. He was, if not the enemy, at least someone to be avoided. Those moments when he'd seemed sympathetic had lured her into saying more than she'd intended. It had been so tempting to tell him everything. She had to keep reminding herself that his duty was to Attwood, not her. Lyn had been right about that.

Clint might be a man of integrity—it was too soon to tell. But he was also a person who probably considered deception a professional requirement. She couldn't trust her reputation and her safety to someone whose loyalty lay elsewhere.

Some part of her still regarded that as a shame. It would have been reassuring to unload her burdens on those strong shoulders.

She dismissed the thought, annoyed with herself. She didn't need anyone to rely on. Just because there had been a moment when they'd touched, when wordless communication flowed, that didn't mean she could trust him.

Leaning back, Rachel forced herself to simulate sleep, but behind her closed lids, her mind was busy. She considered getting off at one of the intermediate stops, but if she headed for the farm too quickly, she might lead any followers straight to Echo Falls. Better to get off at State College in the exodus of students and then backtrack. Each change she made surely would create more difficulties for anyone tracing her.

She'd been thinking about Clint as the follower, but what about the man who'd attacked her? She forced herself to relive those moments. She'd known instantly that it hadn't been Paul. That same instinct told her the man wasn't Clint, either. It wasn't just emotion. Clint was taller, harder, more muscular. Whoever he was, she'd be naïve to assume he wouldn't come after her again.

What had he wanted? Had he thought she knew where Paul was? Or where the flash drive had gone? Surely, if Paul had turned it over to someone else already, the pressure would be off her.

Now that she had time to think instead of react, she began to wonder if the obvious assumption, that Paul had taken the information to sell, was really so simple.

Quite aside from the fact that she couldn't see Paul betraying his friends, surely he'd end up with more continuing benefit when his own firm developed it. Unless he'd had some desperate immediate need for money. If he was in debt, if he were threatened…maybe he would act out of character.

Why didn't Paul answer? He was the only one who could tell her the truth. As soon as she considered it, she realized how ridiculous that hope was. When had Paul ever followed through on his responsibilities toward their marriage? Because like it or not, he *was* responsible for the trouble she was in.

Addicts lie. The unpalatable truth had been spoken by the leader of a group that helped the family and friends of addicted persons. *They lie all the time. They lie whenever it's the easiest thing to do. That's the first thing you have to accept in dealing with them.*

She had no idea if his generalization was true of all addicts, but he'd hit the gold when it came to an assessment of Paul. It had taken longer than it should have for her to accept that, but life had been, if not easier, at least less unpredictable when she had.

Despite herself, she actually fell asleep on the bus, waking only when it pulled into State College. It took a few moments to collect herself, and when she disembarked she looked around with apprehension.

But it was ridiculous to imagine that Clint could have gotten here before her. He might be good at his job, but he couldn't read minds. That was true of anyone else who might be chasing her, too.

Making her way to the counter, she consulted the schedule of outbound routes. There were several possibilities, but only one that would get her out quickly.

Silly, she supposed, but she had a sudden aversion to the thought of sitting and waiting. As long as she kept moving, she felt relatively safe. If anyone had followed her…

But no one had. It was absurd to feel as if unknown eyes were watching her, waiting to see what she did next. She bought a ticket for the first eastbound bus, found it already waiting and boarded. With a sense of urgency she watched the platform, her hand shielding her face, until the driver closed the door and pulled out.

She inhaled deeply, forcing her taut muscles to relax. Everything was going according to plan. There was no reason for her fears.

It wasn't until the last leg of Rachel's trip that her luck ran out. The closest she could get was a stop five miles away from Echo Falls…probably a little less to the farm. There was only one option left. She shouldered the small backpack and started walking.

Five miles had never seemed so long, and her spirits took a nosedive when it began to grow dark. She could have driven from her house to the farm in under four hours, if she'd dared use the car.

As it was, the two-lane blacktop road stretched before her, featureless in the gathering shadows. Telling herself no one knew where she was didn't help when she could still feel hard hands grasping her in the dark.

She was near enough that most of the farms on either side of the road were Amish-owned. Sitting well back from the pavement as the farmhouses did, their dim lights didn't penetrate very far.

Headlights appeared, reflecting from the trees along the verge, and she heard the sound of a motor. A car was coming up behind her, fast.

No reason to think it was someone looking for her,

but it was dangerous to walk along the narrow road in the dark. She stepped off onto the side, weeds brushing the legs of her jeans. The ground sloped down to a ditch, and a leafy branch from a bush tangled in her hair.

The car swerved around the bend in the road, careened crazily across the pavement and scraped the branches of an overhanging bush. Rachel stepped back, up to her ankles in water, heart pounding as the brakes shrieked. If the car stopped—but it was only a momentary pause before the driver straightened the vehicle and sped off.

Idiot. Rachel could breathe again. Speeding drivers were a constant threat to Amish buggies, and most sensible people would drive more carefully in this area after dark. That hadn't been a sensible driver.

Withdrawing her feet from the drainage ditch, she shook them ruefully. Better wet feet than bodily injury from a careless driver, especially when she was this close to safety.

And she *was* close. Only one more farm to pass, and then she saw the white post that held the mailbox at the end of the lane. *Esch*, it read, but people from around here undoubtedly still called it the Byler place, referring to her grandfather, Bishop Josiah Byler. Timothy Esch was Cousin Sadie's husband, and Sadie and Timothy had taken over running the farm when Grossmammi and Grossdaadi were ready to retire to the grossdaadi haus.

Not, she supposed, that her grandfather didn't still participate in the decisions as well as the work of the farm. Timothy and Sadie would expect that, and they'd been happy to have a thriving dairy farm to step into when the time came.

Rachel smiled, thinking of Sadie. She and Sadie were exactly the same age, and they'd been like sisters when they were young, despite the fact that Rachel had been there only in the summer. How they'd cried every year when the time came for her to go back to her mother—Rachel could still remember the sense of desolation she'd felt at leaving.

When she'd gone off with her mother, the unpredictability set in again. Never knowing when Mom might take it into her head to move on, change jobs, change men…

She'd always had a sense of living in two different, contradictory worlds. Learning to adjust had been hard, and it had never grown easier.

Even now, she felt the familiar eagerness to slip back into the even tenor of Amish life, shedding the fears and worries that haunted her. But now she was an adult, and she knew it couldn't be done.

No one could go back, not entirely, to something already lived. She'd be impatient now, living without cell phones and electricity and the internet. But maybe she could have a resting place, at least.

Steps lightening, she hurried along the gravel lane to the farmhouse. She could make out the gaslights showing through the living room windows now, and surely that was Sadie, sitting in a rocking chair, probably with a stack of mending in her lap.

Rachel went automatically toward the back door that led into the kitchen. In the country, family and friends always went to the back. It was only strangers who knocked at the front.

The dogs began barking their alert as she neared. She stopped at the sight of a moving lantern, approaching from the direction of the barn. She couldn't quite make out the dark figure behind it, but she knew it all the same. It was her grandfather, making his last check of the animals, just as he always did.

She took another step, the gravel rattling under her feet, and the lantern lifted. "Who is there?" Her grandfather's voice was as strong as ever.

Rachel dropped her bag, tears stinging her eyes. "It's me, Grossdaadi. Rachel."

"Rachel?" The light swung out toward her, and now she could see the surprised joy in her grandfather's face. "My dear child, komm." He held out his arms.

Rachel crossed the space between them in a stumbling run and threw her arms around him, feeling the soft cotton of his shirt and the still-wiry strength of him despite his age. His arms closed around her, and his soft beard tickled her cheek.

"My dear child," he murmured.

She should explain, say something sensible, but her throat seemed to be blocked, and words were impossible. Instead, she burst into tears.

CHAPTER FIVE

IN RETROSPECT, BREAKING down was probably the best thing she could have done. Nobody asked for explanations because they were so busy comforting her and assuring her that she was home and everything would be all right.

Maybe that was all she'd really needed—to feel someone's arms around her and hear a loving voice tell her everything would be all right. It was exactly how she'd respond to one of her kindergartners who was hurting, and she didn't have any false pride about accepting it.

A half hour later Rachel sat at the kitchen table, a hand-stitched quilt around her shoulders, a mug of hot tea with honey in her hands. She hadn't really been that cold, but sheer relief at being there had left her feeling a bit shaky.

Grossmammi sat next to her, her rosy cheeks crisscrossed with fine wrinkles and her faded blue eyes worried. She patted Rachel's arm, her touch gentle. "No matter what happened, you are here now." She spoke in the soft accents of Pennsylvania Dutch, and Rachel found her mind automatically adjusting to the sounds of her childhood summers. "Is it…him? Paul?"

Grossmammi wouldn't bring herself to call him Rachel's ex-husband, because to her, divorce didn't exist.

Rachel had spared her the knowledge of Paul's gambling. The only consolation Grossmammi could find in her granddaughter's situation was that it had been Paul who'd wanted his freedom, Paul who'd left. Whatever happened, Rachel had always felt her love and support.

"In a way."

Rachel took a deep breath. She'd considered how and what she'd tell them, but now, looking at them, she couldn't find the words. Grossmammi, so worried and loving. Grossdaadi, his worry not quite so obvious, his face stoic and ready for anything. Sadie… Sadie, always as close as a sister to her, wasn't looking at her. Her husband, Timothy, looked perplexed. He leaned toward Sadie, as if to emphasize that he was with her.

Her only choice was to tell them everything, no matter how hard it was, and trust that their love would stretch to cover the situation she'd brought to them.

The words came slowly at first, but as she talked, she began to find she sorted the events and moved through them, not leaving anything out. It seemed to clear her our mind, making it easier to look at what had happened to her in a logical way.

When she got to the attack on her, Grossmammi let out a little gasp, and her fingers clutched Rachel's hand.

"So the only thing I could think of was to come here," she said. "I thought, if only he had a little time, Paul would do the honest thing and that would clear me. If not…" Her voice shook a little. "If not, I don't know what I'll do."

There. It was all said. The decision was up to them now. If they didn't want her to stay, if it was asking too much to involve them, then she would leave.

Her grandfather cleared his throat, looking his most

solemn. As bishop, he'd faced many difficult decisions, but probably never one quite like this, and in his own family.

"Do you think your… Do you think Paul will do as he should?"

With her grandfather's keen eyes on her, Rachel couldn't be less than honest. "I don't know. He has lied to me in the past, often. But he asked me to give him time to straighten it out, and I thought I should."

He nodded, as if he wouldn't expect anything else.

"And this man, Clint Mordan, do you think he's the one who attacked you?"

"No, I'm sure he didn't. His job is to find the stolen file. He may not believe that I don't know where Paul is, but my sense is that he wouldn't do something like that to find out."

Grossdaadi sat, considering, for a long moment. No one else moved or spoke. Whatever he decided, the others would go along with, not only because he was the head of the house or because he was the bishop, but because they respected his wisdom, just as she did.

That was something Paul had never understood. He hadn't been able to look beyond the old-fashioned clothing and unusual traditions to see the very real people they were. And that, she realized, was why she'd never brought him back after that initial visit. He'd actually been ashamed that his prospective wife should have such an odd background. He'd wanted her to be a typical, educated, upper middle-class woman like the other women he knew.

Finally Grossdaadi gave the short nod that meant he had come to a decision. "Rachel is one of our own.

We'll do everything we can to help her. But we cannot lie or break the law."

"I would never ask that," she said, tears welling in her eyes.

"Gut." His gaze swept the others. "Sadie, you can help Rachel with her dress and hair. When anyone asks, we will say only that Cousin Rachel is here for a visit. None of the community will question it, even if it wonders them."

Sadie glanced up at that, almost as if she'd object, but then she nodded. A chill touched the nape of Rachel's neck. Did Sadie, of all people, have doubts about her? The very thought seemed to cut the ground from under her.

But in a moment Sadie had come around the table and touched her lightly on the shoulder.

"You're tired. Komm. I'll see that you are settled for the night."

Rachel nodded. *Tired* was putting it mildly. She wanted to say something, to tell them what it meant to be here, but it was an effort just to get to her feet. She bent to embrace her grandmother, then her grandfather.

"Denke," she whispered softly, her voice choking. "Thank you."

He patted her. "Sleep well. Things will look better in the morning."

She managed a smile, hoping he was right. But somehow she didn't think anything would have changed.

"AT LEAST WE know Rachel Hartline didn't take a plane, wherever she's going." Logan, leaning back from the computer screen he'd been studying, attempted to find a bright spot in the situation.

Clint grunted. It had been a long day, with too few results to suit him, especially when he was driven by the notion that if he'd tried a little harder to get Rachel to confide in him, he might have headed off this ill-timed flight. And if he'd been there when she was attacked… His hands tightened into fists at that. He should have prevented it.

"You'd think, if she and her ex had cashed in on Attwood's brilliant idea, they'd be eager to get out of the country as quickly as possible," Logan added.

"That's assuming they're together." Clint was no longer so convinced of that himself.

His partner eyed him. "You're banking a lot on that supposed attack on the woman, aren't you?"

"If you'd talked to the neighbors, you'd be convinced there was nothing *supposed* about it." Clint sounded irritable, and he knew it. "There's no doubt in my mind that someone went after her, but who? And why? There are too many questions in this mess and not enough answers."

"We're the ones who are supposed to be finding the answers," Logan reminded him. "Still, I wouldn't want to bet that Attwood has told us everything he knows. But when are clients completely honest? Everyone has something they'd rather not talk about. And they come to us with their troubles because they don't want to talk to the police. We agree to respect their confidentiality."

"Not if they're breaking the law," he said quickly. That was where he drew the line. "And what about that story Rachel told me, about how the four of them were actually partners in the firm?" He hadn't had time to look into that, but he knew Logan would have.

"That is interesting, if it's so." Logan flipped through

a couple of computer screens. "The company is registered in James Attwood's name, and from what I've been able to find out, all four of them are currently drawing a salary, including Attwood. If there is an agreement, it must be a fairly informal one."

"Legally binding?" Clinte asked. That was Logan's division, not his.

"That depends on how and whether it's in writing. It could bear some more research, although there may not be any way of finding out unless one of them tells us. It wouldn't have to be registered or recorded in any way."

"Say it's an informal agreement, signed by the four of them and tucked away someplace. In that case, would it be legal?"

"Probably. But how it might affect Hartline's theft, I'm not sure. Still, I'll look into it." His attention to the screen sharpened, and his face grew taut with attention. "Here's something interesting. It looks as if Paul Hartline withdrew funds from an ATM in South Philly this morning."

"When?" Clint was on his feet, leaning over the desk.

"Not until about ten," Logan said slowly. "And at that time…"

"At that time, Rachel had already left her car in the long-term lot and vanished." He frowned. "I'm not sure what that means, if anything."

"She still might have been meeting him someplace," Logan said. "Or, as you seem to think, she may be on the road by herself." He leaned back again to study Clint's expression. "If she is alone, that still doesn't mean she's innocent. In fact, it looks the reverse."

"Yeah." He remained leaning on the desk. "So what do we have on any of the others? Anything more?"

"Bits and pieces." Logan didn't need to refer to his notes now. "Apparently Ian was quite a guy for the ladies up until a few years ago. Trotting out one expensive lovely after another. Since he married and had a kid, it looks like he's turned over a new leaf."

Clint fit that into something else about the man. "Didn't you say that he seems to be living pretty sparsely, given his income?"

"Maybe he's just frugal now that he has a family. Or maybe his wife is. But still, I'd expect someone with his tastes and income to be living in one of the more upscale gated communities rather than a small house in an ordinary suburb."

"No idea what or who he's spending the rest on?"

"No, but I'll get someone looking into it." Logan made a note. "The Gibson woman is something of an enigma. Nice loft apartment downtown, expensive clothes, but not much social life—just a casual date now and then." He shrugged. "I think I told you that much, and I haven't found anything more."

"She may live for her job," Clint suggested.

"True, but the two things don't fit together very well. From the way you described how Attwood Industrial works, she doesn't need designer labels there. But I can't claim to understand women and clothes. Yeah, I know." He answered Clint's unspoken request. "I'll keep digging."

"And what about Attwood?"

Logan shrugged. "On the face of it, he's the one with the most to lose from Hartline's actions. Still, it won't do to accept anything on trust, even if he is our client."

"I've about reached the point of not believing anybody. If we can't find Hartline, and we can't trace Rachel..."

"Hold on a minute." Logan turned back to the screen. "I put someone on to checking cash passengers on public transportation out of Philly. Let's see what this is." He paused a moment and then looked up, smiling. "Okay, I thought that might pay off. A woman answering Rachel Hartline's description took the morning train to Harrisburg."

"Harrisburg." Clint frowned. "I'd have expected New York or Baltimore, if she's trying to hide. Why Harrisburg?" He glanced up to find his partner giving him a quizzical look.

"I don't know. But I expect you'll be trying to find out," Logan said.

"You think this is a wild-goose chase?"

Logan hesitated and then shook his head. "Not if that's your gut instinct. I trust you. Go on after Ms. Hartline, and I'll keep the inquiries running here in the meantime. Attwood finally gave me a list of possible buyers for his project, so I'll start working on them."

"Yeah." Clint ran his hand through his hair, trying to focus. "I'll head for Harrisburg."

"In the morning. Get some sleep first," Logan said as Clint headed for the door. "You look like you need it."

Clint gave a noncommittal shrug. He was tired, but his mind kept dashing off after Rachel.

Still, he'd do it, because it was the sensible thing and would increase the odds that he'd be sharp enough to find her. But it would be hard to rest, not knowing whether Rachel was somewhere safe tonight. Not when he felt this heavy burden of responsibility for her.

"OUCH." RACHEL JUMPED when the point of the straight pin pricked her the next morning. "Let me guess, it's easier to do it on yourself than on someone else." She smiled at Sadie, who responded with a reluctant grin.

Why reluctant? If Sadie was unsure of the wisdom of having Rachel here, she'd be unlikely to admit it, but her expressions gave her away to someone who knew her as well as Rachel did.

They were in the room that had been Rachel's, and during the summer Sadie had shared it with her more often than not. They'd snuggled under Grossmammi's nine-patch quilt, giggling and talking when they were supposed to be asleep, sharing secrets. She'd never had a friend as close as Sadie, and now that friendship seemed to be gone.

Her fault, she thought. Even if Paul wouldn't come, she should have visited more often during those years they were married. But somehow it had been easier not to bring it up, not to start a fight. And after Paul left—well, then she'd been ashamed of her failed marriage, so she'd stayed away.

Sadie pulled out the offending pin and started again. "You'll find it simple when you get the hang of it, yah? Mammi stuck me the first few times she tried to show me how to fasten a grown-up woman's dress."

The straight pins that closed the dress were traditional, if unhandy, like much of Amish life. "I'm willing, but I seem to be all thumbs." Rachel took the next pin and tried to emulate Sadie's movements. "Where are your mamm and daad? I'd love to see them." Her aunt and uncle, always so laughing and loving, were an important part of her childhood.

"Ach, it's a shame, it is, that they aren't here now. They went out to Ohio to stay with Ruthie while her first boppli is born." She smiled. "Though Daad kept saying he didn't know what use he was going to be."

"He can keep Ruthie's husband out of the way," Rachel suggested. "I can't believe little Ruthie is old enough to be starting a family."

"You missed her wedding," Sadie reminded her, and there was an edge to her voice.

Disapproval? Or disappointment? Rachel wasn't sure, but she felt guilty. "It was hard for me to get away on a school day. And Paul…" She stopped herself from saying anything that sounded disapproving of Paul.

For a moment Sadie didn't speak. When she did, her tone had changed. "He doesn't like us much, ain't so?"

"He never understood." And he didn't try. It hadn't seemed worth it to him, Rachel realized. That was a sad commentary on their marriage.

"You could have come anyway by yourself." Sadie, normally very forgiving, was holding on to this.

"I should have. But things were already so difficult between us that I hated to bring up anything I knew would cause a fight." She sucked in a breath. "I should have. I'm ashamed that I didn't."

Sadie didn't speak for a moment. Was she trying to hold on to her anger? But then she touched Rachel's shoulder lightly. "That made it hard for you."

It was the smallest indication of empathy, and Rachel accepted it gladly, putting her hand over Sadie's for a moment.

"Now, let us see what we can do with your hair." Sadie gestured to the bedroom chair, sounding determined to ignore the moment. "It's gut you wear it long."

"Easier to pull it back in a braid when I'm working with five-year-olds." She couldn't push, Rachel reminded herself. If she and Sadie were going to return to the old, easy relationship, she'd have to give her cousin time.

"Yah." Sadie picked up the hairbrush. "You were always gut with the little ones."

For a few moments they were quiet, with only Sadie's nimble fingers moving as she transformed Rachel's hair into the customary braided bun. Rachel could see Sadie's face in the mirror that reflected the rays of the early morning sun streaming in the window behind them.

Sadie's soft brown hair was pulled back from her rosy face in the center part that was customary. Her hair had been lighter once, though never the pale yellow that Rachel's was. Her eyes, a clear, bright blue, had lost the twinkle they'd once had, but maybe that was because of Rachel's arrival.

Sadie glanced up and caught her gaze in the mirror.

"It wondered me…" she began, and then let the words fade away.

"What? You can ask me anything, you know. If it's about the trouble that brought me here…"

"Not exactly." Sadie focused on the hairpins she was sticking into place. "I was thinking about your mother." Sadie glanced around, as if making sure Grossmammi wasn't still lingering in the upstairs hall, able to hear them.

Rachel understood, and her own heart winced. Mom had caused her parents so much pain when she left, and that had never really healed. How could it, when her mother ignored them so completely?

"She's all right, if that's what you're asking." Rachel

kept her voice level. “She lives out in Arizona now in a retirement community.”

“You couldn’t count on her for help then.”

“No.” And not just because Mom was so far away. “She seems happy with her life. Busy with lots of social activities. If I call, I always catch her running out the door for something or other.”

Again that brief touch on her shoulder, as Sadie seemed to understand all the things she didn’t say. Mom had never been the kind of mother a child could rely on, and she could hardly expect that to change now. Rachel had always been an afterthought, or more likely an unpleasant reminder of her father. Their relationship was practically nonexistent now, and the idea of asking her for help in time of trouble was as ludicrous as asking the same from the Tooth Fairy.

“There.” Sadie set the white kapp in place and secured it with hairpins. “Now you look like a proper Amish woman, ain’t so?”

Rachel thought Sadie was probably forcing the light tone, but she went along with it, smiling at the unfamiliar figure that was reflected in the mirror. “Gut job, Sadie. Denke.”

Sadie nodded, a smile lingering on her face until the sound of heavy footsteps on the back porch below them startled her. “Ach, the men are in and wanting breakfast. Komm, we must hurry.”

Following her, Rachel could only hope that she and Sadie had begun to bridge the gap she’d sensed between them since her unexpected arrival. *Give it time*, she reminded herself, but the very thought made her wonder how much time she really had. How long until Clint was on her trail?

By evening, much of Rachel's apprehension had disappeared. Somehow it seemed impossible that any unpleasantness could intrude upon the ordered serenity of Amish life. She had spent much of the day either with her grandmother, listening to her stories and working alongside her at the baking and the mending, or with Sadie's children.

It was hard to believe sometimes that she and Sadie were the same age, especially when she looked at the four beautiful children Sadie and Timothy had produced. Blond and blue-eyed, as Sadie had been before the years turned her hair a few shades darker, they had her rosy cheeks and Timothy's easy, teasing smile.

Anna, the oldest at seven, was so like her mother at that age that Rachel almost felt disoriented when she looked at her. The two little boys were alike enough to be twins, but were two years apart. And the baby, Becky… Well, Rachel fell in love when she held the chubby twelve-month-old. Becky was just beginning to walk, and to see her wobbly, triumphant progress from sofa to chair was enough to swell anyone's heart.

By suppertime, Anna obviously felt that it was her turn to have Rachel's attention, since the younger ones had an unfair advantage in being with Cousin Rachel all day while she was at school.

Now, with the supper dishes completed and Sadie giving year-old Becky and three-year-old Thomas a bath, Anna tugged at Rachel's hand. "You promised to read me a story, Cousin Rachel. Let's go out on the back porch where it's quiet." She shot a glance at five-year-old Daniel, who was playing a rowdy game with his father.

"I'm not sure there's enough light…" she began, but Anna was already moving, so she followed her out to the porch. The sun was sliding behind the ridge and the shadows gathering, but Anna boosted herself onto the porch swing and opened her book.

"Now, we're all ready." She sounded satisfied, so Rachel sat down next to her.

"What are we reading?" Her eyes adjusted to the failing light, and she could make out the print. "*Little House in the Big Woods*. I remember this one. Your mammi and I read it together one summer when we were about your age."

"Did Mammi like it?" Anna leaned her head against Rachel's arm confidingly. Rachel's heart lurched. If her life had been different, she might have a daughter like Anna depending on her now.

"She did—that's certain sure." The Pennsylvania Dutch dialect came easier each time she spoke, welling up from wherever it had been stored. "We used to pretend we were the sisters and try to do all their adventures. Another summer when we were older we read *Anne of Green Gables* and pretended we were Anne and Diana. You probably didn't read that one yet."

"Mammi has it and she says we can read it after we finish all the *Little House* books." She leafed through the book to the right page. "Here's where to start."

Rachel read obediently, finding her voice reflecting the actions on the page automatically, as it did when she read to her kindergartners. But this was different. They were her students, but Anna was connected to her by blood. She didn't know why that should matter, but it did.

Anna and the others woke the longing she'd pushed to the back of her mind for so long—a reminder of the children she didn't have. She'd dreamed for so long of the family she'd one day mother, and she'd pictured herself with a strong, good man beside her, providing her children with the warm, loving, secure home life she hadn't known.

But it had soon become clear that wouldn't happen with Paul. He hadn't wanted the responsibility, hadn't wanted to be tied down, had wanted to remain free. And as the depth of his addiction to gambling became clear—how could she have brought a helpless child into that life?

Now Paul was free, but she couldn't see that it had made him happy. Anna's head resting against her arm seemed to activate that familiar sense of loss—not loss of Paul, but loss of the vision she'd had on the day they married.

"Anna!" The back door swung open. "I didn't know where you were." Sadie seemed to realize her tone was too sharp, and she softened it.

But Anna was already looking at her mother, her blue eyes wide. "But, Mammi, you heard me ask Cousin Rachel to read me a story."

"Yah, I know." Sadie patted her head. "I just forgot for a minute. Run along in and get ready for bed. You can say good-night now. You'll see Cousin Rachel in the morning."

Mollified, Anna nodded, hopping off the swing. "Good night, Cousin Rachel. Thank you for reading my story." She threw her arms around Rachel for a big hug and scurried into the house.

Sadie would have followed her if Rachel hadn't shot from the swing and stopped her. She grasped her cousin's arm, determined to get an answer. "Sadie, what's going on? Why don't you want me to read to your kinder?"

Sadie's face reflected a struggle. Finally, not looking at Rachel, she answered, "It's not the reading. It's coming out here. I don't want you out here alone with Anna."

She wouldn't have been more surprised if Sadie had slapped her. "Why? What do you think I'm going to do to her?"

"Nothing!" Sadie swung on her. "You wouldn't hurt her. But what about those people who were bothering you? What if they follow you here? What if they find you when you're alone with one of my kinder? What might they do?"

The blow struck at her heart. Hurt, pain and mostly shame. She was ashamed of her own thoughtlessness. "Sadie, I'm sorry. You're right. I would never want to put one of you in danger." Shame flooded over her. "I was thinking only of myself. I'll leave."

Now Sadie grabbed *her* arm. "Ach, no. I don't want you to go." Her fingers bit into Rachel's skin. "I'm just… I'm frightened. Mostly for you, I think. If you leave, we won't know what's happening to you." Her arms went around Rachel in a sudden, fierce hug. "Don't go. Just be careful."

"I will. It'll be all right."

Sadie freed herself and rushed off, leaving Rachel to struggle with her own conscience. She hadn't thought of them, only of herself. She'd been seduced into relaxing too much, confident that she was in a safe place. But she couldn't risk other people's safety, no matter how unlikely it was that the man who'd attacked her could find her here.

Finally, growing chilly, she rose. Sitting here in the dark wasn't going to generate any answers, but somehow she didn't feel composed enough to go in and chat.

Instead, she opened the back door and took a flashlight off the hook inside.

Grossmammi, engaged in cutting a cherry pie into slices, looked up and smiled. "Going to the barn, ain't so?"

"How did you know?"

"You always wanted to say good-night to the horses when you were little. Don't stay too long. Pie and coffee are almost ready."

Nodding, Rachel withdrew. Darkness drew in quickly once the sun was behind the ridge, and the flashlight cast a welcome circle of light ahead of her footsteps. She had been worse than thoughtless, not realizing what was troubling Sadie. Of course she was worried about her children's safety.

And now Rachel was. It honestly hadn't occurred to her that she was putting anyone else at risk. She'd been frightened, and she'd run for home automatically, like a child.

If she made an excuse and left, would that help? If someone followed her here, would he assume they were lying when they said she'd gone? Or would he think her grandparents must know where she was, the way everyone assumed she knew where Paul was? The more she thought about it, the more confused she felt.

The barn door was ajar, probably in anticipation of Grossdaadi's late-evening visit. She slid it open a little farther, just enough so that she could get through. There she stopped, standing and taking in the familiar sounds and scents of the barn.

One of the buggy horses whickered softly, probably assuming she'd brought a treat with her. Luckily she remembered where her grandfather kept his supply of carrots.

Fetching a handful, she approached the closest stall. The horse held back for a moment, but when she held out her hand, palm flat, he recognized the familiar movement. Soft lips moved on her palm, daintily taking the carrot.

Rachel laughed softly. “That was an easy way to make friends, wasn’t it? You’re greedy,” she scolded, as the animal investigated her palm again. She patted him. “I’ll come back,” she added, speaking in English for the first time all day.

She turned to the next stall. In the instant she moved she felt something, heard something—a step, a movement—and then arms circled her and a large hand closed firmly over her mouth.

Unable to wield the flashlight, Rachel kicked back, connecting with something that felt like a man’s knee. She felt the breath go out of him, and then a furious voice in her ear.

“Dammit, don’t scream!”

She recognized the exasperated voice even as her body relaxed. He eased his hand away from her mouth.

“Clint Mordan,” she said, angry but somehow not surprised.

She should have known he’d find her.

CHAPTER SIX

Now that he had her, what was he going to do with her? Clint loosened his hold, but he didn't let go. He'd been driven to find Rachel by an impulse as much personal as professional. Now that he had, all he could feel was relief that she was in one piece, combined with the exasperation she'd roused since the moment they met.

"How did you know me?" When she spoke, the question she picked to ask surprised him.

Relaxing a little, he took the flashlight from her hand and moved it enough to show the plain blue dress, the blond hair drawn back from a center part, and a small white headpiece. Amish dress was a surprisingly good disguise. If he'd seen her in a crowd or from a distance, he probably wouldn't have recognized her.

"I didn't," he admitted. "I wasn't sure until I heard your voice. I wouldn't forget that."

Now what had impelled him to add the comment? It wasn't part of his job to get personal.

"I guess I should have stayed with Pennsylvania Dutch, even with the horses."

"You actually speak the language?"

"I spent every summer here when…" She stirred, making him realize he still had his arm around her. "Why are we talking about that? How did you find me? And do you think you might let go now?"

Clint loosened his grasp, but he didn't intend to let go entirely, not until he was sure she wouldn't attempt to run. His eyes had adjusted to the dim light while he waited in the barn. He could make out her features and the delicate oval of her face.

"Finding you wasn't easy," he admitted. "You did all the right things. Leaving the car at the airport, switching from train to bus—you might also be a pro at it."

"I'm not." Her voice was tart. "But you found me so easily after Lyn and I switched cars that I knew I had a pro after me. Not to mention other people. How did you know to come here? Not my mother..." She let the words trail off, as if she'd stumbled across the truth she didn't want to see.

"Your mother," he agreed. "She didn't seem to know anything about your disappearance." Logan had actually made the call, being gifted with more tact than Clint. "But she mentioned her parents' farm, and the rest was easy."

"You didn't tell her I was in trouble." Alarm widened her eyes.

"No, of course not. I'm sure my partner gave her some totally innocent-sounding reason for wanting to reach you. He didn't say that you were missing, just that he wanted to reach you. He's very tactful. But maybe you should send her a message that you're elsewhere, so she won't mention the farm to anyone else."

She rubbed her forehead as if she disliked the idea, but then she nodded. The brief alarm she'd shown at the idea slipped away. "All right. I can tell her something. She wouldn't have been all that concerned."

He wasn't sure whether that meant her mother would have been reassured by Logan or whether she wouldn't have been concerned in any event. He caught a whiff of a troubled relationship. Not his business, but still, he couldn't seem to help wanting to know.

"I gather you didn't consider turning to her." He tried to phrase it carefully.

Rachel seemed to stiffen. "No."

That short response spoke volumes. He'd like to hear the whole story, but now wasn't the time.

"We do try to be discreet. Once we knew you had family in this area…well, Logan had already discovered that you'd taken the bus for State College. I was headed there when he told me about your grandparents."

"And you decided to hide in the barn and grab me." She snapped the words, but somehow there was as much resignation as anger in her voice.

"I was afraid you'd scream. And I was trying to check the place out quietly. I didn't want to alarm the family if you weren't here."

"I suppose I should thank you for that," she muttered. "The family is important to me. I don't want them upset any more than they already are."

"Does that mean that you've told them what's going on?"

She blinked. "Of course. I couldn't stay here without telling them the truth."

"I guess not—not if you care about them." He was beginning to understand her. She'd evade his questions, but she wouldn't lie. And people she cared about got the whole story.

"They're my family." Rachel seemed to think that explained it all, and maybe it did. Whatever her relationship with her mother, she wouldn't lie to these people, any more than he'd lie to his own family.

"Did you tell them about the attack on you?"

"How did you find out?" She didn't seem all that surprised that he knew.

"You weren't at home or at the school, and your friend Ms. Baker wasn't helpful. I went back to the house and ran into your talkative neighbor."

"Mrs. Barton." She sounded resigned. "Yes, she's talkative, but she's the kindest person—always trying to help. If they hadn't come out when they did..."

His arms instinctively tightened around her again. At least she was here, warm and safe in his arms, and not lying in the hospital bed.

"I've heard the story from their perspective. Don't you think I should hear it from you?"

"I guess so." She stirred, glancing around at the silent animals who watched from their stalls. "If we're going to talk, let's get farther from the door. I don't want to alarm anyone."

She led the way past the double row of stalls, and Clint stayed on her heels, aware of the small door at the back he'd used when he checked out the barn.

It seemed Rachel didn't intend to run. Instead, she pulled out a straw bale and settled on it, gesturing to him to sit next to her.

"Now, tell me about the attack." He turned a little more toward her, propping his elbow on the stacked bales behind him. "From the beginning. The intruder wasn't inside?"

She sighed a little, as if tired of explaining things. "No. I parked the car and started for the door. It was dark—I hadn't left a light on. Someone must have been hidden in the shadows. I was looking over toward the

Barton place when he grabbed me from behind." She shot a look at him. "Like you did just now."

"Sorry about that. I was afraid you'd yell your head off if I spoke. But it wasn't me at your house."

"I know."

That surprised him. He'd like to think she was beginning to trust him, but he knew better. "How do you know?"

She shrugged. "I'm not sure. It just… It didn't feel like you."

He'd like to pursue the subject, but that would be an indulgence he didn't have time for. "Did you get any sense of him at all? Height, size, anything?"

Rachel frowned, seeming to think back through those moments. "Not much," she admitted. "I was just too shocked. Things like this don't happen to me. I suppose I lost a few seconds just realizing it was for real. Then I remembered my self-defense classes. Kick, bite, scream, that's what kept going through my head."

"It works," he said, realizing that his hands had curled into fists. If he had his hands on the guy, he'd do some damage. "You did a good job on me, remember?"

Her lips curved. "I doubt that I hurt you, but if I did, you deserved it for scaring me like that."

"Right, I did. So if you connected with him at all, you must have an idea how big he was. My size? Bigger?"

"He was taller than I am, but not as big as you are. Strong, but I didn't get a size of much bulk, if you know what I mean."

"How about what he was wearing? Did you touch his clothes?"

"Dark, I know that, because he blended into the shadows. I felt a sleeve when he held my mouth—not smooth like leather. Fabric."

It wouldn't lead him to the guy, but anything helped. "What about smell? Alcohol? Body odor?"

"Nothing like that." A small shiver when through her.

His hand closed over hers without conscious intent. "It's okay. You're safe here, at least for now. Safer than at your own place, anyway."

Rachel looked up at him, seeming to read something into the words. "Has something else happened there?"

He hesitated, but it was better that she hear it now rather than be surprised, especially if it made her see how serious this was. "I went back to your house early this morning, before I left the city. Someone had been in there again. This time it wasn't a very careful search. I'm afraid you'll find some damage. I'm sorry," he added.

"How bad?" She seemed to steel herself for the response.

Clint remembered the signs of thoughtfulness in the decoration of that cozy, comfortable little house. He could still see her clutching that needlepoint cushion—she'd have done that herself, he supposed.

"Nothing that can't be repaired. A couple of holes in the plaster, the stuffing pulled from some of the cushions, that sort of thing. Some touch-up paint needed here and there."

He didn't want to say how it had affected him—it had struck him as anger toward Rachel, almost as much as a desire to find something. Logic said it would be the same man who'd attacked her, but that sense of malice didn't fit in with the idea of a middleman involved in industrial espionage.

Rachel rubbed her forehead. "I don't… I still can't take it all in. Why is someone doing this to me?"

It seemed obvious, at least to him. "They think you have what your ex took from Attwood Industrial. Or that you know where it is."

"I don't! How many times do I have to say it before you believe me?"

"Seems like it's not me you have to convince." He hesitated, but there was something else that had to be cleared up between them. "Every time I start to believe you, something happens to make me doubt again. Like that little shopping trip you made when you left school early."

Rachel blinked, taking a moment to understand. "You mean the phone."

"Right. The only reason you could want a burner phone is to contact your ex-husband. That doesn't fit with the image of an innocent bystander."

"Paul texted me and asked me to get it so we could communicate. I guess he thought someone might have been able to get access to my regular cell phone." She gave him a quick glance. "I don't suppose you'll believe this, but I only wanted to be able to tell him to give up on this scheme and return what he took."

"And did you? Tell him, I mean." He didn't answer the implied question as to whether he believed her.

"Yes. At least, I texted him, but he didn't answer. And after someone grabbed me at my house…" She hesitated.

"Did he tell you to run?"

Rachel looked startled. "Paul? I told you already, I

haven't heard back from him since I left. I haven't heard anything." Worry set a line between her brows. "I don't understand it. If he knew I'd been attacked, I can't believe he'd do nothing."

He didn't know much about Paul, never having met him, and the picture he was getting of the man was confused, to say the least. "So you think he may not have received your text?"

"I just don't know. I..."

"What? What is it?"

"Paul. The last time I heard from him, he wanted to meet with me at the house. But that was when I was attacked."

It took a second to understand exactly what she meant. "Paul made an appointment to meet you at the house. And when you got there, someone attacked you."

"Yes." Her head came up. "It wasn't Paul. I told you that."

Again he was trying to measure exactly what her feelings were toward her ex-husband. "Rachel, I know you want to believe that, but can you be sure?"

He expected her to flare up at that, but she didn't.

"You think I'm covering up for him, but I'm not. I would have known if it were Paul. But in that case, what happened to Paul? Did the other man know about the appointment, or was it a coincidence?"

Holding his opinion of Paul in reserve, he tried to consider it impartially. "He could have found out about it at Paul's end, I suppose. This phone...has it been out of your control at any time?"

"No, not a chance. I'd only had it for a few hours before that happened."

"Then it's not likely to have had anything to do with your phone."

"No, it couldn't have been." She relaxed a little.

"I don't like coincidences, but if the guy who attacked you had been waiting to get you alone, that might have been his first opportunity. He could have staked out the house, knowing you'd come home sometime."

"I suppose Paul might have been delayed. If he'd arrived when the Bartons were there, he wouldn't attempt to stop."

Possible. Or it was possible that something had happened to prevent him from keeping his appointment with her. Or even that he'd arranged the attack.

"When you texted Paul afterward, did you let him know where you were going?"

He felt her tense at the question. "I texted him that I'd been attacked and was leaving the house. I didn't tell him where."

In other words, she hadn't trusted him with that knowledge.

"Would he be likely to figure it out?"

She rubbed her arms, as if the thought chilled her. "I don't know. I hope not. He'd be more likely to think I'd be with Lyn, probably."

"When all this happened, it didn't occur to you to tell me about it, I suppose."

She just shook her head at that. He didn't have to have it spelled out for him. Rachel didn't trust him, not that much, anyway.

"It wasn't that I thought you were the man." She seemed to sense what he was thinking. "All I wanted was to get out of the way until Paul could settle this situation. Then people would leave me alone. But now you'll take me back, won't you?"

Clint was surprised by his own hesitation. "I don't know." He said the honest thing.

She was so close that he felt, as well as heard, her rapid intake of breath. "You mean you might let me stay?" Rachel turned to him, her face only inches away from his.

"This might be the safest place for you. I don't see how anyone else would trace you here. Your connection to the Amish isn't very well-known, is it?"

"No. That was Paul." The shadow in her eyes was evident. "He didn't like anything that was out of the ordinary. We had to be the typical yuppie couple, as far as he was concerned. Lyn knows, but I don't think she'd tell you. Or anyone else."

His lips quirked. "Your friend wouldn't give me the time of day. As far as she's concerned, I'm the enemy."

Rachel studied his face. "Are you?"

"No." Surprising himself, he touched her cheek lightly with his fingertips. Her skin was soft and smooth, seeming to warm to his touch. For a moment time seemed to stop.

With an effort, Clint got control of himself. He let his hand drop. "I don't want to see you get hurt, Rachel. But my job is to recover the information your ex-husband stole. I'm going to take you at your word that you aren't involved, but you have to do something for me."

"What?" She drew back a little, her gaze wary.

"Promise me you'll let me know if you hear from him. Are you willing to do that?"

Rachel rubbed her forehead, and he could almost imagine the thoughts going through her mind. Could she trust him? That was what it amounted to. He wanted to urge her, to make promises, but he held his peace. She'd have to decide for herself whose side she was on…whether some lingering loyalty to the man she'd once married would make her willing to be complicit in his crime.

At last she nodded. She bent, reaching under the hem of her dress, and he realized that the cell phone was tucked inside an elastic on her leg. She saw him watching, and her lips twitched.

"Haven't you ever seen a leg holster?"

He yanked his mind away from thoughts he'd better not indulge in. "Not for a phone."

"Ordinarily my grandparents wouldn't have any objection to my using a cell phone. I'm not a member of the church. But since I'm wearing Amish dress, it's important to all of us that I try to live the part."

Rachel's sense of ethics was a delicate one, it seemed. It was her loyalty that was causing her grief.

"How does your family feel about the whole situation? Do they get it?" Could people who seemed to live so remote from the real world possibly understand the underbelly of corporate spying?

Her smile flickered again. "Don't underestimate anyone here. My grandfather is an Amish bishop, devoted to his faith. He's also a wise and intelligent man who is quite well read. Very little surprises him." She handed him the phone. "Here. I don't know that I'm as honorable as Grossdaadi, but I'll live up to my part of the agreement."

He took the phone, noting down the number and checking for messages and calls. He added his cell number to the phone and handed it back.

"You can reach me at that number anytime, day or night. Call if you hear from Paul. Or if anything goes wrong." He rose, and the movement seemed to catch her unaware.

She stood, looking up at him, seeming unconcerned by how close they stood. "I can stay here?"

"For the moment, at least." He'd have a job to convince Logan he was doing the right thing. "I'll have to get in touch with my office to see if anything new has turned up. I'm not leaving the area tonight, and I'll be in touch with you again before I go."

"I'll be here." She reached out, clasping his wrist in what appeared to be an unplanned movement. "Clint… thank you."

Okay, there was only so much a man could withstand. He pulled her into his arms, putting his cheek against hers before stepping back with reluctance. "Stay safe, you hear me?"

He turned away, slipping out the back door the way he'd come and vanishing into the shadows.

RACHEL DIDN'T MOVE for several minutes. She wanted to deny how she'd felt in those moments when Clint's arms had gone around her, but she couldn't.

She took a deep breath and headed for the door. All right, she'd reacted. Accept it. Probably it was a natural result of the circumstances. She'd been frightened, upset and knocked out of her normal life catastrophically. And it had been such a long time since anyone had held her that way. A very long time.

A few steps away from the barn she came out of the haze that had enveloped her and saw someone leaning against the old well that had once provided water to the animals before pipes had been laid to the deeper well.

"Grossdaadi." It took an effort to sound normal as she moved to join him. "Have you been looking for me?"

A glance at his face told her the truth. "You heard," she said, before he could speak.

"Yah. I heard your voices and knew you'd met someone."

He didn't ask questions. That wasn't his way. He just looked at you until you felt compelled to tell him. Even the things they'd promised to keep secret as children had come spilling out at Grossdaadi's look.

"Why didn't you come in?" She held off the inevitable with a question.

"I would have, if you'd needed help. He didn't mean you harm, ain't so?"

"No. It was Clint Mordan, the investigator I told you about."

Her grandfather picked up a pebble from the ground and dropped it into the well. She felt a rush of nostalgia, remembering a long-ago summer day and her grandfather explaining that he could tell how much water was in the well by how long it took the pebble to splash. He seemed to listen for the sound, and then turned back to her.

"He certain sure found you fast."

She wasn't going to say how if she could help it. Just the mention of her mother's name might cause pain. "He's very good at his job. He's not with the police anymore, but he and his partner run a security company that is trying to recover what Paul took."

"Yah, I understand that." He was silent for a moment

and then pushed himself away from the fieldstone of the well. "He wants something from you."

Rachel tried to assemble her scattered thoughts. "Yes. Mostly to find out if Paul has been in touch with me, I think. He hasn't," she added hastily. "I would tell you if he had."

"I know that." Her grandfather touched her arm lightly, and they started slowly toward the house, side by side. "Did this man believe you?"

"Yes." She was startled to realize that she didn't have any doubts about it. "He had heard from my neighbor about the man who attacked me, and I think he also wanted to be sure I was safe."

"Gut. He doesn't want to take you away from us, does he?" His disapproval of that idea was plain in his voice.

"No, at least, not right now. He said he thought this was the safest place for me. But..."

He just waited for her to continue.

Rachel forced herself to accept the duty she'd hoped to escape. "Much as I would rather stay here, I won't put all of you in danger. And if there was a way I could get Paul to come to his senses, I would have to do it."

Her grandfather patted her hand. "I wouldn't expect anything else from you." They were only feet from the farmhouse now, and through the window she could see Grossmammi and Sadie moving around in the kitchen. "There is chust one thing I must ask before we go inside."

Pausing, Rachel looked into his face, lit now by the yellow gleam from the windows.

"Do you trust this man?"

Did she trust Clint? She considered, and finally nodded. "Yes, I trust him. At least, I trust that he's an honest man who's doing his duty."

Her grandfather gave his characteristic short nod. "Gut. Then he is wilkom here." His eyes crinkled. "Tell him next time he doesn't need to komm to the back door of the barn."

An unexpected laugh bubbled up in her. "All right. I'll tell him."

And if Clint did come openly to the farm…well, she'd know a great deal about him when she saw how he reacted to her family. To say nothing of what they thought of him.

WHEN THEY STEPPED inside the kitchen, her grandmother was putting slices of cherry pie on the long rectangular table, while Sadie poured coffee.

"So this is what the grown-ups do after the kinder are in bed," Rachel teased.

"This is the reward for tired parents," Grossdaadi said. "Sit now."

Rachel wasn't hungry after the big supper they'd had, but she'd have to eat something. This ritual wasn't because anyone was hungry. Rather, it was a time to sit together, to talk and to share the day's happenings.

Grossmammi seemed to read her thoughts. "You sit down here and eat some pie. It's gut for you after the time you've had. You could stand to gain a few pounds."

Rachel's gaze met Sadie's, and for an instant they shared a thought. Grossmammi never changed, and that was a good thing in a scary world. She always believed homemade food would cure any problem. And it was good to share a moment of communication with her cousin, as well, even if Sadie looked quickly away.

Timothy didn't seem to notice any byplay. "Saying good-night to the buggy horses, were you?"

She nodded, taking the slat-back wooden chair she'd always had when she'd spent summers here. "That little gelding in the first stall was looking for his carrot in a hurry."

"Ach, he's spoiled, that one is. He knows Grossdaadi will give him his treat first."

"Clever, that's all," Grossdaadi said. "He's just a youngster—Timothy and I trained him to the buggy only two years ago."

To Rachel's relief, he didn't mention anything about a visitor in the barn. It seemed that was between them, at least for now.

"What did you think of the pair of Percherons?" Timothy asked.

Sadie leaned across to touch his shoulder in a loving gesture. "You're so fond of those draft horses I'm thinking I should be jealous," she teased. "What do you say, Rachel?"

Fortunately she'd noticed the massive gray pair in the two largest stalls. It would be hard not to. "Very impressive. But I don't think you have anything to worry about, Sadie."

Her grandfather chuckled before taking a long sip of milky coffee. "You might not think so if you could hear him talking to them when he thinks no one is listening…"

His words were cut off by a sound from upstairs—a harsh, barking cough that made Sadie start from her chair.

"Croup," Grossmammi said in a resigned way. "Is it Anna?"

"Yah." Sadie was already halfway to the stairs.

"I'll put the kettle on." Her grandmother started to get up, but Rachel pressed her back down.

"I'll do it." She began filling the big kettle at the sink. "Anna takes after her mother that way, does she?"

Grossmammi nodded. "I'd forgot you'd been here once when Sadie started up."

"Scared me half to death. I'd never heard anyone cough that way."

"You came running to our bedroom looking like a little ghost." Her grandmother pulled out a big earthenware bowl. "We'll need a towel."

Timothy got up. "I'll bring it and check the others while I'm upstairs. We don't want them all up."

The calm, capable manner shown by the family didn't surprise Rachel, but it did make her wonder why her mother had never reacted that way. With her, every small incident of life had been reason for a drama, and Rachel had always found herself in the position of advisor and comforter, as if she'd been the mother. And if she'd been sick or hurt, she'd felt guilty for causing her mother so much trouble.

By the time Sadie came down to the kitchen carrying Anna wrapped in a blanket, the bowl of steaming water was on the table and the towel ready.

"Let's go in your little tent to make the coughing stop," Sadie said, her tone gentle. "Then you'll feel better."

Anna showed a disposition to cry. "It's scary."

Rachel took the towel while Sadie soothed her daughter. "Hush, now. It will make you better."

Anna seemed to doubt it.

"Will you show me how you do it, Anna?" Rachel

held the towel out. "I'll hold it, and you tell me when to put it over your head. I won't do it until you say."

Anna looked at her mother. Getting an approving smile, she nodded. She bent forward over the bowl to inhale the steam while Sadie held her braids back. "I guess now," she murmured, coughing a little as she spoke.

Rachel draped the towel gently over the child's head, smoothing it down around the edge of the bowl. Anna gave another cough or two before her breathing started to ease a bit.

Patting Anna's back, Sadie smiled at her. "You remember," she said softly.

"I've never been able to forget. If I ever have little ones, at least I'll know what to do."

Grossmammi was gesturing to the others to move their coffee and pie into the living room, and she turned the light down a bit before following them. Anna might settle down more easily without her, too, but Anna was holding Rachel's hand, so she stayed, sitting quietly with her cousin.

Sadie didn't speak for a time—she just sat and soothed Anna. When she did say something, it was a surprising question. "Do you think that will ever happen?"

"What?" Then she remembered what she'd said last. "Children? I don't see it. Paul…" She let that trail off. The thought of never having children of her own was a separate little pain in her heart.

She was legally free, of course. But she didn't know if she'd ever be able to trust herself in that way again. She'd watched her mother fail to find a good man time after time, and she'd never thought she'd fall into the same mistake. But she had. And if she and Paul had had a child, what would the current circumstances do to a vulnerable little one?

"Did he never want kinder?" Sadie couldn't seem to comprehend that, of course. Amish couples married with the expectation of starting a family, and she could remember Sadie as young as nine or ten talking about what she would name her children.

"I don't think so. He said he did, but…" She shook her head, giving up any idea of explaining Paul. "In the end, all he wanted was to be free. Gambling was all he thought about. He didn't care that he was taking money we both had earned and just throwing it away. I tried to help him see what it was doing to him, but I failed. I still feel like a failure, but I don't know what I could have done differently."

Could she have made a difference? Would some other reaction or even some other woman have been able to wean Paul away from the gambling that had become an obsession with him? She'd never know. The experts would say that the change had to come from within the addict, not from the outside, but she hadn't found much comfort in that.

Sadie put her hand over Rachel's where it lay, clasping Anna's slack one. "I'm so sorry."

She nodded. "Denke." Her own breathing seemed to be slowing, matching that of the child. She'd just said things to Sadie that she had been reluctant to say to anyone else. The atmosphere of this place seemed to take all of her protective barriers down.

Anna moved, leaning back against her mother. Her breathing was even and easy, her eyes closed. Sadie slid the now-damp towel away but held it, ready to use again if necessary.

"Do you think she's over it?" Rachel kept her voice low.

"I hope so. I'd best keep her here for a bit longer, in case it starts up again." She glanced at Rachel. "She wouldn't notice if you slipped away. You don't have to stay."

"I'll sit with you."

Sadie's lips tilted slightly. "Best cousin friend."

Rachel smiled in response. It was what Sadie had once called their relationship. She was relieved to feel it coming back strong again.

"About what I said before…" Sadie's fingers tightened on hers. "I'm sorry. I didn't mean to make you feel bad about coming. You belong here. Always."

She had to blink back a quick tear. If she could mend things with Sadie, maybe things were looking up.

The cell phone picked that moment to vibrate against her leg. It was a harsh reminder. Nothing was really resolved. She couldn't fool herself into thinking anything else.

She slipped her hand away from theirs. "I…need to go upstairs for a moment. I'll come back."

Sadie nodded, but she looked at her rather oddly as she scurried from the room. The cell phone vibrated again when she was on the stairs, and then it stopped. A message from someone. Paul? Clint?

Racing into the bathroom, she pulled the cell phone free of its strap and fumbled with it.

The text was from Paul. She read it twice, and still didn't know what to make of it.

Tried to call, but you didn't answer. I had to change phones again, so haven't heard from you. Remember that day in June? We never thought we'd end up like this. Sorry. Stay safe.

Rachel tried to rub away the headache that stabbed her at his words. What did he mean? More important, why didn't he come forward and resolve this mess if he felt that way about it?

Questions, but no answers. She'd have to show this to Clint. She'd given her word. Her throat tightened at the thought.

She didn't have to do it now, not this late and with a sick child in the house. She'd already texted him the message from her grandfather, and he'd said he'd come to the farm the following day.

Turning off the phone, she longed to cut out all intrusions from the outside world as easily. But today's worries were enough for today. She'd deal with this tomorrow.

CHAPTER SEVEN

CLINT DROVE UP the long lane to the farmhouse in mid-morning, hoping this was a good time to come. Farmers got up early, especially on a dairy farm like this one. He'd spent the night in the nearby town of Echo Falls…the kind of place that might have appeared on a calendar of typical American small towns. Tree-lined main street, brick courthouse, a clock tower chiming the hour—it might have been the town in Ohio where he'd grown up. If small towns were dying, as some people suggested, the good folks of Echo Falls weren't recognizing it.

He'd breakfasted at a coffee shop run by a cheerful Amish woman who'd brought him what looked like a home-cooked breakfast and lingered at the table to talk. He was a visitor, yah? He was a little early for the peak of fall color, but he'd find some pretty walks if he liked to hike.

A query about the town's name brought forth a spate of information about the falls, which proved to be on the ridge above the town. She was enthusiastic enough to walk out with him when he'd finished to point out the silvery line plunging down the ridge. Clint managed to show interest while at the same time parrying her obvious determination to find out what he was doing in Echo Falls.

If he'd been able to relax, he might have enjoyed the drive to the farm. The trees on the ridges were already showing color, and the fields lay golden in the sunlight. This place might have been any of the farms he'd passed on the way, the white farmhouse and red outbuildings forming a loose rectangle with pastures and cornfields surrounding them.

He really needed to talk to Rachel, but he suspected he'd have to be polite to her people first. Well, he could do that, even if he wasn't as good at chatting people up as his partner was.

As Clint pulled to a stop at a wider part of the lane, he realized that a small knot of people was clustered in the nearest field, almost looking like mourners gathering around a grave. But no, the object in the middle was a large—make that *very* large—tree stump.

As soon as he got out of the car, one of the figures turned and gestured to him. Rachel wore a green dress today. It would probably bring out the deep sea green of her eyes, and her hair glinted golden in the sunlight. The woman who stood next to her was similar enough to be a cousin. They each held a small child by the hand, as if restraining them.

Assuming the gesture was an invitation, Clint started across the field toward them. If the two men were planning to get that massive stump out, what they needed was a front-end loader.

Rachel turned to meet him as he approached. "Good morning. I didn't expect you quite so soon."

"It seemed best to get an early start." His voice sounded stilted to his own ears, but it was hard to sound normal when he was aware of all those listening ears.

Including those of the small boy who clung to Rachel's hand. He looked about the age of her kindergartners, with hair so pale a yellow that it was almost white and round blue eyes. He didn't expect any of her students would be wearing black pants and suspenders, though.

He smiled at the boy. "Who's this?"

The child hid his face in the folds of Rachel's skirt, but one blue eye peeped out at him.

Rachel patted him. "This is my cousin's boy, Daniel. And that is Sadie with young Thomas."

He nodded politely at the cousin, whose level gaze seemed to measure him with what he suspected was disapproval. Thomas was a slightly smaller version of Daniel.

"Here is my grandfather, Josiah Byler, and Sadie's husband, Timothy Esch. Everyone, this is Clint Mordan."

Timothy was holding a large shovel, but he didn't look threatening. He had a tanned, open face and a light brown beard, fairly short.

The grandfather was another story. His long beard was nearly all white, and his lean face was laced with wrinkles. The faded blue eyes were still sharp, and he had a quality of dignity and assurance that compelled respect.

Clint realized he should have asked Rachel how to address an Amish bishop. It wouldn't do to cause offense right off the bat. He nodded to the younger man and after a moment of hesitation held out his hand to the older one.

"Sir. Thank you for letting me come."

The man's hard hand clasped his. "My granddaughter says you can be trusted. So you are wilkom." His English was good, but with a slight guttural intonation.

So Rachel had said he was trustworthy, had she? He glanced at her, noting that her cheeks were a bit pinker than usual.

"Clint is not a name I've heard often," the old man said.

"It's short for Clinton. I was named after my uncle, my father's brother."

Byler nodded. "We often use family names, as well. What does your uncle do?"

Apparently he was in for a third degree before he'd be approved, despite the words of welcome.

"He's a police officer in Cincinnati. My father is also in the police, but in a small town outside the city. I don't know if you know the area..."

He let that taper off when Rachel's grandfather nodded.

"There is an Amish community in that area. We have been there for weddings and other family events." His gaze sharpened a little. "But Rachel says that you are not in the police."

"No, sir." He was beginning to feel like a kid called to the principal's office. "I was, but after an injury on the job I had to take another position. Rachel will have told you what my interest is in the situation."

Another short nod, and the man turned toward the tree trunk, saying something to Timothy in dialect. The inquisition was over. Clint hoped he'd said the right things.

"That's a pretty big stump," he said, not wanting to walk away, especially when Rachel was making no move to ease the situation. "Can I give you a hand?"

The two men seemed to consult wordlessly, and then Timothy grinned. "If you don't mind getting dirty, we could use another pair of hands." The younger man's English was easier and more colloquial.

"The stump is old and breaking down. It should komm easy." The grandfather, after a measuring look, handed him an ax. "Timothy is clearing soil away from the roots. Then the big ones must be cut."

He couldn't resist the feeling that this was some sort of test. If so, he'd do his best to pass it. So he nodded, stepping into the trench Timothy was digging around the stump.

"Got it."

Timothy glanced at his shoes. "You need boots for muddy work."

"It's not that wet. I'll be fine." He smiled. "I've been dirty before. Let's get at it."

Needless to say, the job wasn't quite so easy as the grandfather expected, but Clint found it satisfying to do something physical after days of talking to people. He liked the feel of the ax in his hands and the sound it made when it bit into the wood.

Soon he was barely aware of those watching. He and Timothy worked in tandem, making their way around the stump. It reminded him of working with his dad, doing his share to keep their acre lot looking the way his mother thought it should. Dad was a great believer in the value of hard work.

The ax went clear through the last of the thick roots. He gave the trunk a tentative nudge, using the ax head as a lever. It rocked gently in response.

Timothy nodded, smiling. "I think we have it. Want to give it a try?"

"Why not?" He set the ax out of the way, glancing at the two little boys, who were watching intently. He grinned. "Your boys are sure interested."

"Yah. They want to be big enough to help." He said something to the boys in dialect, and they giggled, jumping a little in their excitement.

"What did you tell them?"

"I said, 'Watch while we get it out in three tries.'"

Clint nodded. "Guess we'd better do it, then."

Timothy positioned himself next to Clint, and they planted their hands against the rough trunk. "Ready? On the count of three."

They pushed, and the stump rocked reluctantly, roots pulling.

"Again," Timothy said. This time they got a rending sound, and the roots began to tear from the soil. They looked at each other.

"One more, right?"

Timothy nodded. He said something to the others in dialect, and they all joined in the counting. On three Clint threw all his weight into it, shoving until he felt the muscles strain all the way to his feet. The stump rocked, groaned, protested and then toppled out of the earth, sending up a shower of roots and dirt and sending both of them sprawling.

The little boys were cheering, jumping up and down with excitement. Clint rolled to his feet, grinning at Timothy.

Timothy pounded him on the back. "Who says we couldn't get that old thing out? All it took was some muscle. Let's go wash up and get a drink."

Rachel smiled, lips quirking as if she was as much

amused as pleased. She and the other woman and kids headed for the house, and they followed.

After sluicing cold water over his face and draining two cups of it, brought by the older boy with a shy smile, he reluctantly decided it was time to get back to his real work. Before he could say anything, Bishop Byler grasped his shoulder.

"Gut job. You can help anytime." He paused. "Maybe our Rachel should show you around the place. In the daylight," he added. He didn't smile, but his eyes crinkled in amusement.

He realized Rachel was watching. Her face relaxed in a smile. "I'd best do that before Timothy decides to enlist you to help with any other little chores."

"Ach, there's not much to hand. Just a roof to patch on the shed and an ash tree or two needing felled. Ash borer's been bad lately." The smile lines around Timothy's eyes deepened. "Go on now."

"Yah, Clint's done enough for one day," the grandfather put in. "Lunch will be ready when you get back," he added. He said something to Timothy, and they headed toward the barn.

Rachel gestured to a stand of fruit trees beyond the barn. "Let's walk out to the orchard."

He fell into step with her, enjoying the stretch of muscles that had gotten a workout. The whole setting was so deceptively peaceful—the fields gleaming gold in the sunlight, the reds and oranges that had begun to show on the wooded ridges, the quiet, broken only by the lowing of a cow and the twitter of the birds among the branches of the apple trees.

And the woman who walked by his side. He had to force his mind back to business. He had things he had to say, but he'd let Rachel begin the conversation once she felt they were far enough away to be private.

Rachel darted a sidelong, smiling look at him. "You might almost have been Amish in that blue shirt, swinging an ax."

"Not quite." He rubbed his chin. "No beard."

"Only married men have beards. You don't have a wife someplace, do you? If so..."

"No, I'm unattached," he said quickly. Was she thinking about the way he'd held her the previous night? For an instant, he could almost feel her body pressed against his again.

Maybe he should apologize. Explain. But what was there to say? He didn't have any reasonable explanation. He had never before had that unreasoning need to embrace a witness in a case. The feeling was still there—subdued, but ready to jump to life in an instant.

Rachel didn't pursue the subject. She patted one of the apple trees—an old one, its branches wide and spreading. "Sadie and I used to sit in this tree and exchange secrets when we were kids." She nodded to another, taller one. "And I climbed too high in that one and was afraid to climb down."

"How'd you get down? Fall?"

She chuckled. "Not as bad as that. My grandfather talked me down."

"I can see he'd be good at that. Kind of hard not to do what he says, isn't it?"

She nodded, and silence fell between them for a moment. Maybe she was at a loss to know how to begin.

When she spoke, her voice was somber. "Is there anything new in the investigation? Anything you're going to tell me, that is," she added, giving him a challenging glance.

"You don't think I'd hold out on you, do you?"

"Yes." But she smiled.

He certainly didn't intend to tell her what Logan had thought about his willingness to leave her relatively undisturbed. In the end, he didn't suppose his partner had been totally convinced, but at least Logan trusted his judgment.

"Logan looked into that partnership business you told me about," he said abruptly.

Rachel glanced at him, seeming a little startled. "I'd forgotten we talked about it. You know, I'm not sure there was ever anything in it more than Paul's—" she hesitated, looking for a word "—well, optimism, I guess. He was always so sure his pot of gold was just around the next corner."

"Common enough with gamblers."

"I suppose you've looked into that, as well as every other aspect of our lives." Bitterness laced the words, reminding him of the distance that had to exist between them.

"It was a reasonable avenue of investigation under the circumstances." He hoped he didn't sound defensive. "Was that what..."

"Broke up our marriage?" She finished the question for him. "I suppose, in a way. He got tired of making promises he never managed to keep. In the end, he just wanted out." Her lips pressed together, as if she were determined not to say more about the subject of her broken marriage.

He had no good excuse for probing deeper, other

than an interest that went beyond his professional responsibilities.

"In any event, Logan talked to Claire about the initial agreement among the four of them." He frowned. "Would you say she'd be an unbiased source?"

They paused, looking down the slope toward the barn and the old well.

"I don't know. The four of them were always very close, at least in the early days. I'm not sure any of them could be unbiased about the others." Quite suddenly her eyes crinkled. "Don't ask me to be fair about Claire. She's the kind of woman other women either envy or dislike. Always a bit cool and superior."

"Popular with men?" he questioned.

"You'd be able to tell that better than I would," she protested. "But that's hardly the point. What did she say about their agreement?"

"According to Logan, she implied that it had been a temporary expedient, just to get the company up and running. Salaries and bonuses have taken the place of any idea of shares in the profit." He studied Rachel's face. "You're not surprised?"

"I suppose it was like all those other dreams." For some reason she stopped abruptly. Frowning, she bent to retrieve the cell phone. "This text came last night." She thrust the phone into his hand as if eager to have the deed accomplished before she could change her mind.

He was tempted to ask why she hadn't let him know immediately, but he knew the answer to that one, didn't he? Rachel was still struggling with what loyalty she owed to Paul. He'd have said she didn't owe him a thing, but he was probably prejudiced. Besides, she'd never ask him for an opinion. He understood her well enough now to be sure she'd battle it through on her own.

Clint studied the text. Now it was his turn to frown. "That's it?"

"Not very helpful, is it?"

"It looks that way." He glanced at her, wondering if she was marshaling a defense of her ex.

"He says he's sorry, I guess for getting me involved in his problems, but he still doesn't explain." She hesitated, her eyes somber. "It almost sounds as if he's saying goodbye."

He'd like to ask how she felt about that, but that would be pushing their relationship too far. "It's not the explanation we've been hoping for. What does he mean about a day in June?"

She shook her head, and the breeze caught a strand of hair that pulled loose from the bun. "I guess it's a reference to our wedding. We wanted an outdoor wedding, so we were married in June at a park outside the city." She smoothed her hair back with a hand that was slightly unsteady. "It seems a long time ago now."

"Did you respond to this?" He held the phone out to her.

"I tried again later. Twice." She didn't take it. "He hasn't responded."

"Try again. Ask him where he is. Tell him we'll help him settle this so there won't be a need for the police."

For a moment Rachel seemed to hover on the verge of an argument, but then she took the phone. She keyed in the message, frowned over it and handed it back to him. "Okay?"

Nodding, he hit *Send.* He didn't suppose it would be

of any more use than Rachel's other pleas, but it was worth a try.

Putting the phone back in her hand, he paused awkwardly. "Look, I know it's hard. But I don't see what else you can do."

Before she could answer, Clint's own cell buzzed. He yanked it out. Logan. Now what?

"What's up?"

"Nothing much. Just a lead that you might run down from where you are."

He glanced at Rachel. "About what?" He kept his voice guarded.

"A friend of the people who interest us, name of Michael Leonard." Obviously Logan had picked up on the fact that he was with someone. "Apparently this guy was one of their little group initially, but he broke away from them early on—about the time they were starting the company. Seems like he might have some insight into their inner workings. Worth a visit?"

"Sounds like it." The chance of an unbiased but knowledgeable opinion on that foursome was worth looking into. "Where is he?"

"Maybe a two-hour drive from you. I figured you may as well check it out since you're practically there."

He did some rapid calculating. If he could meet with the man today, it would be perfect. "Okay, text me with the phone number and name, anything else you have. I'll set it up."

When he ended the call, he realized Rachel was watching him, openly curious.

"Sorry. Logan came up with someone who might shed some light on a few things we'd like to know." He hesitated. "Did Paul ever mention someone called Michael Leonard to you?"

She frowned, seeming to scour her memory. "I don't think so. Who is he?"

"Apparently a college friend of his." He didn't want to snub her, but he wasn't quite ready to confide everything. He glanced at his phone. "I'd like to get in touch with him…"

"And you'd like some privacy," she finished for him, her lips quirking. "Fine. I'll start back. Just be sure you come in for lunch when you finish."

"You don't need to feed me. That's not part of the deal, is it?" He smiled to take away any sting in the words.

"You don't know my grandmother. Don't try to get out of it, or she'll be offended."

"You sound like a teacher I once had. 'She who must be obeyed,'" he quoted.

"Every teacher worth her salt has a voice like that," she told him. "And don't you forget it."

"Yes, ma'am. I'll be in directly."

He watched her go, still smiling, until she was out of earshot. Then he punched in the number.

RACHEL'S SMILE VANISHED as she walked back to the house, trying hard to pull up any connection with the name Clint had mentioned. Michael Leonard. Mike Leonard. She tried it using the nickname, and it roused a faint buzz in her memory. A college friend, according to Clint. She wouldn't necessarily know him then, but it did seem she'd heard the name.

"There you are." Grossmammi turned from the stove at the sound of the door. "Is he coming?"

"He's on his way. He had to make a phone call first."

"He could have used the telephone in the shanty," Grossmammi protested. Rachel thought her grandmother was struggling between her innate hospitality and her wariness with a stranger who might cause trouble for her precious granddaughter.

"That's nice of you." She gave her grandmother a quick hug. "But I think it was easier just to use the cell phone."

Grossmammi wrinkled up her nose at that and seemed about to give them her view of cell phones. Sadie, rolling her eyes, intervened.

"Here's Clint. You sit down, and I'll get the food on the table."

Rachel hid a smile at the thought of Clint's reaction to what Grossmammi considered an appropriate lunch—bowls of steaming chicken pot pie, cooked dried corn, green beans, applesauce, cabbage slaw—she was used to cooking for men who worked out in the fields all day.

Sure enough, Clint came to a stop and stared at the table for just an instant before he recovered. "It smells wonderful in here. And everything looks delicious."

She had to award him points for not protesting that Grossmammi shouldn't go to so much trouble. She wouldn't have appreciated that, but she did know how to react to a compliment, moving her head as if to shake it off but smiling, nonetheless.

"This is my grandmother." She put her arm around Grossmammi's waist for a moment.

Clint nodded, smiling at her.

"Right here, Clint." Timothy pulled out the chair next to his.

The others took their usual places, with Sadie sliding into the chair nearest the stove to handle refills. The baby, plopped on her lap, reached for the spoon and had her small hands wrapped firmly in Sadie's. A hushing sound reinforced the gesture.

Clint seemed to pick up on it quickly, and he bowed his head along with the others. Whether he expected the silent grace or not, he sat quietly, probably taking a furtive glance to see what to do.

Rachel, used to the time of silent prayer, no longer even needed to watch someone to see when it ended. It was automatic, and at the same moment everyone was moving, picking up serving dishes and starting the food around the table.

Helping the two boys fill their plates, Rachel found her mind occupied with the question of whether to tell Clint that she found the name familiar. Still, it seemed a useless bit of information. Unless and until she remembered something definitive, she couldn't help. But what did they think this man might be able to tell them about Paul?

When she could attend to the adult conversation again, her grandfather was asking Clint what he'd thought of the town of Echo Falls.

"Seems like a nice place. Friendly people, and I like the settled old buildings and locally owned businesses. I didn't see any falls, though, until someone pointed them out to me, up on the ridge."

"Right. The falls isn't in town at all," Timothy said. "So they could have named it anything."

"Ach, what an idea," Sadie said, offering baby Becky a piece of crust dipped in potpie. "How would folks know to look for the falls if they named the town something else?"

Timothy grinned, used to her teasing. "They could put up a big sign."

"You can see the falls from up by the orchard if you know where to look," Rachel said. "It's near the top of the ridge, but the trees make it hard to see this time of year. There's a lane that goes up from the neighbor's place."

"Makes for a nice walk in the woods, going up there," Timothy added.

Clint nodded, looking as if he hoped no one was going to suggest a hike today. "With all these miles of wooded hills, you must get good hunting around here."

"Now you've done it," Sadie said, addressing Clint directly for what might be the first time. "You'll never get them off the subject."

She and Sadie exchanged smiles as Grossdaadi and Timothy launched into hunting talk. "Small game season now..." Timothy began.

"Antlered deer season coming up right after Thanksgiving," Grossdaadi added. "We should be thinking about that soon. You hunt?" This was directed at Clint.

"I used to go all the time with my dad, but it's been hard to get back there during hunting season the past few years. You probably have better whitetail hunting here than we did out in our area."

That, of course, reminded Grossdaadi of the year so many family members had gotten their deer that they'd shared the venison with every family in the church. Timothy capped that with the story of last year's surprise snowfall on the first day of deer season.

Sadie leaned across toward Rachel. "Look at the boys watching them. By the time they're old enough to hunt they'll be just as bad."

"Ach, I know full well it's the time together out in

the woods they like, not just the hunting," Grossmammi said placidly.

"That's so." Sadie smiled a little, watching her husband. "Timothy's that tenderhearted he's always a little sad when he actually gets a deer. But he still looks forward to it. And venison makes good eating."

"They'll talk about it forever," Grossmammi said. She reached across to put another helping of chicken potpie on Clint's plate, just as she would for Grossdaadi or Timothy.

It certainly looked as if they would. Even now, Clint was telling the others about building a tree stand with his uncle, and he was as relaxed and at ease as if he'd known them for years.

They looked the same. The thought hit Rachel like a splash of water in the face, and she blinked. There was Clint, a stranger and maybe an adversary, sitting at her grandparents' table and talking hunting as if he belonged here. And the rest of her family smiling and at ease with him.

She tried not to compare this with the one visit Paul had made here, but she couldn't help herself. She could still see Paul, stiff and uncomfortable, making stilted conversation with her grandfather. And her family, trying valiantly to accept him for her sake, and all the while wondering what she was thinking of.

It wasn't a fair comparison, she told herself. But a small voice in the back of her mind had a question. Why? Why isn't it? Paul came here embarrassed and ready to dislike them. Clint was treating them just like anyone else, and they were responding. They liked him.

Maybe that was the trouble. She liked him, too. Entirely too much for current circumstances.

CHAPTER EIGHT

CLINT DROVE AWAY from the farm, realizing that he was smiling with a pleasure that had no place in the investigation of a case. Still, it was normal to enjoy meeting people as nice as Rachel's family, wasn't it? He'd hit it off with the men quickly. Despite the clothes, they had a lot in common with his own father, uncle and grandfather. They'd understand each other, he thought.

But now he had to focus on what was important. This might well be a wild-goose chase. Still, he had the feeling that much of what happened lately had its roots in the relationships of those four people. He couldn't look at the theft, if that's what it was, in isolation. If he could get an honest insight in the way those people worked together, it could go a long way toward explaining what had happened.

It wouldn't resolve the question of where Paul Hartline and the missing material were, but it was hard to tell what might be important. Besides, there was nothing he could do in Philly that Logan and their staff couldn't do as well.

A couple of hours' drive brought him to the small city in New York State that was home to Michael Leonard. He exited the interstate and followed the GPS toward the thriving electronics division of a major company.

The facility was so spread out that he wasted time

trying to find the right building, but eventually he was seated in a bland conference room that looked just like every other one he'd been in. Across from him, Michael Leonard sat, frowning. He'd agreed to meet, but looked like he wasn't happy about it.

Clint took a couple of minutes to assess the man before plunging into the topic of his visit. Midthirties, he'd guess, with already thinning hair and a slightly stooped look, as if he spent his time bending over schematics. He seemed fit enough, though, and gave the impression of someone suited with his place in life and not eager to take on anything that might upset it. Too bad he hadn't invited Clint into his office—a personal office told a lot more about a man.

"You wanted to talk to me about Paul Hartline." Leonard seemed to get tired of waiting for him to begin. "Is Paul in some sort of trouble?"

He hesitated, but he sensed he wouldn't get much unless he was relatively forthcoming. "He may be. It looks as if he might have tried to share Attwood Industrial secrets to another firm."

Leonard's frown deepened. "That isn't what I thought you were going to say. People change, of course, but I'd have said Paul would be loyal to Attwood's clique no matter what personal failings he had."

Clint raised an eyebrow. "You knew about his gambling habit, did you?"

The man relaxed. "If you know about it already, then I don't have to be tactful. Yeah, even as far back as when I first met him, he couldn't resist making a bet on anything and everything...whether you were going to have a pop quiz in class, whether it was going to rain on Saturday... especially the results of any sporting event. He even organized betting on the football team." His mouth slid into a slight smile. "He'd bet against his own college team if he thought he'd win."

"But you still say he'd be loyal to Attwood?"

Leonard looked down at his hands for a moment. "I would, yeah. Thing was, Attwood needed that kind of loyalty."

"Needed?" His ears perked up at that.

Leonard met his eyes, suddenly suspicious. "I thought it was Hartline you wanted to know about."

"All four of them, in fact." He hesitated. "Like I said on the phone, our security company is supposed to sort this situation out. It's hard to do that without understanding the dynamics among those four."

"I get that. It always was." He smiled suddenly. "But you've got it wrong in one way. Originally there weren't four, there were five."

"Five," Clint repeated. "Including you, then."

"That's it. Five of us, planning how we'd conquer the world over beers in the tavern and in late-night gab sessions. We figured we could do it all, and among us we'd have the different talents we needed to make a go of it."

"You were in the same field as Attwood, then?"

He nodded. "Me, James and Ian were the scientific brains, of course, but Ian always took the subordinate role. He knew he didn't have that spark of invention James and I had, but he had a gift for testing the most unlikely ideas until they were proved or disproved. Claire was our business manager, and Paul could sell anything, including himself."

Clint realized the man was enjoying his reminiscences, smiling a little at the thought of those days. Still, something had clearly gone wrong.

"So what happened?" he asked bluntly. "They're in Philadelphia running the company you planned and you're here."

"This is a good place to be." He said it defiantly. "I've got a decent lab and plenty of money behind me. To say nothing of a wife and kid. I don't need to chase jackpots anymore."

"I can see that," he said. "Most people settle into the lives they want eventually. Still, it isn't what you'd planned. So what happened?"

Leonard's face hardened. "What happened was that I discovered all that loyalty to each other only extended so far. When push came to shove and a big grant was in the balance, someone sabotaged the work I was ready to present."

"Attwood?"

He shrugged. "It could have been any of them. We'd gone out celebrating, and my computer was accessible to all of them. In any event, the grant went to Attwood. He swore he had nothing to do with what happened. Maybe he didn't. I wouldn't put it past any of them to figure that James Attwood was the better meal ticket. Anyway, that ended our relationship. Good thing, too. I'm better off."

Clint suspected Michael Leonard wasn't quite convinced of that himself—maybe still suffering from a sense of having been done out of what was his. But whether he meant it or not, it might well be true. Someone was going to take the fall for what had happened at Attwood Industrial, and Leonard might consider himself well out of it.

RACHEL SPENT ANOTHER good day with the family, but she couldn't help thinking about Paul. Where was he?

How likely was it that he could resolve his problems in a way that left her in the clear?

And what was Clint finding out from that college friend? She realized she was hoping he'd return to the farm before heading back to the city. Only so she'd be kept up to date, she told herself. Not because she wanted to see him again.

By evening, Rachel felt a passionate desire to be alone. Solitude was one thing that was missing in Amish family life, and she'd grown used to having time on her own each day. So once the children had gone off to get ready for bed, she settled on the back porch swing. If Clint did call, she'd have a little privacy.

On the heels of the thought, her grandmother pushed the door open and stepped out on the porch. "It's getting chilly out here. I brought you a wrap." She swung a black shawl of her own around Rachel's shoulders.

Rachel scooted over. "Sit with me, unless it's too cold for you." It was one thing to long for privacy and quite another to say so to someone who loved you.

Sitting, Grossmammi's feet barely touched the floor. She noticed Rachel's glance and smiled. "We grow smaller when we get old. Your grandfather teases me about getting a ladder so I can reach the kitchen shelves."

"He'll just have to get things down for you." Rachel put her hand over her grandmother's, realizing that the bones felt as fragile as a bird's. She should be coming to visit more often, instead of just when she needed something.

"Have you heard from your friend yet?"

"Clint? No, nothing yet." She wasn't sure how to explain the relationship between herself and Clint, but she didn't think it was friendship. "He may not be able to tell me everything he finds out, because it's his job, you see."

She nodded. "Josiah said he seems to be an honorable man."

If her grandfather had said that, it was high praise based on a very short acquaintance. She'd have to hope he was right.

"You are still feeling sorrow for Paul, ain't so?"

The simple question opened up a whole train of thought she'd rather not focus on. "I guess I am." She tried to stop at that, but words seemed to force themselves out, almost against her will. "If I'd paid attention, I'd have known when I brought Paul here that a marriage between us would lead to grief. All of you tried, but you didn't like him, did you?"

Grossmammi was silent for a moment. "Let us say rather that we didn't trust him with our precious girl's happiness."

"I'd like to convince myself that you saw more than I did, but that wouldn't be true. I knew, even then. The warning signs were all there, but I rushed ahead, anyway."

"Yah." Their hands were clasped, and Rachel felt her grandmother's warmth. "We understood. You were longing for the settled home your mammi never gave you. We have always felt so guilty about it."

"Guilty?" That shocked her out of her self-absorption. "You weren't to blame for what happened. My mother rushed into marriage under the spell of infatuation, leaving behind everything that should have been important to her. And when it wasn't what she expected, she rushed on to another relationship. It certainly wasn't your fault. You did your best for her and for me."

"Not enough." She smoothed her palm over Rachel's hand and patted it. "Is she… How is she now?" Pain threaded the words.

Rachel longed to say something that would make it better, but there weren't any words for that. "She seems well," she said carefully. "The place where she lives has lots of activities for older people, like card parties and trips. I'd say she's as content as I've ever seen her."

Tears glistened in her grandmother's eyes. "Poor child. She spent her life looking for happiness. But happiness isn't something you find. It's something that comes along unexpected when you're doing the right thing."

Rachel's throat was too choked for words. Her grandmother had summed up a whole philosophy of life in a few words. How much of her own regret came from looking for happiness as if it were a hidden treasure she could find?

Before she could find a way to respond, the phone buzzed. Rachel hurried to pull it out. "It's Clint."

Her grandmother slid off the swing and patted her cheek in what almost seemed a blessing. "I'll leave you to talk."

As the door closed behind her, Rachel connected, discovering that her breathing had quickened. Maybe Clint would have some answers.

"What took you so long to answer? Is anything wrong?"

Rachel didn't want to be warmed by his concern or annoyed by his barking at her.

"My grandmother was leaving to give me some privacy to talk. Nothing's wrong, except that I've been hoping to hear something from you all day. Where are you?"

"On my way back to the city. Any problems there?"

So he wasn't coming back here, after all. She tried not to feel disappointed. "No problems. I realized that the name of the person you were looking for seemed familiar, but I don't think I ever met him."

"No, I guess you wouldn't have. He was apparently fairly close to Attwood and the others when they were in school. In the same line of study, in fact."

"I see." But she didn't. "Was he helpful? Did he know anything about why Paul did it or what he's going to do now?"

There was a pause, as if she'd caught him by surprise. "He hadn't heard from Paul in years, from what he said."

"Right. I understand."

She had to remind herself that Clint's primary purpose was to regain the file. He'd want to learn anything that might help him with that, but she suspected he didn't think Paul was likely to do the right thing in his situation. And he probably thought he already knew Paul's motivation. Money.

"It's natural to be worried when someone you care about is missing." He sounded awkward. Strained, maybe. "But there's nothing new on him."

Did he think her concern meant that she was still in love with Paul? She hovered on the brink of trying to explain herself but rejected the idea. It didn't matter what Clint thought of her motives. Nothing mattered except finding Paul and getting him to do the right thing before he took her down with him.

“If he doesn’t turn up soon, Attwood will probably go to the police, won’t he?”

She cringed away from that thought. Attwood had threatened to prosecute her. If that happened, even if nothing was ever proved against her, the resulting publicity could destroy her teaching career. Worse, it could hurt the school she and Lyn had worked so hard to build. A small private school like theirs lived and died by its reputation.

She wouldn’t take that risk. If the worst happened, she had to separate herself from Lyn and the school.

“He doesn’t want to go to the police. My partner says he’s still determined not to unleash any negative publicity, especially since, according to him, the idea they were developing might turn out to be a dud, anyway.”

“I hope that’s true. I mean, not that it’s a dud, but that it doesn’t become public knowledge. About this man you saw today…”

“Look, we’d better wind this up.” Clint’s tone was hurried. “Your grandparents…”

She got the message. He didn’t intend to share what he’d learned, if anything. She tried to convince herself that was only to be expected.

“They understand that I have to cooperate with you, under the circumstances. Anyway, I’m out on the back porch where there’s no one to be bothered.”

“Bad idea,” he said quickly. “I told you not to go off on your own, and…”

“Don’t be ridiculous. I’m perfectly safe sitting on the back porch within shouting distance of the whole family.”

“Go inside, and then you won’t have to shout.” He sounded exasperated again.

"Fine. Goodbye." Thoroughly annoyed, she ended the call. Maybe nobody had ever told Clint that snapping at someone wasn't a great way to gain their cooperation.

She stowed the cell phone away. She'd have to charge it again soon—the generator that ran the milk cooling tanks should work, but she wasn't foolish enough to go wandering out there after dark, no matter what Clint thought of her judgment.

She would not hurry inside just because Clint thought he knew better than she did. She'd sit here and enjoy the peace and stillness. Wrapping her grandmother's thick black shawl around her, she settled back on the swing.

The stars were so much brighter here than they could ever be in the city, and the sliver of a crescent moon hung above the ridge. It was quiet…so quiet that even from this distance she could hear the movement of the buggy horses in their stalls.

And something else. Focusing, she tried to isolate the faint rustling noise, realizing it came from the row of blueberry bushes off to her right. An animal of some sort, moving in search of prey under the cover of darkness. At the moment, all her sympathies were with the hunted.

The relaxation she'd hoped for eluded her. If only she could pick up the phone and talk with Lyn, her friend's common-sense attitude might bring the world back into something approaching normal, but she didn't dare.

Telling herself she was being paranoid didn't help. If she couldn't do anything else about this mess, she could stop turning to Lyn, involving her. It was too hard to separate Lyn's role as head teacher from her role as good friend.

She had to act on her own. It was the right thing to do. It was also very lonely.

Another rustle came from the blueberry bushes. She turned, the swing creaking as she did, trying to see what was there. The rustling noise ceased in that instant, as if the hunter were alarmed by her presence.

Hunter. Hunted. She didn't like that train of thought. No one could know where she was, she reminded herself. But her peaceful moment was destroyed, and her nerves jangled with alarm. The memory of arms grabbing her from behind was suddenly too vivid to be ignored.

She stood, leaving the swing lurching, and hurried into the house.

CLINT FROWNED AT the phone. Now what did she have to be annoyed about? He was just trying to keep her safe. Almost at once another call came through. He hit the answer button.

"Hey, what's up, Logan?"

"I just got a report. Paul Hartline's car has been found abandoned in St. Davids."

His adrenaline began to pump. Finally, a break. "Stolen?"

"It doesn't look like it. I'm going down to check it out, but I figured you'd want to see for yourself. What's your ETA?"

He checked his watch. "I'm nearly to the blue route. I'll meet you there."

After getting the address, he focused on what came next. Search the car, and maybe there'd be a lead on where Hartline had gone. And maybe he'd come back for it. Wouldn't that be nice if he'd walk right into their hands?

An hour later, he shoved himself away from Hartline's car and glared at it. "Finding the car should have led us somewhere, but it's just another dead end."

"This case is full of dead ends," Logan muttered. "I could do with seeing a little daylight."

"Yeah. Well, let's get out of here before some helpful neighbor decides to call the cops. It's not leading us…" Clint stopped, looking at the idea that had just popped into his head. "We didn't check underneath."

Logan blinked. "What for? You think he rigged the car in some way?"

"Not that." He knelt and swung the flashlight beam under the vehicle.

A car drove slowly past and then pulled into a driveway a few houses down. "Hurry up," Logan muttered. "We're going to have company in a minute."

"Just wait." He had to stretch to reach it, but his fingers closed around the object attached to the frame. With a quick jerk, he pulled it free and got to his feet.

Logan gave a low whistle. "So somebody wanted to know where Hartline went."

"Who?" This raised more questions than answers. "More important, did they find him?"

Logan ran a hand through his hair. "Inquiring neighbor headed this way. Let's find some coffee before we start analyzing. I don't want to explain what we're doing to the local cops."

A half hour later they were sitting in a booth at the nearest coffee shop, hands around their now-cooling mugs, still trying to hash out some answers. Or at least find the right questions to ask.

"Okay," Logan said, blowing out a frustrated breath. "Let's start with the obvious. The only reason I can see for anybody to put a trace on Hartline's car is that he hasn't turned over whatever it was he took."

"Right. That would also explain the repeated searches of his apartment and Rachel's house. And the attack on her. So this thing…idea, schematic, invention… whatever the heck it is, is still out there." He stopped, thinking over what he'd just said. "You know, that's what's really bugging me about the whole thing. We've been at a disadvantage from the beginning by not understanding what's missing or even what the internal workings of the company are."

"All we have is Attwood's description of it as a valuable new way to do something, with no explanation of what that something is." Logan glared at his mug and signaled the server for a refill. "Something technical, obviously. And unproven, as yet. Maybe Hartline acted too fast."

Clint nodded his thanks when the server topped off his cup. "According to his ex, Hartline wasn't involved in the technical aspect of the business at all. He handled the marketing exclusively. Would he even know enough to find and access whatever it is he copied?"

"Good point. I suppose if he'd been recruited by a rival company, he might have been told what to do, but it's hard to understand how they'd know exactly how to get at it." His gaze met Logan's across the table. "So what are we saying? That someone besides Hartline from the company was involved?"

"We've seen stranger things," Logan said. "If so, that person might have been smart to use Hartline to keep suspicion away from himself. Or herself. The bottom line is that we need to know more about the day-to-day running of the company from someone other than Attwood."

Clint found he was picturing Ian Robinson turning up at Rachel's door to help her clear up after the intruder. Rachel seemed to relate to him more than anyone else at Attwood Industrial.

"What about bringing Robinson into the loop? He probably knows as much about the technical side as Attwood himself, and he's a close friend of Hartline's."

"About Robinson..." Logan was shaking his head. "I didn't have time to tell you something that came to light just before I left the office."

"Robinson put a foot on the wrong side of the line?" His eyebrows lifted. He hadn't cared for the guy himself, but at least his concern for Rachel had seemed genuine.

"When I ran a routine credit check on him, everything seemed fine. But apparently he had an extra card—one that had only *his* name on it, not his wife's, with the office address. And the charges were for nights at various hotels and some extravagant restaurant options."

Clint grinned. "Everyone doesn't agree with you that a fast-food joint is fine dining, you know." He sobered. "Still, it's odd. Could it be a card kept separate for expenses on business trips?"

"Most of the hotels were right here in the Philly area."

His eyebrows lifted. "So what was this successful married professional doing staying at a hotel when he could easily have gone home to his wife and child?"

"I don't know, but we'd better find out before we put any trust in what he tells us. Maybe one of the technicians can put us on to how things work..."

Logan broke off when Clint's phone rang. As Clint frowned at the screen, Logan's face took on a questioning look.

"The ex-wife again?"

"No." His frown deepened. "Her friend." Why was Lyn Baker calling him when she'd seemed so determined to avoid telling him anything at all?

The woman started talking as soon as he answered, her clipped tones at odds with the anxiety underlying her voice. "We've had a break-in at the school. In Rachel's classroom, to be specific. The police have been and gone without seeming to find much, but it occurred to me that you ought to know."

"Right. Thanks." His mind struggled with the ramifications. "I suppose you can't tell if anything's missing." That would be too much to hope for.

"Not really," she said. "But I found a few of her files tossed on the desk, and I know they weren't out at the end of the school day on Friday. I came back for a music concert and to prepare for tomorrow, and just walked through to check her room."

"Any specific files out?" He didn't think Rachel had told her friend where she'd been headed, and he didn't want to give it away with his questions.

"They seemed to be pictures she was saving, maybe to display on different subjects." She apparently realized how little she had to tell, because a note of doubt had entered her voice. "I don't know how important it is, but if you're in touch with Rachel, you ought to know, I guess."

"You did the right thing," he reassured her automatically, wondering whether this was a false alarm. "Was the school actually broken into? You said there was an event going on."

"Yes, that's what the police pointed out. I think they thought some kids just slipped away from the concert and made a mess."

Kids, or someone else using the concert to cover their activities. "Don't you have security cameras?"

"We're a small, private elementary school." She sounded exasperated, probably thinking about how parents would react. "We operate on a shoestring. The only cameras are on the outside entrances."

"So someone could have come in with the crowd and slipped off."

"They could," she admitted. "If you want to come by and see for yourself, I won't put anything away."

"I'll stop by tomorrow, either before or after school. In the meantime, I can contact Rachel and see if she has any ideas."

"Good." Her voice had become crisp again. "She seems to be trusting you. I hope she's not mistaken."

He could hardly blame the woman. "I'll make sure she's all right."

"You'd better." It didn't sound like a threat—rather a statement of fact.

"Count on it," he said shortly.

Logan was already putting some money on the table. "Trouble?"

"I don't know. I don't see what it means, but someone broke into Rachel's classroom. I've got to contact her—make sure there was nothing that could give away her location."

"We'd better get out of here so you can talk." Logan slid out of the booth.

He grimaced. “It’s not that easy. She’ll probably have the phone turned off at this point. I’ll text and have her call me back.”

“Okay.” Logan glanced at his watch as they headed for the car. “I’ll drop you off. Tomorrow we can get busy finding a source of information at Attwood’s. I’m not a fan of going behind the client’s back, but I also don’t like working blind.”

Clint didn’t either, especially not where Rachel was concerned.

CHAPTER NINE

Morning sunshine slanted across the backyard as Rachel handed one end of a wet sheet to Sadie and stretched out to pin her end to the clothesline. On a day as warm as this, it was hard to believe that the first frost could be just around the corner.

"Oops, look out!" She scooped up Sadie's three-year-old to keep him from running right into the sheet. "Thomas, I thought you boys were helping."

"I'm helping, Cousin Rachel." Daniel gave up chasing his little brother and hurried to her with a handful of clothespins. "I'll hold these for you."

"Me, too." It was the immemorial cry of the younger sibling coming from Thomas. At a look from his mother, Daniel handed him some of the clothespins.

"Here. You hold them for Mammi."

Rachel set him on his feet and he trotted off eagerly to his mother. She and Sadie exchanged smiles over the children's heads. Sadie's boys were being raised in the typical Amish tradition, learning early to work and to be kind, and with a single look, Sadie had reinforced both of those lessons.

But the helping didn't seem destined to last very long, because a buggy drove up to the house, and both boys went running.

Rachel felt a flutter of uneasiness. “I don’t suppose I can just stay busy out here, can I?”

“Not unless you want to make folks talk,” Sadie said. She linked her arm with Rachel’s. “Komm. Just act natural.”

That actually worked fairly well, right up to the point at which Rachel recognized one of the two women in the buggy. Sarah Burkhalter was a neighbor, and she’d certainly known Rachel well enough to know she wasn’t Amish.

Sadie carried the encounter off with flair. “Sarah, how nice to see you. And your great-aunt, too. This is my cousin, Rachel, who is visiting us for a bit.”

The older woman’s face sharpened inquisitively. “Rachel? I didn’t know you had a cousin Rachel. What side of…”

Sarah Burkhalter interrupted the question by leaning across her, smiling. “Rachel, how gut it is to see you again. It’s been years. But we don’t want to take you away from your visiting. I just thought we’d pick up your cookies for the school lunch and save you a trip.”

“They’re all ready,” Sadie said, exerting a gentle pressure on Rachel’s arm. “Rachel, will you give them to Daniel to bring out? I don’t want to keep you away from Grossmammi any longer.”

“For sure.” She turned away with a sigh of relief. Grabbing Daniel’s hand, she led him quickly into the kitchen. The cookies were ready on the counter, so she put the container into his hands.

“You’ll take care, now, yah?”

“I’ll be careful.” He wrapped both arms around the plastic container and marched out, mindful of his responsibility.

Rachel kept herself out of sight until the buggy had driven away and the boys had run off. When she rejoined Sadie she could feel laughter bubbling up in her. "Sarah knew, and she played up beautifully. Who would have guessed the two of you could improvise that way?"

Sadie chuckled. "As soon as I saw Sarah's great-aunt, I knew we were in trouble. She is without a doubt the nosiest woman I've ever known. Kind, mind you, but she always wants to know everything that's happening."

"Obviously Sarah is used to it. She did it all without being rude or saying a false word." She shook her head. "Pretending to be Amish requires a lot of cooperation from people who care about you."

Sadie smiled. "You have that, always."

It wasn't until they'd finished hanging the sheets that Rachel realized she hadn't turned her phone on yet this morning. She powered up, saw a text from Clint and slipped up to her bedroom in the daadi haus to call him.

"About time you were calling back." Clint sounded as if his patience was running thin. "Didn't you get my message?"

"Sorry. I had the phone turned off overnight to conserve the battery. Someone broke in at the school?"

"It's not a big deal," he said, as if he heard the fear in her voice. "Someone got into your classroom, apparently during the concert. Your classroom seemed the only place disturbed."

Revulsion grabbed her at the thought of someone making a mess in a place that should be safe for the children. "How bad was it?" She couldn't help picturing the mess in her house.

"I told you—not much. Just some folders taken out of the filing cabinet. Your friend saw the room wasn't the way it had been left, so she called the police. She suggested I come over to have a look at it, as well. But was there anything there that might lead to you?"

She sank down on the bed and tried to focus. Her mind skittered through the contents of her desk and file cabinet. "I don't see what there would be. Was Lyn specific about what was disturbed?"

"She said some files had been left out, presumably by the intruder. But as far as she could tell, they were mostly pictures you'd saved to illustrate something for the kids."

Baffling, that was all she could think. "I just can't imagine what anyone might hope to find there. Are you sure it's connected?"

"I don't mind admitting that coincidences happen, but this one is stretching the odds a bit too far. The police seem to think it was kids, skipping out of the concert, but why would they go to the kindergarten room?"

"No place else showed signs of someone getting in?"

"Not that Ms. Baker could see. The intruder didn't attempt to get in the office at all, and that's where he might find cash or something of value. I'm going to stop by the school so she can show me."

The shadow of her trouble was already touching the school. Tension tightened on the nape of her neck—tension that had been noticeably missing since she'd arrived at the farm. "Have you made any progress otherwise?"

He was so quiet she thought she'd lost the connection. "Paul's car has turned up," he said.

"What? Where?"

"It was sitting in a quiet residential block in St. Davids, undisturbed."

"Was there anything in it that might lead to him?" She assumed he'd have found a way to get past the locked door. That seemed to be a requirement for his job.

"Neat as a pin. No papers, no maps, nothing. The glove box contained the owner's manual and the usual insurance and registration."

She shook her head, even though he couldn't see her. "That doesn't sound like Paul. His car always accumulated papers, wrappers, maps… He'd only clean it out once a week."

"Well, either he parked it there right after his cleaning, or he intended to leave nothing that might lead to him."

It seemed very unsatisfactory to her. "You're sure the car wasn't stolen?"

"A thief wouldn't desert it in pristine condition in a nice residential area." He sounded as if he was exhibiting patience. "They're not that thoughtful as a group. It'd either be in a chop shop or wrapped around a tree."

"I suppose that's true." The reminder of Paul increased the pressure of taut muscles. "Why would he walk away from it?"

"Why not? You did."

That was different, she wanted to say, but what good would it do? Maybe to Clint there wasn't any difference between her actions and Paul's.

Where had Paul gone? If he really did regret what he'd done, why hadn't he come forward?

Her phone gave a warning beep, and she realized she was running on very low battery. "I've got to put my phone on the charger. Is there anything else you wanted to say?"

"Just be careful. All right? I don't want anything to happen to you. Among other things, your friend Lyn would beat me to a pulp if I let you get hurt."

She smiled, warmed. "I promise."

CLINT HUNG UP, annoyed at the sense of failure that kept creeping up on him. Logan felt the same, he knew, but in this case, sharing the misery didn't improve it. Neither of them relished the idea of failing on this one—they'd never be able to consider it part of the game.

They probably never would feel that way, no matter how busy and successful the agency was. They both came from a tradition that put duty first—the police in his case, the military in Logan's. They didn't expect to fail.

This wasn't going to be the first time, not if he could help it. He'd get on with the task of finding someone from Attwood Industrial who would talk freely about the place. Michael Leonard had been willing enough to talk, but of course he no longer relied on Attwood for his future.

If someone else had been involved with Paul in the scheme, it seemed to him Ian Robinson was the most likely—he was an old friend of Paul's, his job was second only to Attwood's on the scientific side and his occasional weekend activities needed to be explained. But proof would be helpful.

By the time Clint reached Rachel's school that afternoon to check in with her friend, he was actually feeling encouraged. The talkative technician he and Logan had unearthed seemed perfectly willing to gossip about his fellow workers at Attwood Industrial, and everything he said bolstered the idea that Robinson had something to hide.

Furthermore, he'd once run into Robinson and Claire Gibson, Attwood's assistant, having an intimate chat in a downtown restaurant. He'd had a few salacious comments for that. And people said women were the nosy ones.

Nothing like finding someone willing to gossip to shed light on the inner workings of an institution. Any dalliance between Robinson and Ms. Gibson might have nothing to do with the matter they were investigating, but it certainly raised questions in his mind, as well as doubts about the man's reliability.

Walking into the school was like swimming against a tide of children. A steady stream of them poured out the walk, heading for the circular drive where parents were waiting to pick them up. By the time he made it inside, the hallways were emptied of students and the head teacher waited to greet him.

"Thanks for coming. I'm not sure there's much for you to see, but I kept out everything that had been taken from the filing cabinet."

"Never hurts to have a look myself." He fell into step with her as they walked toward the kindergarten room. "Did you hear anything else from the police?"

"No. I got the impression that they thought I was making a mountain out of a molehill. If it hadn't been Rachel's room..."

"Exactly. Anything out of the ordinary touching on her could be important."

She glanced at him. "I won't ask where Rachel is, because I know she doesn't want me to know. But you can tell me if she needs anything, can't you?" Her concern for her friend was clear in the way she spoke.

"Rachel's fine, and as far as I can see, there's not a thing she needs except answers that probably only her ex-husband can provide."

"I won't tell you what I think of him, because the language would be unbecoming to my position here."

The acid tone made him glance at her, a little startled at discovering someone so close to Rachel who shared his opinion of Paul Hartline.

"But I'm relieved to know she's okay." She didn't seem to expect a response to that. She opened the door and led the way into the kindergarten classroom. "The things I found were lying on the desk, and a couple of the pictures were on the floor between it and the filing cabinet. Here they are. If I hadn't checked the room before I left, I wouldn't have thought anything of it."

She spread pictures out on the desk, and he saw photos of animals, fish, plants, seasonal landscapes and bodies of water. All of them perfectly harmless, telling the intruder nothing at all.

So why did he or she get them out? "Where would these have been stored?"

The woman indicated the filing cabinet against the wall. "In here. Teachers keep things like this for bulletin boards and to illustrate something they're teaching. Rachel has always been organized about what she saved. These were in the third drawer down—it had been left open, but I had to close it before the children came in, of course."

He nodded, sliding the drawer open to find manila folders, each neatly marked. He leafed through them, seeing nothing unusual. His fingers stopped, feeling one out of alignment. Funny. It seemed to have been put in backward. Somehow he couldn't imagine Rachel doing that, not when everything else was so well organized.

Clint pulled out the file, turning it over. The label made his muscles tense. Photos of Grandfather Byler's Farm, it read. He flipped it open. The file was empty.

He heard a sharp intake of breath and turned to find that the woman had leaned over to see what he'd found.

"I had no idea Rachel still had those here."

"You'd seen them before?" So much for the idea that the search wouldn't have told the intruder anything.

Ms. Baker nodded. "Of course. She had pictures she'd taken at the farm enlarged for a display we did in the hallway about where food comes from. It was a couple of years ago, so she's probably forgotten all about it."

"Yes." His mouth clamped on the word. "What should be in here? Do you remember?"

She frowned, obviously trying to recall, and finally shook her head. "I don't know, not specifically. There were probably ten or twelve that we used, but she might have had more. Pictures of cows grazing and being milked, that I do remember. Fields of corn, a silo." She shrugged. "That sort of thing. Suburban children often have no idea where food comes from, other than the grocery store."

"Any that might be identifiable as a particular place or even give a hint to the location?"

She shook her head, clearly upset. "I don't know. She's at her grandparents' farm, I suppose. I thought as much, although I didn't say anything. And now someone has taken the photos. I should have realized what was missing, but I didn't… Well, never mind that. What are you going to do now?"

He was already on his way to the door. "Call and warn her. And then get up there." Not breaking his stride, he yanked out the cell phone and punched in Rachel's number.

It went straight to voicemail. Leaving a terse warning, he jumped in his car and headed down the street, calling Logan as he went.

Logan, at least, was answering his phone. In a few short sentences, he gave his partner the gist of the situation. "I'm heading straight up there. You'll handle things here?"

"Right. I think, under the circumstances, it wouldn't be a bad thing to put a man on to watch Ian Robinson. If he was in this and Hartline double-crossed him, he might be willing to do almost anything to find him."

"Good." He came to a halt at a red light and sat fuming. "Worst time of the day to try to get anywhere in a hurry. I just hope Rachel checks her messages and has enough sense to get somewhere safe."

He ended the call and thought about calling the police in Echo Falls. If he did, he'd be in for lengthy explanations, and even then, there was no guarantee they'd do anything about it. And if they showed up at the farm, sirens blaring—

He could imagine Rachel's reaction to that. It was everything she didn't want to inflict on her family. That wouldn't stop him, but another thought did.

He knew what Rachel would do if that happened. She'd leave. She was so determined that no one else would suffer for her affairs that she'd get out again. And this time there might be no way of finding her. No, he couldn't risk it. If she got the message, or even if she followed the reasonable precautions he'd urged on her, no one would attempt anything in broad daylight with witnesses around. But he had to get there by dark.

As he focused on the best route to get him away from city traffic, tension buzzed in his mind. What if she didn't check her messages? What if she was still wandering around the farm on her own, protected only by two men who'd sworn never to use violence? What if he didn't make it in time to keep her safe?

RACHEL SPENT A good part of the day with her grandmother, and by the time she'd helped with supper and cleaning up, she realized it was getting dark out and she hadn't yet retrieved her cell phone from the charger in the milking shed. She went to the back door and looked out at the shadows.

It wasn't that dark out, but Clint's warning kept repeating itself in her mind. No, she wouldn't give him a chance to accuse her of stupidity. She turned and went back to the living room, where Grossmammi sat knitting, Grossdaadi read a copy of the Amish weekly newspaper and Timothy tinkered with a toy boat he was trying to fix for Daniel.

It was a shame to disturb anyone, but her memory of sensing someone behind her in the dark was still strong. "Grossdaadi, are you going to the barn this evening? I thought I'd walk out with you."

He looked pleased. "Yah, I'd like fine to have your company. Chust let me finish reading this article, and I'll be ready."

Impossible to insist on doing it sooner, so she sat on the footstool by her grandmother's rocker, watching the rapid movement of the needles as they clicked. Now that she'd reminded herself, she was suddenly anxious to check the phone again.

What if Clint had called or there had finally been a message from Paul? Still, she'd checked the phone in midafternoon, and there'd been nothing new then. She could hardly go running out to the milking shed every five minutes.

Finally putting the paper aside, her grandfather planted his hands on the arms of his chair and pushed himself to his feet. Catching her expression, he smiled.

"Ach, Rachel, don't look that way. Old bones get stiff from sitting, but I'm gut for a few more years yet, if so God wills it."

"I'm sure you are." She took his hand, just as she'd done so often when she was small. "You always were the strongest man I knew, and you still are." She kept pace with him as they walked to the back door.

He was slowing down. Despite her words, she couldn't help but see it, just as she'd seen that her grandmother was growing more frail. She should have come back more often to visit, no matter what Paul had thought. This had been the closest thing she'd ever known to a home when she was growing up, and she could never repay them for their loving support.

Grossdaadi switched on a flashlight when they stepped out the back. "It gets dark quick this time of year. Before you know it we'll be setting the clocks back." He chuckled. "Too bad we can't convince the cows to switch time. They still go by the sun, no matter what the clock says."

"So do you," she said lightly. "You can't fool me on that one."

"Ach, I try. But the school keeps to government time,

just like the grain mill and the feed store. So I have to adjust. Other folks don't understand that farmers live by nature's timetable."

She turned that over in her mind, thinking of the truth of what he'd said. "If I ask my students where milk comes from, they'll say, 'the grocery store.' They miss something, living in their comfortable suburbs, I'm afraid."

"We miss things, too, living separate. But the rewards more than make up for anything we don't have."

Rachel squeezed his hand. "I'm glad I can come here sometimes, just to slow down and remember."

"You'll komm more often now, yah?" Her grandfather seemed to have read a great deal in her few words.

"Yah," she said, smiling.

They'd reached the barn, and she helped slide open the door enough to walk through. Then she took a step back.

"I'm going to run over to the milking shed to get my phone. I'll be right back. Save some carrots for me to give them."

"I will. Take the flashlight, then." Her grandfather handed it to her. "I have the battery lantern if I need more light."

She wouldn't have asked for it, but the metal cylinder felt cold and solid in her hand. "Denke. I'll just be a minute."

Grossdaadi was already turning in answer to the whickers of the horses greeting him, and she had to smile. Animals knew who cared for them.

Still smiling, she stepped away from the barn door. Without her grandfather's comfortable presence beside her, the night suddenly seemed darker. Silly to be nervous. He was only a shout away, and it wasn't more than twenty feet to the milking shed. Fumbling with the switch of the flashlight, she set off toward the generator and her cell phone.

The old well loomed up to her left, and her shoes were silent on the grass. Even the usual night sounds seemed muted. Then the faintest whisper of sound behind reached her. Had Grossdaadi decided…

Something snapped around her neck, tightening instantly. It forced her head back, stifling her cry. Her hands flew to the cruel band, flailing helplessly. A body pressed against her, forcing her against the stones of the well.

It was like a kick to her heart. Her blood pounded, her adrenaline surged. *Fight*, her mind screamed. *Fight.*

The pressure on her throat, nearly cutting off her breath, panicked her. She kicked backward, hampered by the dress, unable to connect. Blackness swam before her eyes, blotting out the stars.

The pressure eased, ever so slightly.

"Tell me," a voice whispered, harsh in her ear. "Where is it? Where is it? Tell me!"

She sucked air in frantically, and the thing around her neck tightened as if in warning. "I don't know," she gasped.

"Wrong answer." The whisper came, soft as a lover's, and her breath was cut off again.

How can I tell you? I don't know. But she couldn't get the words out. The darkness closed in. *Do something*, she ordered her body, but it didn't obey. Slip down, let the black close in…

No! Forcing her fogged brain to work she remembered the flashlight, still clamped in her hand. Her only chance. Letting her body slump, she felt the cruel grip ease slightly. Now or never. She swung her arm back over her head, putting everything she had in the movement. She felt…heard…the flashlight connect.

He stumbled, swearing, pushing at her. She tried to push back, but her body wouldn't obey. Lights seemed to flash, cutting the darkness, and then she was falling, falling, screaming, grabbing for anything that would stop her downward plunge.

Something brushed her arm. She grabbed, caught, snagged it with one hand. And stopped with a jerk that nearly pulled her arm from its socket.

She was alive. She struggled to breathe again, trying to get her mind working. He'd pushed her, she'd fallen… the well. She'd fallen into the well, and now she dangled, pain jabbing her shoulder, demanding she let go.

Gasping, she brought her other hand up, feeling her whole body swing precariously at the movement. She grabbed on, taking some of the weight, and the pressure eased. But if she moved… The slightest movement could jar her hands free. And nothing was below her but the blackness, the water and the rocks.

MOVEMENT FLICKERED FOR an instant at the edge of Clint's headlight beams, and an instant later a scream cut the night, loud enough to hear even inside the car. He jerked the car toward the sound, bumped over the edge of the lane into the long grass and came to a halt. In an instant he was out and running, headlight beams spreading a path toward the old well by the barn.

The well—that was where the movement had been. Rachel—

Someone else was running—no, more than one person. A dark, man-shaped shadow bolted for the woods and faded into the shadows. The other figure resolved itself into Rachel's grandfather running toward the well, calling out.

"Rachel!"

At the name Clint flung himself forward, reaching the stone well a step ahead of the old man. Steeling himself, he looked down, prepared for the worst.

Rachel's face was a pale oval in the gloom, looking up at him. Her hands clung tight to the well rope.

"Are you all right?" Fear made his voice sharp.

Rachel's grandfather was calling something in dialect he didn't understand. His hands gripped the edge of the well. "Rachel, child." His voice broke.

"Okay." The sound was weak. Distant. "I can't hold on..."

"Yes, you can." Clint forced a confidence he didn't feel. "We'll get you out. Just hold on."

He shot a glance at the older man and lowered his voice. "How deep?"

Byler's face was a taut mask. "The water is shallow now. Rocks underneath. If she falls..."

"We won't let her." He gripped the older man's shoulder for an instant. "First thing we need is some light to see her."

"She had a flashlight." Byler dropped to his hands and knees to search. "Here." He was up again, thrusting a cold metal torch in Clint's hand.

Clint flicked the switch, blessing the strong beam of light, and turned it to penetrate the darkness of the well. Rachel, about ten or twelve feet below them, closed her eyes against the brightness.

"You're going to be all right."

He tried to sound reassuring. But the well stretched twice as far below her, with only her hands, gripping the rope, between her and disaster. Her body swayed a little, the rope making tiny movements. He had to force himself not to think about the results if she fell twenty or thirty feet onto stones.

"Are the rope and the winch strong enough to pull her up?"

The older man seemed to be measuring Rachel's probable weight against the rope. Finally he nodded. "Yah. It's the best way. We couldn't get a ladder down without the risk of hitting her. The others are coming."

Clint didn't bother to look, but he could hear footsteps on the back porch and startled cries. He focused all his attention on Rachel, clinging desperately to a rope that must be cutting into her hands.

"We're going to pull you up. The rope might slip down a bit when we start, so hang on, okay?"

"Okay." She sounded more controlled now. She must be terrified, but she would hold the fear at bay, he thought.

Clint grasped the handle with both hands. Timothy, reaching them, didn't ask useless questions. Seeing that his hands wouldn't fit on the handle, he grasped the metal bar that connected it to the spindle. The grandfather, apparently conceding that they were stronger than he, prepared to release the wheel.

"On three," Clint said. "One, two, three."

The pull on the handle slammed into him. Fighting the pain, he held it steady, not daring to look down at Rachel…

"It's all right," Byler said. "The rope is holding. She's got a gut grip."

Clint started to push, feeling the pressure against him as the rope tightened. Slowly he began to wind the rope up and Rachel with it. Timothy's strong body braced next to him. Together they turned the handle, movements matching; even their breathing was in sync as they worked in unison.

"She's coming." Sadie leaned over the edge. Her grandmother had her hands clasped together, her lips moving in what seemed a soundless prayer.

Slowly, very slowly, Rachel inched her way upward. He fought to keep his attention on the spindle turning, the rope winding steadily. Her grandfather and Sadie reached out to her, waiting for the moment when they could clasp her in their arms and draw her to safety.

A stab of envy went through Clint. He wanted to be the one to lift her out, to put his arms around her and hold her close. But that wasn't his job. His job was to wind the rope up, muscles screaming, and bring her to safety.

And then she was out, safe in their arms, and they were all crying.

CHAPTER TEN

CLINT AND TIMOTHY released the handle, and the bucket fell, clattering to the bottom, as the rope spun out. Timothy grinned at him.

"Hard on the muscles, yah?"

He nodded, not sure he could speak. Rachel's grandfather put an arm around each of them to clasp their shoulders. "Gut work." His voice was unsteady, and he took a deep breath. "Komm. Let's get Rachel into the house."

They surrounded her, half leading, half carrying her toward the back porch. He lingered a moment, scanning what he could see of the woods into which the shadow had vanished.

"You saw who did this thing?" Timothy followed the direction of his gaze. "Did he go into the woods?"

"Yeah, he went that way. I didn't see him close enough to identify."

He fought back any bitterness at having let the man go. He couldn't have done anything else, not with Rachel in imminent danger.

"Should we go have a look?" Timothy took a step in that direction.

"Don't bother." Clint put a hand on his shoulder. "He's long gone by now." If he called the police—

But reason told him that even if he convinced the

local boys of who he was and what had happened, they'd be too late to get roadblocks up, aside from the fact that they wouldn't know what kind of vehicle they were after or who the driver was.

But whoever he was, he was willing to take serious risks to get to Rachel. Why? He must believe she knew more than she was saying.

They headed toward the house. "This is a bad thing," Timothy said, his voice solemn. "We know there is wickedness in the world, but to have it come so close to home, after one of us. Poor Rachel."

"She's just an innocent bystander, but she's become a target. I have to find out who's behind this." He was actually speaking to himself, he realized, but Timothy was nodding.

"You will." He clapped Clint on the shoulder. "You'll keep our Rachel safe."

With that, they'd reached the house. Timothy led the way into the kitchen.

They found Rachel sitting at the table, wrapped in a voluminous quilt, while her grandmother patted her hand and Sadie urged a steaming mug of hot chocolate on her.

"Yes, I'll drink it." Rachel sounded as if she'd agree to anything to get her cousin to stop fussing. She wrapped both hands around the mug, seeming to welcome its warmth, and looked up, her gaze meeting his.

Her eyes looked huge in her pale face. "Thank you." She moved slightly, the movement taking in the whole group. "All of you. If you hadn't been there…" She let that trail off.

"I should not have left you alone for a moment." Her

grandfather touched her cheek lightly, as if making sure she was really safe.

"You couldn't know." She put her hand over his. "I should have been more sensible." She glanced at him. "Clint will tell you so."

"I'll tell you that you should have checked your phone. What were you thinking?" His exasperation was a welcome relief after the fear she'd put him through. It seemed, oddly enough, to make the others relax.

"I had it charging. I did check it earlier." A little color came into her face. "In fact, I was going to get it when..."

"Too late." He frowned at her, and then realized that the others were exchanging glances.

"You need to talk. We can leave." Her grandfather gestured toward the hall.

"No, don't," Rachel said quickly. "I'm the one who has to leave." Her gaze caught his again. "That's what you were going to say, isn't it? I must go back to the city."

He inhaled, trying to swallow the exasperation that he recognized was a reaction to the terror he'd felt thinking he was going to lose her. The image of his partner, dying in that alley, slithered through his mind.

"I think it's best if you go back." He forced himself to sound calm. "We could call the police here..."

"No." Her voice was strong on the word. "I won't bring the police here."

"If it will keep you safe..." her grandfather began.

"It's not the answer," Clint said, confident that he was right. "This trouble started in the city, and that's where the answer is. We'll find a safe place for you to stay." He glanced at her grandfather. "We'll keep a guard on her constantly, I promise."

Her grandfather gave him a long, level look and then nodded. Clint breathed a little easier. He turned back to Rachel, forcing himself to sound calm. Detached.

"I don't want to make you relive it, but was there anything at all that you noticed about the man?"

She shook her head and then hesitated. "I think…I think it was the same person as before. I can't tell you why. It just felt that way."

He nodded. "I'd guess there was something you noticed subconsciously. Don't try to pull it out now. Just let it surface when it will. Did he say anything?"

"Just, 'Where is it? Where is it?'"

"It, not him?" His mind spun into gear. So the assailant wasn't looking for Paul, just for the flash drive. That must mean something, but what?

"That's right." Rachel's eyes widened as she caught the implication. She looked as if she'd question him, but then she shook her head slightly. "That was all. Then I hit him with the flashlight, and he stumbled, and I went—"

"That's all for now," he said quickly. He couldn't bring himself to make her relive the experience at the moment. "Leave it for now. We'll talk later."

"I'll get my things…" Rachel began, moving a little.

"Not now." He pressed her back into the chair. "You're too shaken to set off tonight. And I don't want to run into that guy on a dark road. We'll head back tomorrow. In the meantime, my partner will fix up a safe place for you to stay."

"That's right," Byler said firmly. "Now you must get some sleep as best you can."

Somewhat to his surprise, Rachel didn't argue. She rose, carrying the cocoa mug, and went out, the quilt trailing behind her. Her grandmother and Sadie went with her.

When they'd gone, Timothy poured out a mug of coffee from the pot on the stove, then a second, which he handed to Byler. He gave Clint an inquiring look. "Coffee? Or will it keep you awake?"

"I'll take it, the stronger the better. I need to stay awake anyhow. I'll settle on the porch and keep an eye on things, just to make sure our friend doesn't return."

"We will take turns," Byler said, in a tone that didn't brook any argument. Timothy nodded agreement.

"Yah. I'll set up a cot in here so you can sleep when I'm on duty," he said. "We'll leave the dogs out, too. We won't let anyone get near the farmhouse tonight."

Clint didn't waste time trying to dissuade them. If he could catch a few hours of sleep, he'd be better able to deal with tomorrow.

They sat in companionable silence until Sadie returned. She looked at him steadily for a moment.

"Rachel wants to speak to you," she said, and he couldn't tell whether she disapproved or not. "This way."

Clint followed her down the hall and up the stairs. "We put her to bed in this side of the house, instead of her room in the daadi haus," she said. "That way there are more people around to hear her."

"Good idea," he said, and found he was addressing her back.

She reached the room and paused, her hand on the knob. "Not too long," she warned. "She needs to rest."

He nodded, and she swung the door open so he could enter. To his surprise, she didn't follow him.

"We'll wait outside while you talk," she said. Her grandmother rose from her chair next to the bed, kissed Rachel lightly and joined them in the doorway.

"Afterward, I'll sit with her until she falls asleep," the grandmother added. They both went out, closing the door.

Rachel was sitting up in bed, pillows stacked behind her. Her hair, loose for once, lay across the shoulders of a white cotton nightgown that didn't reveal an extra inch of skin.

"I'm a danger to them," she said abruptly, as if daring him to argue with her. "I've got to get out of here so they'll be safe."

He wasn't surprised that she'd returned to the assault immediately. He moved to the chair her grandmother had left and sat down. "More important, we need to be sure that joker sees you leave, so he knows not to come back here again. Tomorrow is better for that."

She didn't look convinced. "If we went out now, headlights on, surely anyone watching would notice."

Clint was already shaking his head. "He's not hanging around. Right now he'll still be running, afraid someone is coming after him. He doesn't know if you're all right, but he's sure to guess we're watching for him. In the unlikely chance he hangs around, he'd notice us go in the morning. It's safer, as well. Honestly."

The tension seemed to ebb from her face, leaving her exhausted. "I thought you would be insisting on calling the police."

"I would, if it would do any good, but it's useless now." He knew, no one better, how police worked in small rural communities. He'd grown up with it, hearing his father's frustration on being constantly shorthanded when anything came up, having to juggle his priorities.

Rachel seemed relieved to accept that. "How did you know to come when you did?"

"If you'd had your phone on…" he began, but stopped when she glared at him. "Your friend Lyn. We found a folder that was missing its contents. It was marked Photos of Grandfather Byler's Farm."

He saw the realization dawn on her face. "I'd totally forgotten. But how could anyone find me through that? It contained photos of things around the farm, looking like any other dairy farm."

"There must have been something that was identifiable enough for him to find you, because he did. That can't be coincidence."

Her expression changed as she considered his words. "I suppose," she said slowly. "Maybe the mailbox or a road sign showed in the background of a picture."

"Maybe so. It doesn't matter now. Just get some sleep. We'll have plenty of time to talk tomorrow." He moved then, switching from the chair to the side of the bed. "Good night."

It was no good—she was too close, too vulnerable-looking. He bent to kiss her.

It was meant to be a gentle, reassuring kiss. But her lips came to life under his, and desire seized him—desire coupled with an intense longing to protect her, keep her safe, to free her to smile again.

Her arms were twined around his neck—her body pressed against his. Did she even realize it? Or was she instinctively seeking comfort? He couldn't stop, not until he felt a faint awareness touch her, making her withdraw, very slowly.

He pulled back, his lips an inch from hers, their breath mingling. "Good night, Rachel. Get some sleep. We'll deal with everything tomorrow." Rising, he released her slowly. "Don't be afraid. We'll get through this. I promise. Now sleep. We'll be on watch."

CHAPTER ELEVEN

To Rachel's surprise, she actually did sleep soundly, waking when the first rays of the sun slipped in the window. She moved, felt pain in her arms and shoulders and remembered.

So that particular nightmare had been reality, not a dream. Before she could plunge into reliving it, she pulled herself away from reliving it. It had been bad, but it was over. This morning she would go back to the city, taking the danger with her. Whatever happened, she would not risk harm to those she loved.

She dressed in her own clothes. Grossmammi must have brought them over from the daadi haus after she was asleep. That meant they'd accepted the idea that she was leaving this morning.

Rachel took a few minutes, carefully hanging up Sadie's things. Her fingers lingered for a moment on the fabric of the blue dress. In a way, her usual pants and sweater felt strange on her, as if she were putting on someone else's clothes, ready to live someone else's life.

But it wasn't. It was hers, no matter what it brought her.

When she reached the kitchen, Sadie and Grossmammi were both there. Sorrow shadowed her grandmother's face, but she managed a smile.

"You are ready to be Englisch again, ain't so?"

“As ready as I can be. Where’s Clint?”

“The boys convinced him to go out and see the baby chicks.” Sadie’s eyes crinkled. “Maybe you should rescue him. Breakfast will be ready when you come back.”

There wasn’t much left to say, it seemed. They were prepared for her to vanish as suddenly as she’d come. Trying to smile in return, she hurried out into the bright, chilly morning.

Daniel and Thomas had taken Clint into the chicken pen, it seemed. Sadie was probably right about the rescuing. She didn’t know much about Clint’s background, but she couldn’t imagine it had included chickens. She headed toward them.

When Rachel was close enough to get a look at Clint’s face, it startled her. He was clearly beat and looked as if he’d be the better for a mug of strong coffee. Or maybe a nap.

“Good morning. I’m surprised you’re up already. You couldn’t have gotten much sleep.”

She’d have to be careful what she said in front of the little ones. Thomas wouldn’t understand the English words, but Daniel seemed to pick up more every day.

“I’m okay. I just need some coffee.”

“You’ll get that, and breakfast. Sadie has it ready for us.”

“Cousin Rachel, Clint is going to hold one of the peeps,” Daniel said, bouncing with impatience. “You can, too. Komm in.”

Obviously he’d be disappointed if they rushed off to breakfast without admiring the peeps.

“Only if he wants to,” she cautioned, and moved the latch to slip through the opening before any of the hens could go exploring. Had Clint ever held a baby chick before?

But Clint was already cooperating, seemingly unconcerned about the hen that was squawking around his feet. He bent over the boys while Daniel put a yellow ball of fluff in his cupped hands.

She watched him, surprised that she could still smile. "Having fun?"

"Sure. Who wouldn't find this fun?" He straightened, holding out the peep. "Did you ever feel anything so soft?"

Rachel touched the tiny creature with a gentle finger. "Never." She glanced at the two boys. "You seem to have made a hit with my little cousins."

"I figured maybe they were hoping I'd shriek and back off."

"Oh, no. They're too kind to play tricks on people they like."

"Then I'm glad I'm included in the like category." His intimate smile hinted at a double meaning to the words, and he studied her face. "Did you sleep?"

"Like a rock," she said. "I'm sorry you… Did you sit up all night?"

"No, Timothy and your grandfather took turns with me."

"I didn't realize—I guess I was pretty out of it by that time." But she hadn't imagined that embrace, and the thought of it sent the blood rushing through her.

"That's not surprising. I'm glad you got some rest, because it will be a long day."

She looked at him with a question in her face. "The drive back isn't that exhausting."

"No, but we have to get you settled in a new place.

And I think we should sit down and go over everything with Logan, just to be sure we're all on the same page."

"Yes." Rachel said the word reluctantly. It was time to leave this sanctuary, and Clint's mind was already back in the city in spite of the fact that he stood here in the chicken coop.

Soon she would be, as well. She'd have to face what Paul had done. And face, too, the fact that he apparently wasn't going to clear her.

She was right back where she'd been before she ran away.

No, not quite. She rejected that thought instantly. She was better, stronger, for having spent even a short time with family who loved her unconditionally. And there was more.

She studied Clint's intent face. Now she was sure whose side he was on. She wasn't quite ready to face whatever that meant, but at least she was willing to try.

CLINT HAD EXPECTED Rachel's goodbyes to last forever, but now that the time had come, she seemed almost eager to get them over with. Maybe she feared breaking down. In fact, although tears glistened in her grandmother's eyes, they all seemed intent on making the farewells simple. He overheard Sadie telling the children that Cousin Rachel had to go back to her schoolchildren, but she'd come again soon.

Well, he didn't actually understand her words, but she saw him watching and translated for him in a quick aside, adding, "The boys will miss you, too. Komm back and see us."

He could say only something noncommittal to that, because it seemed unlikely Rachel would want him in her life when all this was over. For a few minutes the previous night he'd convinced himself they were at a beginning, rather than an ending, but in the cold light of day, he didn't buy it.

Final hugs, final goodbyes. He didn't understand what her grandmother whispered to Rachel, but it made her blink back tears, whatever it was. Then Timothy was clapping him on the shoulder with a blow that nearly knocked him off his feet.

"We do gut work together, yah? Komm again."

He nodded, smiling in return.

Suddenly Rachel's grandfather was in front of him, and Clint didn't know what to say. Or whether he needed to say anything. The old man seemed capable of looking right through him and out the other side. If he had something to hide, he wouldn't want to meet that steady gaze.

He extended his hand. "Goodbye, sir."

His hand was seized in a firm, wiry grip. "Denke, Clint. You kept our Rachel safe last night. See that you take care of her."

"I'll try. But she might have something to say about the idea of anyone taking care of her. Rachel seems to prize her independence."

"Yah." His voice deepened on the word. "Rachel has been let down too often by people, especially her mamm. It makes it hard for her to trust. And all the more important she have someone looking out for her safety."

This was no time for questions, but he understood what the man wanted from him. Suppressing his own doubts, he said what he felt. "I won't let her down."

That was all, nothing more. Either he meant it or not, and this wasn't a man to be swayed by empty promises.

There was silence between them, and after a moment Byler nodded. "Gut."

After a few more hugs, Rachel slid into the passenger seat. With a final wave, he drove off down the lane, reached the main road and made the turn that would take them away from the farm and back to Philadelphia.

Rachel had her face turned toward the window, maybe straining her eyes for the last glimpse of the place. Even when it had completely vanished from sight, she stayed in that position, probably trying to hide the emotion she felt at leaving.

Clint cleared his throat, looking for something appropriate to say. "I'm sorry," he said at last. "I wish you didn't have to go back, but I don't see any other way."

"No." She settled into the seat and stared down at her hands, clasped in her lap. "There isn't one. I was wrong to think running away would help."

"At least you had a chance to see your family. I'm guessing that helped you."

"It did. And I had a chance to see you out of your own setting." She sounded like a person deliberately steering the conversation away from a sensitive subject. "I don't imagine you are often expected to hold baby chicks or dig out stumps."

He smiled in response. The least he could do was go along with her, if it made this easier. And they'd have plenty of time to discuss the immediate future.

"Apparently it's like riding a bike. You never forget how to do it."

"Really? You mean you've actually spent time on a

farm? That seems an odd background for someone in your line of work."

"Not so strange. I grew up in a small town, and my grandfather had a farm, mainly just a big garden and a few chickens for the eggs. But some of my friends lived on working farms." The memories always brought a smile. "I got pulled into quite a few chores in my day. Anything so my buddy could finish his work and we could go play baseball or football or whatever was on our agenda for the day."

"Your parents are still there?" She almost sounded as if she envied him.

"My dad's retired from the police force now, but they wouldn't consider moving away. Their whole lives are bound up in that place."

"It sounds nice," she murmured.

Apparently her childhood hadn't been so stable, from what she'd let drop and what her grandfather said. But if she wanted to hear about his family, he didn't mind.

"My two sisters still live in the same town. You couldn't catch the folks moving away from their grandkids." He smiled again, thinking of the way they doted on those kids. Come to think of it, he was pretty good at that himself. "At least now that they're supplied with two boys and two girls, I'm off the hook."

"You don't want children?"

Something in her voice hinted that might be a sensitive topic for her. Obviously she and her ex hadn't started a family, but a man with a gambling addiction wasn't a good bet in the fatherhood sweepstakes.

"I wouldn't go that far," he said. "But finding the right woman comes first. For a while there, every time I went to see my folks, my mother would introduce me to some single woman she thought might be a suitable mother for her potential grandkids. At least now she's stopped doing that. I was tired of being embarrassed."

Rachel turned toward him with a smile that seemed to ease the tension from her face. "It's a shame. I'd like to have seen you showing embarrassment. I doubt that you can."

"I'm not always on the job." He returned the smile, and for a moment they were just two people feeling their way toward knowing each other without the background of guilt and danger.

All of a sudden he'd reached the point that he wanted to know what made her the woman she was. He'd gotten a piece of it through seeing the kind of environment where she'd spent her summers as a child, but it seemed clear that whatever her mother had done affected Rachel in ways she might not even recognize.

He'd like to ask, but he didn't have the right to do that. Not when he still hid the black part of his own life—the moment that had robbed him of his career and left him with a burden of guilt for the person he hadn't been able to save.

Right now Rachel seemed willing to trust her safety to him. He couldn't kid himself about that—she was doing it only because she had no other choices. Circumstances had combined to wrap the two of them together, for good or ill.

But if she knew his story, all of it, how willing would she be to trust him to protect her?

CHAPTER TWELVE

THEY DROVE ANOTHER fifty miles with very little said, and Clint began to think they'd reach Philadelphia without another word. Then Rachel spoke, so abruptly it startled him. "You must have been wondering about my mother. I suppose you realized that she had left the Amish."

Careful. He had to be careful. He was torn between wanting to know everything there was to know about her and the fear that one day she'd hate herself for having told him.

"I figured that was the case. But obviously she still had a relationship with her family, since you went there every summer."

"Yes and no." Rachel was staring at the road ahead of them but probably not seeing it. "She ran away to marry my father. He left before I was born."

The dry tone in which she said that didn't invite sympathy. "She didn't return to her family?"

"No. She liked the outside world too much. But she was happy to send me there for the summers. It gave her a little freedom, you see. Each time I went back, she'd embarked on a new romance, but they never seemed to last."

He had to say something, even if she didn't welcome it. "That must have been rough on you."

She shrugged. "I had the summers to look forward

to. No matter how often we moved, or how much our lives changed, the farm stayed the same. It was home."

Obviously this was what her grandfather had meant about people letting her down. Small wonder if she found it hard to trust.

"Logan seemed to think she was settled in a retirement community now." Logan had also said that she hadn't seemed very interested in her daughter's whereabouts, but he didn't see a need to report that fact.

"She married again after I was on my own. He passed away after a couple of years, but he left her comfortably off, and she stayed where she is." Her lips twisted a bit. "My grandmother says she was always looking for happiness, as if it were a treasure that could be found."

He considered the words. "Is that what you think?"

"Grossmammi would say that happiness comes from doing what is right, not from looking." She avoided answering the question about herself.

"I guess I never thought too much about whether I was happy or not. After I passed the age of expecting the perfect Christmas present under the tree on Christmas morning, that is."

She smiled, seeming to relax a little. "Maybe that's the key. Don't be thinking about how you're feeling all the time—taking your emotional temperature, a friend of mine calls it."

"Lyn, by any chance?"

The tension had left her now, and he thought she was reassured by his light question.

"As a matter of fact, yes. How did you guess?"

"She seems like a woman with a practical approach to things."

"She is." Her voice sobered. "I wish I thought…" She

stopped and shook her head. "I'll have to resign from the school. She'll try to talk me out of it, but I want to be clear of there before anything breaks in the newspaper."

He was in no position to give her advice, but the urge was too strong to resist. "I wouldn't jump into that too quickly. If Attwood has his way, there will never be anything in the newspaper. He's dead set against any publicity. Anyway, there's no rush."

"Isn't there?" Her tone was bleak. "Someone is still willing to attack me to find that flash drive. And Paul has vanished, presumably taking it with him. I don't see any happy ending coming from all of this."

He wanted to reassure her. To solve the problem in a way that didn't harm her. But he couldn't. All he could do was try to find answers to a lot of uncomfortable questions.

RACHEL MUST HAVE fallen asleep, because when she woke the car was approaching the Schuylkill Expressway just outside the city. Oddly enough, given how she'd felt earlier, she was more optimistic now. She'd get past this trouble—she had to. And she had a strong ally on her side.

A glance at Clint told her he was focused on the traffic, frowning.

"Sorry I've been such bad company. I didn't intend to fall asleep."

"No problem. I didn't need a navigator for this trip."

The words were light, but not Clint's expression. Not that it was ever easy to see past that stoic mask he wore on duty.

She straightened, hands smoothing her hair, and

looked around her. Clint had taken the ramp into Center City. "Where are we going?"

"My office, to meet my partner, Logan. We need to make some decisions."

If he'd been interested and sympathetic earlier, all that had vanished now. His face and his voice were businesslike.

Rachel's brief sense of ease vanished, and the strain rushed back. She'd returned to face a situation that grew worse by the moment, at least from her perspective. Was that how Clint, as a professional, saw it, as well?

"How far is it to your office?"

Clint focused on turning a corner before he answered. "Maybe ten minutes. Logan will be waiting for us."

An uneasy silence fell between them. Had she imagined that wave of warm sympathy earlier? Or was it a tool to be turned on and off?

"Logan may have something more definitive for us by now. We can hope, anyway."

Soon enough for her Clint drove into an underground garage. The renovated building above must house offices, including that of Angelo and Mordan, Security Specialists. Clint parked, and in another moment they were gliding smoothly upward in an elevator.

Rachel read through the business listings on the wall. Clint's firm was on the fourth floor. She was too jittery to stand there in silence while the elevator carried them toward the next phase of her troubles.

"Has your office always been here?"

Clint emerged from his distraction. "Since we started together, four years ago." He was silent for a moment but then seemed to think he should be more forthcoming. "We've known each other for years. He left the military after a serious injury at about the same time I left the police. Same reason." He grimaced. "I could have stayed on in a desk job, but that wasn't for me."

"I can see that." She wanted to ask about his injury, but it seemed the No Trespassing sign was up on his face again. Anyway, they had arrived.

Clint hustled her through an outer office, past a middle-aged receptionist, who looked at her with curiosity, and on into his partner's domain.

Logan Angelo rose to his feet when he saw her. Rangy, taller than Clint and not as solid, he eyed her for a moment before speaking.

"Ms. Hartline. Please, have a seat. You don't look as if you're too much the worse for your ordeal."

Oddly enough, other than the pain when her body protested her movements, she hadn't been reminded of those moments. Maybe that was for the best, although she didn't think it would last. When she was away from Clint's protective presence, she'd probably relive it again and again. "I'm fine. Is there anything new?"

"Nothing dramatic," he said, settling back behind his computer.

"I hope there's something." Clint sounded like a man hanging by the last thread. "I've had enough of running around in the dark."

Instead of answering, Logan posed a question. "Any reason for alarm at your end?"

"We weren't followed back from the farm, if that's what you mean. I'm sure of that."

She hadn't even realized he'd been watching for someone following them. Obviously she wasn't well prepared for life on the run.

"Good. That means our opponents don't have limitless resources," Logan said. "I find that encouraging."

"Glad it makes you happy." Clint perched on the corner of the desk. "Let's get to it. What have you found?"

"Nothing on Paul Hartline's whereabouts, unfortunately," Logan said. "As for the other members of the upper echelon at Attwood's, aside from Robinson's mysterious hotel stays, nothing. Ms. Gibson is apparently devoted to the business, lives well and dates casually. Attwood himself seems to have no social life at all or any interests outside the firm."

"You're investigating them?" Rachel said. Clint had mentioned the theory that someone else was involved, but… "They couldn't be in on this—they have everything to lose. Besides, neither Ian nor Claire would double-cross Attwood."

"Why not?" Clint asked. "Paul did."

A probably irrational need to defend Paul swept over her. "I know it looks that way, but when he contacted me, Paul said this was not what it looked like."

"He hasn't given you any information to back that up, has he?" Clint seemed just as irrationally determined to think the worst of her ex.

"You might try keeping an open mind until the truth emerges," she snapped.

Logan, who had been looking from Clint to her and back again as if watching a tennis match, intervened. "Nobody knows anything definite about your former husband's motives yet, so let's not jump the gun. All we can do is follow where the information leads us while we keep Ms. Hartline safe."

Clint blew out a long breath and seemed to force himself to relax. "Right. Do you have a place for Ms.

Hartline to sleep for a few nights? I don't want her alone in her house until we get a lead on who's behind this."

"I booked a room at the Fairfield Hotel for the moment. It's close to the office, and they had an upstairs room at the back."

They were talking about her as if she weren't there—another reason to feel annoyed. But there was little she could do about it unless she wanted to be off on her own again. Easy prey.

Nodding as if he were familiar with the place, Clint stood. "If there's nothing else, I'll run her over there now," he said.

"My backpack is in the car, but I'll need some other clothes from my house." She made a small attempt to seize some control of her life.

"I'll pick them up. Make a list." Clint clasped her elbow, then released it when she winced. "Sorry." Regret darkened his eyes as he piloted her to the door. "Just wait in the outside office for a few minutes, while I check a few things with my partner." Then, apparently noticing her expression, he added. "If you will."

Rachel marched out. He ought to be getting the message that he was overstepping the line if he had any sensitivity at all. But what was the chance of that? Those tender moments the previous night might never have been.

Or maybe that was the reason for this. He regretted what happened between them, and now he was busy drawing the line between investigator and witness again.

Clint joined her in less than five minutes, and if his expression was anything to go by, that conversation with his partner hadn't softened his mood any. They didn't exchange more than a word or two during the time it took to drive to the hotel, check her in and go to the room.

Rachel expected him to leave her at the door since he seemed eager to be rid of her, but he moved past her. "I'll just have a look around."

She nodded, not bothering to protest. He was trying to keep her safe, she knew. Clint checked the bedroom and bath thoroughly before nodding.

"Okay. Logan says that Attwood would like to see us this afternoon, and we think it might help if you come along. Can you grab a late lunch and be ready to leave around four?"

A chat with James Attwood was low on her list of things she'd like to do. "What can I do to help? There's nothing helpful I can tell him. I assume you're reporting everything to him. And the last time I saw him, he threatened to prosecute me for involvement."

"He must know he wouldn't have a leg to stand on in a case against you," he snapped. "That wasn't too clever on his part, assuming he is the genius everyone says."

"A genius in his own field, but not when it comes to people. That's why he needed the others, I think."

"We've told him you urged Paul to bring back the information, so he shouldn't be blaming you. We'd rather you're there because something may come out when we have fresh eyes on the situation. Even some reaction from one of them to you might tell us something."

She shrugged. "Maybe. But my eyes are anything but fresh." Why was it so hard to convince people she didn't know anything?

"Look, you know these people better than we do." Clint sounded impatient, as if he had other things to do than debate the subject. "You may sense something off-kilter that we'd miss. If one of them was involved with Paul in what went on, we need to know."

It was easier to agree than to keep arguing. "Very well. But I can't go anywhere without a change of clothes."

"Give me the list. I'll stop by your house." He extended his hand.

Somewhat reluctantly she held out the list she'd jotted down while she had been waiting for him. Another woman would have no trouble figuring out what she wanted from the list, but she had her doubts about Clint. Her fingers tightened on the paper.

"You'll never figure out what to bring. I could ask Lyn to do it."

"No!" He snatched the list from her. "Until we understand the danger better, no extraneous people should know where you are."

"I can't live like this!" She flared up as if he'd touched a match to dry tinder. "I'd rather take my chances than be unable to trust my closest friend."

The effort Clint made to get hold of himself was almost visible. When he spoke, he clearly tried to sound, if not conciliatory, at least reasonable.

"It's not a question of trusting your friend. Someone searched your classroom, remember? Whoever is looking for you knows about your friendship. You don't want to do anything to put your friend in danger, do you?"

She spun away from him, fighting to control the emotions that kept ricocheting wildly from one extreme to the other. She pressed her fingers against her forehead, willing herself to calm.

Finally she was able to speak. "You're right. I wasn't thinking. We'll do it your way."

Clint was silent. She heard him take a step, and thought he was leaving until he put his hands on her shoulders. "Sorry. Usually I have just a little more tact. Try to get some rest while I'm gone. And if I forget anything, I'll go buy you a replacement. Okay?"

Composing her face, she turned back to him. His hands dropped instantly from her shoulders. "I'll make do. You don't have to buy me a lollipop to get me to be good."

"No, I guess I don't." He gave her a rueful smile. "Sorry. I don't usually have this much trouble staying civil. I'll be back as soon as I can."

He left quickly, and Rachel moved to throw the bolt on the door, locking herself in.

CLINT STOPPED BACK at the office after dropping Rachel off. He didn't have long, but Logan wanted to hear about his conversation with Michael Leonard, the college contact he'd dug up. As soon as they were finished, he had to run over to Rachel's house to get the things she needed, so he was keeping track of the time.

"Stop looking at your watch." Logan didn't normally sound so irritated. This business was getting to him, too. "So you're saying Leonard didn't give you a thing that helps."

"I didn't say that." He leaned back in his desk chair, wishing he had time to put his feet up and just think this whole thing through.

"What then?" Logan grimaced. "Sorry. I've got the wind up about this whole business. Ms. Hartline could have been killed, and we're still no closer to a solution."

"Leonard didn't say anything that would help there, but it was still worth seeing him." Clint went through that interview in his mind. "From the look of things, Leonard has been plenty successful on his own. Nice car, wife, kids, a mini-mansion in an upscale suburb."

"I'm glad he's doing well."

"Sarcasm doesn't become you," Clint retorted. "The point is, apparently at one time the four musketeers were actually five. Leonard was part of their little group. An important part, to hear him tell it."

"He might be biased," Logan pointed out.

"True. But from everything you unearthed about him, I don't think so. He apparently rivaled James Attwood for top honors in their department at the university. Despite that, they teamed up."

"You mean they planned to go into business together? What happened? Did Attwood ditch him?"

"Not exactly. At least, not from his perspective. He claims he found Attwood a little too willing to cheat to get his way. Or one of the others was willing to do it for him. There was sabotage to a project he was working on. When it came time to draw up a partnership agreement, Leonard decided he wouldn't trust his future to someone he thought played fast and loose with ethics."

Logan frowned, flipping a pen in his hand, usually characteristic of deep thought. "In other words, James Attwood isn't the sterling character he's been painted. And sabotage sounds familiar, doesn't it?"

Clint shrugged. "It's a possibility Attwood is playing some game. It's also a possibility that Leonard was wrong, or that someone else acted without Attwood's knowledge."

"The company has a clean reputation, from everything I've been able to find out."

"I'm sure. And before you say it, I don't see how it can play into this business, anyway. On the surface, it looks like Attwood is the one person who'd have no interest in taking the file. He already had complete control of them."

"That's what I'd say, all right," Logan said. "I was hoping the guy would give us a lead on why someone might want to betray him, but this doesn't help."

"I guess not." But something was swimming around in the back of Clint's mind. Unfortunately, it refused to come out and show itself.

He shoved himself to his feet. "Well, it's something to toss into the mix. I'd better get those things for Rachel."

"You seem to be getting pretty protective where she's concerned." Logan's comment stopped him before he reached the door.

"We can't afford to have a witness wiped out, can we?"

"You sure that's all there is to it?"

He had to admit his partner had a right to ask. What he did reflected on both of them. But since he didn't know himself what was driving him where Rachel was concerned, he couldn't very well come up with an answer.

He was taking too long. He had to say something. "Whatever I might or might not feel when it comes to Rachel Hartline, I know where to draw the line."

Logan studied his face. "I hope so. And not just for the sake of the firm. I don't want to have to pick up the pieces if you come to grief."

"Don't worry." He made an effort to sound convincing. "I'm a big boy now. I'll deal with it."

He took off before Logan could say anything else.

HE HAD TO get a grip, Clint told himself for the fiftieth time as they walked into the offices of Attwood's company. He and Logan had met difficult challenges before, and good solid investigating had brought them to a resolution. It was no different this time.

Right. He kept Rachel between him and Logan as they entered. Nothing could happen to her here. There was no reason to be spooked, but he was.

Claire Gibson swung around at their entrance, her startled look at the sight of Rachel quickly hidden. Instead of greeting them, she reached for the door into Attwood's office. "I'll just tell Mr. Attwood that you're here."

Clint was sufficiently intrigued to move swiftly, so that they entered the office on her heels. If she wanted to alert Attwood that Rachel was here, he'd like to know why.

The Gibson woman was already announcing them when Rachel appeared behind him. For just an instant, some emotion Clint couldn't identify froze Attwood in place at the window. Then he was moving behind his desk, his expression cool and businesslike.

"Thank you for coming in. I didn't realize you were bringing Ms. Hartline."

"We thought it might be helpful to pool any information we have, and Ms. Hartline has been most cooperative."

"I see." He nodded to her. "Rachel."

Clint could sense Rachel's uneasiness as she stood

next to him, but it couldn't have been detected in the calm way she greeted Attwood. Claire Gibson fussed about, arranging seating and incidentally buying time, if any was needed.

"I expected a report from you by now." Attwood seized control. "Have you found my file?"

"Not yet." Logan was crisp and unapologetic. "We have a few additional questions. From what we've been told, it seems Paul Hartline knew very little about the technical side of the business. How do you suppose he was able to access that particular file so easily?"

"I've no idea. That's your job. I expected you to have located it by this time."

The attack didn't rattle Logan. "We can't operate if we're kept in the dark. What exactly is this new project of yours?"

"Knowing that won't help you. Find Paul, and you'll probably find the information he stole."

Clint stirred. "You can help us do our job by answering our questions. Was this particular file protected in any way? Did Hartline know of its existence? Had he worked with it in the past?"

Attwood's gaze shifted from him to Rachel and back again. "I suppose this is necessary. Yes, all my files are password protected."

"We haven't considered protecting them from each other," Claire Gibson pointed out. "The four of us have been working together for a long time. I wouldn't be surprised if Paul could guess your password."

"That could be," Attwood said grudgingly.

"Had Hartline worked with this particular file?" Logan took up the questioning again.

Attwood hesitated, and the woman answered for him.

"I don't think he had, had he, James? But he knew of its existence. We all did."

Attwood's gaze rested on her for a moment, completely expressionless. Then he seemed to make an effort to change the tenor of the meeting.

"Claire's right. We had all been excited about the possibilities of the new program. Unfortunately, I've been working over my figures again, and I'm afraid that there may be a flaw in the project." He paused for a moment, and Clint thought he was struggling with the admission. "If so, Paul may have tried to sell it and failed."

"Then what happened to him?" Rachel's tone was impatient, as if she'd sat silent as long as she could. Obviously she still cared about her ex. But then, he'd already figured that out, hadn't he?

"He ran away, I suppose. It doesn't matter."

Claire Gibson intervened quickly. "Naturally we're worried about him. We've known Paul a very long time. What James means is that it doesn't matter about the project."

"Yes." Attwood's tone was crisp. "I doubt we'll be doing anything more with it in any event. So if you haven't found it by the end of the week, you can turn in your final report."

He and Logan exchanged glances. That was all they were going to get, apparently. Short and not so sweet.

His jaw tightened. Attwood might be ready to dismiss the whole thing, but he wasn't. Not when they hadn't learned the truth. And not when Rachel remained a target.

CHAPTER THIRTEEN

ALMOST BEFORE SHE knew what was happening, Rachel found herself ushered out of Attwood's office. She turned to Clint to protest, but before she could say anything, Claire Gibson surprised her by putting her arm around her.

More than surprised. She and Claire had been cordial, she supposed, but never on hugging terms. Or was this pity, rather than friendship?

"I'm sorry about the way James handled that. It's not for lack of caring, I promise you." Claire's words seemed aimed at all of them. "We're used to the fact that James comes across as unfeeling, but I know how it affects other people." She turned back to Rachel. "He really does regret the fact that you've been hurt by all of this. And he's actually cut up by Paul's actions. All of us are."

Rachel caught at the vanishing threads of her composure. "I know you've been friends for a long time."

"I gather that's one of your roles in the company," Logan said. "Interpreting Mr. Attwood to other people."

Claire gave a graceful shrug, spreading manicured hands. "Someone has to. We're all aware that he can't be turned loose on an unsuspecting client if we're to keep the account. That's where Paul was so good. I don't know how we'll get along without him."

"In your opinion, could Hartline have known enough about this new idea not only to be able to access it, but to find a buyer?" Clint returned doggedly to the question, and Rachel realized he still wasn't satisfied that Paul had been alone in his actions.

"He must have been able to," Claire said. "That's what he did, isn't it?"

They weren't going to get anywhere with her. Rachel had never seen that cool, sophisticated exterior ruffled, and she didn't think Clint's questions were going to do it. Besides, Claire would never have joined Paul in such a crazy scheme. She certainly didn't need money, if her clothes were anything to judge by. And Rachel couldn't imagine her acting on an impulse. If she were involved, there would have been no glitches.

Rachel caught an exchange of glances between Clint and Logan. She imagined them telling each other there was nothing here. The motive was obvious. Paul needed money—he always did. Further digging wouldn't lead to anything else.

That was true. She'd known that already, going right back to the day she'd tried to use the debit card in the grocery store only to have it declined. Paul's excuses had made sense for a time, but maybe she'd been a slow learner. Her conviction that he wouldn't betray these people seemed ridiculous in the face of all she knew about him.

She turned, more than ready to leave a place in which she'd never had a part. This had been Paul's world, not hers.

But before she could start toward the door, it opened and Ian Robinson came in. He stopped abruptly at the sight of her. Odd, that he hadn't been around for this meeting, as well. Or hadn't Attwood wanted him there?

"Rachel. I'm so glad to see you. I've been calling, and I stopped by the house but you weren't there. We were getting worried." He came forward and clasped her hands in his, projecting worry and sympathy.

"I decided to get away for a few days." That had seemed the best answer to any casual questions. "I'm sorry I didn't return your calls."

Ian glanced up at the interested gazes of Clint and Logan and dropped her hands. "That's all right. I can understand your wanting to get away from the house after having a break-in there. That's enough to shake anyone. Look, why don't you come and stay with us for a few days? Julie would love to have you, I know. I'll just call her."

Rachel could almost feel the silent pressure of Clint's strong will. *Any of them could be involved.*

"That's so kind of you, Ian, but I'm already settled at the moment. Please give Julie my love. Maybe we can get together when things calm down."

"Well, all right." He gave in readily, and she suspected he'd made the offer before thinking of the ramifications. "But you know you're always welcome." Ian nodded to the others before turning into his own office.

Rachel held her breath until he'd disappeared from sight, half-afraid Clint was going to stop him with questions. Not that she objected to Clint questioning anyone. He had to do his job, but not when she was there. Hearing them tackle Attwood was one thing, but she'd been friends with Ian and Julie.

Apparently Clint had caught her feelings. Or else he'd decided questioning Ian would go better without her. He led the way out and down the narrow stairs to the ground floor.

As soon as the three of them were outside, she turned to Clint. "Don't ask me to do anything like that again. It was so uncomfortable."

It was Logan who smiled. "No use saying that. I've tried. Clint will just tell you that you have to go outside your comfort zone to find out what you need to know."

Clint nudged him with his elbow, as if to suggest he stay out of it. "Difficult interviews come with the territory. I wanted to see how they'd react to having you there."

"I hope you got something from it, because I certainly didn't." They'd reached the car, and she yanked the door open before Clint could grab it.

He waited until she'd slid in, then closed her door gently and went around to the other side. Making a statement about her bad temper, maybe. Apparently he was taking her back to the hotel, because Logan headed for his own car without waiting.

"Is Attwood always that uncooperative?" Clint started the car and pulled out of the lot, his attention seeming to be on the passing traffic rather than her.

"Uncooperative?" She pushed her feeling aside and considered it. "He doesn't have any social skills, I suppose. The others were always used to his ways and just seemed to accept them. I don't know that he was less cooperative than normal. He's always been impatient with everyone else's responsibilities, from what Paul used to say."

A noncommittal grunt was Clint's only response, and he didn't say anything else until they were out of the maze of small streets around the building.

"Did you sense anything off-key about how they responded to you?" He returned to the attack once they were back on the main road.

Rachel struggled to sound cooperative. "I've never really talked to James Attwood that much, so I can't say. As for Claire… Well, she was friendlier than I'd have expected. I suppose she felt some regret for the circumstances. As for her interpreting Attwood to other people—that's true enough. I've heard her do it in the past."

"I'm glad you had enough sense to turn down Robinson's invitation."

"I'm not that foolish, whatever you might think." She couldn't help the tartness in her voice. "Give me a little credit."

"Sorry." He glanced at her with a trace of a smile. "Maybe I need someone to translate for me. Just for a minute, when he asked you, I was afraid you'd give in. It's natural to want to be with friends at a time like this."

"If I were going to do that, I'd be calling Lyn, not Ian."

"Funny. I got the impression you and Ian were pretty close." He concentrated on the turn ahead of them. "From the way he acted the time he walked in on us, that is."

That startled her. "You mean after the house had been searched? He was reacting like anyone would at something like that happening to a friend. Well, anyone who wasn't a police officer, I suppose."

"Meaning I got used to such things? Maybe so, but I don't take them lightly. And at that point I didn't know what side you were on."

"I guess I can't blame you for that," she admitted, hoping it didn't sound as grudging as it felt. Her feelings seemed to be bouncing all over the map. "As for Ian and his wife, yes, we were friends, but it was really because Ian and Paul were so close. I hadn't seen either of them much since the divorce." She shrugged. "Friends of the divorcing couple have to choose, I guess."

"Regrets?" He glanced at her, something questioning in the depths of his dark eyes.

She didn't answer for a moment. There were too many regrets, and she'd be foolish to confide them in someone she'd never see again after his job was finished. If they'd met under other circumstances…

"Don't we all have regrets?" she said lightly. "I'm not immune to that, but I try not to dwell on them."

The car slid down the ramp to the garage under the hotel. "If you succeed, you're better at it than I am." Something real and painful seemed to thread through his words, leaving her breathless and at a loss.

Clint pulled into a parking space. "I'll walk you up." He'd gone back to his usual businesslike tone…the one that said arguing was useless.

He opened her door. She slid out, the movement bringing her very close to him. Their gazes met, and emotion shimmered between them, shaking her by its intensity.

Then he stepped back, closing and locking the door without a word. Together they walked toward the elevator.

When they reached her room, Rachel fully expected Clint to leave, his duty done. Even though his last few comments had been a bit more relaxed, his face had settled into those stoic lines that gave no clue to his thoughts.

But she was wrong. Taking the key card from her

hand, he entered the room first and began the routine of checking. She sat down on the edge of the bed, suddenly wiped out. Was it only this morning that they were standing in the chicken pen at the farm, laughing over the baby chicks?

Clint went in the bathroom, and she heard the rattle of rings as he thrust the shower curtain back. When he emerged, she was looking at him, eyebrows lifted.

"Haven't you forgotten something? You didn't check under the bed."

His lips twitched, just a little. He bent solemnly, lifted the floral bedspread, and peered under the bed. "Nope. Not a monster in sight."

Finally a smile from him. Good.

"Too bad you weren't around when I was about eight. Most of my nightmares involved something under the bed. My mother was not amused."

"Not just the usual monsters in the closet?" he asked.

"I'll have you know I was a very imaginative child. My nightmares ran the gamut from ogres to trolls to creatures from outer space to headless spooks and things grabbing me from the dark."

That came a little too close to reality, and Rachel couldn't help the shiver that ran through her. She fought it off and managed a smile. "Well, now that you know I'm safe, you can call it quits for the day."

Clint studied her face for a moment. Then he pulled over the desk chair and sat so that he was knee to knee with her.

"You really are safe now. No one knows where you are, and even if they did, just put the dead bolt on when I leave. But they—whoever they are—don't know."

She nodded, trying to project an air of confidence.

"Right. I'll be fine." She rubbed absently at her shoulder, wincing when her fingers hit a sore spot.

He was on that at once, of course. "Hurting?"

"Just a little. Apparently my usual workout doesn't prepare me for hanging from a rope. I feel as if I've been stretched out on a rack. And I must have banged against a few stones on the way up. But I got out, thanks to you."

Before she could guess his intent, Clint leaned forward, putting a large warm hand over her shoulder. His fingers pressed lightly.

"Those muscles have so many knots it's a wonder you can lift your arms. You need some liniment."

"I don't think the hotel stocks that in the minibar." The words were slightly breathless. He was massaging both shoulders now, his hands moving with the gentlest of pressure, smoothing and warming. Impossible not to relax, yielding to the touch.

She shouldn't. *Say something, anything, before he guesses how it makes you feel.* "I actually do have a massage therapist, but I don't suppose you'd like for me to go see her."

"You suppose right." His fingers followed the taut muscle that ran up her neck and into her skull. "I had no idea teaching kindergarten was that physically taxing. Are those little kids rough on you?"

"You try getting down to the floor and up again a hundred times a day and see how it makes you feel."

His lips twitched again. "As I recall, my kindergarten teacher sat behind her desk all day. If she wanted to see one of us, we went to her."

"Old school," she said. "We don't teach that way anymore."

"I guess I have a lot to learn about it."

"Your work doesn't involve you with many kindergarten teachers, I would think." *Keep it light*, she reminded herself.

"Not many, no. But I'm always interested in learning something new."

"I could lend you a book on the theory of teaching young children," she offered. "Well, I could, if I had access to my own house."

His hands paused. "If it's any consolation, I don't think we can justify keeping you away from home much longer. Especially if Attwood closes our investigation."

"Will he really do that? Without ever knowing?"

Clint shrugged, his eyes shadowed. "It's not what we want, but he's the client." He hesitated, his mind seeming far away for a moment. "You know, what you need when you go home is a dog."

"A guard dog? I can't keep a big dog in that small house when I'm out all day." That was assuming she had a job left to go to when this was over.

"It doesn't have to be a big dog. Just one with a loud bark. You could even borrow Buster for a while."

She smiled, relaxing into an almost mindless pleasure at his gentle touch smoothing the tension away. "I doubt the Bartons could do without him."

"Maybe not." He smiled in return. Then his eyes seemed to darken, and she could feel the touch of his gaze on her face just as clearly as she felt the warmth of his hands.

She couldn't speak. She couldn't move. *This is a bad idea*, some part of her mind insisted. Then his lips covered hers, silencing the thought.

This time the kiss was slow, gentle, almost questioning, then deepening when she responded. He drew her close, and she wrapped her arms around him, not thinking, only feeling.

When, finally, he drew back, he was smiling a little ruefully. "I don't think I can apologize," he murmured. "But it's bad timing, I know."

"Yes, it is." But some part of her wished he had swept his scruples aside. "One thing is sure… I won't be having any nightmares tonight."

He touched her face lightly and slid his chair back. "Glad to know that."

"It's important," she insisted, trying to cover her feelings with something light. "You wouldn't know, of course. I'm sure if a monster invaded your dreams, you'd just walk right over it."

His face tightened, his eyes darkening again, but with pain, not desire.

Rachel's breath caught. She'd hurt him. All unaware, she tramped on something he wasn't willing to admit. Something painful, hiding behind his indomitable facade.

Clint stood, glancing around as if to be sure he hadn't forgotten anything. "I'd better get going."

"Yes, of course." She pulled herself together. "Thanks for… Well, thanks."

He nodded, striding to the door. Just as he reached for the handle, she thought of something.

"When you have a chance, could you pick up my cell phone for me? It's in the closet at my house, tucked inside a boot. I know, you don't want me to call anyone, but I'd like to see what messages I have."

"Yes, fine." He yanked the door open. "I'll get it." The door closed, and he was gone.

When Clint picked Rachel up the next morning, he had a couple of concerns on his mind. The first was the question of whether or not to let her move back to her house, not that he could stop her if she was as determined as she'd sounded on the phone earlier. And the second was whether or not he should come clean about the fact that he'd already had her cell phone when she asked for it, and that Logan had searched it for any telltale information.

There hadn't been any. He hadn't expected it. Rachel had been honest with them. He suspected honesty was her default setting, but that it could become snarled when it came into conflict with her sense of loyalty.

As far as he was concerned, Paul Hartline was a loser who'd never deserved a woman like Rachel. Not that anyone would ask for his opinion on the subject.

Shelving the question of what to say about the cell phone, he held the door while she slid into the seat. She seemed in a brighter mood this morning. He considered asking her if her sleep had been free of nightmares, but decided not to push his luck. That subject went a little too close to his own nightmares, and he had no intention of sharing them with anyone.

Rachel was looking at him when he got behind the wheel. "I hope you realize I only agreed to yet another search of my house because I want to get back in it. What could there possibly be left for you to find? And I feel quite sure you had a look around after I turned up missing."

She didn't sound annoyed, so he risked treating it lightly. "Can you blame me? One minute you were insisting you didn't know anything about Paul's misdeeds, and the next you'd run away."

"Don't forget the fact that I went to a lot of trouble making sure you couldn't find me." She sounded as if she were scoring a point, and he grinned.

"I did find you," he reminded her.

"Only because your partner conned my mother. Isn't that against the law?"

He lifted both hands in a momentary sketch of surrender. "Turn me in, why don't you?"

"I'll let it pass this time."

"As it was, I nearly got caught by your helpful neighbors. They seemed to be looking out for you."

"They're nice people." She smiled. "I always think they look like a set of Santa and Mrs. Claus figurines I had when I was little."

"That's it," he said. "I wondered who they reminded me of."

The lightness seemed to last, for a time at least. He wondered what she was thinking. She was leaning forward as he took the route that led to West Chester. Eager to get back to her home? Obviously it meant a lot to her.

But she was going to sell. He'd nearly forgotten her mention of the reason she'd met her ex to begin with that day. She'd been trying to get him to sign off on a sales agreement.

He glanced at her again. Why? Money? Her salary might not be enough to pay the mortgage. Or she might be reluctant to continue living in a place where, presumably, she'd once been happy.

That was like biting on a sore spot. Maybe Rachel didn't want the reminder of her ex. Maybe a lot of reasons, none of which were his business. But he'd liked that little house of hers. It had a sense of home about it that he'd missed in the last few years. A man could be happy in a place like that…as long as it came with the right woman.

"You're very quiet all of a sudden," Rachel said. "Are you worried? Or did something new turn up about Paul?" Her voice sharpened on the second question.

"There's nothing new." He hesitated for a moment, and then decided to level with her. "There is a reason for wanting to search your place with you there."

Her eyes grew wary. "What?"

"I'm hoping going through your belongings may trigger a hint of where Paul might go if he needed a place to hole up. Or where he might think to hide something small if he didn't want to carry it around with him."

"The flash drive." The wariness faded. "But I thought, from what Attwood said, that he wasn't concerned about the flash drive any longer. He seemed to think that program had some problem."

"That's what he said."

"Don't you believe him?" She sounded as if the thought had never occurred to her.

"I don't have any particular reason to think he wasn't telling the truth," he said, careful not to plant any suspicion when he didn't have proof. "But we were hired to recover that flash drive, and if I start something, I have a duty to finish it. And when it comes to Attwood…as an investigator, I'm inclined to doubt everyone until I have good reason not to."

Rachel was silent for a moment. "That's not a necessary qualification for a kindergarten teacher."

"Good." His lips twitched a little. "I'd hate to think you were cross-examining five-year-olds."

But she didn't smile in return. What was she thinking?

"Do you still doubt me?" She didn't seem angry,

which he might have expected after what passed between them the previous night. But in any event, he owed her the truth about that.

"No." He glanced at her to make sure she believed him. "I know you now. Maybe that's one positive thing that came from tracking you down. I know you well enough to be convinced you're innocent of any connection with what Paul did."

"Thank you." The words were a soft murmur.

As for whatever remaining loyalty she might have toward Paul…well, he couldn't see that affecting the case at all, except to cause her added grief if Paul ended up in jail. His fingers tightened on the steering wheel. That aspect of it wasn't remotely fair, but he didn't see what he could do about it. He admired the conviction that would make her sacrifice the work she loved rather than bring possible harm to the school. If he could spare her that decision…

"Is something wrong?" she said.

He realized he'd been silent too long and let his face reflect his feelings. He didn't ordinarily allow that, but his usual rules didn't seem to apply when it came to Rachel.

"Just hoping you won't be too upset when you see your house. That last searcher must have been in a bad mood." That really was enough to make him grim.

"I'll soon see, won't I?" She said the words lightly, but her hands were clasped tightly in her lap.

A few minutes later he was pulling into the driveway. Rachel slipped out quickly, and he hurried to catch up with her before she opened the door.

His presence didn't help. She winced when she stepped into the living room, her breath going out as if she'd been punched in the stomach.

"I'm sorry. I'd have tried to clean it up, but if we'd had to call in the police, that would cause more problems."

"I know." Rachel blinked rapidly, probably trying to prevent any tears from spilling over. "I thought I was ready for it, but hearing about it isn't like seeing it."

He stooped to grab a lamp table that looked as if it had been tossed across the room. "I'm afraid the lamp is a lost cause."

Rachel stared at the shattered glass globe. Then she straightened. "I'd like to sweep up the glass before we do any searching. I don't want broken glass ground into the carpet."

"Right. We may as well straighten as we go. That'll help you see if anything is missing."

It might also help her in the event she was determined to stay here tonight, and he couldn't convince her otherwise. He didn't really have the right to keep her away, little though he liked admitting it, but he could probably convince her to take some safety precautions first—dead bolts on the doors, at the very least.

Of course, the damage might put her off so much that she felt she couldn't bear to come back ever, but he didn't think she'd give in to what she'd see as weakness.

Rachel went to the kitchen and came back with a broom, dustpan and small electric sweeper. He took the broom and dustpan from her hands and knelt to pick up the biggest pieces first before trying to sweep.

"Funny." Her voice didn't sound as if she saw anything humorous. "I thought maybe seeing it like this would make me less upset about the necessity of selling. It doesn't. It just makes me want to fix it all up again, the way I did when we bought it."

He looked up at her, hands pausing. "I wondered

if you felt it was too painful to go on living here after the divorce."

Rachel actually seemed startled at the idea. "Money," she said crisply. "If I could afford the mortgage payments, I wouldn't let the house go for anything. It was my first real home."

After meeting her grandparents and learning about the life she'd lived with her mother, he could understand her feeling. A home of her own was more important to Rachel than it might be to people like him, who'd launched their lives from a solid family base. And he had begun to feel the yearning for a real home—at least since he'd met Rachel.

He carried the lamp remains to the trash bin in the kitchen. When he returned, she'd finished vacuuming the carpet and was restoring the drawer to the lamp table.

"Is everything you normally keep in that drawer there?" He picked up a handful of coasters.

She nodded, replacing the coasters, a notepad and a couple of pens to the drawer. "When you asked about my feelings for the house—were you picturing Paul and me planning the decorating or painting the walls together? That never happened."

"You were the one with the paint brush, I take it."

"I'm not bad with a paint roller, either." She was making a visible effort to sound at ease. "I loved every minute of decorating this place. Picking the colors, waiting until I'd saved enough to get just the right lamp…" She glanced ruefully at the spot where the lamp used to be.

"You wouldn't care for my preferred style of interior design, I'm afraid." He wanted to take that sadness from her face.

"Why? What do you like? Danish modern pale wood? Or shiny chrome and black leather?"

"It's more like Early Gym Classic. I have an exercise bike for television watching and a weight bench complete with a full set of weights."

That brought a smile to her face. "I gather you don't entertain very much."

"It's not as bad as all that. If I have anyone over, the weight bench can double as a coffee table."

"Genius," she said solemnly. "I admire pieces that can do double duty."

He grinned. "I can tell."

"Is there no lady in your life to object to your furnishing style?"

"No, not now. There's never been anyone serious enough that I take decorating advice from, anyway."

He looked at Rachel, and for an instant he felt again the upsurge of desire that had overcome him the previous night. Maybe she felt it, too, because she turned away instantly.

"We'd better get on with the search, although I don't think there's anything in here that would give us a clue." Her tone had become brisk.

He couldn't blame her. The situation was far too complicated even without the error of becoming emotionally involved.

Did that excuse him from answering honestly her question about his love life or lack thereof? He knew more than she could imagine about her marriage and divorce as well as her social life since the divorce—a life limited to the occasional girls' night out. He didn't like the way his evasion made him feel.

CHAPTER FOURTEEN

RACHEL REALIZED THEY'D worked their way through the living room and kitchen with barely a word spoken between them. Clint was giving a final wipe to the kitchen floor he'd insisted on mopping once he'd swept up the contents of the flour canister. She studied what she could see of his averted face.

Something had been said that had brought that stoic mask back to his face, and she couldn't think what it had been. Was it her comment about his having someone in his life to give opinions on decorating?

She fought back a surge of embarrassment. She hadn't meant anything by it. Or had she? Didn't she, at some level she didn't want to recognize, long to understand his personal life?

That was natural, wasn't it? He had come so far into her life…farther, maybe, than anyone else in years. He couldn't expect that to run only one way.

But clearly he did. And just as clearly this train of thought was getting her nowhere.

Clint straightened, surveying the floor with satisfaction. Obviously he was a man who took pride in a job well done.

"If you hire yourself out, I'm sure I could find you a few jobs."

He smiled, but that shadow lingered in his eyes. "I

might have to turn to that eventually. Coming up blank for a client isn't the way to build a good reputation in this business."

"I hadn't thought of that." No, she'd been too absorbed in her own troubles to look beyond them. "Surely one dissatisfied client won't hurt you."

"Don't worry about it. Logan would say I have a constitutional dislike of loose ends. And speaking of loose ends..." He picked up his jacket, hanging on the back of a kitchen chair, and pulled out her cell phone. "There you go."

"Thanks so much." She'd never considered herself one of those people who grew permanently attached to their cell phone, but she was ridiculously glad to have it back.

Clint cleared his throat, bringing her gaze to him. "We had to look through it. I'd apologize, but..."

"But you're not really sorry."

"At that point, I was desperate. I had to do anything I could to find you."

"And to find out if I was involved." She shook her head when he started to speak. "Never mind. I'm annoyed, but I'll get over it. I understand your reasons. You had no reason to believe you could trust me."

"I wanted to."

For an instant his words hung between them, and she wasn't sure how to respond. Did he mean... Was he saying his instincts had told him to trust her, just as hers had said the same about him?

He moved, not meeting her eyes. "Let's move on to the bedroom."

Wordless, Rachel led the way. She'd been putting this off, and she knew why. If any remnants of her marriage were left, they'd be stowed away in the dower chest her grandmother had given her. And that stood at the foot of the bed.

"Anything stored under here?" Clint knelt to peer under the bed, reminding her of that moment in the hotel room when he'd done the same.

"I'm not a believer in under-bed storage," she said. "Collects dust. That would be the Pennsylvania Dutch hausfrau coming out in me."

"Inherited from your grandmother, no doubt." He replied lightly, but the words didn't cover the way he winced when he got up from the floor.

Humiliation drenched her when she realized what she'd done. "I shouldn't have let you mop that floor. Your injury..."

"It's nothing." The brusque tone told her that he didn't accept sympathy. "It doesn't bother me now."

His brush-off annoyed her, and the words burst out of her. "Of course it's something! You had to give up your work because of that injury, so it was serious. Don't tell me it's nothing."

"Yes, ma'am." He eyed her warily. "You always get that riled up by little white lies?"

"When they're used to shut someone out they're not so little."

She could see him pondering that, fitting it together with what he knew about her. *Addicts lie.* He probably knew that, could probably see exactly why lies affected her the way they did.

Rachel pressed her lips together. She gave entirely too much away each time she talked to Clint. She ought to shut up entirely.

"I'm sorry." She hurried the words. "I didn't... I shouldn't push in where I'm not wanted."

"It's not that. Believe me, it's not." He sounded as if he meant it, but how could she be sure? "I don't like to talk about it."

She shrugged, turning away. She'd made a fool of herself enough for one day, it seemed. The silence hung heavy between them. And then he took a step toward her.

"My partner and I were following a small-time drug dealer, hoping he'd lead us to the bigger fish behind him."

Clint spoke very deliberately. Rachel looked at his face, and her breath caught. He'd understood exactly what she was thinking, and why. And he was making amends in the hardest possible way, telling her the thing he didn't want to.

She was afraid to listen, but also afraid not to.

"The guy led us into an alley behind some boarded-up stores. My buddy wanted to call for backup, but I was afraid we'd lose him. So we went in. It was a trap."

His pain was so obvious. Just remembering turned his face white and brought out a line of perspiration on his forehead. How could she ever have thought him stoic?

"I'm sorry. You don't have to..."

Clint's sharp gesture stopped her. "He was hit first. I headed for him, cursing myself for not listening to him. The next round hit me. I tried to reach him, but turned out my hip was shattered and my spinal cord affected. I couldn't move. I could just lie there, watching. He bled out before help reached us."

"I'm so sorry." Tears choked the words, and she reached out a tentative hand to touch his. "That's a lot to carry around with you." It was so little to say, but she sensed he couldn't handle anything more.

"Most people don't see that." His voice was taut with

pain. "It was part of the job, they think. One of the risks cops take."

"Most people aren't very observant. Including me." Her throat closed, making it difficult to get the words out. "Thank you for telling me."

"Yeah." He squeezed her hand. "I've gotten into the habit of shying away from talking about it."

"Until I yelled at you and bludgeoned my way in." She tried to ease the weight of emotion. "Not one of my more attractive qualities, I'm afraid."

"But effective." The tension in his face eased. "You deserved an answer, given how much I've probed into your life. I wish…well, I was going to say I wished we'd met under other circumstances, but we probably never would have."

"I guess that's true." It was difficult to imagine her life without him now, but that was a dangerous place to go. She might very well have to.

Rachel forced herself to move away from such emotional territory. "If we're going to look for any remnants of my marriage, the place to start is with the dower chest." She nodded at it. "If there are any reminders of Paul here, that's where they'd be."

"Okay." He went to the chest, sitting down on the floor in front of it. She sat cross-legged next to him, her knee brushing his leg.

She undid the clasp and lifted the lid, surveying all the things she hadn't had the heart to get rid of. She couldn't do it before, but with Clint next to her, she felt strong. It was time to deal with it and be done, once and for all.

THE NEXT DAY, Rachel decided, counted as a red-letter day. She was moving back into her house. And she was driving her own car once again. Either Clint or Logan had rescued it from the airport lot.

Amazing how freeing that was, being able to drive her own car and go where she wanted to. She hadn't realized that until she was confined, first at the farm by her own choice, and then here, because Clint was so determined to keep her safe.

She turned into the drive, hit the garage door opener button and pulled in. It was good, very good, to be back. But even so, she didn't close the garage door until she'd had a thorough look around.

Satisfied, she carried her few belongings to the front door, dropping them on the porch while she unlocked the door. Home again.

Carrying everything inside, she turned to lock the door and discovered a new addition. The door bore a shiny new dead bolt. Her heart twisted. Clint. He had known he couldn't keep her away from her home any longer, so he'd done the practical thing. As a homecoming gift, it couldn't be better.

She locked the door turning the knob on the dead bolt. She'd have to unlock it when Lyn arrived in a few minutes, but that was better than taking chances. Clint would approve of her caution.

At least, she supposed he would. He hadn't wanted her to come back yet, but she'd assured him she'd be fine. And then he'd said she should wait until he could come with her. But she'd grown impatient waiting for his call, so here she was, home again. And the first thing she saw was his determination to protect her.

He wasn't going to be happy with her for coming without him. She glanced at her phone, half expecting an irate call. But if she'd waited, she'd still be sitting in that hotel room.

She walked through the house, making mental notes of what had to be done to restore it. She wasn't surprised to find that there was a dead bolt on the back door, as well. She was fortunate that he hadn't seen fit to install a guard dog, too.

She and Clint seemed to have crossed some sort of a bridge in their relationship the previous day. It would take a while to get used to the new normal, once she figured out what it was. They were no longer investigator and suspect, or protector and protected, though she suspected Clint still wanted to believe that. And *colleagues* wasn't the right word. Friends? If she ignored her uncontrollable shiver of attraction whenever she was near him, that might be it.

Carrying her bag into the bedroom, she hung up the few things she had with her. When she turned to the dresser, the first thing she saw was the manila folder containing photos from her marriage. She'd left it out after they'd finished looking through the contents of the dower chest, thinking she should get rid of it.

For a few minutes she stood irresolute, holding the folder. Then she walked into the kitchen, intending to throw it away. Her marriage was over and nothing would be gained by holding on to reminders of it.

The doorbell pealed, and she dropped the folder on the table. Lyn. She hurried to the door, remembering to look through the peephole to confirm that it was actually her friend, and opened the door.

Lyn, carrying bags from their favorite Chinese takeout place, nodded approvingly. "That's right. Now lock everything up again. I don't want any nutcases wandering in here."

"If anyone came, I doubt they'd be wandering." Rachel locked up and led the way to the kitchen. "I know it's a little early to eat, but I'm hungry. I hope you want to eat and talk at the same time."

"My idea exactly," Lyn said. Together they got out plates and wineglasses before opening containers. They'd done this so many times since Paul moved out that it had become a pleasant routine.

"You got Crab Rangoon!" Rachel seized the package. "I thought we agreed we'd only indulge in that for special occasions."

"This is a special occasion. You're home, and that's worth celebrating."

"Good, because I intend to be greedy." Silly, that such a simple thing could lift her spirits so much.

Lyn dumped a generous portion of sweet and sour shrimp on her plate. "Just this once, it's all for you." She took a sip of the wine she'd brought and her expression turned blissful. "Now this is the appropriate end to a stressful day."

"Problems at school?" Even as Rachel asked the question, the longing overflowed to be back in her classroom, seeing the children's faces as they mastered something new.

"Nothing that won't be cured when you come back. So when is it going to be? Tomorrow?"

"I wish." She forced herself to cling to what she knew was right. "Not until I'm sure there's not going to be any public kickback from what Paul did."

"You're just being stubborn." Lyn put her chopsticks down. "Honestly, nobody could possibly blame the school for something done by the former husband of a teacher."

"And you're being too optimistic. Of course they could. You should know our helicopter parents better than that. After all, my classroom was invaded because of Paul's actions. If I had a child..."

She hesitated, hit by another foolish wave of longing. Where had this come from? Had she been that affected by seeing Sadie with her children?

"If you had a child, you wouldn't turn into a helicopter parent," Lyn said tartly. "And you wouldn't allow fear to overrule your judgment."

"But plenty of people do," Rachel said, trying to make her tone final. "So I won't come back until I'm sure it's safe. Please don't make me miss it any more than I already do."

Lyn studied her for a moment, and then sighed. "All right. I see you're determined, so I promise not to push."

"And I can count on your not breaking that promise more than ten times a day," Rachel added, smiling.

"I'm a natural-born pusher." Lyn grinned. "But I'll try. Let's talk about something else. That'll help. What's this?" She picked up the folder that lay on the table.

"Feel free to look."

"I'm going to." Lyn flipped it open and started leafing through the photos. She stopped at one taken of the wedding party, standing in front of the lake where their outdoor ceremony had taken place.

"That wasn't such a long time ago. Why do we look so young?"

Rachel leaned over to see. She and Paul, flanked by Lyn and Ian, who had been their only attendants. The rustic bower where the ceremony had been performed formed an arch over their heads.

"Maybe we've aged a lot in the last few years?"

Lyn sniffed. "I'd prefer to think I took a little more care with my makeup that day. You were lucky it didn't pour."

"That's the risk of planning an outdoor wedding. As it turned out, the weather was fine. It might have been more appropriate to the outcome if we'd had thunder and lightning."

As usual, Lyn saw what was behind the words. "You couldn't have foreseen what was going to happen. Paul was an expert at putting on a good front."

"I wish I could believe that. The truth is that I looked at him and saw what I wanted to be there. And he probably did the same with me. No wonder we were disappointed in the end."

Lyn returned the photo to the stack and closed the folder. "You were in love. People in love do that. It's just human nature." She lifted the folder. "This is the past. How about getting rid of it?"

"Give me a little credit. That's what I was about to do when I heard you at the door." Seeing the doubt in Lyn's face, she nodded toward the trash bin behind Lyn. "Go ahead. Toss it in."

Lyn held it a second longer, and then she dropped it into the bin. "Good. Why did you have those pictures out? Brooding over them?"

"No, I wasn't. Clint wanted to see anything I still had that related to Paul, so we went through the house." She seemed to see Clint straightening up, wincing in pain. Seemed to hear his story again, echoing in her thoughts.

Lyn was watching her again, and Rachel could read

the concern in her eyes. "I'll be glad if you can drop all those regrets about Paul. Just…don't jump into caring for someone else too quickly."

She couldn't pretend not to understand what Lyn was driving at. "It's not…it's not that way with Clint. Really." The fact that she had to emphasize it was a dead giveaway. "I'm grateful to him for his help, that's all."

"Tell that to someone who doesn't know you as well as I do. I've seen your expression when you mention him." She waved Rachel to silence when she'd have protested. "Don't bother. You're a smart woman. You'll figure it out. I just don't want to see you depend on somebody you don't really know."

It was good advice. And true that she didn't really know Clint in the sense of knowing his tastes and his habits and the kind of movies he liked. But what she did know about him went deeper than surface details because of the situation that had thrown them together. She knew he was dogged, determined to do what he saw was his duty, and honest.

Circumstances had pitchforked them past all the externals to what really counted at the heart of a person. Clint was a man of integrity. And if she were wrong about that, she'd just have to take the consequences.

"NOTHING." CLINT SLAPPED his hand down on the desk, rattling the remains of the take-out meal he and Logan had shared. "We've been over every scrap of information we have, and I don't see another thing to pursue."

"Yeah." Logan's more equable temperament didn't lead him to smack inanimate objects, but he was exasperated. "How does a guy vanish so completely? It'd be different if he were a pro, but we're assuming this is his first venture into illegal activities. Or are we?"

Clint caught his drift. "The gambling? Yes, he might have met some questionable types that way. But would he be likely to turn to them for help with such a specialized theft? Seems unlikely."

"Good point. But there's no doubt he's done a disappearing act. It's been three days since anything turned up on his ATM or his credit cards. And there's money sitting in his bank account that hasn't been disturbed. Why? People don't leave valuable assets behind."

"No. Which makes it look as if he hadn't originally intended to flee, but something made it necessary."

Clint didn't like it. Paul wasn't behaving the way he should be if he'd ripped off his employer. And yet they knew he had.

Logan shrugged. "Could be that Attwood's guess was right, much as I hate to admit it. Maybe Hartline turned the files over to his buyer, and said buyer found they were flawed. He might well think Hartline was trying to con him."

"If so, Hartline would have a good reason to disappear," Clint agreed. "But if he'd planned it that way, surely he'd have made sure he had everything ready to get away."

It just kept moving in circles with no end in sight. Clint didn't like it.

"I suppose he might have been naïve enough to think the buyer wouldn't notice. Or wouldn't pursue him afterward."

"Maybe." Logan sounded as unhappy about it as he felt. "And maybe this is one of those cases that drizzle off to an unsatisfactory conclusion. So we turn in our final report and back out as gracefully as we can. Unfortunately, it still leaves Rachel Hartline hanging."

"You think I don't know that?" It came out as a snarl. "And there's one strong reason not to make that assumption about the information on that flash drive. Someone was still looking for it very recently. Someone who wanted it badly enough to risk killing Rachel to get it."

"I haven't forgotten. Just I guess that means we're not going to close the file and walk away, no matter what Attwood says." Logan's response was mild, probably because he saw more than Clint wanted him to. "I was surprised you agreed to her going home today."

"Agreed? Who agreed? It's not like I had a choice. We have no right to keep her away. At least I told her not to go until I could be with her."

His inability to sway her decision still irked him, leaving a residue of guilt and also of fear for her. And time was marching on. She'd be wondering why he hadn't called.

"I wish..." He stopped, not wanting to go there.

Logan grinned. "Right. I know what you wish."

Clint threw a ball of crumpled paper at him. "It's not like that. There's such a thing as professional etiquette."

"And there's also such a thing as being human. Face it. You haven't exhibited a healthy interest in a woman in a long time. You're overdue."

"Inappropriate." He snapped the word, more than annoyed that he'd shown his feelings.

Logan considered. "Not really. She's neither a client nor a suspect. And once Attwood signs off on our report, we're done. I don't know about you, but I'd rather not continue to handle security for someone who keeps us in the dark. Life's too short."

Clint remained stubbornly silent. Maybe what Logan said was true, but it wasn't everything that was involved here. He'd met Rachel when she was in a vulnerable place. And even worse, she was still carrying a load of loyalty toward her ex. He might be reasonably sure that Paul Hartline wasn't worth it, but given Rachel's family background, it wasn't surprising that she couldn't just let it go.

He shot out of his chair. The only way to disrupt that kind of destructive thinking was to do something. He became aware that Logan was watching him, smiling.

"What?" he growled.

"Let me guess. You're going over to see Rachel and try to talk her into staying put."

"Okay, yes. But it doesn't mean what you think it does."

Logan didn't even dignify that with a response. He just smiled. Clint slammed his way out of the office.

RACHEL WAS PUTTING the few dishes they'd used in the dishwasher when the doorbell chimed. She closed the door and wiped her hands on the kitchen towel. Lyn must have forgotten something.

She actually had her hand on the lock when she woke to her actions. Just because Lyn's visit had been a return to normality, that didn't mean she could relax her guard. She looked out the window to find Clint on her doorstep, looking impatient.

Or annoyed. He'd wanted her to wait for him.

Unlocking the dead bolt, she swung the door open. "Coming to check on me?"

He paused halfway through the door. "You sound like Logan."

So his partner had…what? Teased him about coming over here? She focused on relocking the door, wondering at a state of affairs that had such an idea warming her.

When Rachel turned to him, Clint was frowning. "I thought you were going to wait for me. Do you know how I felt when I reached the hotel and you'd checked out?"

"I told you I wanted to get over here because Lyn was coming. You didn't show up."

"You could have waited. Or called me." He glared at her, and she realized he really was upset. "After all this, don't you trust me enough to do a simple thing like that?"

Trust. That was the word she'd shied away from. "It wasn't a question of not trusting you."

His expression treated that with the contempt it deserved. "Yes, that's exactly what it is."

"That's not fair," she protested, even though she knew it was true. "I just… I wanted to do something on my own. I'm a grown woman."

"I'm aware of that." Something intruded on the anger in his eyes. "The truth is that too many people have let you down—your father, your mother, Paul. Well, I'm not any of those."

"I know, but…"

"You might think you have reason to believe otherwise, but whatever else happens, I won't let you down."

Remorse was like a flood of acid through her. How hard was that for him to say, carrying, as he must, the weight of his partner's death? If he said he wouldn't let her down, it was no idle promise.

"I'm sorry." She wanted to reach out to him, but she

wasn't sure how. The chasm that had suddenly opened between them was so huge, so deep, that she was afraid she'd never span it. "I don't doubt you. I know you'll do what you say you will. But don't you see? It's important to me to make my own decisions to…to balance out all the mistakes."

Clint's iciness seemed to thaw as she watched. "Not that many mistakes," he said. "Just one big one."

She was shaking inside, but she had to keep going. "It seemed like the most important thing in the world at the time. You'd think I could have taken a little more care about it."

He shook his head, and the last of his anger flicked away. "Impossible. Nobody takes care when they're falling in love. You just have to hope your instincts aren't leading you wrong."

Rachel was finally able to smile. "In that case, I must have terrible instincts."

"I doubt it." He took her hand, swinging it lightly. "But maybe you weren't listening to them."

"Maybe not." She felt a little breathless. Were they really past the anger that had flared up between them like a fierce summer storm? She wanted to believe it.

Clint glanced around the room. "I thought you were having company. You said Lyn was coming over."

"Lyn came. We had supper and talked." The memory of what they'd talked about gave her pause. "She left a few minutes ago. After all, tomorrow is a school day for her."

His left eyebrow lifted slightly. "And for you."

"You're as bad as Lyn is." She led the way to the sofa and gestured for him to sit. "I told you the same thing I told her. I'm not going back until I'm sure there's no chance of any reflection on the school from what Paul did."

He waited until she'd settled before pulling a chair closer to her. "I'm glad to hear Lyn agrees with me. You're letting your scruples carry you too far. You know you want to be back there, and it would be good for you."

"Yes, I do want to be back!" Her longing sought relief, and Clint was a handy target. "But I won't let my own desire risk what's good for the school."

"Sorry." He reached across the space between them to enfold her hand in his. "I shouldn't push."

She managed a smile. "That's what Lyn said, too. But she admitted that she's one of the world's greatest pushers when it comes to people she cares about."

She stopped. Did that make it sound as if she assumed he cared about her? She hadn't meant to. At least, she didn't think so.

"Okay, so you're not going back until you feel it's safe. Attwood did say he expected our final report on Friday. Once he's signed off on it, the case is over as far as he's concerned."

"It'd be nice to think it's done with. But what if the file surfaces? Or Paul gets in touch? Or someone comes after me again?"

"You haven't heard anything from Paul, have you?" Clint was instantly alert.

"I'd have told you if I had. But still..." She wasn't sure herself what caused her hesitation. She'd be delighted to think this was finished, but she couldn't quite accept it yet.

"Logan and I were just talking about that." He released her hand, leaning back in the chair. "Nothing at all has shown up to indicate Paul is still in town, and it should have. He can't live on air."

"You're convinced he's run off, then." She tried to assess what she felt about it. Relief, primarily. "That's what James thinks, too."

"Seems likely, but..." Clint didn't look satisfied.

"But what?" Her heart seemed to sink. "You don't agree?"

"I can't figure out why he'd leave money in his bank account if he was going to disappear. Can you?"

That startled her. "Not a chance. Unless he's changed a great deal in the past year, it's impossible. I know he'd talked about turning over a new leaf, but in this situation... He'd be more likely to turn everything he owned into cash if he planned to leave. Anyone would."

"That was my thinking, too. We could be wrong. Or he might have had to change his plans in a hurry. There's nothing to stop him from cleaning out his account here from a distance."

She tried to come up with an answer and failed. She just couldn't imagine a situation in which Paul wouldn't try to get his hands on every bit of cash he could.

Finally she shook her head. "I'm out of ideas. How about some coffee? I made it for Lyn, and it's still hot."

"Sounds good. Maybe it'll clear my brain."

Clint followed her into the kitchen. When she turned back to him, a mug of coffee in her hand, she found him surveying the wine bottle Lyn had dropped on top of the trash.

"Looks like you two had a party."

"I'm afraid that was mostly Lyn, though I had some, as well. She does like Pinot Grigio with Chinese food.

Put that in the recycling bin, will you? Right next to the trash."

Setting his coffee on the table, she poured a cup of herbal tea from the pot under the tea cozy. "I can't handle coffee in the evening, even decaf. I have enough to keep me awake."

"My mother always insists on hot chocolate for a good night's sleep. I keep telling her chocolate has caffeine, but she won't believe me." He picked up the folder that lay on top of the trash can and looked at her, eyebrows lifting.

"I decided it was time to get rid of those reminders." She found she wasn't meeting his gaze.

"Anything in particular make you decide that now?" His voice seemed to have deepened, and it woke an answering hum along her nerve endings.

"I...I don't know." She glanced at him and as quickly looked away.

"Sure you don't?" He covered the space between them in a long stride and took the tea mug from her hand, setting it on the counter before he put his hands on her arms. "Think hard," he murmured.

Rachel looked up at him, knowing she shouldn't. Knowing she couldn't stop herself. Longing shimmered between them. He drew her against him, and her arms slid around him.

This was what she wanted. Why did she keep denying it to herself?

Their lips barely touched when the doorbell rang, jerking them apart as if it had been a shot.

CHAPTER FIFTEEN

In the instant after the doorbell chimed, Clint was all business.

"Are you expecting anyone?"

"No." She smoothed her hair back, her hand trembling just a bit. "I'd better see who it is."

"Don't open until I say so," he warned.

Not necessary to tell her so. She didn't feel particularly brave. But a quick look out the peephole told her it wasn't anyone threatening.

She took a few steps away from the door. "It's Claire," she whispered. "What's she going to think of your being here at this hour?"

"It's not exactly the middle of the night. Anyway, she'll have seen my car, so it's too late. Better let her in."

Sure enough, as soon as she opened the door, Claire's eyes went from her to Clint, standing now in the kitchen doorway.

"Claire, how nice to see you. Please come in." Rachel hoped she sounded cordial, but behind the words, her mind was questioning. *Why are you here?*

"I just wanted to be sure you weren't alone on your first night back home." Claire obviously intended to stay, since she walked in and dropped her handbag on the sofa. "But I see you're well taken care of by Clint."

She would not let herself blush. Or look guilty. Because she wasn't.

"Ms. Hartline has been allowing us to go through some old papers that belonged to her husband." He held up the file folder. "I'm just clearing up a few details."

Claire looked from him to Rachel. "I don't want to interrupt. I should go."

Since she didn't move to pick up her bag, this was clearly meant only to embarrass.

"That's not necessary," Rachel said, sitting down on the sofa. "Please, join me. We'll let Mr. Mordan get on with his work."

"Right," Clint said. "I'm working on the kitchen table, so I won't disturb you. Nice to see you, Ms. Gibson." He closed the kitchen door, leaving it ever so slightly ajar. So he planned to listen in on the conversation. Rachel wasn't surprised.

"May I get you anything? Coffee, tea?" She sincerely hoped this would be the last visitor of the evening.

"No, no, I don't have time to stay long."

In that case, why are you here? "It was nice of you to come by."

"When we heard at the office that you were coming back home, everyone was concerned. You had such a bad experience here with the break-in and the attack on you. I should think it would make you very nervous."

"I'm fine. I suppose these days we have to assume that we'll be a victim at some point in our lives. It could have been much worse." She gestured toward the scar on the wall where the intruder had flung a crystal vase that had been a wedding gift. "There are a few things I still have to fix, but fortunately most of the damage was cosmetic."

"But the attack on you." Claire gave an elaborate

shiver. "I should think you'd start reliving it the minute it got dark outside."

"Not a tremor." She held out her hands in emphasis. If she wasn't afraid, it sounded as if Claire intended to make her so. "How did you say you heard that I was moving back in?"

Something disturbed the cool superiority of Claire's face. "I'm not sure. Someone at the office mentioned it, I suppose. Everyone seemed to know. At any rate, we were all worried, so I said I'd stop over this evening and make sure you were all right."

How? she wondered. *How did everyone know?* She couldn't imagine that Clint would go out of his way to spread the word. But she didn't think she'd gain anything by pressing Claire on it.

"Well, if it doesn't bother you, I'm sure you're relieved to be back in your own house again." Claire was quick to change the subject. "Were you staying with friends?"

Rachel nodded. If Claire didn't know about her family, she'd prefer to keep it that way. "But we always want to be in our own place, don't we? And things seem to be returning to normal."

"I certainly hope so." Claire looked genuinely concerned. "All this worry has been bad for James. Creative people like James do need to be shielded from distractions."

Was that what the disruption of her life and Paul's disappearance were? Distractions?

"James is fortunate he has you to handle such things for him."

"Yes. I have to remind him of that sometimes." Claire

gave a little laugh, inviting Rachel to share the joke, all girls together. Claire seemed impervious to sarcasm.

"I hope you're adjusting to doing without Paul at work." Rachel began to think she'd shortly run out of polite, meaningless conversation.

"I'm not sure it's possible to do without him. We've all been together so long. I doubt that anyone new could fit in." Claire shook her head. "I still can't quite believe that this whole business is what it seems. You never had any hint that Paul was planning it?"

"Certainly not." If that sounded sharp, it was the way she meant it. "I've seen very little of him in the past year. And I was only at the company at the wrong time by accident. I'd been trying to get Paul to sign the necessary papers so that I can sell the house."

"Surely you don't have to part with it." Claire glanced around without any particular admiration that Rachel could see. "It's such a sweet little house."

Any woman would know instantly how a comment like that was meant. Rachel wondered if Clint caught how derogatory it was.

"I like it," she said firmly. "But not on a teacher's salary, I'm afraid."

"That really is too bad of Paul. If only you could talk to him about it…" She let that trail off invitingly.

"Impossible, I'm afraid, since I have no idea where he is."

"Surely you've heard something from him." Claire leaned toward her, intent. "I'd do anything I could to make this right again. After all, we were very good friends. *Very* good. You can count on me."

Rachel pulled back, repelled by the avid interest that seemed so out of place from self-contained Claire. "Not a thing." She stood. "If you were as close as all that, I'm surprised he hasn't contacted you directly."

For a moment the woman's face froze, and then she produced her usual cool smile. "Naturally he'd get in touch with you, first. You were his wife." She rose, picking up her bag. "I won't keep you any longer, since you have another guest."

She was not going to attempt any explanation. "Thank you for stopping by."

When they reached the door, Claire paused again even as she stepped out. "Do tell Paul to give me a call."

Rachel kept her lips firmly pressed together. Apparently giving up, at least for the moment, Claire left.

Rachel closed the door with a bit more emphasis than necessary and snapped the locks.

"If I were guessing, I'd say you didn't like the woman much." Clint spoke from behind her.

She turned to him, banishing the irritation Claire had engendered. "I'd say the feeling was mutual. Funny. Before tonight, I'd have said Claire never gave me a thought. Certainly not to the extent to dislike me. I wonder why."

"Who knows? I wouldn't let it worry you. Maybe she just resented anyone else horning in on the close relationship the four of them had."

"Maybe." But she doubted it. Claire didn't seem troubled by the fact that Ian was married. Why should she be? "She seemed to be implying that there had been something going on between her and Paul. But why should I care? I hadn't even met him at that time."

She realized that Clint was studying her face as if waiting for something to hit her.

"I see. You think she meant that there's been something between them more recently." She tried to weigh how she felt about the possibility, but it was no use. She'd been so battered by all the other revelations about Paul that she was past feeling anything.

"Does that bother you?"

Rachel rubbed her temples. "No. Or maybe I'm numb. Our marriage was over long before we filed the papers. I'd just like to have my life back."

An uneasy silence fell between them. She'd try to recapture that moment between them, but she was just too tired to think.

"Nobody can blame you for that." Clint squeezed her shoulder and strode to the door. "I'm off now. Be sure everything is locked up and then try to get some sleep. You obviously need it. But take your cell phone with you."

He left, not waiting for a response.

RACHEL WAS NURSING her second cup of coffee the next morning when the cell phone announced the arrival of a text. She stared blankly at her cell for a few minutes before realizing the buzz hadn't been on her regular phone. It had been on the disposable phone she'd bought because of Paul.

Heart thudding, she dug in her bag for the phone. She'd stopped expecting a call from him…had nearly convinced herself that he'd left town, that she wouldn't hear from him again. And here he was again. For a moment she hesitated, then she opened it.

The text was brief. Meet me at my place as soon as you can. Don't fail me. Paul.

Her immediate reaction was of annoyance. How like Paul to assume, after everything that had happened, that she'd rush to his aid. She dialed his number. She'd have an explanation before she went rushing over there.

But Paul's cell went straight to voicemail. Rachel stared at it, trying to think of an appropriate message. There didn't seem to be one. Frustrated, she tossed the phone back in her bag. Go? Or ignore it?

She couldn't ignore it. Not if this was the only chance she'd ever have to convince Paul to come forward and accept responsibility for his actions. He had to, or how could she ever be safe from whoever wanted him so badly they'd risk her life?

A doubting voice in the back of her mind questioned the likelihood of his doing any such thing, but she was already grabbing her jacket. Maybe there were those who could walk away, but it seemed she wasn't one of them.

Rachel was already on her way to the car when she realized that she hadn't done as she'd promised—she hadn't let Clint know that she'd heard from Paul. And she was going off to meet Paul without telling him. Given his reaction the previous night, that probably wasn't a good idea.

She stopped, pulling out her phone to call him. But his phone, like Paul's, went straight to voicemail. Was no one where they should be this morning?

Biting her lip, she frowned at the phone. If she waited to hear back from Clint, Paul might very well be gone by the time she got there. She couldn't risk that—not when seeing him could result in clearing this mess up once and for all.

Quickly, she left a message telling Clint about the text. Telling him she was going. And then, trying not to sound needy, she asked if he'd meet her there.

It wasn't that she was afraid to meet Paul, but she'd feel a lot better knowing Clint was on his way. The truth was that she'd come to rely on his steady presence. She shouldn't, but she did.

Violating her own policy about cell phones in cars, Rachel kept the phone on the car seat beside her as she drove to Paul's. Hoping…well, she wasn't quite sure. Was she waiting for a call back from Paul? Or from Clint?

In any event, she could have saved herself the trouble. No one called, and she pulled into the parking lot at Paul's apartment with no other options. She'd have to rely on herself. Decide for herself. Wasn't that what she claimed she wanted? Now that she had it, she wasn't so sure.

So she'd see Paul, and make one final effort to convince him to do the right thing and get her off the hook. Whether he did or not, she was done. The divorce had never felt so final.

A young woman with a baby in a stroller was coming out as Rachel went in. Rachel paused, holding the door and complimenting the baby, then slipped through without the need for buzzing Paul's apartment. The waiting elevator carried her quickly upstairs… Just as well, since the last thing she needed was to obsess about what she'd say to Paul.

The upstairs hallway stood empty. Most people would be at work at this time of day. Was that why Paul had chosen now to come back here?

She reached the door, her hand raised to knock, and saw that it stood ajar. She pushed it with her fingertips. "Paul?"

No answer. The living room, furnished in what she

thought of as motel modern, stood silent. Leaving the door open behind her, she crossed to the small kitchen, but she could see already that no one was there.

"Paul?" she called again, louder. If he'd brought her over here only to play games, she wasn't amused. "You wanted me to come, so here I am. Let's get this over with."

Still nothing. She considered walking out. The silence had begun to prey on her nerves, and her skin prickled.

Nonsense. Once again, Paul had let her down. She shouldn't be surprised at that. She strode to the bedroom door. If he was there, he'd better have some convincing explanation for this whole thing.

She pushed the door open. Paul was there, but he wouldn't be giving any explanations. He lay on the floor, and the back of his head—

She retched, clutching her stomach and trying to breathe. The college track trophy he'd won had always stood on the left side of his dresser, wherever they'd lived. Now it lay on the floor, the golden runner thick with blood.

Rachel took a step back, then another, groping in her bag for her phone. She had to call help. It might not be too late.

But it was. She knew it. Holding the thought at bay, she punched in 911.

"What is the nature of your emergency?"

She stood, staring at the phone, not knowing what to say. Even as the 911 operator repeated her question, the outside door swung open. Two uniformed patrolmen stepped in, looking as surprised to see her as she was to see them.

"What's going on here?"

She could only gesture toward the bedroom. The

phone spoke again, and she thrust it into the hand of the nearest officer, stumbling to a chair. Her head was spinning, and blackness seemed to be closing in on her. She collapsed into the seat, bending forward, her head between her knees. *Hold on.* She had to hold on.

For a confusing interval the room buzzed with activity. One of the cops was asking her questions, but she couldn't seem to focus. Finally, either taking pity on her or giving up on getting a straight answer at the moment, he went to the kitchen, returning with a glass of water.

Rachel sipped at the water, trying to make some sense out of what had happened. But she couldn't.

One officer knelt by her chair. "Can you tell me your name?"

She nodded. "Rachel Hartline." Realizing he'd want more, she gave him her address.

He jotted down notes, his face serious. He was young, she realized. Probably not as old as she was, and his face had a greenish tinge at the moment. Maybe, like her, he hadn't seen anyone who'd died by violence before today.

"And the man in the other room?"

She swallowed hard. "Paul Hartline. He's my ex-husband."

Ex-husband. It really was final now, and a shudder went through her.

The two officers seemed to exchange glances. Did they think she'd done it? That she'd be capable of picking up the trophy Paul was so proud of and hitting…

A confusion of noise at the door heralded the arrival of more police. In a moment the small apartment buzzed with activity. People came and went past her, into the bedroom. She couldn't see what they were doing—didn't want to see.

An argument seemed to erupt at the door, and she heard Clint's voice. He was obviously refusing to be turned away, and she caught a word here or there as he argued. Apparently he was successful, because soon he was kneeling next to her, gripping her hands.

"Are you hurt?" His voice was rough with demand, but she heard the caring under it and was thankful.

"I'm…I'm all right. But I found him. Paul. He wanted to see me…"

"I know. You left a message. I'm sorry I didn't get here faster." He squeezed her hands, his grip painful. "It's all right. Just tell me what you found when you got here."

"Maybe she'd better tell me, too, Mordan." Another cop, in plain clothes this time.

"Ms. Hartline's too shaken for any questioning, Phillips. So don't be pushing."

They knew each other, then. She wasn't sure if that made it harder or easier. At least the officer was allowing Clint to stay.

"It's all right." She pushed a strand of hair back from her face, trying to collect herself. As long as she didn't think of what she'd seen, she'd be all right. "I'd rather tell you what happened. I had a text from Paul, wanting me to come over and meet him. I told you." She fixed her eyes on Clint, and he nodded.

"Why was that?"

Rachel blinked, looking at the other man. "Why did he want to see me? Or why did I tell Clint?"

"Both." He gave her an interested look that was probably meant to encourage her to talk.

"I don't know what Paul wanted," she hedged, not sure whether she should mention the business with Attwood Industrial or not. "My phone…" She waved a hand toward the uniformed officers. "I gave it to someone."

"That's all right, Ms. Hartline. I have it. I may have to hold on to it."

She felt Clint stiffen, but she just nodded. "That's all right. You'll have seen he didn't say what he wanted. But he was going to sign a sales agreement to put the house we owned on the market, so it may have been that. Or…"

"Or?"

Rachel looked at Clint, hoping for guidance. He shrugged.

"You'll see from Ms. Hartline's phone that she'd been trying to reach him. That was at my request. Or rather at the request of our client James Attwood. You're familiar with the firm?"

The other man nodded. "Some kind of think tank for tech products, isn't it? You run their security, do you?"

Clint nodded. "Hartline didn't turn up for work one day about…well, over a week ago now. Attwood thought his files had been tampered with, so he called us in. We've been trying to locate Hartline."

"Industrial espionage, was it?"

Clint shrugged. "I can go into that with you at length later. Or James Attwood can. If you can finish up with Ms. Hartline, I'd like to take her home."

"Not just yet. I have a few more questions."

Rachel sensed a silent battle between the two men. Evidently the detective won, because Clint shrugged.

More questions. Exactly when she'd arrived, who

might have seen her, when was the last time she'd heard from her ex. She answered as exactly and as briefly as possible. Attwood wasn't going to like her saying anything, but the situation had become too serious to cater to him. Paul was dead.

Her head spun again, and Clint's hands tightened on hers. She heard their voices as if from a distance. Whatever Clint's argument, it must have been convincing, because a few minutes later Clint was taking her out to his car, one arm wrapped firmly around her.

RACHEL LOOKED A little better by the time Clint drove away from the apartment building. Not good, but better. He didn't want to remember how he'd felt when he'd arrived and seen the police there.

"My car..."

"Don't worry about it. I'll arrange to pick it up. Want to give me your keys?"

She nodded, fishing in her bag for a few minutes before seeming to remember that she kept them in an outside pocket. She handed them over, and he tucked them in the console.

"Thanks." Rachel pressed her fingers to her temples, the way she did when upset or trying to think. "I'm glad you got there before they started questioning me. I didn't know what to say about Attwood. He won't like being involved."

Clint shrugged. "I'm afraid Attwood will just have to lump it. It's impossible to keep the information quiet now. At least the cops have another trail to pursue." He stopped, knowing he'd said too much.

But Rachel didn't seem surprised. "Besides me, you mean. Isn't an ex-wife who finds the body automatically the chief suspect?" Her voice quivered only a little on the words.

"Maybe so, but the first steps they take will show it wasn't you. Since you didn't go into the bedroom at all, they won't find any evidence you'd been there. And I'd be surprised if the person who swung that trophy didn't get blood splattered."

She winced, exhaling as if he'd punched her. Remorse swept him.

"Maybe someday I'll learn to stop coming out with everything that enters my head. I'm sorry, Rachel."

"It's okay." She clasped her hands firmly in her lap. He wanted to stop the car and pull her into his arms for comfort, but he couldn't do that on a busy highway. "You actually made me feel a little better. What you said is true. I didn't take even a step inside—just stood in the doorway for a moment. I…I could see there was nothing I could do."

"That trophy. I couldn't get a close look, but I assume it was his?"

"First place in the state in the long jump when he was in college. He…he was proud of it." She firmed her voice and went on. "It always stood on the left side of his dresser, so I suppose that's where it was."

Handy, he thought. The killer might have known it was there. Or a quarrel might have sprung up suddenly and the trophy snatched up. Or the killer might have seized it rather than use a gun, if the death had been planned.

"The woman I saw coming out of the building." Rachel was obviously thinking back through her answers. "If they find her, she might be able to tell them what time it was."

"Right. She might not, of course, if she's not a person who notices such things, but it's worth exploring. And they had the time of your 911 call. That will show you weren't there long enough for a quarrel to escalate to that extent."

"If she didn't notice, there's no one to say what time I left the house."

She was starting to brood, most likely listing the possible evidence against her.

"Look, I know Phillips. He's a good cop. He's not going to jump to conclusions, especially without any physical evidence. So try to put it out of your mind."

That wasn't the brightest thing he'd said. He pulled into her driveway. Of course she wasn't going think of anything else, at least for a time.

"You don't need to come in," she began, but he ignored her, going around to help her out of the car and hold on to her as they walked to the door. Just in case, he told himself. Or maybe because he wanted to touch her, support her.

He spotted the movement of a curtain at the house next door and hoped Mrs. Barton wasn't going to rush over full of concern and sympathy. But apparently she thought he had things under control, because she didn't emerge.

Once inside, he deposited Rachel on the sofa and pulled a quilted throw over her. "I'm going to make you a cup of tea. Just sit."

"I'll be fine by myself. Really." But she didn't sound convinced. "And I'm sure you have things you have to do."

She was right about that, but most of them could

wait. He did have to call Logan right away. He could do that while the water boiled.

"What's going on?" Logan demanded. "I had a call from a cop to verify that you were my partner. What have you been up to?"

"Nothing, but Paul Hartline is dead." Turning his back on the other room, he gave Logan a quick rundown. "Naturally Rachel had nothing to do with it."

"Naturally," Logan replied.

If he'd detected any sarcasm in that, Clint would have jumped down his throat, but there was none.

"Fortunately, it should be able to establish that she didn't arrive until after he was dead." A thought hammered at his skull. "It makes me wonder about that text she got, asking her to meet him there."

"A setup." Logan caught on at once. "Easiest thing in the world to send a text on someone's phone once you've slugged him. But we're right back to who, aren't we? I wouldn't expect anybody to be willing to kill over that idea of Attwood's."

"No." That was bugging him, too, he realized. "I had a glimpse of the body. He hadn't been dead long, by the looks of it. So you're right—it was a deliberate attempt to implicate Rachel. Maybe a brainstorm on the killer's part when he realized he had a body on his hands."

The kettle began to steam. "Listen, I'm going to need to stay here until I can get someone else to stay with Rachel. And if the cops come calling, I don't want her talking to them without me."

"I did figure that out," Logan said. "I'll get onto Attwood and let him know what's happening."

"You may as well warn him to prepare for questions. I had to tell them about the connection to Attwood's and why I was there. I said as little as possible, but I know Jim Phillips, the lead cop on it. He's not going to rest until he knows every detail."

"Murder puts it out of our control. Attwood will have to understand that. He might be able to ignore the attacks on Rachel since she wouldn't report them, but not this. It's already in police hands. And if he doesn't, I don't figure we've lost anything. I'll call you back after I've talked to him. Stay in touch."

"Right." He picked up the kettle and poured. "And thanks, buddy."

"Anytime. Take care of her." He broke the connection.

CHAPTER SIXTEEN

HIS MIND EASED after sharing the burden with Logan, Clint carried the mug of hot tea into the living room. "I may have overloaded it with sugar, but drink it, anyway. It's good when you've had a shock."

Catching her expression, he grinned. "My mother taught me that, too."

"She must have a secret connection with my grandmother, then." Rachel wrapped both hands around the mug. Some of the tension seemed to drain out of her face, and she leaned back against the cushions.

He sat next to her, his arm along the back of the sofa so that he could turn toward her. No questions, not now. Better to let her adjust in her own time.

But apparently she couldn't do so, because soon enough she was looking at him, frowning slightly. "The police will want to talk to me again, won't they?"

He couldn't say something soothing, not when she wanted the truth. "Probably, but it's routine. It's common to take a witness over their story several times. Something may come back that he or she didn't remember the first time through. Or, if a person is lying, there's a possibility of catching it." He reached out to touch her shoulder. "You're telling the truth, so no one can trip you up."

She nodded. "I am, but even so, I don't relish the idea

of going over and over it." She shuddered. "It was bad enough the first time. I still can't believe it happened."

"Unfortunately, it's real."

His thoughts spun around and around what they knew about Paul and his motivations. Money, that had always been their assumption. A reasonable one, since gamblers always needed more cash.

But murder didn't seem to fit into the scenario of industrial treachery that they suspected. What if Hartline had been killed for some other reason entirely? But if so, what was it?

"Will I have to formally identify the…the body?" Rachel's fingers gripped the mug until her knuckles were white and strained. "I'm afraid the extent of my knowledge about these things comes from TV."

Clint wrapped one hand around hers, very gently. "It may come to that. You're not his wife any longer, but you may be the closest thing the police can find to a relative. Where are his people?"

"I don't know. I don't think he has much family. He never talked about them, except to say they didn't have anything to do with each other." She moved restlessly. "I tried to get him to look them up when we became engaged, but he refused."

"Failing relatives, the police may be satisfied with someone who knew him well—anyone from Attwood's, I suppose."

"Better me than James Attwood. But I suppose Ian might. He knew Paul longer than I did."

He nodded. "I'll suggest that to Phillips."

"You knew him, didn't you?" She set down the mug and turned toward him, seeming relieved to get away from the question of identification. "The detective, I mean."

"Not well, but we were at the police academy at the same time. And I know of him. He's a good cop. Like I said, he's not a man to jump to conclusions."

"I guess that's the best I could expect. It just seems so…" Her voice choked, and she stopped, fighting for control.

Heart full, Clint drew her gently into his arms. Holding her against him, he hoped that human warmth and caring might help at a moment like this. She moved against him with a little sigh, and he felt a few tears dampen his shirt.

He smoothed his hand up and down her back. "It's going to be all right." It was the only thing he could think of to say, but it appeared to be the right thing, because he felt her relax more.

Too bad he couldn't do the same. Anyone with human feelings would weep over the unexpected death of someone close. But he couldn't help wondering if Paul still had such a large place in Rachel's heart that there was no room for anyone else.

They might have sat like that the rest of the day, but soon enough his cell phone sounded, like a call to duty. He turned a little to reach his pocket, and Rachel drew back.

Logan. He punched the button. "What?"

"Sorry. I just got off the phone with our friend Attwood. Not a happy man, as we expected. He wants to see us both. Today. In about an hour."

He muttered a suggestion as to what Attwood could do.

"I couldn't agree more," Logan said. "But we did sign a contract with the man, and I think we should clean things up as best we can. Can you get away?"

Clint released Rachel to look at his phone. "I might be able to. Let me make a call, and I'll get back to you."

Rachel moved away from him, pulling the throw around her. "If you have to leave, I'll be fine by myself."

"I'm not leaving unless someone else is here, and that's flat. What's Lyn's number?"

"You can't call her in the middle of a school day." She sounded scandalized at the thought.

"Yes, I can. And never mind, because I have her on my cell." He clicked on the name, and almost immediately Lyn came on the line.

"Is something wrong? Is Rachel okay?"

Rachel was trying to snatch the phone from him, in fact, so he got up and moved out of range. "She's all right, but Paul is dead." He figured he didn't have to sugarcoat that for her. "And Rachel's the one who found him."

"Where is she now?"

"I brought her home, but I don't want to leave her alone, and I have to go out. If you're listening, you can hear her protesting in the background over my interrupting you in the middle of a school day."

"I'll be there in half an hour. Tell her to be quiet and let her friends take care of her for once."

"I will. And if the cops show up while you're here, call me ASAP and then stall them. I don't want her answering any questions until I'm with her."

"Don't worry. They won't get past me."

He grinned, irrationally relieved. "I'm sure."

She'd already hung up. He pocketed the phone and turned back to Rachel.

"She's coming, so there's no use in you making a fuss about it. You'd do the same for her in a minute."

Rachel opened her mouth to argue and then shut it again. "All right," she said finally. "But I don't like people making arrangements for me as if I were a child."

"Too bad. You don't have a choice this time." He thought of what her grandfather had said when they were leaving the farm. "I've got to call Logan back, and I'll stay until Lyn gets here."

Apparently giving up for the moment, she nodded.

Good. Maybe he was overreacting, but he'd rather do that than make any sort of mistake where Rachel was concerned.

RACHEL HAD EXCHANGED the quilt for a warm sweater by the time Lyn had spotted the police car pulling up in front of the house. In fact, Lyn had insisted on her staying in the bedroom until Clint arrived, and she'd been too frazzled to argue.

In any event, the interview with Detective Phillips had been far less harrowing than she'd expected. He'd led her over the details of her actions, but with Clint nearby and Lyn looking ready to pounce, she'd found she could go through it.

No, she hadn't seen anyone else at the building other than the woman and child. No, she didn't go into the bedroom at all, just stood in the doorway. And no, she had no idea who might have wanted to kill her ex-husband.

Now, from where she stood at the front window, she could see Phillips standing outside on the sidewalk, talking to Clint. Actually, it looked as if Clint was doing most of the talking.

"What do you suppose he's saying?"

"I don't know." Lyn moved closer to the window,

trying to see more. "I wish I'd learned lip-reading. It'd be very useful at a time like this."

She smiled, as Lyn had probably intended. "You do know some sign language. That's useful." She and Lyn had taken a course one winter, anticipating the arrival of a hearing-impaired child who was now in the third grade and doing beautifully.

"True, but not at the moment." Lyn transferred her attention to Rachel. "I can guess at the content, if not the exact words. He's telling that detective all the reasons why he'd be an idiot to suspect you."

Rachel steered her thoughts away from the idea of being a suspect. "You seem to have changed your mind about Clint. Weren't you the one who warned me about trusting him?"

"When you're wrong, you may as well admit it." Lyn gestured with her hands, as if tossing her previous opinion away. "Your Clint seems to be one of the good guys."

"He's not 'my' Clint," she began, and closed her lips on the rest of the sentence since Clint walked back in at that moment.

"Okay," he said, seeming to banish a frown when he looked at her. "That wasn't so bad, was it?"

"I guess not, but is he really satisfied?"

"Of course he is," Lyn said abruptly. "He's not an idiot, and it would be idiotic to think you had anything to do with this." She grabbed her jacket. "Look, I'm going to run home and pick up what I need to stay the night. You'll be here until I get back?" The question was directed to Clint, who nodded.

"I don't need babysitting," she began, but it was too

late. Lyn was already out the door, and Clint had settled himself in the armchair.

She turned to him, but the bland look he gave her was so disarming she had to smile.

"All right, I give in." She sat on the sofa, kicked off her shoes and curled up against the cushion. "But now you answer the question. Is that detective convinced?"

Clint leaned forward, elbows on his knees. "It's not a matter of being convinced of your innocence. It's a question of what the evidence tells him. And right now the evidence tells him that unless you're Houdini, you couldn't have attacked Paul." He hesitated. "They found the woman with the baby, and she confirmed the time you arrived. They also have the times of the text from Paul's phone and your call to me. You just didn't have time."

She blew out a long breath, relaxing the tension that had an iron grip on her. "That's good. But it's not over, is it?"

"You'll have to go into the station, make a statement and sign it. I'll go with you," he added quickly. "It's nothing to worry about. And Robinson is going to do the identification, not that there's any doubt about it. The police will keep digging, of course, but I think you're out of it."

The way he phrased that snagged her attention. "You're still worried, aren't you?"

"Of course I'm worried. There's a killer on the loose, and he tried to involve you. I don't like anything about this situation."

"I guess this isn't the sort of conclusion you want when you take on a client."

Clint shook his head almost angrily. "Never mind that.

I don't care about Attwood now. He gave us the push seconds before we were going to do the same to him."

She considered that. "He wouldn't like any suggestion that Paul's death was connected to the company."

"No. And it may not have been. We don't know what else Paul might have been involved in. The police investigation may turn up something."

It was all oddly dissatisfying. Rachel pressed her fingers against her temples. So…incomplete.

"Do you have an attorney?"

The question, coming out of the blue, shook her. "What…why? Why do I need an attorney? If the police…"

"No, that's not why." He reached out to clasp her hand. "Sorry. I need to think before I speak. I'm assuming there will be legal complications, since you and Paul owned this house together. A lot depends on how the mortgage was set up, whether he had a will and probably some other things I don't know about. An attorney could save you a lot of hassle."

"I hadn't even thought of that, but I'm sure you're right. What happens to his share of the house?" Her mind started spinning again.

"Okay, stop." He squeezed her hand. "That's what the attorney is going to handle for you, so there's no point even thinking about it."

Rachel took a breath and tried to turn off the spinning thoughts. He was right. "Has anyone ever told you that always being right is annoying?"

He grinned. "A time or two. Get a lawyer."

"The woman who handled the divorce can probably do it. She's already familiar with our finances. Such as they are."

She couldn't help it—her thoughts went over the

well-worn paths again. She'd been determined not to repeat her mother's mistakes, but she'd fallen right into the same mess. Worse, she was still entangled with Paul no matter what she did.

Clint said something, and she tried to recall her wandering attention.

"I'm sorry. What?"

He rose. "Lyn's coming. And I have to get moving."

"Right." She collected herself with an effort. "I can't thank you enough for today. If you hadn't—"

"Forget it." The words were brusque, and he was already heading for the door. "I'll check in with you in the morning. Try to get some sleep."

He and Lyn passed each other in the doorway. Rachel heard him say a few words to her, and then he was gone.

Lyn came in, tossing a backpack on the end of the sofa. "Where was Clint rushing off to?"

She shrugged. "I've no idea. He was probably afraid if he hung around I'd cry all over him again. Men hate that, so he was only too happy to turn me over to you."

Lyn stared at her for a long moment. "Don't be an idiot."

The sharp tone shocked her, and Rachel could only stare back. "What?"

"You heard me. For probably the first time in your life, you've run into an honorable guy who wouldn't take advantage of you when you're—if you'll excuse the word—vulnerable. Don't throw that away."

Leaving Rachel gaping, she pulled out her phone and proceeded to order a pizza.

CLINT PACED THE office until Logan pitched a wad of paper at him.

"Next time it's going to be something heavier," he

said. "Will you stop prowling and start talking? What are you so worried about, as if I didn't know?"

Clint planted his fists on Logan's desk. "Don't tell me you're not frustrated, too, because I won't believe it. We can't just walk away from this mess."

"Our client seems to think we can. In fact, he's put an end to it. Which means we won't get any cooperation from anyone at Attwood's."

"I don't know about that," he said slowly. "With all that's been going on, I didn't tell you about Ms. Gibson's visit to Rachel the other evening."

"Claire Gibson? I wouldn't have guessed they'd be on visiting terms." Logan seemed to consider that, frowning. "What did she want?"

"Good question. I just happened to be in the kitchen at the time."

"Where you just happened to hear everything that was said," Logan finished for him. "So?"

"I'd say she what she really wanted was a lead on Paul's whereabouts, but she also kept landing little jabs about how close she and Paul were. Hints with sharp edges."

"Did it bother Rachel?"

"Not to notice. She seemed to think if there ever had been anything between them it would have been before she even met Paul." He shrugged. "Maybe the Gibson woman would be willing to talk, even if her boss did close us down. She doesn't seem to be in awe of him, anyway."

Logan nodded. "Worth a try. Do you want to do it, or should I?"

"You, I think." Clint was reluctant to let anything out of his hands at this point, but he had to admit Logan would probably do a better job than he would. "She's probably connecting me with Rachel, especially after seeing me there last night."

"Okay, will do." Logan gave him that raised eyebrow look. "So why might she be connecting you with Rachel?"

"Don't start. I've already heard your opinions."

Logan grinned. "Play it your way, then. I'm just surprised you left Rachel alone."

"She's not alone," he said, too fast. "Her friend is with her." He frowned, considering. "She ought to tell her family what happened so they can support her, but I don't suppose she will. Too determined to handle things on her own."

"Maybe a good friend could let them know what's going on."

The suggestion hung there in the air for a moment while Clint speculated on the probable outcome. Rachel would be annoyed with him, no doubt. It just might be worth it.

He pulled out his phone. "I'll probably have to leave a message and wait for a call back. Their phone isn't in the house." He could see the question in Logan's face at that, but now wasn't the time for a lesson on Amish tradition.

He'd just left his name and number on the answering machine when someone picked up.

"Clint? Is that you?" It was Timothy's voice. "I was chust walking past the phone shanty when I heard the machine. Is Rachel all right?"

"She's okay, but something bad has happened." He paused, wondering if he should ask for Rachel's grandfather, but maybe it was better to use Timothy as a go-between. "Her ex-husband has been killed."

"Killed? An accident?" Timothy sounded surprised, but not shocked. "Was Rachel with him? Was she injured?"

He was assuming a car accident, Clint realized. It was probably the worst thing he could imagine.

"Rachel wasn't with him. But it wasn't an accident." He hesitated, but they had to be told, and better it came from him. "He was attacked and killed. Unfortunately, it was Rachel who found him afterward, so she's pretty shaken."

"Wait, wait, hold on." Timothy obviously turned away from the phone, shouting for Sadie. In a moment, it seemed, there was an excited gabble of voices in Pennsylvania Dutch, all speaking at once.

Finally a voice came through clearly, and it was Rachel's grandfather's. "You're sure Rachel is safe?"

That would be his first concern always, Clint knew. "She's safe, and she has her friend Lyn staying with her for tonight, at least. But she's pretty shaken by what happened."

"Our poor child. Timothy said that she found him?"

"That's right. She'd received a message from him asking her to meet him at his apartment. He was dead when she arrived."

"By herself?"

The question made him feel guilty. "I got there a few minutes later, so I was able to help her deal with the police and their questions."

"They must see that she couldn't have done this terrible thing." His tone was sharp with anxiety.

"I don't believe they suspect her, but she still has to

answer questions and make a statement. And there will be a lot of business to take care of."

"Yah, I see. Wait a moment."

Again Clint heard the jumble of voices, the grandmother's soft and tear-filled, Sadie's rapid and anxious, Timothy's slow and steady.

"Clinton, are you there?"

"Yes, I'm here. Don't worry. We won't leave her alone."

"We are thinking that Sadie should komm and stay with her. We can hire a driver to bring her." He paused. "Her grandmother and I would be there, too, but Sadie says that might be too much. What do you think?"

He thought that Rachel would be ready to strangle him if he brought her whole family down there. She'd be as determined to protect them as they were to protect her.

"I'd say you should talk to Rachel first, before you decide what to do. Right now I think just talking with you would help her more than anything else." He was beginning to think he'd unleashed more than he'd bargained for with this call.

"She should have called us herself. We're her family."

"I know." He cleared his throat. Family was family, no matter what it looked like from the outside. "She's just been too overwhelmed with everything to think of it."

He wasn't sure the older man believed that, but he seemed to accept it.

"It was gut you called us. Denke, Clint. We won't forget your kindness."

"I left my phone number on your answering machine. Don't hesitate to call me. For anything."

"Da Herr sie mit du," he said gravely.

Clint translated the words with his barely remembered high school German. *The Lord be with you.*

"Take care. I'll call if anything else happens that you should know about." He ended the call.

Logan was studying him thoughtfully. "Nice people?"

"Very nice." He blew out a breath. "Rachel will think I was interfering, but it'll be good for her to talk to them."

"When are you going to talk to her?" That eyebrow lifted again. "Honestly, I mean. Tell her what you feel."

"Not now. Not when she's trying to get used to the fact that her former husband is dead. It wouldn't be right."

"Far as I know, a woman never objects to hearing that a man cares about her, no matter what else is going on. And assuming she feels the same, of course."

He turned his back on Logan, but he couldn't keep the words out of his head. That was the whole point, wasn't it? Whether or not she felt the same.

This wasn't the right time. He felt sure of it. And he didn't know if it ever would be.

CHAPTER SEVENTEEN

"THAT WASN'T SO BAD, was it?" Clint asked her the question once they were safely away from the police station where she'd been signing her statement the next day.

Rachel managed a halfhearted smile. "I guess not if you're used to police stations and people standing over you while you're signing a statement."

"This wasn't bad. You should see Phillips when he wants to be intimidating."

"No, thanks, I'll pass." She glanced at Clint as he stopped the car at a traffic light. "Thanks for going with me. I admit that made it easier, having you there."

"All part of the service."

The light changed, and he stepped on the gas. Rachel realized she was watching his strong, tanned hands on the wheel and focused her eyes on the road instead.

"So, was calling my family part of the service, as well?"

Clint gave her a wary look. "I wondered when that was going to come up. Are you mad at me?"

"I should be. But it was so good to hear their voices..." Her heart swelled at the memory. How could she ever think that she didn't have a home when she had them?

"I thought it might be." He sounded a bit smug.

"Yes, well, don't get too self-satisfied. I would have told them about it, but..."

"But you didn't want to alarm them, or make them worry or feel responsible," he finished for her.

"That's about it," she admitted.

"Isn't that what families are all about? Worrying, scolding, taking responsibility? Loving?"

She hated to admit just how right he was. "They were going to let Sadie come down here to stay with me. Can you imagine her leaving her kids just to keep me company?"

"She'd know that her children would be well taken care of while she was here." He grinned. "I could hear them arguing, each of them wanting to be the one who came. I might not understand Pennsylvania Dutch, but they sounded just like my family when they get going. I think Sadie won by having the loudest argument."

"I wouldn't be surprised at that." Her cousin was still one of her best friends, it seemed.

"Is she coming?"

"I managed to talk them out of it for the moment. I told them that Lyn is staying nights with me for now, and I hope to go back to teaching on Monday."

"Really?" Clint looked so pleased anyone would have thought it was his good news instead of hers.

"If nothing else happens," she added quickly. "It seems the substitute hasn't been working out too well, and Lyn was pretty persuasive. I just hope she's right."

Clint pulled into the driveway and stopped. "Mind if I come in? There's something else I'd like to talk about."

For some reason, Lyn's words about Clint popped to the forefront of her mind, and she felt a rush of heat to her cheeks. Turning her face away as she unbuckled her seat belt, she nodded.

"Sure, come in. There's probably some leftover pizza if you want it for your lunch."

"I'll pass on the pizza, but I wouldn't say no to a cup of coffee."

"I think I can manage that." Together they went into the house.

Rachel headed straight for the kitchen to start a pot of coffee, grateful for something to occupy her. Clint followed her, propping his long body against the counter and watching her.

"You said you had something else you needed to talk to me about," she reminded him.

"Yeah." He frowned. "Logan and I had a long talk after Attwood shut us down. We're not satisfied."

She nodded, trying to look intelligently interested, and she didn't know whether to be sorry or relieved that what he had to say wasn't personal.

"I'm not either, but I don't see what you can do about it. I mean, if James won't pay you to continue..."

"Some things are more important than money. There are too many loose ends flapping in the breeze to suit me. And Logan," he added quickly.

"He won't give you access to any of the firm's records, will he?" Knowing Attwood's passion for secrecy, she was surprised they'd had any access to begin with.

"No, but he can't keep us from probing around. Somebody wanted to buy that flash drive from Paul, and something has happened to it. From what we understand, there would be a limited number of firms interested enough and cutthroat enough to do a deal with him. And to pursue him, and you, when he backed off, assuming that's what he did."

"I see. I'd like to believe that Paul reconsidered betraying his friends, but I don't know anymore. Maybe I never did know him. But you… Do you always go above and beyond what the client wants?"

He grinned. "Part of the service, remember?"

"Even if Attwood doesn't want that service?" She poured coffee into two mugs and handed one to him.

"Right at the moment I'm more concerned about your safety than his happiness." He sat at the kitchen table, and she slid into the chair at a right angle to him.

"I'm grateful. But things have been quiet. Maybe, whoever it is, he got what he wanted from Paul when he attacked him."

"Could be," he agreed. "Or he could have given up, thinking that the secret to where it is died with Paul."

"That's probably how it is," she said. She didn't like the idea of never knowing the truth about all of this heartache, but she might have to learn to live with it.

He shrugged. "I agree that's most likely, but I don't want to make any assumptions where your safety is concerned." He hesitated. "And there's another thing. That text, the one asking you to meet him."

It took a moment for his meaning to drop into place in her mind. "You think it may not have been from Paul?"

"I think it's a pretty close-run thing as to timing, and so does Phillips. Someone could easily have picked up Paul's phone and sent that text, ensuring you'd be the one to find him."

A shiver went through her. "Just out of meanness? Or was it intended to incriminate me?"

"Could be either way." His brown eyes darkened. "I don't like it."

"No. I don't, either." She rubbed her arms, chilled. "That's not a welcome addition to all the rest of the things I have to worry me."

"You're not stressing about the property, are you? That's the lawyer's job. Let him get on with it."

"Her," she corrected. "And actually, I've already talked to her this morning." She couldn't help brightening a little. "She has all the information together already from the divorce. And I'd forgotten, until she mentioned it, that if either one of us passed away before the house was disposed of, the other inherited their share."

"So the house is yours, free and clear? Smart attorney, getting that included."

"I think it's usual, from what she said." She hesitated. "But I suppose that's another reason for the police to suspect me."

"Not a very strong one, in my opinion. And with the timing working out the way it did, they'd never bring a case on that motive alone."

"I hope that's how they see it. But there's another piece of news. Paul had agreed to keep me the beneficiary of his life insurance for a period of time after the divorce. Just as a safeguard so I couldn't lose the house. So I wouldn't have to sell unless I wanted to."

"I see." He spoke slowly, and his mask was back in place, making her wonder what he was thinking. "It sounds as if your divorce was fairly friendly."

She winced a little at the words. "No divorce is really friendly, but I have to give Paul credit for what he did do. He was more thoughtful than I expected."

"He should have been, after what he'd put you through." He sounded impatient, or maybe annoyed.

"That's not really fair." Her temper flared. "You never even knew him. Besides, he's gone now, so..."

"So what?" Clint shoved his chair back and shot to his feet, setting the coffee mugs rocking. "So now he's an angel, just because he's dead? That doesn't change the fact that he made you a target."

She stood, as well, stiffening herself against the sudden attack. What was the matter with him? She'd thought he was understanding and fair, but he seemed to relish the idea of attacking Paul's character. It hurt, more than it should, and she knew why... Because she'd begun to trust him, maybe to love him. Was she just plunging in over her head again, making the same mistake of caring about someone without really knowing him?

She choked back her pain and disappointment. "I'm the one who's affected, not you."

"That's the way you want it, isn't it? You have to shut me out because you can't really trust anyone."

"That's not true. And you have no right to say it." Anger was the only thing that kept her from dissolving in a puddle of grief.

He just stared at her, his jaw clenched as if to stop him from saying anything else. Then he spun and walked out, leaving her trying to figure out what had just happened.

Rachel stood frozen for a few minutes, staring at the door that had closed behind Clint. She pressed her fingers against her temples, moving them in small circles in an effort to calm herself.

She hadn't meant that Paul was an angel. Far from it.

She was just beginning to grope her way toward forgiving him for what he'd done. She had to do that, for her own sake as much as for his. Clint didn't understand that… Why should he? She hadn't explained.

Had she been making excuses for Paul again? She didn't think so. She'd fallen into that trap too many times during their marriage.

Clint had taken what she'd said the wrong way. She managed to bring back that flame of anger at him. He didn't understand—no one could possibly understand unless they'd walked through this particular desert. Being married to an addict, no matter what the addiction, wasn't like anything else.

So many times she'd longed to see again the sweet, charming man she'd married. Sometimes she'd caught glimpses of the old him, when life was going well.

Be honest, she told herself. Those moments had come when he was winning. They hadn't lasted, because his streak of good fortune had never lasted.

Trying to shake off the feelings, she carried the coffee mugs to the sink and emptied them. Maybe she'd just been maudlin, and Clint had been justifiably impatient.

She could talk it over with Lyn when she returned this afternoon. Until then she wouldn't let herself think about it. She'd start a decent supper for the two of them. No more take-out food. There ought to be the ingredients for her favorite chicken and broccoli dish.

She bent to pull out the freezer door and something stuck between the refrigerator and trash bin caught her eye. Reaching in, her fingertips closed on the corner of a paper that must have missed the trash bin.

Someone rapped at the back door, startling her. The paper slipped from her fingers.

She went cautiously to the door. Mrs. Barton stood on the minuscule back porch, holding a covered plate. The woman smiled and waved one hand.

Taking a steadying breath, Rachel opened the door. "Mrs. Barton. How nice of you to come over."

Her neighbor stepped inside, pressing the plate she carried into Rachel's hands. "It's just some pumpkin muffins. We thought you might like to have something." Her blue eyes filled with ready tears. "We're so sorry about what happened to Paul."

So the news was out already. She'd have been naïve to think otherwise. "Yes, it was terrible."

"We were just so shocked." Mrs. Barton pressed her hand. "I know you weren't together any longer, but it's still just so sad."

Rachel nodded. It *was* sad. She'd been so battered by the rest of the circumstances that she hadn't come to grips with the simple sadness of a life cut short.

"Now, we don't want to intrude. You have friends and others who are helping you, I know. But if you need anything, anything at all, remember we're right next door."

After all that had happened, it was this small thing that brought her nearly to tears. "Thank you," she managed. "You're so kind."

"Not at all. That's what neighbors are for." Mrs. Barton turned, nearly stepping on the bit of paper on the floor. "Oops." She picked it up before Rachel could. "I'm so sorry. Goodness, I nearly stepped on your picture."

No, it wasn't paper. It was a photograph. One of the pictures from the folder she'd tossed.

Mrs. Barton took a quick glance before handing it

over, and her face grew more sorrowful. "I'll be off now." But she paused at the door. "It is sad, my dear, but you know, it doesn't do to dwell on the past. Take care." She slipped out, closing the door.

Ironic, given what she'd just been thinking. Mrs. Barton must have thought that she'd been looking through old pictures, mourning Paul. Maybe, eventually, she would have done so in normal circumstances, but nothing that had happened had been normal.

She glanced at the picture. The photo had been taken on their wedding day. She and Paul had stood, hand in hand, in front of the arbor by the lake.

Her throat tightened with tears she had no intention of shedding. They'd looked so young, so untried. The past few years had made their mark upon her face, if not on Paul's.

The small outdoor gathering place hadn't had anything remotely approaching an altar, but its benches faced the vine-covered arbor. They were standing behind the sundial that served as a focal point for the area.

Why a sundial? she remembered wondering at the time. And Lyn had pointed out the lettering around the edges: *Count only the sunny hours.* That was ironic, given how their marriage had turned out.

Still, those had been happy moments, full of promise for the future. She smiled, touching the photo lightly. Paul, eager to get the perfect photo setting, had grabbed the top of the sundial…the triangular blade that cast its shadow to tell the time. And it had pulled right out in his hands.

He'd turned red, grinning, standing there with the blade in his hand, revealing a small hole that its end slid into.

"You've done it now," she'd said, laughing. "They'll probably charge us for a new sundial."

"Not a chance." He'd plucked a tiny daisy from her bouquet and dropped it into the hole, then slid the end of the blade back in place. "See? Our wedding will be recorded there forever and a day."

Rachel looked at the photo for another moment. Then she dropped it back into the trash bin. The daisy might still be there, though she doubted it, but their marriage had certainly not lasted forever and a day. A few short years, most of them filled with the struggle to help Paul deal with his addiction. And then he'd wanted out.

Turning her back on the trash bin, she moved the chicken package to the refrigerator and looked for something to have for lunch. The leftover pizza was still there, but her stomach lurched at the thought of it. Maybe she'd wait until later.

Her cell buzzed, announcing a text, and she grabbed it. Clint? No, it was Lyn, asking what she should pick up for supper. She quickly texted the chicken plan and clicked *Send.*

For a moment Rachel stood, phone in hand, as another text filled her mind…the text from Paul with that odd reference to their wedding day. Her nerves began to tingle. Paul, desperate about what he'd done, had taken time to mention that day. To bring that place back to her mind. Why?

The idea was ridiculous. It didn't make sense. Paul wouldn't have, couldn't have, been telling her the location of the flash drive.

She could go and look. She rejected the thought as soon as it occurred. No, it would be foolish to get herself any deeper into Paul's mess. Besides, it wouldn't be there. It was a silly notion.

But it wouldn't leave her alone. If the flash drive were there… Well, what if it were? No one would find it. It could sit there until it disintegrated, and no one would ever know.

That was the coward's way. If it were there, she had to give it back to Attwood. Besides, she couldn't pass up the chance to get out from under it once and for all. No one could imagine she knew anything once the flash drive had been found and returned.

But would that be an end to it? Or would they assume she'd known all along where it was? Did she want to take that risk?

Her thoughts moved back and forth, unable to settle. Finally she shook her head. She'd put it out of her mind for now. Instead, she'd focus on preparing her lesson plans for next week. Then she'd cook Lyn a nice dinner, they'd sit and talk, and she'd concentrate on the future.

BUT THE NEXT MORNING, Rachel wasn't so sure of her decision. She and Lyn had had a pleasant evening, talking about the school, focusing on the future. But she hadn't brought up the situation with Clint, and she hadn't mentioned the photograph of the sundial.

Why not? She stared out the kitchen window at a gray wet day after Lyn had headed out to run some errands. She'd have said she could talk to Lyn about anything, and certainly she valued Lyn's common-sense approach to things, as well as her fierce partisanship of Rachel. But she hadn't told her.

Maybe because this was a decision she had to make

on her own. She could pretend she'd never had the thought about where the flash drive might be.

No, she couldn't. She'd spent too much time denying the truth—the truth about Paul's gambling, the truth about the mistakes she'd made. For someone who claimed to value honesty, that was a pretty sad admission.

She had to do something. The only question was whether she should look for herself or confide her suspicions to someone else.

If she drove out to the lake and checked, she'd know for sure whether this suspicion was fact. If she found nothing, she'd be relieved and she could forget it. But if she found the flash drive, then what? She'd be in possession of stolen property, making herself a target again.

Call Clint. Rachel reached for her cell phone and stopped. She and Clint hadn't parted on good terms. Her chest felt tight suddenly, and she rubbed it, as if she could rub away the ache. She wanted to make that up—to explain, if she could, why she'd said what she did about Paul.

If she called him with this…after the things she'd said… She hated to turn to him with yet another problem. Rachel rubbed her forehead, tired of the direction of her thoughts.

She and Clint had been brought together because of Paul. She wanted to believe that they had found something beyond that, but it was hard—hard to imagine a relationship with Clint where Paul was no longer a factor.

Still, he was involved. She'd have to call and let him know. And somehow try to do it without thinking of the quarrel that had sent him out of here in such a temper.

It was the right thing, so she'd do it. She picked up the phone.

After all her rationalizing, it was disappointing to find herself sent straight to voicemail. She hesitated, but she'd have to say something. He'd know she'd called. But to tell him the whole thing in the message—no, that wouldn't work. So leaving a message saying that there was something she wanted to tell him, she hung up.

Clint wasn't available, but the itch to do something grew worse. What about Ian? He had offered to be a go-between, making peace between Paul and Attwood. Did that still apply now that Paul was gone?

Assuming she found the flash drive, Ian could advise her on the best course. Should she return it to James Attwood? Or would it be better, since he'd already declared it was worthless, simply to destroy it?

Without giving herself time to consider it any further, she spun and hurried into the bedroom. She'd dress, drive down to Attwood Industrial and sound out Ian. Then she'd have a better sense of what to do. If the flash drive was hidden in the base of the sundial, it certainly wasn't going anywhere. She had time to make the best decision.

By the time Rachel reached the offices she was firm in her mind about what she intended to do. Unfortunately, she still couldn't prevent the spasm that gripped her stomach at the very thought of walking inside.

Never mind. She'd get through this as she'd gotten through everything else. At least then, the whereabouts of that flash drive might no longer be hanging over her. She could settle the remaining business resulting from Paul's death and then be able to move on.

What that moving on would look like, she wasn't

sure. She had thought…hoped…that it might include Clint. In any event, it would certainly include more time spent at Echo Falls. Thanksgiving break would be here before she knew it, and she could go home for several days.

Maybe, as her grandfather had suggested, she might bring someone with her.

She didn't recognize the receptionist in the lobby, but after a brief phone conversation, the young woman directed her upstairs. Just as if she'd never been here before.

In a way, that was a relief. She'd probably have enough knowing glances once she reached the offices.

As luck would have it, the outer office was empty except for Ian, who'd obviously been waiting for her.

"It's good to see you." He flushed slightly. "I'm so sorry—we should have come to see you, to find out if you needed anything, but…"

"Don't worry about it."

She suspected he hadn't been that eager to align himself with her, given what had happened. That hadn't occurred to her. Was she really that naïve? He might very well prefer to know nothing at this point.

But she was here now, and she'd go through with it.

"I'm sorry to bother you at work, but something has come up that I'd like your advice about."

"I…" He cast an apprehensive glance at Attwood's office door and then took her arm. "Come into my office so we can be private."

Once inside, Ian closed the door with something that looked like relief. His office was a replica of what Paul's had been, but where her picture had sat on Paul's desk, Ian had a photo of himself with Julie and the baby, to say nothing of the row of pictures of their little one, which decorated the top of the bookshelf. There must be a new one for every month of her young life.

She turned back to Ian, noticing the way he still stood by the door. Was he hoping she'd go right back out again?

"I'm sorry." The impulse to apologize overtook her. "I shouldn't have come. I'm sure at this point no one here wants to be associated with me."

To do him justice, Ian looked embarrassed. He gave a rueful smile, relaxing a little. Pulling out two leather-padded visitors' chairs, he gestured her to a seat and took the other one.

"No, I'm sorry. James has just been in such a mood lately that no one knows which way to jump. But we're friends. Tell me what's going on."

For an instant, sitting bolt upright on the comfortable chair, she was tongue-tied. How to begin a story like this one? The only way was to come right out with it.

"Something occurred to me last night having to do with the location of that flash drive Paul had." She hesitated, startled by the shock on Ian's face. But then they, like her, had assumed the flash drive was gone for good with Paul's death.

"You know where it is?" He cast an apprehensive look behind him, as if to be sure the door was completely closed. "Do you have it?"

"No, no, nothing like that. I'm not even convinced myself that this means anything, but once I thought about it, I…well, I couldn't just ignore it."

"I suppose not," he said, but his expression belied the words.

She drew in a breath, trying to relax taut muscles. This was proving to be harder than she'd expected.

"The last text I received from Paul..." Well, the last one that she was certain had actually come from Paul. "It contained something that struck me as a little odd. It's stuck in my mind, and I started wondering if he meant it as a way of telling me where the flash drive was."

Ian was frowning. "But... Forgive me, Rachel, but why would Paul want you to know? I'm sure you had nothing to do with his taking the information, so I wouldn't think he'd involve you that way."

"I wish he hadn't, believe me. It seems to me that he might have seen it as a sort of safety precaution. If something happened to him, I mean."

Her throat tightened as the image of Paul, lying on the bedroom floor, flooded her mind. She fought back nausea at the vivid sight and scent of the blood.

Ian, preoccupied with his own thoughts, didn't seem to notice her reaction. "I see. Yes, that would be like Paul. He'd know that you would do the right thing if you found it."

"I hope so. The trouble is knowing what the right thing is. If, of course, it's there at all."

"Where? You haven't told me what Paul said, or where you think he'd pointed you."

"I haven't, have I? I'm afraid my mind is spinning too much to make sense. In his text, Paul made reference to our wedding. It seemed out of context, somehow. Why would he, when he was involved in such a mess?"

Ian nodded. "The park by the lake. But I still don't get it. How could he put something there and trust it would be undisturbed for several weeks. Surely that's risky."

"Yes, but he may have felt desperate enough to take a chance. And there is one spot…" She stopped, having a belated onset of caution. Perhaps it was safer not to be too explicit. She trusted Ian, but even so, she ought to be cautious.

"That's okay," he said quickly. "Come to think of it, I don't want to know. That might be the best thing for you, too."

"You mean pretend I never thought of it, don't you?" She was disappointed, but she understood. Ian probably didn't want to be handed a hot potato, either.

Ian fidgeted with his wedding ring. "Honestly, I think that might be best. James seems satisfied that it's never going to show up. Now that Paul is gone, well, I'm afraid it's been a relief to him. The whole thing is over with as little publicity as possible."

What he said made perfect sense. It was the logical thing to do. Unfortunately it was the one thing she knew she couldn't live with.

"You're probably right, but I think I have to look."

Ian looked as if he'd expected it. "That's your decision."

"You don't understand. I'm not being sentimental. I'm being realistic. As long as the flash drive is thought to be out there, I remain a target for anyone who wants it."

"Oh, but surely…"

"Ian, my house has been searched repeatedly. I've been attacked twice. I can't live this way."

Now she'd startled him. "Rachel, I had no idea you'd been attacked. I'm so sorry. I can see why you feel that way. But if the flash drive is there, what are you going to do with it?"

"That's the question. The only way for me to be clear of the situation is for it to be known that it's found. So should I turn it over to Attwood? Or to the police?"

He frowned, and she thought he was torn between what he thought was best for his own position and his affection for her. After a long moment he spoke.

"Honestly, Rachel, I'm not sure. Will you give me a chance to think about it? After all, if you don't find the drive, then it's a moot point."

Ian, passing off responsibility as quickly as possible—she wasn't really surprised. Paul had always said that was his pattern. She had a fleeting thought of Clint, who never handed off unpleasant jobs to anyone.

"Maybe that would be best." *For you.* She rose. "Thanks, Ian. I'll let you know what I find."

He nodded. "But...don't come here. Call me on my private cell, all right?"

Very eager not to accept responsibility, it seemed. "Yes, all right. Thanks."

She went out quickly, not waiting for him to escort her. The outer office was still empty and quiet, and she hurried downstairs and out to her car.

Once there, she thought for a moment. *What next?*

Clint. Whatever he might think about it, he wasn't a man to pass off responsibility, and she wanted someone to know where she was going. More to the point, she wanted someone with her.

She called again, but the phone still went to voicemail. Rather than leave a message, she texted him quickly, telling him where she was going and why. With what must have been the final bit of battery, the text sent, and then the phone shut down.

Great. She hadn't charged it the previous night. But she'd had considerably more on her mind at the time, as it happened.

It didn't matter. Clint knew where she was going. All she had to do was see if the drive was there. Then she'd turn it over to Clint, tell him what Ian had said, and let them take over disposing of it. Dropping the phone in her bag, she headed for the lake.

CHAPTER EIGHTEEN

CLINT WAS STILL feeling frustrated and annoyed with himself as he drove to Attwood Industrial the day after that stupid conversation with Rachel. He should have been more sensitive. That didn't seem to be his strong suit, especially when he found himself wanting to hit anyone who'd hurt her.

What was it with him? Was he really that jealous of her ex? That was ridiculous. But he'd let a few kind words send him into a tailspin, mainly because he still didn't know where he stood with her.

Worse, he'd let his own feelings get in the way of doing his job and also in the way of helping Rachel. All right, so he was upset to think she was still hung up on her late husband. He didn't have the right to let that interfere with being a friend when she needed one.

Now, thanks to his hasty words, she probably wouldn't turn to him when she needed help.

He drew up on the side street next to Attwood Industrial. No sense in advertising the fact that he intended to catch Claire Gibson when and if she went out to lunch. Logan said she'd been doing a great job of avoiding his calls. Well, she couldn't avoid him if he was right there, and if she knew anything, he wanted to know it.

He'd settled himself for a wait, parked where he could see both the parking lot and the front entrance to the building. At least the rain had stopped, so his visibility wasn't obstructed. The heavy rain clouds looked ready to drop another load any minute, though, and the streets were already slick with wet fallen leaves.

His cell phone buzzed, and he yanked it out. He'd missed a call from Rachel at some point, and also had a message from her—ridiculous to feel exhilarated because she was contacting him, wasn't it? He scanned the text, his earlier joy replaced by growing fear for her. She'd been here, but she'd left, heading for the place where she and Paul had been married. She thought the flash drive might be there.

Why? Where? He hit the steering wheel in frustration. He remembered the photos, all right, but she hadn't mentioned specifically where the wedding had taken place. A lake, a park, outside the city…but where?

He started to call her, but glanced up first just in time to see Ian Robinson's car pull out of the lot. Startled, he saw it wasn't Ian driving. It was James Attwood.

Instinct sent alarms racing through him. This didn't feel right. He pulled out as soon as traffic passed and followed Attwood at a safe distance. Once he felt convinced he was headed for the Schuylkill Expressway, he picked up the phone again and called Rachel.

No answer. And he remembered her saying, on that drive back to Philly, that she never used her cell phone while driving. When the phone went to voicemail he left a quick message, then followed it up with a text, basically saying *where are you* and *don't do anything until I get there.*

He'd like to believe she'd listen. In the meantime, his instincts told him to follow Attwood, to see what he was doing slipping off in the middle of the day in someone else's car. Something wasn't right about that, and Rachel was out there somewhere by herself.

Following Attwood worked out fine, right up until the time he lost him. A fender bender right in front of him caused an inevitable delay, and by the time he was clear, the car was nowhere in sight. Attwood could have turned off at any one of several exits.

All right, so he'd find out where Rachel was another way, since she hadn't called back. He punched in the number for Lyn, waiting impatiently. If she were in the classroom or doing any one of a hundred things she might be doing, she wouldn't answer.

But she did.

"This is Clint. Quick, tell me where Rachel and Paul got married."

Inevitably she said, "Why?"

"Just tell me. It's important."

The strain in his voice must have gotten through to her.

"Bentwood County Park. Out on…"

"Yeah, I know it." He hung up.

He pulled off at the next exit, mentally plotting a course to the park. *Think.* Why did he have this sense of urgency? Was it justified or an overreaction?

Rachel thought she knew where the flash drive might be. Instead of waiting until he could deal with it, she'd headed out on her own. He couldn't deny that she was a strong woman for all her obvious gentleness. But in this case she may have taken on more than she could handle.

Okay, think. So she'd gone to see Ian, someone she considered a friend of Paul's. Why? Obviously for some reason connected with the flash drive. If she'd told him where she thought it was…

But in that case, why was Attwood the one who seemed to be following her? The possibility came clearly. Because Attwood was the one primarily concerned with the flash drive. Either Robinson had told him or he'd learned some other way what Rachel intended.

It might be perfectly innocent. He could have made arrangements to meet Rachel there so that she could turn over the flash drive to him. But his gut told him it wasn't that easy.

He didn't like James Attwood—hadn't from the beginning. The man struck him the wrong way. But that didn't mean he was up to something underhanded. After all, why would he be? He'd already said he'd found a flaw in the design, rendering the flash drive worthless. Whatever the pot of gold invention that Paul had expected to share in, this apparently wasn't it.

That set up another train of thought. Rachel had said that there had been an agreement among the four of them to share the fruits of Attwood's ideas. According to Claire, that agreement had been superseded by the time the company was successful. But what exactly had that agreement said?

He called Logan, quickly told him where he was and what was going on. "Listen, maybe I'm jumping the gun, but I don't like this situation. Get hold of either Robinson or the Gibson woman and press them for exactly what was in that original contract that the four of them signed."

"Any leverage I can use to get them to cough it up?" Logan asked only the pertinent question, sizing up the situation and trusting Clint's judgment.

"Probably not, but I'd say try Robinson first. He looks like the weaker link to me. He knows, if I'm not mistaken, what Rachel is doing. Press him on it. And if necessary, you might point out all those records you found that show him in posh hotels when he should have been home by the fireside."

Logan grunted. "That should do it. I'll call you as soon as I have something."

Clint cut off the call without another word. They didn't need words—that was one of the great things about their partnership. If it could be done, Logan would do it.

In the meantime, he had to get to Rachel, but the rain had started again, inevitably slowing traffic and annoying drivers eager to get somewhere before rush hour. He gritted his teeth, clenching the steering wheel and glaring at the vehicle ahead of him, trying to deny the increasing sense of danger.

RACHEL KEPT REMINDING herself there was no hurry as she battled the rain and the traffic. Either the flash drive was there or it wasn't.

She turned off onto the narrow two-lane road that led into the park. Here, too, the rain and wind had stripped colorful leaves from the trees, changing them to a sodden brown slush underneath. The picnic groves were deserted, and it looked as if not a soul had ventured into the park on a day like this.

The road meandered its way through wooded areas. She passed the turnoff to the boat dock, and she could see, through the opening, the glint of the lake and the thin stripe of the walking trail that wound around the lake. The next turnoff should, if she remembered correctly, lead to the spot she wanted.

Yes, there it was. A rustic sign told her this was

the lane to the Willow Amphitheater, a rather generous term for the collection of benches facing the arbor and the lake. She pulled into the gravel parking lot and stopped, glad she'd worn a rain jacket with a hood. The driving rain had slackened to a chilly drizzle, but as she stepped out it managed to drip directly down the back of her neck.

After pulling the hood up, she locked the car and headed down the path, hands shoved in her pockets against the cold. Too bad she hadn't made up her mind to do this the previous day, when the sun had gilded the world with the golden glow of autumn.

Actually, now that she considered it, this was a better day for her task. She'd hardly have wanted families picnicking in the area when she was about to dismantle a park landmark.

When she stepped out into the clearing the lake spread out before her, gray and uninviting on such a dark, dreary day…so very different from the last time she'd seen it. Then the now-wet benches had been filled with friends, and sunlight had glinted off the water that sparkled in the background.

She and Lyn had come early to decorate the arbor with flowers before rushing off to change for the ceremony. Ian and Paul had been there supposedly to help, but mostly they'd clowned around and gotten in the way. Paul had been in such good spirits that day, filled with an elation and enthusiasm she'd seldom seen afterward except when he'd had an unexpected win on the horses or in a poker game.

It appalled her now to think of how long it had taken her to catch on to what was happening. How could she have been so blind? Apparently the initial bloom of love had that effect on even the sensible.

Rachel forced herself to walk steadily down the aisle between the benches where she'd once gone with a singing heart. Now that she was here, the weather actually seemed appropriate to her task. Finding the flash drive, holding in her hand the evidence of Paul's duplicity, would put a definite period to that part of her life.

A chill breeze ruffled the surface of the lake as she approached the sundial, sending up little whitecaps that chased one another across the water. She stopped, planting her hands on the rim of the sundial.

Count only the sunny hours. There had been few enough of them to count, as it had turned out. Today was yet another example—the sundial couldn't tell anyone the time today.

Taking a deep breath, she put her hands on the gnomon, the triangular blade that, when properly oriented, gave one a rough idea of the time on a sunny day. Paul probably hadn't noticed whether he'd put it back correctly. If not, some maintenance person may have come along and had it out again, exposing anything the lay beneath.

She twisted, lifting. Nothing. It didn't budge. Maybe it had been secured in place since that day. How deflating if, after all her talk, she couldn't even get it out.

The thought gave her strength, and she tugged at it again. It popped out so suddenly that Rachel stumbled back a step or two, gripping it in her hand.

For a moment she hesitated, feeling an irrational desire to put it back without looking, walk away and try to forget. But that was cowardly and probably impossible. She took a step forward and peered down into the opening.

She expected dirt, but it was surprisingly dust-free, apparently because it was such a tight fit. In the moment before her eyes adjusted, she thought it was empty. Then she saw. At the bottom lay the remnant of a withered flower, brown and disintegrating. And on top of it, in a plastic case, was a flash drive.

Steeling herself as if she had to touch something hot, she grasped the flash drive with her fingertips and pulled it out. For a moment her fingers lingered on the remnants of the flower. It would crumble to dust if she tried to take it out, just like the hope it had symbolized.

Withdrawing her hand, she stood looking for a moment at the small, innocent plastic case on her palm. She'd been right in what she'd felt. This really was hot, in the sense that it affected anyone who touched it. It may very well have caused Paul's death.

The voice from behind her had her hands closing over the drive.

"Rachel. So you knew where it was all along."

She spun around to find James Attwood standing not more than ten feet away from her. For an instant she could only gape. How had he known she was here?

Then the meaning of his words penetrated. "No, no, of course I didn't. I only realized it last night, when I started to think about that last text I received from Paul."

Behind the black-rimmed glasses he wore, James's eyes grew blank. "Asking you to meet him at his apartment? How would that bring you here?"

"Not that one. He'd messaged me earlier, referring to our wedding." She gestured, realizing she still held the triangular blade in one hand. "Here. You remember."

"Yes, I remember." He glanced around. "Looks a little different today."

She almost said that everything was different, but held her tongue. There were more important things than her particular failure.

"James, this proves it, doesn't it? Paul put the flash drive here, thinking it would be safe. Doesn't that show that he'd reconsidered? He wasn't going to sell it, after all."

He was looking at her hand…the one holding the flash drive. He seemed to force himself to focus on her words.

"I suppose. It doesn't matter now."

"It matters," she said, stung. "Paul may have been tempted, but in the end he didn't betray his friends. Please…there's no need for all of this to come out, is there?"

Again she had that sense that his attention was elsewhere. The silence was just a little too long before he answered. "No, of course not. You're right. It's best if it isn't mentioned again at all. I'll destroy the drive, and that will be the end of it."

"Good."

But it wasn't good. Something was off about this whole conversation. She stood there, fingers clamped around the drive, and listened to her instincts. Something was wrong.

"Give it to me." James held out his hand for the drive, taking a step closer.

A wave of fear flooded over her, and she knew what felt off-key. James had assumed she was talking about the message to meet Paul at his apartment when she'd spoken of the final text. How had he known about it? No one knew except Clint and the police, and she couldn't see them confiding in James.

He'd know if he were the one who'd sent it. A small voice in the back of her mind made the observation.

Impossible. What reason could he possibly have? But she couldn't ignore the impulse that had her gripping the flash drive so tightly she'd have to pry her fingers away.

"Rachel, give it to me, and I'll take care of it. You won't have to worry about anything coming out, I promise." He smiled, possibly meaning it to be reassuring, but the smile didn't reach his eyes. They were cold, very cold.

He took a step toward her, and she said the first thing that came into her mind.

"Clint is coming to meet me. I… We should wait for him."

The smile vanished. "I see. You don't trust me."

"It's not…" Her disclaimer vanished when he pulled a handgun from his jacket.

"I really am sorry, Rachel. I didn't want to do any of this." He must have seen her panicked glance toward the parking area. "Are you looking for your friend Clint? I'm afraid he won't be along. He was following me, you see, but I managed to lose him. He's probably sitting in traffic somewhere. So it's just the two of us." He raised the weapon, pointing it directly at her. "I don't want to use the gun. Just give it to me."

CLINT HEARD THE words as he neared the clearing. He froze, heart stopping. Rachel. He had to get to her. He took a few silent steps forward. He was nearly there, but not close enough. He moved cautiously behind the branches of an evergreen and looked toward the lake.

The scene spread out in front of him—the gray lake, the man with the gun and Rachel, standing by the cement sundial he'd seen in the photos, clutching something in her hand. Mind working feverishly, he calculated the distance between himself and Attwood, between Attwood and Rachel. Not good. If he tried to rush the man, Attwood would have plenty of time to get off a shot before he could get anywhere near him.

He was carrying, of course, but his weapon didn't seem likely to do him any good as long as Attwood's gun was trained on Rachel. Even as he thought that, he saw Rachel's face change as she spotted him.

Unfortunately, Attwood saw it, as well. Still holding the gun on Rachel, he looked back at Clint. Then he took a step closer to Rachel, aiming the weapon directly at her face.

"I might have known you'd get here. A little too soon, as it happens."

"James, this is crazy." The words burst out of Rachel. "We agreed to destroy the drive, didn't we? All I want is that Paul not be considered a thief."

"That's not what Attwood is worried about."

Clint took a step forward. Maybe, if they kept Attwood distracted, an opportunity would come to rush him. Or at least to get the weapon pointed at him instead of Rachel. He had to give her that chance.

"You think you've figured it out? I doubt it." Attwood had that superior attitude down pat. He honestly didn't think anyone else was as smart as he was.

"You want the file destroyed because if anyone else who understood it got a look, they'd recognize it for the breakthrough it is. Not the failure you've been trying to make everyone believe."

"Stop right where you are," Attwood ordered, and the expression on his face told Clint he'd been right. "Take your gun out very slowly with your left hand and toss it on the ground."

When Clint didn't obey instantly, Attwood's weapon moved a few inches closer to Rachel's face.

"Okay, okay, just back off." His fear for Rachel was nearly uncontrollable, but he had to master it. He had to push it to one side if he were going to find a way to save her.

Carefully, using two fingers, he took out his weapon. He held it at arm's length for a moment, and then tossed it to the ground about five feet in front of him.

While Attwood's eyes were on him, Rachel moved slightly to one side. Careful not to let his face betray him, Clint watched her. *Good. Get out of the line of fire. Get ready to run.* He willed the words at her.

But Rachel took a firm grip on whatever it was she held in her hand…a piece of the cement sundial, he realized. Heavy, capable of doing damage.

But not in her hands. He didn't want her taking any risks that might encourage Attwood to fire. In the instant Attwood glanced back at her, he shook his head slightly, hoping she got the message.

Don't. Don't do anything, not yet. Just keep talking. He thought the words so strongly it seemed he could see his message flying through the air to her.

"James, please stop this nonsense." She'd managed to keep her voice almost normal, and Clint felt a spurt of pride in her. She wasn't one to give up or get hysterical, not his Rachel.

Ignoring her, Attwood spoke to Clint. "You've become a problem. I thought, having hired you, I'd be able to control what you found out. I had to do something when the file was copied or it would have looked suspicious if anyone found out. But you pushed too far."

"That was a miscalculation on your part, wasn't it?" Antagonize the man? It was hard to figure how he'd respond, but Clint had to try. “But then, you’ve miscalculated right along, haven’t you? You thought that agreement you all signed way back when would get you what you wanted. You didn’t see it coming back to bite you in the end.”

“But I thought that contract wasn’t in force any longer,” Rachel protested, bringing Attwood’s gaze swinging back to her.

Good. We’ve got to keep him off balance. Rachel seemed to understand that.

“That’s what he wanted us to think, and he apparently convinced Claire Gibson of that. But Paul wasn’t one to let any profit slip through his hands, was he?” He forced Attwood’s attention back to himself. “He didn’t buy the story you tried out on him, the idea that the project wouldn’t work. So he took a copy to find out for himself.”

“Ridiculous.” He practically spat the word. “Paul was too stupid to analyze it himself. He thought he’d find an expert to tell him. Too many people would know. So I had to stop him. Told him I’d be happy to strike a deal if he would meet me at his apartment and how to avoid any of you seeing him… He admitted no one else had seen my work and didn’t realize how that made him expendable until it was too late. Like I said, stupid.”

“I must be stupid, as well, because I don’t understand. If this new project really was a breakthrough, why would you want to convince everyone it wasn’t?”

Rachel was doing her part, just as if they’d planned it. Clint edged a little closer…closer to Attwood, closer to his weapon while Attwood looked at her.

“You didn’t want to share, did you, Attwood?” He let his contempt show in his voice, hoping he wasn’t reading the man wrong. “You knew that the project had the potential for a big payoff, and under the terms of the contract you signed with the others, they'd share."

"Why should they get any of it?" He was angry enough to wave the gun so that it no longer pointed at Rachel's face. "They did nothing to earn it. I did all the work. It was my idea, not theirs."

"It was their work that allowed you to start the company to begin with," Rachel said.

"Right, but he didn't want to consider that part of it." Clint came back quickly, praying they were keeping Attwood off balance. "He probably intended to fake a crisis, let the company fold and then he'd be free to market his discovery and scoop the pot. Greedy, like I said."

"It's mine!" Attwood's icy control burst entirely. "This would have worked perfectly if it hadn't been for Paul. And then Rachel, showing up where she didn't belong. I had to find out what she knew and stop her from talking. Ian and Claire didn't know anything about it, and they'd believe anything I told them." He swung the weapon back at her.

"You were the one who searched my house. The one who attacked me." She flung the words at him.

"I had to find that drive. It's not my fault you got in the way. It's Paul's."

"Nice rationalization." He'd been focused on Rachel too long. "You can't admit it was your own trickery that did you in, can you?"

Attwood turned, aiming at him, regaining his calm. Too calm. He'd been waffling, not eager to take the last step—to kill two more people to keep his secret. But now he'd decided. Clint could read it in his eyes.

"No more talk. This ends now." The weapon was trained on him. Even a poor marksman couldn't help but connect at this range.

I'm sorry, Rachel. I'm so sorry. I let you down.

Attwood's finger tightened on the trigger. A flash of movement—Rachel raising the object in her hand, flinging it straight at Attwood.

It struck him full in the back of the head as the gun went off. Clint was already rolling to one side, hoping to dodge the shot, to buy Rachel a few more seconds of life. But it wasn't needed. Attwood crumpled face-down into the grass.

Clint's roll brought him to his feet again. Scooping up his own weapon, he darted forward, kicking the gun away from Attwood's hand. When the man didn't move, he bent to check him.

"I didn't kill him, did I?"

He looked up into Rachel's white face, then stood and held out his hand to her. "No, you didn't kill him. He's just knocked out." And that was too good for him, but Clint didn't suppose Rachel would want to hear him say that.

She came to him, looking down at Attwood with a dazed expression. "I didn't know what else to do. I couldn't let him shoot you. But I didn't want to hurt him."

"I know."

He understood. Rachel didn't want to hurt anyone, ever. It was one of the things he loved about her. He pulled her against him, feeling her body shake under the damp jacket.

"It's over," he murmured, pressing his lips against her forehead. "There's just all the mopping up to do. But you're free of it."

She turned her face so that her cheek rested against his. He wrapped his arms around her and held on tight, his heart swelling until he thought it would burst.

Finally he realized how cold she was. And how much remained to be done.

A time and place for everything, he reminded himself. This was definitely not the place or time to show Rachel how much she meant to him, not with Attwood lying unconscious at their feet.

"You saved my life. And your own. He couldn't afford to let us live, knowing what we did. You understand that, don't you?" He didn't want her ever feeling guilty over what she'd had to do.

"I know. I probably couldn't have done it otherwise."

He managed a smile, hoping to lighten the mood. "I never knew you had such a pitching arm."

Her smile wobbled a little, but it was there. "Kindergarten teachers have many talents. I keep telling you that."

"I believe it." He glanced down at Attwood again. By the look of him, they'd need an ambulance as well as the police. "I'll have to call this in. It's going to be a long day, I'm afraid." He nodded toward the benches. "Better sit down. This will take some time."

And explaining. He'd try Phillips first, he decided. At least he knew the background situation. And they had Paul's killer, although how they were going to prove it, he wasn't sure.

But Rachel was safe. His heart seemed to overflow as he looked at her, her wet hair clinging to a face as white as paper. They'd lived through it. And if she'd ended up saving him instead of the other way around… well, that didn't seem to matter much.

CHAPTER NINETEEN

THE NEXT HOUR passed in a haze for Rachel, with police coming and going, an ambulance, questions, questions and more questions. She held it together with the knowledge that Clint was by her side, sending out a constant flow of support that never varied, whether she seemed to need it or not.

At least Phillips knew some of the background, so the whole story didn't sound quite so fanciful. Even with that, so much had to be explained and gone through that her head had begun to spin.

She squirmed on the damp bench, and Clint put his hand over hers.

"Cold?"

"Down to the bone." She shivered. "Somehow I don't think I'll ever want to come back to the park."

Clint glanced around at the police activity. "Guess it's spoiled the memories you had of this place."

"That doesn't really matter." Her conviction surprised her. "I think…" She fumbled for the words. "What happened in the past affects me, but I can't let it run the rest of my life. That's up to me."

Phillips came back to them just then, so Clint didn't have time to answer, but he squeezed her fingers before letting go.

"Suppose we go back to the station. We could all

stand to warm up, maybe have some hot coffee, before we get to official statements."

Clint stood, drawing her up with him. "I'll drive Ms. Hartline and meet you there." His look seemed to challenge Phillips, but the man just nodded.

"My car is here..." she began.

"I'll have one of my people drive it back." Phillips held out his hand. "Your keys?"

After a startled moment, she handed them over. Did he want to search her car? He could feel free. Nothing there would contradict the truth, and that was what counted now, not that she was sure she understood it.

She could at least use the drive back to get an explanation from Clint of those extraordinary claims of his about Attwood and the contract. How could he know all that? When she started to climb into his vehicle, he stopped her with a hand on her jacket.

"Wait a minute. This thing is soaked. Do you have anything else in your car that you could put on?" At her blank look, he shook his head. "Never mind. Get that off. I've got a jacket in the back. You ride back to the station in that wet thing, you'll catch pneumonia." He caught her look and his eyes crinkled. "And yes, that's one of the things my mother always said."

She shed the jacket and changed into a warm, fleece-lined one that seemed to hug her when she pulled it around her and settled into the seat. Clint bent, and before she could stop him, he'd pulled off her canvas shoes.

"At least your socks are dry. I don't have an extra pair of those handy. Tuck your feet right under the heater. You'll warm up as soon as we get going."

She'd argue, but it hardly seemed worth it when he made her feel so good. Cherished. It was like coming into her grandmother's kitchen and feeling welcoming arms around her.

Once they were back on the main road, Rachel turned to him. "I've waited long enough. Explain, please. How did you know it was James?"

"I didn't, not for sure. But a lot of things just didn't seem to add up. And there you were, saying Paul wouldn't betray his friends." He darted a glance at her. "I'll be honest. I didn't want to believe anything good about him. But that seemed to ring true. He was a compulsive gambler, but he'd never messed with the company."

"No." She considered that. "He took from us, lied to me, but I knew he'd never do that to them." She grimaced. "That should have told me something a lot earlier than it did."

"Not your fault," he said. "You loved him."

"Partly my fault," she countered. "I loved the person I thought he was, and I let that blind me. I guess the truth is that everyone has to have something or someone to whom they'll always be true. We didn't happen to be that to each other."

"That doesn't mean it's impossible for you."

He was staring at the road, and she wasn't sure whether to take that as personally as she'd like. Maybe it was safer not to make assumptions, at least not at the moment, when they were coming off a pretty emotional experience.

"Was that all? That wouldn't lead you to James, in particular. It might have been Ian or Claire."

"I didn't forget about them." He darted a glance at her. "It may not have to come out, but the two of them have been having an affair for the past few months."

That stunned her into silence while she absorbed it.

"I guess, at some level, I'm not as surprised as I should be. But how could Ian risk losing his family that way?"

"He probably thinks no one will ever know." Clint shrugged. "Someone always knows. Anyway, once we understood what they were hiding, it seemed to me that they were preoccupied enough without getting involved in whatever Paul was doing. Then there was that old classmate of theirs I talked to."

It took a moment. "You mean the guy you went to see when you came to Echo Falls?"

"That's the one. He gave me an interesting perspective. Even granting that he wanted to make himself look good, it came through loud and clear that in his opinion, Attwood was only concerned with himself—his research, his ideas, his success. And that brought me back to that contract the four of them agreed to in order to start the company."

"I thought it no longer applied. That was what Claire said, anyway."

"Claire could have been persuaded to back up James on just about anything, I imagine. When you managed to vanish today—"

"I didn't vanish. I texted you to tell you where I was going."

"Where, as in where you and Paul got married. All I knew was that it was a park with a lake."

She closed her mouth on a retort. "I didn't think. It was so clear in my mind that I guess I thought you knew." She darted a look at him. "You seem to know everything else about me."

It was his turn to look at her, and his expression brought the blood to her cheeks. "Not everything," he said.

"Anyway, about the contract…" she said quickly.

"I told Logan to put pressure on Ian. Find out what you told him, where you were going and what the story was on that contract. Turns out that, despite the company being in Attwood's name, he was obligated to share the profits from any new invention with the other three. That was to be their reward for sticking with him instead on going on to lucrative jobs of their own."

"I see." She let her mind play around with that because it explained so much. That was Paul's pot of gold—the dream that was always just out of reach.

"As for what I told Attwood about Paul's motives in taking the flash drive...well, there was no way of knowing that for sure, but it seemed a likely possibility. At the moment I just mainly wanted to keep Attwood talking so he wouldn't start shooting."

She shivered. "I knew that was what you were doing. I was terrified you'd try to charge him and get yourself killed." Her voice shook a little. "I still can't believe we both got out of that in one piece."

"We're here. We're all right, and your nightmare is about over. As for us..."

Her heart gave a little leap and started fluttering. She couldn't—didn't want to—go there right now. Besides, they'd already reached the station.

"Look, there's Phillips gesturing to us. He must want you to park there."

Muttering something uncomplimentary about Phillips under his breath, Clint pulled into the parking space.

BY THE TIME all the questions were answered and statements signed, Clint suspected only willpower was keeping Rachel upright. He'd been thinking for the past few hours that once he took her home, he'd finally have a chance to tell her how he felt.

How could he? With everything else this day had brought, how could he put yet another emotional burden on her? After all they'd been through in recent weeks, Rachel might well have begun to loathe the sight of him.

At that moment she caught him watching her and smiled. It was a feeble effort, at best, given the fact that her face was white and strained.

Okay, so maybe he could eliminate the loathing part. That still didn't mean she'd want to hear it now. A rest from all this trouble, that was what she needed. A chance to get her life back. Then, maybe then, he could call her, ask her out and start to build a relationship with her that didn't depend on an investigation to get it started.

Phillips finally came out of the office he'd been holed up in for the past ten minutes. He gave Rachel a sympathetic glance, letting the real person slip from behind the police mask.

"You can leave now." His look included Clint. "Both of you. We have all we need for the moment. We'll be in touch."

"I bet you will." Clint look Rachel's arm. "Let's get out of here. I'll take you home."

"Just one thing," she said, holding back. "What's going to happen now about…well, all of it? The company, the new invention, the whole thing. If James goes to jail for Paul's murder…" She let that trail off.

Clint thought he knew what was worrying her. "You're thinking about all the people who depend on Attwood's."

"Ian, Claire, all the technicians—even Charlie, the

security guard. Do they just lose everything they've worked for?"

Phillips shrugged. "Not my department, I'm afraid. At a guess, someone could be brought in to manage it, or it may just fold. Like I say, not my area."

He turned away, and Clint squeezed her arm. "It's not your department, either. I know you're sorry for them, but none of it was your responsibility."

"I know. Really," she added, when he looked doubtful. "I just can't help caring about them."

"That's your specialty, isn't it?" He brushed a strand of hair away from her cheek. "Love and caring, given away without regard to worth."

"It's better than the opposite." She looked at him with those clear green eyes, deep as a silent pool.

"Yes." His hand lingered for a moment on her skin. "Yes, it is."

A door opened on the other side of the hallway, and he drew his hand away slowly as Claire Gibson came out, followed by Ian.

He gave the man a short nod. He supposed he should be grateful—at least Ian had come out with the truth when Logan pressed him, allowing Clint to work it out. Even so, he'd barely gotten to Rachel in time.

"Rachel." Ian stopped, looking at her, a mix of emotions chasing across his face. Embarrassment, shame, defiance...he couldn't seem to settle on one. "I'm glad you're all right. I'm so sorry I told James what you said. I—"

"You told him? So that he could come after me?" Her green eyes weren't so calm now.

"I didn't...I didn't realize what he was going to do.

Honestly. I just didn't want to take responsibility for the decision."

"No. You don't like to take responsibility, do you?" Rachel looked from him to Claire, who was already walking away.

Robinson flushed an unbecoming shade of red. "I don't… There's nothing serious between us. If we want to enjoy some time with each other, we can. We're both adults."

"You're an adult with a wife and a child."

His effort to justify himself collapsed abruptly. "You're not going to tell Julie, are you?"

"No. There's a big difference in telling you what I think and running to Julie with something that will only cause her pain. But that doesn't mean she won't find out. Do you want to lose them?"

There was nothing gentle and caring in Rachel's tone now. This was the part of her that wanted the truth at all costs. And Clint loved that about her, too.

Robinson blanched. "It's not that serious, really."

"To you, maybe. To Julie?" She turned away from him, back to Clint. "We can go now."

Clint nodded. "Right. Let's go."

Rachel was quiet all the way back to her house. Clint glanced at her from time to time, not sure whether he should speak or not. Finally he couldn't handle the silence any longer.

"Tired?"

She turned toward him, seeming to return from a distance. "A little. Mostly just…spent. Is it really over?"

This he could understand. He'd been there a time or two himself—that moment when you couldn't quite believe the trauma had ended and didn't know whether to count on it or not.

"Hard to believe, isn't it?" He considered. "It's over in the sense that the truth is out now. But there will still be legalities to go through. And if it comes to a trial, we'll have to get through it."

"If?" Anger flared in her eyes. "He's not going to get away with it, is he?"

"I hope not. Attwood will certainly be charged. But there's always the possibility he'll plead guilty to avoid a trial. Or that his attorney will strike a plea deal to let him plead guilty with a chance of parole after a good long time. You can never predict what a court might do."

"I'm not vindictive." She said the words slowly, as if she were feeling her way. "When I think about what he's done, it makes me angry, but if I've learned anything, it's that I can't let anger and disappointment affect the rest of my life." She looked at him, green eyes huge and serious. "Or guilt."

Clint felt as if she were looking right into his heart and seeing the pain and guilt that had taken up residence there after his partner's death. But like her, he'd come through it to the other side.

"You're going to be all right," he said. "So am I." Smiling at her, he pulled into her driveway.

Rachel sat still for a moment, and then she returned his smile. "Come in?"

In answer he got out, came around the car and clasped her hand as they walked to the door.

Once they were inside she turned to him, something questioning in her face. All the resolutions he'd made about taking it slow, giving her time, starting over…they just melted away. He drew her close, wrapping his arms around her and knowing he never wanted to let her go.

It was enough. In that moment it was enough just to hold her…to know she could step out of the cloud that had followed her and start to live again.

Finally she pulled back, just a little, studying his face. "Is this too soon? We've only known each other for a few weeks, but I feel as if we've always known each other."

"Me, too." He smoothed the hair back from her face. "We know the important things about each other. Nobody could go through what we did and not get that. The rest of it…" He cradled her face between his hands. "What kind of movies you like, your favorite foods, my pet peeves… We can catch up with those while we go along. Don't you think?" He couldn't help there being a little anxiety in the question.

"Yes, I think so."

He heard the confidence in her voice, saw it in her eyes, and knew it was going to be all right. He took a deep breath.

"I wasn't going to say this yet. I was going to take my time, move slowly, work up to it. But I can't. I love you, Rachel. I love everything about you, and when I know all there is to know, I'm just going to love you more." He paused for breath, hardly able to believe he'd said it. "Is that all right with you?"

"Oh, Clint." Her eyes were shining, so he knew she wasn't going to say no. "I was so confused, so sure I couldn't trust myself where men were concerned, and then you burst into my life at the worst possible time, and I finally got it. What happened in the past…it has nothing to do with us. With you and me. I don't need to go slow or be cautious. I already know everything that's important about you, and I love you."

Hands on either side of his face, she drew him down for a kiss. Somewhere in the midst of all the rockets that were going off he felt it—felt the solid sureness that this was right. He'd nearly messed it up by his stupid jealousy of Paul, but Rachel seemed able to forgive him, maybe because she'd come to terms with the past. They both had.

This was good, and it was forever.

EPILOGUE

RACHEL LIFTED A massive bowl of mashed potatoes over the heads of Daniel and Thomas as they ran through the kitchen. The aroma of roasting turkey filled the whole house, proclaiming that it was Thanksgiving. A day for giving thanks, and she had so much to be thankful for.

The kitchen was filled with women, but Sadie had everything organized. Each person had a job to do, and if she could do it and talk at the same time, so much the better. Her cousins and their wives were here, leading a horde of small children being corralled outside for the moment. Rachel exchanged a smile with her aunt, home at last after superintending the arrival of her new grandchild.

She held her breath as Sadie's boys scooted around Grossmammi, who was sprinkling brown sugar over the top of the sweet potatoes, but her grandmother had long experience in avoiding small children while cooking.

"Out, out." She waved her hand at the boys, who were suffering from the usual overexcitement of the entire family gathered for Thanksgiving.

Clint, grinning, picked up one boy under each arm and carted them toward the door. "Let's go, guys. We're in the way, and that only leads to trouble. If you want your share of a drumstick, you have to leave the cooks alone."

They probably didn't understand the English words, but they caught the meaning, giggling as he hauled them out into the crisp November sunshine to join the other young ones.

Grossmammi looked after them for a moment, smiling, and then turned the smile on Rachel. "You've got yourself a gut man there, Rachel. Don't you let him go."

"I won't, believe me." She hugged her happiness to her heart. To be here, with the family she loved, celebrating, and to see how they loved and accepted Clint—what more could she ask of life?

Sadie shook her head. "Ach, Rachel, don't stand there in a lovesick haze. We've got to get this food on the table while it's hot." But she scolded with an understanding smile, and the other women smiled. Sadie understood. Even better, Sadie was happy for her.

They all were, she knew. She'd been restored to her right place in the family.

Maybe, if life had gone on the way she once thought she wanted, she'd never have come home again. She wouldn't have been a part of this, and all through her own foolishness.

What's more, she might never have met Clint, never have had the love that filled her life and spilled over onto everyone she met.

But Sadie was determined not to let anyone stand around and think when there was a meal to serve. Rachel was swept into carrying food to the tables, set up everywhere a table could be squeezed in. With this number of people, it had to be done. Grossmammi was determined that they wouldn't eat in shifts. They'd all sit down together and give thanks.

She was surveying a table to be sure everything was

there when someone moved behind her. She knew without looking that it was Clint.

He rested his hands on her shoulders.

"This is the first real Thanksgiving I've had since I left home," he said. "I'd forgotten how much I was missing."

She put her hands over his. "That first of many real celebrations to come. Did you get through to your mother on the phone?"

"I called. Mom and Dad's place sounded about like this, and I'm sure I heard Dad arguing with someone about who would get the drumstick. They send their love." His breath touched her cheek. "I told them you sent yours right back."

"Good. Did you tell them we'd be there for Christmas?"

He laughed, low in his chest. "I thought Mom was going to come right through the phone, she was so delighted. Of course she made noises about how maybe we wanted to have our first Christmas in our own home together, but I could tell she didn't mean it."

"That does sound tempting." She leaned against him, just for a moment. "But it's important that we go to them this year. Besides, I want to experience all of your family's traditions."

"Fine. Just don't let Mom convince you to try some lutfisk, or you'll regret it."

"Lutfisk? That's a new one on me."

"Mom's family is Swedish. It's a tradition. And before you say you want to experience it, let me warn you it tastes like rotten fish."

She laughed. "You've convinced me."

Clint drew her a little closer, so that she could feel

the steady beat of his heart. “We’ll have lots of celebrations ahead of us. Time to blend a lot of traditions together and maybe invent some new ones of our own. A lifetime of them.”

A lifetime of celebrations with the man who loved her—what more could anyone ask? Grossmammi would remind her that everyone got their share of sunshine and shadows, and she didn’t doubt that there would be difficult times. But whatever came, they’d meet it together.

Together, bonded in a love and a promise she could trust forever.

* * * * *

HOUSE OF SECRETS

CHAPTER ONE

CATHERINE MORLEY STARED in frustration at the black wrought-iron gates of the property known as Morley's End. *Frustration* had been the key word of this entire trip. Her flight from Boston had been delayed, the car rental people at the Savannah had been extremely polite but also extremely slow, she'd gotten lost twice finding St. James Island and now the caretaker, promised by her late great-aunt's attorney, wasn't here to let her in.

She reached in the car window to hit the horn. Its blare sent birds fluttering from the branches of the live oak that overhung the gate, making the Spanish moss sway as if it were alive. The lush, secretive maritime forest had frightened her on her one previous visit as a confused eight-year-old, sent away to a great-aunt while her parents tried futilely to patch their broken marriage. She wouldn't allow it to frighten her now.

Still, Catherine couldn't help glancing over her shoulder. She'd turned off the main road, where the new vacation houses of the wealthy had changed this end of the island beyond all recognition with their manicured grounds that tamed the teeming low-country growth. And then there was Aunt Henny's place—thirty acres of prime building land and beachfront, enclosed by an uncompromising metal fence.

The stone pineapples on the posts at either end of

the gate were hidden by rough wooden boxes, painted with a stark message. *Keep Out!* Typical Aunt Henny. If Catherine were safely back in Boston dealing with the multiple responsibilities of being a junior partner in her father's law firm, she'd find it amusing. Since she was here, executor of Aunt Henny's estate and unable even to get inside, it wasn't funny.

But there, finally, was the caretaker, ambling toward the gate as if he had all the time in the world at his disposal. She resisted the impulse to blast the horn in his ears and contented herself with a glare that would have dented an alligator's hide. It didn't seem to have any noticeable effect on him. Six feet of solid muscle, marred by a faint limp, thick black hair countered by a pair of the bluest eyes she'd ever seen, a lazy smile that seemed to find amusement in the sight of her standing hot and fuming in front of the closed gate—this didn't look like any handyman she'd ever seen.

"I expected you to be here to open the gates when I arrived." She matched him stare for stare. "My aunt's attorney assured me I wouldn't have any trouble getting in."

"Relax, sugar. Henny always said you'd hurry yourself into a heart attack if you didn't learn to slow down." He pressed a hidden button and the gates slid smoothly back.

She bit back a retort about his use of her aunt's first name. Henny had been the eccentric one of her father's family, causing her Boston relatives endless embarrassment over her antics. It would be like her to be on a first-name basis with the help. "Thank you," she said shortly. "Has Mr. Adams arrived yet?" Why had the attorney insisted on meeting her here rather than at his office in Savannah? Surely that would have been easier for him, and then she could have visited the house alone and said goodbye to her aunt in her own way.

He nodded, so she yanked the car door open and got in. Before she could turn the ignition, the caretaker had reached the passenger's side and slid in next to her. He gave her a bland smile that didn't quite mask the impression that he knew something about this situation she didn't. "Might as well ride back as walk," he drawled. "I don't reckon you mind, do you, Miz Catherine?"

Up close she could see the scars, white against the tanned skin, running down his right leg from khaki shorts to battered sneakers. She looked away, but not before she caught the tightened lips that said he'd caught her staring. "That's fine. But the gates—"

He held up the remote in his hand. "Got it covered, sugar."

"Don't call me that," she snapped, and something about the words seemed oddly familiar, as if they'd had this exchange before. She drove through, the gate closing smoothly behind him. Closing them in. The tangle of dark pines, gnarled live oaks, dangling moss and dense undergrowth crowded the car, and the lush, fecund smell of the salt marsh stirred memories—of herself, too high on the wide branch of an oak, of a boy's laughter as he teased her to get down.

She stopped the car and frowned at him. "Who are you?"

"Just call me Nathan, ma'am." He accentuated the drawl to the slow trickle of molasses.

"Nathan Corwin." She said the name slowly. One of her aunt's eccentricities had been to keep her own name through two marriages. The fact that both husbands had been wealthy had alleviated the embarrassment slightly in her family's view. Daniel Corwin had been her second husband, coming into the marriage with a son. Nathan. "Why are you pretending to be a handyman? Just out of a need to embarrass me? As I recall, that was one of your many talents." She'd been eight, so he must have been ten—an age to resent having an unknown little girl foisted on him as a relative-by-marriage he had to entertain. He'd coped by tormenting her with typical little-boy tricks.

His dark brows lifted. "Looks like little Cathy has developed a sharp tongue. Guess that goes along with being a Boston lawyer." He shook his head. "Disappointed Henny, that did. Figured it meant you were turning out just like your father."

"That's none of your business, even if you are my—" She stopped, unable for a moment to put a name to their relationship.

"Step-uncle, maybe?" he drawled. Yes, definitely laughing at her.

"We aren't related at all, so drop it. You still haven't told me why you're pretending to be Aunt Henny's handyman. The last I heard, you were working in Atlanta." And that had been ages ago. Obviously something had changed in Nathan's life.

"I happen to be a very good handyman. And, to use your elegant words, anything else is none of your business." The undertone of bitterness in his voice silenced any retort.

"Fine." She reached for the gearshift. His hand closed over hers, sending an unexpected jolt of warmth up her arm.

"Wait a second." He took his hand away slowly, the

movement almost a caress. "There's something you have to know before you go up to the house and face Henny's lawyer and her other relatives-by-marriage."

She glanced at him, and the intensity in those deep blue eyes had her suddenly breathless. "What?"

"Your aunt's will has disappeared. And I don't buy the idea that her death was natural."

CHAPTER TWO

CATHERINE'S HEAD WAS throbbing in time with the babble of voices that had followed the announcement by her aunt's attorney. The will had, indeed, disappeared.

Bradley Adams, the lawyer, sat behind the massive mahogany desk in the room Aunt Henny had called her workroom. It had certainly never been a formal parlor. The desk surface still held stacks of books, papers, magazines, a basket of yarn and knitting needles, and a half-finished piece of needlework. Across the room, the latest flat-panel television was flanked by a dartboard and an easel, and the walls held everything from faded prints to garish posters. Aunt Henny might have been eighty-two and in poor health from diabetes, but she'd never lost her interest in everything and everyone.

Catherine cleared her throat. "Surely you have a copy of my great-aunt's will."

Adams's shock of white hair, bushy white brows and drooping moustache hid his expression to some extent. "Your aunt was a very strong-willed woman. She wished to have the only copy. I've looked in all the obvious places, but I haven't found it."

The rambling old beach house had a dozen or more rooms, attics, walk-in closets with hidden panels and a widow's walk that gave a view of the ocean. It had been Nathan's father's house, she remembered, brought by him into the marriage and renamed Morley's End in honor of Aunt Henny. Now his son claimed to be the handyman. She looked for Nathan and found him across the room, leaning against the fireplace with his arms crossed over his chest. Their gazes locked. Clashed, and again she felt that odd sensation of warmth, as if they were connected.

"Still, you must know what was in it." Flora Judson leaned on the desk, hands planted. "You can tell us. We're all family."

Not exactly, Catherine thought. Flora was the niece of Henny's first husband, a stout, motherly woman who'd been a nurse and had done her best to take care of Aunt Henny, she said, during her final illness. Unfortunately, Flora's motherly instincts seemed wasted on her only child, Bobby Jon, a surly, tattooed teenager.

"Mr. Adams can't tell us. It wouldn't be ethical." The third member of the trio spoke up with an apologetic smile. Clayton Henderson was Bobby Jon's cousin, but probably neither of them took any pleasure in that. Clayton's lightweight suit was immaculate in spite of the humidity of the May afternoon, and the stylish cut of his blond hair and his finely groomed hands made him look as if he'd just stepped from an expensive salon. "I may just be an accountant, not an attorney like Cousin Catherine, but I know that."

So she was Cousin Catherine now. Everyone seemed to be eager to get along with her, probably because as executor of the estate, they assumed she wielded some power. Everyone except Nathan, she amended. He wasn't any more conciliatory now than he had been at ten. And as for that outrageous claim of his—

Still, he'd been right about one thing. The will was

missing, and whatever hope she'd had of winding things up quickly had vanished along with it.

"It not only wouldn't be ethical," Adams said. "It would be fruitless. According to witnesses I've spoken with, the will Henrietta made in my office wasn't her last. She made and signed another will just a month ago. If we find it, it is the valid will."

Flora turned an alarming shade of purple, but before she could speak, Bobby Jon slouched toward the door. "I'm outta here, Ma. I'll wait in the car."

Adams stood. "I believe it's time we all left. Catherine must be tired from her trip, and until she finds the will—one of the wills—we can do nothing."

His words only increased her headache, but at least the others began moving toward the door. She needed a bit of peace and quiet to consider what she had to do. Call her father, that much was obvious, and tell him her absence would be extended.

Flora paused next to her, looking as if she'd hug her but only patting her arm. "I left some food in the refrigerator, and if you need anything, you call me." She tilted her head closer to Catherine's. "You want to be careful, with that Nathan staying so close in the caretaker's cottage. Maybe I should stay here with you."

"No. Thank you," she added. That was the last thing she wanted. "I'll be fine."

Flora shook her head, graying locks bobbing. "Just lock your doors." She darted a glance at Nathan. "That boy can't be trusted. Your aunt knew that—they fought somethin' fierce. And she made him stay out in the cottage, not in the house."

Saying she could take care of herself wouldn't allay

Flora's fears, but Catherine wasn't afraid of Nathan. He was annoying, not dangerous.

Finally they were all out. All except Nathan, that is. He left his guarded position by the fireplace and approached her. "I saw dear Flora getting in her two cents' worth. I trust she warned you against me. Would you like me to put an extra chain on the door?"

"That won't be necessary." She hesitated and then made up her mind. "Look, I know you've never liked me, and there's no reason to start now. But I'd like you to level with me. Why did you say you think there's something wrong about Aunt Henny's death?"

He frowned, dark brows drawing down over those very blue eyes. His stubble of beard was dark against his tanned skin. "This." He gestured. "All this mix-up with the wills. I know it doesn't look like it, but Henny was very organized about business. She wouldn't have left things in a mess for you to clear up."

"She may have thought she had time to get things in order." Sorrow tightened her throat. She would like to have said goodbye. She would like to have done a lot of things differently. "Maybe she didn't realize how sick she was."

"Maybe." But his tone said he doubted it. "Listen—" He touched her wrist, and then released it as if it were hot. "Lock your doors tonight. Put the chain on."

It was the same advice Flora had given, but she'd been talking about him. Nathan slouched toward the door, the limp a little more pronounced.

"What did you and Aunt Henny quarrel about?" she asked impulsively.

"None of your business." His smile took the sting out. "And you were wrong about one thing, Cathy."

She blinked at the effect of that smile. “What?”

“When you said I never liked you. I did. I still do.” He went out, closing the door.

CHAPTER THREE

Catherine leaned her elbows on the windowsill of the room she'd occupied as a child and looked out at the sultry southern night. After she'd eaten Flora's sandwiches and had a glass of too-sweet tea, she'd started searching the workroom. She'd gotten through one set of shelves before the exasperating call from her father. How did he expect her to have prevented Aunt Henny's shenanigans with the two wills?

The glow through the trees had to be Nathan's cottage. She thought again how odd it was that he lived in the handyman's cottage of the estate that had been his father's. Unfair, but surely Aunt Henny had a good reason for that. She'd never been unkind.

Beyond the pale strip of beach, the dark sea moved restlessly. A vague memory of Nathan and a tidal pool teased her mind. She slid into bed, reaching for Aunt Henny's Bible. She'd brought it from Henny's bedside table. Struggling to keep her eyes open, she slid back against the pillows. The Bible slid from her hands.

A sharp noise roused her from a foggy, frightening dream in which she struggled desperately toward someone—or was it away from someone? She couldn't seem to remember. Then she heard the sound again and realized it was the doorbell.

She tried to focus on the clock. Three in the morning, and the doorbell pealed. Something wrong. She stumbled out of bed, dragging her flannel robe around her. She couldn't find her slippers, so she fumbled her way barefoot to the door.

Out the door into the dark hall she went, feeling as if she waded through waist-deep water. The doorbell pealed again. "Coming," she muttered, and grabbed the stair railing, feet slipping from hardwood floor in the upper hall to carpeted stairs.

Start down, hurry, bell ringing—something bit into her leg, stinging. She was moving too fast, her body lurched forward, hands grabbing for something, anything to grab on to. She couldn't catch herself. She was falling, ricocheting down the stairs—

NATHAN RAN TOWARD the house, the flashlight swinging in his hand, grimacing at the stab of pain from each step. Good thing he'd opened the windows tonight; good thing he was a light sleeper, or he might not have heard that persistent ringing of the doorbell.

Something was wrong. Catherine—he felt a little stab of fear. If something happened to Catherine, was it because of what he'd told her or in spite of it? He stormed up the steps to the door. Whoever had been ringing the doorbell was gone, maybe alarmed at the sight of his approaching light. He pounded on the door with the heavy flashlight.

"Catherine! Cathy, it's Nathan. Open up."

Nothing, and the instinct that drove him told him that wasn't good. He fumbled for the key ring he'd shoved into his pocket, found the door key, hands stiff and awkward as he shoved it into the lock, turned it, pushed the door—

It opened three inches and stopped. She'd put the chain on, of course. He'd told her to. He maneuvered the flashlight through the opening, scanning the hall. The beam hit a stream of pale hair, a white face, a splash of blood on the forehead. Cathy sprawled at the bottom of the stairs, headfirst, limp and still.

"Cathy—" The other doors would be locked, too. He'd seen to that. Without letting himself think too much, he drew back and flung himself at the door. A creak of dry wood, a snap, and he was in, stumbling and nearly falling as his bad leg took the full agonizing weight of his forward lunge. He sucked in the pain and dropped to the floor next to Catherine, his fingers feeling her neck for a pulse.

She was breathing, thank heaven, and her pulse seemed steady under his fingers. He straightened her legs, then her arms, checking for damage, finding nothing except the cut on her forehead, and that didn't look deep enough for stitches.

It couldn't be good that she was unconscious. His stomach twisted at her pallor. He'd have to call the St. James Clinic and hope someone was on duty at this hour. The only alternative was across the bridge to Savannah, and that would take too long. He yanked the cell phone from the pocket of his shorts, but before he could dial, she moaned.

Dropping the phone, he patted her cheek. "Cathy, can you hear me? Open your eyes. It's Nathan. Look at me."

As if responding to his voice, her eyelids flickered. Her hand moved, groping for something, and he caught it in his, holding it firmly. "Come on, Cathy. Open your eyes. I promise not to chase you up any more trees." As an attempt at humor it wasn't great, but she responded, moving a little, groaning and putting her hand to her head.

"What happened?" The words came out in a slur. She opened her eyes slowly, as if the lids weighed a ton.

Shock stabbed through him. Her pupils were dark, dilated and unfocused. He grabbed her shoulders. "What did you take? Tell me, Catherine. What did you take?"

She shook her head and winced. "What do you mean?"

"I mean your pupils are dilated and you're clearly out of it. What did you take? Sleeping pills? Tranquilizers? What?" He couldn't keep the fury from his voice. He'd feel that way at discovering that anyone he knew was doping. It wasn't because it was Catherine, with her cool eyes, her sharp mind and that vulnerable curve to her lips.

Her eyes shot open. Normally a clear green that reminded him of mountain springs, they were blurred, but full of indignation. "Are you crazy? I don't take things like that."

He shook her lightly. "Be honest with me. If I have to take you to a doctor, I want to know what to tell him or her."

She slapped his hands away, and that return to her usual attitude heartened him. "I am telling you the truth." She enunciated the words carefully. "After you left, I searched for a while, and then I had the sandwiches and tea Flora had left and went to bed. I didn't take so much as a vitamin pill."

The truth sank in then. It was better than thinking she'd taken the stuff herself, but not much. "Wake up, Cathy, and think. You need to be alert, because if you didn't take something yourself, then somebody—somebody with access to this house—drugged you tonight."

CHAPTER FOUR

"NO MORE, PLEASE." Catherine tried to push away the coffeepot.

Nathan filled her mug anyway and then sank down into the kitchen chair opposite her. He'd finally let her stop walking, as much for his sake as hers, since his leg wouldn't hold him up any longer. But he wanted to be sure that dazed gaze was completely gone. His stomach still churned at the thought of how she'd looked when she'd first opened her eyes.

"Are you coherent enough to talk yet?" He leaned across the table for a closer look at her face. Innocent of makeup, with her blond hair falling to her shoulders instead of fastened back in that sophisticated twist she'd worn when she arrived, she looked more like the little girl he remembered, but with the allure of the grown woman she was now.

"I'm fine." The glare was convincing enough. "Talk away. This conspiracy theory is yours, not mine."

He slapped his palm down on the table. "Facts, not theory. Someone drugged you tonight, probably in the food Flora left, since you say you didn't have anything else."

"I don't just say it. It's true." The chill in her voice would cool down a gallon of sweet tea.

"Then someone else did it. And tied a nice strong

cord across the stairs. And rang the doorbell, to make sure you'd come stumbling down them, too dazed to save yourself."

He could tell she didn't like admitting it, but she was too much of a lawyer not to recognize the truth when it stared her in the face. "All right," she snapped. "Who?"

He lifted an eyebrow. "Do you have any enemies who are likely to have followed you to St. James?"

"That's ridiculous. I'm a corporate attorney, not a prosecutor who makes enemies."

"Personal? Jealous ex-boyfriend?"

Her eyes flickered a little at that. "No boyfriend, period."

"That sounds a little lonely." That sounded a lot lonely, but he was no better.

She shrugged. "Just take my word for it, okay? If this isn't a figment of our imagination, it has something to do with Aunt Henny. She's my only connection to this place."

"All right. The people potentially involved with Henny's will are the ones who were here today. Adams, the lawyer. Flora and her disgusting offspring. Pretty-boy Clayton."

"Not very fond of them, are you?" Her gaze was steady and assessing.

"Not especially. Flora did her best to carry every bit of gossip about me she could find to Henny. Bobby Jon will pick up anything that's not chained down. And Clayton—well, Clayton and I have never had much use for each other."

"Aren't you forgetting someone?"

"You mean Adams? He's honest enough, just maybe getting a bit past his prime."

"No." She looked at him. "I mean you."

Funny, that her doubt could hurt that much. Natural enough, he supposed. He wasn't anything to her but the vague memory of an oaf who'd teased her as a child. He shrugged. "Well, putting motive aside, I suppose I could have had access to the food Flora left. I knew about it—Flora announced her good deed to everyone. I could have tied the cord, rung the bell, then broken in to rescue you. But why would I?"

"Why would anyone?" She ran her fingers through her hair, wincing a little when they brushed the bandage he'd applied to the cut. "What does anyone have to gain? My only function here is to carry out Aunt Henny's wishes as expressed in her will. If I don't do it, the probate court will simply appoint another executor."

"That's assuming you find the will. Either will."

She frowned. "That business with the second will is odd. Adams told me that the witness who came forward is a nurse at the clinic, very reputable. She doesn't know what was in the will, but Aunt Henny asked her and the gardener to witness it one day when she was doing a home visit."

"A month ago." He tried to remember what had been going on at that time. "Henny had had a couple of bad episodes. Flora was always coming in and fixing the most unappetizing food imaginable and lecturing her if she didn't eat it."

"I suppose that just made Aunt Henny all the more determined to eat what she wanted."

Something about sitting there alone with her in the quiet kitchen, the sun brightening the sky, made him ask the question he'd never intended to ask. "Why didn't you come? You were the only blood kin she cared a thing about, and you never came to see her."

She jerked back as if he'd hit her, cheeks paling. "Because I didn't know how ill she was. I saw her in Boston at Christmas and she seemed fine then. Complaining about the cold and saying I'd have to come to St. James for Christmas next time, but feeling well for her age."

Did he believe her? He wanted to, but— "She wanted you to come, that last month. Talked about it a lot. I thought she'd asked you to come."

"And you suppose I'd ignore a request like that and then lie about it? How flattering. You don't know me in the least." She sat there in an old flannel robe with her hair around her shoulders, but her eyes flashed as if she argued a case in front of a judge.

"Maybe I don't. But maybe you really are your father's daughter."

Her chin came up at that. "I suppose you know what you're talking about. I don't. But there's something you're ignoring."

"What's that?" It might be safer to quarrel with her than to imagine he felt something.

"According to you, you were as close to her as anyone. If you knew she was sick, knew she wanted me, why didn't you send for me yourself?"

CHAPTER FIVE

SHE DIDN'T FEEL too bad, considering the number of bruises under her slacks and long-sleeved shirt. Cathy went cautiously down the stairs. The wonder was that she hadn't broken her neck, falling that far.

She hadn't seen Nathan since he'd stormed out of the house after their quarrel. She supposed it was a quarrel, when two people were determined to think the worst of each other. She paused at the bottom of the steps, listening. Was someone in the dining room? That sounded like a drawer closing.

She went quickly across the hallway. Bobby Jon turned from the china closet, hand on the drawer that probably held the silver flatware. "What are you doing?" she snapped.

He slouched toward her. "Nothing. What's it to you?"

"As the executor, I'm responsible for the contents of the house. If you took anything out of that drawer, put it back."

"Or what?" He came close—so close that she was aware of his wiry strength and the sense of wildness that emanated from him. "You want to search me?"

She stiffened, but before she could reply, Flora bustled into the room, a dust cloth in her hand. "Catherine, there you are. Bobby Jon and I came over to help you look for those wills." She sniffed. "Not that I believe there ever was a second one."

"That's very nice of you." *And do you believe you're mentioned in one of the wills, Flora?* "But I'm afraid that wouldn't be proper. As executor, that's my job."

"But we're family. You can trust us." Flora looked ready to take offense.

"Of course, but it's not a question of that. Mr. Adams was very specific about it." She ushered them toward the door. "I appreciate the offer, though."

Flora paused on the threshold. "Guess you've got to do what Adams says. But don't you go letting Nathan into the house, either." She glanced toward the cottage. "He takes drugs, you know. I saw the evidence with my own eyes. Your great-aunt knew, too."

She wouldn't let her expression change. "Thank you, Flora. I'll see you later, I'm sure."

She waited until they'd climbed into a rusty pickup and driven away. Then she headed for the cottage, fueled by determination. It was past time for Nathan to level with her.

She skirted the drainage ditch that ran along the path, catching her breath when a small alligator slid into the water at her approach. *The low country can be a dangerous place.* She could almost hear Aunt Henny's voice. *Dangerous, but beautiful.* Aunt Henny had known every inch of this land, and every creature that lived on it. She'd taught Cathy to respect it.

A shiver went down her spine. It wasn't the gators she feared.

The cottage door stood ajar, so she walked in, rapping as she did. "Nathan?" She stopped. Exercise equipment crowded the space.

Nathan, on a leg-press machine, grimaced as he pushed and then released. "Don't you believe in knocking?"

"I just had a visit from Flora and son. You were right about him. I think he was trying to get at the silver service."

He grunted, getting up and mopping his face with a towel. "That place needs a guard dog. I suppose Flora offered to help look for the will."

"She did." She could see the pain in his face when he moved, and her heart clutched. He'd probably reinjured himself getting to her last night. "She said something else." *Just say it, Cathy.* "She said you were into drugs, and Aunt Henny knew."

He tossed the towel away, face averted. "Believe what you want." Pain etched the words and echoed in her heart.

She walked to him deliberately and touched his arm. "I believe you're an honest man. Aunt Henny trusted you, or you wouldn't be living here. So tell me. Please."

For a moment it hung in the balance. He looked into her face, and apparently whatever he saw there satisfied him, because he nodded. "Henny and I had our ups and downs. I always thought she was too bossy. You're a lot like her, you know?"

"I'll take that as a compliment."

His smile flickered. "She wanted me to become a naturalist, because I loved the island and its creatures like she did. But that was too tame for me, so I became a cop. We fought about it."

She wouldn't let herself look down at his leg. "You got hurt on the job."

He nodded. "A drug dealer smashed me against a

brick wall with an SUV, leading to more operations than I want to remember. The irony is, I became dependent on the pain meds." He took a breath. "Not anymore. Thanks to Henny, I made it. She set this up for me." He gestured toward the equipment. "Bullied me through the bad times. Gave me my life back and never asked a thing in return."

Tears stung her eyes. "Yes. She always thought she knew what was best for you, and most times she was right."

"Any particular thing she was right about for you?" He was so close the question seemed to brush her skin.

She didn't step away. "When she came at Christmas. I'd been dating someone. She sized him up in a minute and a half and told me he was a stuffed shirt and a pretentious snob. Which he was."

Nathan chuckled deep in his throat. "I trust he's out of the picture now." He touched her cheek, skimming his fingers back into her hair. "Because I intend to kiss you, and I wouldn't want to—"

She turned her head slightly, and their lips met, cutting off his words. The room seemed to fade as she let her eyes close and leaned into the kiss. She felt as if she'd come home at last.

CHAPTER SIX

"Did you know Henny kept all the pictures you sent her?" Nathan held up a drawing he'd just unearthed from the workroom cabinet, smiling at Cathy's expression when she saw the stick figure.

"She should have thrown that away." Cathy knelt in front of the bookcases, pulling things from the bottom shelves. "I never could draw."

"She wanted it. She loved you." He could understand the feeling. Cathy was lovable, especially when she forgot about her life and career back in Boston and relaxed. Henny had always said that the island brought out what was real in people.

"Well, if she wanted us to find her will, she should have saved a little less stuff. Or put it somewhere obvious, like the safe." She pulled a stack of books from the shelf, and a carved wooden box came with them.

"That's mine, Cousin Catherine."

Nathan jerked around. Fine watchdog he was. Why hadn't he heard Clayton approach?

Cathy glanced from Clayton to him before replying, and he knew what she was thinking. Was Clayton, like Flora, eager to join the search for the missing wills?

She turned the box over in her hands. "I'm sorry, Clayton, but nothing must leave the house until after the will has been found. I'm sure you understand."

"But that's mine." Clayton took a step toward her. "You have to give it to me."

Nathan eased away from the cabinet, muscles tightening. "No, she doesn't." For a moment they faced each other, and he could feel the tension radiating from Clayton.

"I'll tell you what." Cathy scrambled to her feet. "I won't open it, and I'll keep it safe for you. Once I've gone through everything, we can sort this out. All right?"

For a moment longer Clayton stood rigid. Then he nodded. "Yes. Thank you." He took a step toward the door. "I guess I should go." Before they could speak, he'd hurried out.

He looked at her, eyebrows lifting. "Maybe you ought to see what's inside."

She shook the box experimentally. Paper rustled. "I promised. But I'd love to know how important this is to him."

"Enough to try to get you out of the way, you mean? Frankly, at this moment I don't trust any of them. He might have been kin, but Henny didn't trust Clayton any more than she trusted—" He stopped, realizing he was about to go too far.

Two red spots appeared on Cathy's cheeks. "Than my father. That's what you were going to say, isn't it? I know they didn't get along, but he's not a bad person."

He no longer suspected that she was involved in her father's scheme, so he shouldn't say any more. "If you say so. You know him. I don't."

She shoved the box onto the shelf and planted her hands on her hips. "Don't patronize me. If you imagine you know something about my father, you can't just imply he's not trustworthy and let it go."

"All right. Fine." The anger he'd felt at the time surged to life. "Did you know your father was here six weeks before Henny died? Did you know that he pushed her to sell Morley's End for some condo scheme he was involved in? And that when she refused, he threatened to have her declared incompetent?"

Cathy's face had been red—now it was ashen. "That's not true. My father wouldn't do something like that. He wouldn't!"

"Wouldn't he?" He'd gone too far, but he couldn't back down now. He owed it to Henny. "If you don't believe me, ask him. Just ask him."

CATHY SAT ON the bed in the room that had been hers as a child. She'd cried herself out after the phone call to her father, and now she had no more tears. She faced the truth—that her father was a man who'd badger a sick old woman because of his own greed.

I didn't know, Lord. I didn't know, and I wasn't here to help her. Please, show me what to do now.

Aunt Henny's Bible still lay on the bedside table. She picked it up, her throat tightening when she saw the bookmark that stuck out of it—an image of Jesus as shepherd, pasted together with a child's care. She'd made it in Sunday School and sent it to her. The passage that it marked was one of Aunt Henny's favorites, the 23rd Psalm.

Aunt Henny had underlined several verses, as she always did when she found something that spoke to her.

She read through the familiar chapter, then closed the Bible and put it back. The words had comforted her, as no doubt they'd comforted Aunt Henny. Now it was time to take action. She owed Nathan the truth.

The house was silent as she hurried down the stairs and out the door. The setting sun touched the marsh grasses with gold, and a mockingbird swooped over her head as she trotted down the path.

Her heart was in her throat as she approached the cottage. She had been so angry with Nathan, and now she had to apologize. Had to admit that her own father had behaved just as badly as Nathan had said.

Her mind flickered back to that kiss they'd shared. How odd it was. If someone had asked before she'd come back, she'd have said that she barely remembered Nathan. And yet they'd moved so quickly to the point of arguing and caring as if they'd been together for years. Maybe, in a way, that childhood summer had created a bond that had been there ever since, even though she hadn't seen it.

She rounded the corner of the cottage, her mind focused on what she had to say to him. And stopped, breath catching in her throat.

Where the porch had been there was nothing but a pile of jagged boards and protruding timbers, and Nathan lay, half-covered, in the midst of it.

CHAPTER SEVEN

"I'M FINE. STOP fussing over me," Nathan snarled.

The tall, stately Gullah nurse who'd met them at the clinic smiled at Catherine and continued wrapping an elastic bandage around his wrist. "Might as well stop resisting, Nathan. I've known you since you were a tadpole, and it's not impressing me."

"Are you sure that's not broken?" The vise Cathy had felt around her heart when she saw Nathan trapped in the wreckage of the porch had loosened a little, but she still shuddered when she thought of it.

Esther Johnson shook her head, gold earrings swinging against her skin. "He's fine. Just try to keep him out of trouble." Her gaze zeroed in on the bandage on Cathy's forehead. "You two look as if you've gone a round with a gator. Take care out there at Morley's End."

Things came together in her mind then. "Mr. Adams told me that a nurse from the clinic witnessed my aunt's will. Was that you?"

The woman nodded. "I knew what it was, of course, but I don't know what was in it."

"I guess you've heard that we haven't been able to find either will." Nathan winced as she fastened the bandage. "Did you have any sense of what she was doing with it?"

"No, can't say as I do. It was on the desk in her workroom when I left."

"WE'RE NO FURTHER along than we were before." Nathan leaned against the passenger seat as Catherine drove down the narrow lane to the house. "Maybe worse, with me banged up." He flexed his hand, and she could tell by the way he stiffened that it hurt.

"We can't keep going this way." The concern she felt must have shown in her voice. "Maybe we should go to the police. That porch didn't collapse by itself."

"And tell them what?" Nathan just sounded frustrated. "That we think one of Henny's relatives is trying to keep us from finding the will? What can they gain by delaying us?"

It was irrational, to feel so pleased that he kept saying "us," as if they were a team. "I've given up wondering why. I just want to find the new will and get this settled."

"So you can rush back to Boston?" Nathan's voice deepened a little, as if her answer was important.

"I don't know what I'm going to do," she said slowly. "There hasn't been enough time to figure it out. But I know I'll be leaving my father's firm."

Nathan reached across the seat to touch her wrist in a comforting gesture. "I'm sorry I was the one to tell you. I didn't want to hurt you."

She took a deep breath to ease the pain in her heart. "It's better that I know the truth. It explains why he was so eager for me to come. He probably hoped I'd inherit and that I'd agree to his plans. Which I wouldn't. This place meant too much to Aunt Henny." She hesitated. "And to you. Whatever the will says, this place rightfully belongs to you."

Nathan stiffened. "My father left it to Henny, and

she had the right to dispose of it however she saw fit. I have no desire to change that."

"Then we'd better find that will, and fast." She drew to a stop in front of the house. "I still think it has to be in the workroom somewhere. That was her special place."

"Let's get looking, then." He opened the door with his good hand. "I'm not stopping until we've gone through every single inch. I don't want to risk any more little accidents."

"Agreed." She slid out, wanting to help him but afraid he'd be offended if she tried. "You start looking while I go make us some coffee. It's going to be a long night."

IT WAS DARK outside by the time Cathy sank down in the middle of the books she'd removed from the shelves. "Maybe we were wrong. Maybe she put it someplace else."

Nathan looked worse than she felt, his face white with fatigue and pain as he shoved aside his own stack of books. "What about her bedroom? Did you take a look up there?"

She nodded. "I did that earlier. Unless she had a secret hiding place under the floorboards, it's not there. You grew up in this house—can you think of anything?"

"I've already checked all the hiding places I know about." He gave her a strained smile. "I didn't wait for the executor to arrive from Boston—I'd already started looking as soon as I knew the will was missing. I didn't want to let her down. Maybe if I hadn't gone to Savannah that night—"

"You couldn't have known. You said she seemed to be feeling well that day."

"I hate it that she died alone." His voice choked. He was letting her see how much he'd loved Henny, and she sensed that he didn't show that depth of emotion easily.

"She wasn't alone," she said softly. "'Even though I walk through the valley of the shadow of death, Thou are with me.' That was her favorite passage, remember? I've been using her Bible, and she had it bookmarked and underscored."

"I remember." He jerked a nod toward a sepia-toned print on the wall, with its flock of sheep settled against a quiet hillside. "That's why that's hanging in here, so she could see it from her desk."

Cathy stared at the familiar print, feeling a tingle of excitement moving through her. "She'd underscored the words in her Bible. Recently—the ink wasn't faded. What if—"

Nathan was on his feet almost before she'd finished speaking. He couldn't manage the heavy frame with one hand, and she rushed to help him tilt it from the wall. The new envelope was white against the brown backing of the print. She pulled it out, fingers trembling.

"Last will and testament of Henrietta Morley. We've found it!"

"Now you can give it to me."

They turned. Flora stood in the doorway, smiling, and in her plump hands was clutched a deadly looking rifle.

CHAPTER EIGHT

NATHAN FROZE, HIS good hand still holding the heavy picture frame. Helpless—why did he have to feel so helpless? Flora had the deer rifle aimed right at Cathy. She might be a lousy shot, but at this distance, she could hardly miss.

"Flora." Cathy found her voice first. "What are you doing? Put that thing down."

"Not until you give me the will."

Flora didn't budge from the doorway. She wouldn't come within range, so that meant he had to move. He eased the frame back against the wall, assessing the distance between them and the clutter of books they'd left on the floor, now an obstacle course for a man with only one good leg and one good arm. *Lord, be with us now, or we don't stand a chance.*

"You mean this?" Cathy held the envelope up, moving several steps away from him.

Way to go, sugar. Put some distance between us, so when I move she'll aim at me, not you. A cold hand seized his heart at the thought of the damage that rifle could do.

"Stop that! Stand still!" The barrel of the rifle wavered between them. "Just give me the will, and no one will get hurt. I have the first one, so once this one is destroyed, everything is okay."

"Destroying a will is a criminal offense," Cathy said. Her voice was perfectly calm, as if she faced a potential murderer every day. "The court won't let you inherit if you do that."

"No one will know." Flora's face hardened. "Henny never should have written it. She said she was going to do it—going to change her will after she found out about the few little things we took from the house."

"What did you do?" For an instant rage consumed him, and he beat it back. No good cop went into a confrontation against a weapon with his control shattered by anger.

But Cathy understood the implication. She gasped, taking an unwary step toward Flora. Toward the weapon. "Aunt Henny—you did something to her. Flora, what did you do?"

"She had everything. Everything! And she begrudged us a few little pieces of silver. She sat up in her bed like a queen with that Bible open on her lap and told me we'd have to be content with whatever we'd already taken."

Flora was so angry that the rifle shook, and he moved to the side, searching for a clear path to her.

"You killed her." Cathy took another step, as if she knew what he planned and was drawing Flora's attention further and further from him. "You're a nurse—you'd know how to make it look as if she overindulged and let her sugar get out of control."

"I didn't want to do it. She made me. I have to think of my son. She never had any kids, so she didn't know what that was like." She seemed to be asking Cathy to agree.

Cathy nodded, as if that actually made sense. The

heavy rifle sagged a little. He reached toward the desk, groping with his good hand for anything he could throw.

"You must have been shocked when Adams said there was a second will," Cathy said.

"I had the first one. But I couldn't pretend to find it if there was a second one, so I had to stop you until I could get it and destroy it." She raised the rifle again. "Now give it to me."

"Fine, take it." Cathy thrust the envelope toward her, then let it drop. It fluttered toward the floor.

Cathy bent as if to pick it up. His hand closed over the brass lamp and he threw with all his strength. Flora stumbled backward, tripping on the threshold, and he lunged at her, knocking the rifle away.

It fired, and he looked toward Cathy, his heart clutching, but she came toward them, shaking but in one piece. "I think you just shot Aunt Henny's dartboard," she said, and dropped to her knees next to him.

CATHY HURRIED BACK to the workroom after seeing Adams and Clayton off, with Clayton clutching the box Aunt Henny had left him in her will. Evidence of some malfeasance on his part? Well, if so, he was safe now. Bobby Jon hadn't shown up for the reading of the will. In fact, no one had seen him on St. James since his mother's arrest.

Nathan stood in front of the print, straightening it. He turned as she entered, giving her a smile that made her knees turn to water. "You know, I was never too crazy about this picture, but it's growing on me. What do you think? Should we leave it here for good?"

She walked toward him slowly, not sure how to put what she wanted to say. "Just because Aunt Henny left the property to both of us, you don't have to consult me about everything. It came from your family, so rightfully—"

"If you tell me that it belongs to me, I might just have to chase you up a tree again."

"Well, I just meant that I might not be here to make decisions," she said. "I'm out of a job, remember?"

"That makes two of us, but there's no rush. Turning the land into a nature preserve, like Henny asked, is going to take some time. After that—well, we both know his law practice is getting beyond Adams. I'll bet he'd be happy to have a bright young woman come on board as a partner."

"Are you saying you want me to stay?" She'd made so many mistakes about people, including her own father, that she had to be sure she did it right this time.

As an answer, Nathan reached out and pulled her close against him. She went willingly, her doubts evaporating in the strength of his embrace. He kissed her until she had to cling to him to keep from falling, and then he leaned just far enough away to see her face.

"You know what's the only thing that bothers me about this?" He grinned, all the marks of grief and pain gone from his face. "It's exactly what Henny expected would happen. We've just proved her right again."

* * * * *

SPECIAL EXCERPT FROM
Love Inspired Suspense

When his infant nephew is abducted,
Texas Ranger Dallas Sanders
will stop at nothing to find the kidnappers,
before it's too late...

Read on for a sneak preview of
Texas Baby Pursuit *by Margaret Daley,*
the next book in the Lone Star Justice miniseries,
available in August 2018 from
Love Inspired Suspense.

Texas Ranger Dallas Sanders parked in the back of the sheriff's station in Cimarron Trail, his home for the past few years. Although he worked out of the Texas Rangers' office in San Antonio, he loved returning to the smaller town northwest of the city at the end of a long day at work. Now that he'd wrapped up an intense case involving a turf war between two rival gangs that had lasted six months, it was time he introduced himself to the new sheriff, and then all he wanted to do was go to his ranch and spend quality time with his daughter, Michelle.

When he slid from his SUV and started for the building, his cell phone's ringtone played "The Yellow Rose of Texas." He smiled when he saw who was calling him. "Hi, princess. I should be home in half an hour."

"Dad, I'm not at the ranch. I'm babysitting for Aunt Lenora. Grandma drove me here, and Aunt Lenora will bring me home in a couple of hours."

His thirteen-year-old daughter was the reason he'd bought a small ranch right outside Cimarron Trail rather than living in San Antonio. Yes, it added an hour to his commute to and from work, but it was worth it.

Some of his relatives lived nearby, and after his wife had walked out on their marriage, his daughter needed family around her for support. "How about dinner?" he asked as he opened the rear door into the sheriff's station.

"I'll let you know. Aunt Lenora has a committee meeting that might run over. If I get hungry, she has stuff to eat here. The reason I'm calling is that the store where I want to buy my electronic keyboard is open until nine, and I have enough money after Aunt Lenora pays me. Can you take me later when I come home?"

He glanced at his watch. Three o'clock. All he had thought about on his drive home was relaxing and spending some quality time with Michelle now that he didn't have to put in fourteen-hour days.

"Dad, please."

He released a long breath. "Sure, if we have time. If not, we can go tomorrow. I'm taking a few days off."

"I think I called the wrong number. Are you sure you're Dallas Sanders?"

He laughed. "I know, princess. I've been working way too much, but I promise I'll make it up to you."

"I'm holding you to it. Gotta go. Brady's crying."

When he disconnected the call, he slid his phone back into his pocket. He smiled as he scanned the large room where most of the deputies worked. Michelle was his life. When Patricia left him a few years ago for another man, he'd spiraled into a depression that he'd had to fight his way out of for the sake of his daughter. Without Michelle, he might have wallowed in his misery for years.

Dallas approached Deputy Carson, a member of his church. "Mark, is the new sheriff here?"

The young man gestured toward a closed door off the main room. "I know you don't work this county, but I was expecting you last week."

"I was working a big case that rapidly blew up. The good thing is we have the main perpetrators safely in jail now. My life will get back to normal."

Mark chuckled. "But for how long?"

"Please don't say that. I want only positive thoughts." Dallas strolled to the closed door and knocked.

"Come in," a female voice said.

He entered the office and found a woman dressed in a brown uniform with her head bent over a paper she was writing on. His gaze latched onto her shoulder-length auburn hair, which fell forward, framing her face as she looked up at him. Crystal clear green eyes locked on his face for a few seconds before she noticed the Texas Ranger star pinned to his white shirt over his heart.

She rose, came around her desk and extended her hand. "I'm Sheriff Rachel Young. Since you aren't the Texas Ranger who covers my county—because he's on vacation—I'm assuming you're here on one of your cases. How can I help you?"

He shook her hand. "I'm Dallas Sanders, and no, I'm not here on a case. I live right outside Cimarron Trail and wanted to welcome you to the area as well as let you know if you ever need extra help, I live at the Five Star Ranch. I understand you were a sergeant for the Austin Police Department before becoming sheriff."

Her smile lit up her whole face and made him feel at ease. "When my father retired, I jumped at the chance to fill his position and run for sheriff. I grew up in Cimarron Trail."

"I dealt with your dad a couple of times when a case I was on involved this county, too. I didn't think he would retire for years."

"He finally decided to become a rancher. It was a childhood dream besides being a police officer. His place is northeast of Cimarron Trail. The Safe Haven Ranch, which is really a refuge for abandoned animals, is three hundred acres, small by Texas standards." She gestured toward a chair in front of her desk. "If you have time, take a seat. I'd like your view of what's happening in the area. I want to be proactive rather than reactive. My first ten days have been quiet. Too quiet. I feel like I'm waiting for the other shoe to drop."

Dallas sat while the sheriff took another chair nearby. "I assume your father filled you in."

"About the county, yes. But what I mean by the area is the other counties nearby, including Bexar County."

"I just wrapped up a case involving a turf war between two gangs. At least for the moment it's quiet between them, although I'm not naïve enough to think that will last. There have also been smuggling activities up and down I-35."

His cell phone sounded, and he slipped it from his pocket to see who was calling. Michelle. Again? Maybe her plans watching Brady had changed. She usually texted him while he was working, but a call twice in fifteen minutes was most unusual. "I need to answer this."

He tapped the on button. "Michelle—"

"Help! They're taking Brady!"

Her frantic words, followed by a scream, urged Dallas to his feet. "Michelle, what's going on?"

Then it sounded like she dropped the phone, sending chills down his spine. "No! Don't," she cried out.

"Michelle!" Everything went silent.

He rushed out into the main room, aware the sheriff had followed him. He glanced back. "Something's happened at my sister's house. Can you follow me?"

With her keys in her hand, the sheriff nodded and said to a deputy, "Follow, too."

As Dallas hurried toward his SUV, he kept repeating his daughter's name into his cell phone, but there was only silence. The phone was dead. His heart pounded against his rib cage as he started his car. His sister's house wasn't far from the sheriff's station, but every scenario involving kids that he'd encountered as a law enforcement officer raced through his thoughts. He recalled the semitruck full of human beings smuggled into the United States—children included—discovered just this month in a parking lot during the heat of summer in a suburb of San Antonio.

After he slammed to a stop in his sister's driveway, he ran toward the front door, trying not to think about the smuggling rings bringing people in and out of this country. He couldn't rid his mind of it. Fear spurred him to go faster.

When he spied the front door wide open he drew his gun, and his professional facade fell into place. Whatever had gone down, the perpetrator could still be inside—with his daughter.

Sheriff Young and her deputy entered the house right behind him. Dallas motioned for them to go right while he went left toward the bedrooms. His heartbeat drowned out other sounds as he moved down the hall, checking the rooms. When he stepped into Brady's, its emptiness mocked him. *Brady is gone. Where is Michelle?*

* * *

As Rachel moved into the kitchen, the first thing she noticed was that the back door—just like the front door—was wide open. She gestured for her deputy to circle the room while she headed to the exit, leading to a screened-in porch.

Lying on a blanket on the wood floor was a young teenage girl, her arm stretched out toward a smashed cell phone, blood pooling onto the coverlet. “Call 911,” Rachel yelled to her deputy as she rushed to the child and knelt next to her.

The girl’s eyes fluttered, opened for a few seconds, then closed.

“Michelle. I’m here to help. Your dad is, too.” Rachel felt the teenager’s pulse on the side of her neck. Her fast heart rate might indicate a concussion. She examined the injury on the side of the girl’s head, blood still flowing from it, but she couldn’t tell how deep the wound was. “Michelle.”

The young teen moaned and lifted her eyelids as she tried to sit up.

Rachel gently restrained her. “Don’t get up yet.” She spied a white hand towel on the blanket and snatched it up, then pressed it against the girl’s wound to try to stop the bleeding.

The child’s brown eyes grew wide as she stared over Rachel’s shoulder. “Dad.”

Rachel had been so absorbed in the teenager she hadn’t heard Dallas coming out onto the porch. She looked over her shoulder at Texas Ranger Dallas Sanders, over six feet tall. His stiff posture and clenched jaw warred with the smile flirting at the edges of his mouth as he looked at his daughter.

A half grin won out. "I'm here, honey. You'll be okay. I promise."

Rachel was amazed at the calmness in his voice. Now she understood why her father had mentioned Dallas when discussing potential allies for her in the area. He kept his composure in a situation that would throw most into a panic.

Dallas squatted on the other side of Michelle and took over putting pressure on the injury to stem the blood flow. "What happened?" he asked in a soft, soothing voice.

"Brady." Michelle turned her head to the side—the movement causing her to wince and displace the cloth on her wound. "They...took him, Daddy." She waved her hand toward an area with scattered toys on the blanket. Tears ran down her face.

Again the teen tried to rise, but this time Dallas clasped one of her shoulders. "Don't move until you're checked out." He re-covered the injury with the cloth. Worry engraved deeper lines on his face.

"Your dad's right," Rachel said. "An ambulance is on its way. You're in good hands."

"But Brady—" Michelle's eyelids half closed "—is gone..." Tears drenched her cheeks, her eyes dulling.

Rachel glanced at Dallas. Their gazes locking for a few seconds gave her a brief glimpse into the suppressed fear in his eyes, so dark they were almost black. "Michelle, I'm Sheriff Young. I'm here to look for Brady. You don't need to worry. I'll take care of him."

While Dallas hovered over his daughter, trying to reassure her everything was being taken care of, Rachel rose and covered the distance to Deputy Jones, who was one of her investigative officers. "Call for backup. A baby was taken. We need help looking for Brady." She started for the screen door that led to the yard. "I'll be out here canvassing the yard. Let me know when more help arrives."

"Yes, ma'am," her deputy said with a nod.

Rachel started for the exit, glancing back at Dallas and his daughter.

"I'll be right back, princess."

Michelle clutched her father's arm. "Don't leave me, Daddy."

"I'm not. I need to talk to the sheriff for a moment."

The teen slipped her hand away and held the cloth over her injury, her arm shaking. Dallas rose and quickly bridged the short distance between himself and Rachel. "I'll get what information I can from Michelle and contact my sister and mother."

"I'll need a description of Brady and what he was wearing, and if possible, a recent picture. It'll help with the Amber Alert. How old is he?"

"He's eight months old and crawling. Not walking yet. He has dark hair and blue eyes."

Rachel nodded, then turned toward the door as the EMTs came onto the porch. The screen door was slightly open. The kidnapper came in this way or left out the back. She descended the steps but paused a moment and again looked at Dallas, standing back from his daughter, running his fingers through his short brown hair. A tic twitched in his jaw while one of the paramedics stooped to check Michelle.

Rachel's throat thickened. She had a daughter who would turn one in a month. All she wanted to do was drive out to her parents' house, pick up Katie and hug her. Never let her go. The only good thing that had come out of her marriage was Katie.

This case would be hard for her. She'd only been sheriff for a couple of weeks and had dealt with minor crimes so far. The honeymoon was over.

She scanned the area—open with few fences except one along the back where a dirt road ran behind the houses on the street. The kidnapper could have parked on that road by the southern border of the Fowlers' ranch and easily climbed the rear fence. But then, if that were case, why was the front door open?

As she walked toward the rear of the property, using the most direct path, her gaze swept the ground around her. About ten feet away, she spotted a Binky on the grass. She took out her phone and snapped a picture. After putting on a pair of gloves, she leaned over, picked up the blue pacifier and put it into an evidence bag. From the looks of it, it hadn't been outside long. Possibly dropped by Brady, which meant the kidnappers had left by the back door and headed for the road behind the house. She'd need to know from Michelle how the kidnappers got into the house, since both entrances were wide open.

Most likely the perpetrators entered through the front door, because it had been wide open when Michelle and Dallas arrived. Maybe they fled out the nearest exit. And ran around to the front to leave? She hoped a neighbor had seen something—the kidnappers or the getaway car with a license plate number.

It was even possible they'd come into the place through the back screen door and gone out the front because their car was on the street. But wouldn't Michelle have seen them approaching from the rear? Only the top half of the porch was screened. Rachel shook her head and looked back at the house.

Her stomach tightened into a hard ball, and she held up the evidence bag with the Binky in it. Or they'd come in the front and gone out the back, their car parked on the dirt road behind the property. She had to check everything out. Timing was important in cases like kidnapping.

She climbed the fence rails and paused above the ground and road, staring at several sets of different tire tracks. She knew they were freshly made because the day before it had rained hard. She would have casts made of all of them. Maybe one would give them a lead. She inspected the barren earth that had only a few weeds sticking up. Two pairs of boot prints crisscrossed the tire tracks. Michelle had said "they." Were there two intruders or more, having something to do with one of the back ways into the Fowlers' ranch?

She would have this blocked off and processed, but she would also need to pay Houston Fowler a visit to find out which of his employees had used this road in the past twenty-four hours. Even if no one had, maybe one of them saw something.

As she hopped down and started back toward the house, her cell phone rang. She glanced at the caller ID and punched the on button. "Is everything all right, Dad?"

"I've got a call there's been a kidnapping."

"An eight-month-old baby."

"Whose?"

"Lenora and Paul Howard's. How's Katie?"

"She's fine. Your mother is feeding her. Don't worry. I won't let anything happen to my granddaughter."

Her dad knew her well. Rachel reached the porch. "I need to go."

"I don't want to butt in, but I'll help in any way you need."

"Thanks, Dad. Right now, just keep Katie safe." Rachel disconnected the call and opened the screen door to the porch, then entered.

Deputy Jones finished taking photos of the area. "Texas Ranger Sanders went with his daughter to the regional hospital."

Thinking of the nasty bleeding gash on the side of Michelle's head, Rachel asked, "Was she still responsive when she left?"

"Yes. He called his sister and brother-in-law. They should be here soon. Also, the word's getting out and already a couple of reporters have arrived."

"But not on the property?"

"No. Standing in the street along with some of the neighbors."

"I'll go around front and meet the parents. Send a deputy out to make castings of the tire tracks along the dirt road behind here as well as the two sets of boot prints."

Instead of going through the house, Rachel headed around the side of the building and came upon a large, muscular man wearing a hoodie standing behind a group of tall bushes, peeking in a window. When he spied her, he whirled around, plunged through the thick vegetation and raced across the Howards' neighbor's back lawn.

Rachel took out after him. Her heart pounded as quickly as her feet against the ground. The suspicious man disappeared around the corner of a home two away from the Howards'. As she chased him, she pressed her mic and said, "I'm in pursuit of a guy at the Howards'. I'm two houses away heading west. I need backup."

Who was this guy? Why was he there? What was he looking for?

Rachel chased the man around the side of the neighbor's place, colliding into the solid wall of his body, his head down, hood masking his face. She stumbled back, fighting to stay on her feet. As she regained her footing, she raised her head just as a fist plowed into her jaw, then her eye. The world swirled, and she collapsed.

Don't miss
Texas Baby Pursuit *by Margaret Daley,*
available August 2018 wherever
Love Inspired Suspense books and ebooks are sold.
www.LoveInspired.com